PENGUIN CLASSICS

PENGUIN ENGLISH POETS
GENERAL EDITOR: CHRISTOPHER RICKS

ALFRED LORD TENNYSON

Selected poems

ALFRED LORD TENNYSON was born in 1809 at Somersby, Lincolnshire, the sixth of eleven children of a clergyman. He went up to Cambridge in 1828 but did not obtain a degree. He never had any occupation other than poet. In 1850 he was created Poet Laureate and in 1883 he accepted a peerage. His first important book, *Poems, Chiefly Lyrical*, was published in 1830, and was not a critical success, but his two volumes of *Poems*, 1842, which contain some of his finest work, established him as the leading poet of his generation. Nine years earlier his close friend Arthur Hallam had died and this event had a lasting influence on his life and writing. *In Memoriam*, a series of lyrics and speculations on mortality in tribute to Hallam, appeared in 1850. This was followed in 1855 by *Maud*, which J. R. Lowell described as 'the antiphonal voice to *In Memoriam*'. The principal work of Tennyson's later years, *Idylls of the King*, was composed in two creative spells (1856–9 and 1868–74). T. S. Eliot wrote of Tennyson: 'He has three qualities which are seldom found together except in the greatest poets: abundance, variety and complete competence. He had the finest ear of any English poet since Milton.' After a short illness Tennyson died in 1892 and was buried in Westminster Abbey.

AIDAN DAY was educated at Queen Elizabeth I Grammar School, Horncastle, and the University of Leicester, where he gained a BA in English, followed by a PhD. He has taught at the University of Hull and is now Reader in English Literature at the University of Edinburgh. He is the author of a number of articles on Tennyson and is co-editor, with Christopher Ricks, of *The Tennyson Archive*, which reproduces Tennyson's poetical manuscripts in facsimile (thirty-one volumes, 1987–93). He has also edited, with a critical introduction and commentary, *Robert Browning: Selected Poetry and Prose* (1991). He is the author of *Jokerman: Reading the Lyrics of Bob Dylan* (1988) and *Romanticism* (1996).

ALFRED LORD TENNYSON

Selected Poems

EDITED BY

AIDAN DAY

PENGUIN BOOKS

PENGUIN BOOKS

Published by the Penguin Group
Penguin Books Ltd, 27 Wrights Lane, London W8 5TZ, England
Penguin Putnam Inc., 375 Hudson Street, New York, New York 10014, USA
Penguin Books Australia Ltd, Ringwood, Victoria, Australia
Penguin Books Canada Ltd, 10 Alcorn Avenue, Toronto, Ontario, Canada M4V 3B2
Penguin Books (NZ) Ltd, 182–190 Wairau Road, Auckland 10, New Zealand

Penguin Books Ltd, Registered Offices: Harmondsworth, Middlesex, England

First published 1991
7 9 10 8

Filmset in Ehrhardt 453 (lasercomp)

Printed in England by Clays Ltd, St Ives plc

For my sister, Hilary

CONTENTS

PREFACE

Except where noted otherwise, the poetical texts in this selection are based, with a few minor corrections, on the Eversley edition of *The Works of Tennyson*, edited by Hallam Lord Tennyson (9 volumes, Macmillan, 1907–8).

The selection concentrates, in the first place, on poems of Tennyson's 1830, 1832 ('1833') and 1842 volumes; it presents the two great works of Tennyson's middle period, *In Memoriam* (1850) and *Maud* (1855); and some representative shorter poems from Tennyson's later volumes. The selection includes only the complete texts of poems. The one exception to this rule is that songs and lyrics have been extracted from *The Princess* (1847), but by certain criteria these may stand as entire poems. The substantial work of Tennyson's later years, *Idylls of the King* (1859–85), is not represented, partly because of the principle of including only complete works and partly because there is a full Penguin English Poets edition of *Idylls* edited by J. M. Gray (1983). Tennyson's interest in Arthurian material is illustrated by his 1842 'Morte d'Arthur', which was later incorporated within 'The Passing of Arthur' in *Idylls of the King*. The poems are arranged in chronological order of publication, with works not published in Tennyson's lifetime included according to date of composition. A symbol [▲ ▲ ▲] marks the conclusion of each group of poems.

The Notes give basic details of dates of composition (where known) and publication, and of influences on the poems.

ACKNOWLEDGEMENTS

I should like to express my gratitude to Christopher Ricks. My debt to his superlative work on Tennyson will be apparent in the pages that follow.

TABLE OF DATES

1809	(6 August) Born at Somersby, Lincolnshire, fourth son of Revd George Clayton Tennyson, Rector of Somersby, and Elizabeth Tennyson (née Fytche). Alfred Lord Tennyson's childhood and youth were overshadowed by family feuds (his father was all but disinherited in favour of a younger brother, later Charles Tennyson d'Eyncourt of Bayons Manor) and by his father's mental instability.
1816–20	Pupil at Louth Grammar School. Subsequently educated at home by his father.
1827	(April) *Poems by Two Brothers* by Tennyson and his brother Charles, with a few contributions by another brother, Frederick. Tennyson's poems were written 'between 15 and 17'. (November) Enters Trinity College, Cambridge.
1829	Meets Arthur Henry Hallam (probably in April), also a student at Trinity, who was to become Tennyson's close friend and the fiancé of his sister Emily. (June) Wins the Chancellor's Gold Medal with his prize poem 'Timbuctoo'. (October) Becomes a member of the 'Apostles', a Cambridge debating society to which most of his university friends belonged.
1830	(June) *Poems, Chiefly Lyrical* (July–September) Visits the Pyrenees with Hallam.
1831	(March) Death of Tennyson's father. Leaves Cambridge without a degree.

1832	(May) Harsh review of *1830* by 'Christopher North' (John Wilson) in *Blackwood's Magazine*. (July) Tours the Rhine country with Hallam. (December) *Poems* (title page dated 1833).
1833	(April) Vicious review of *1832* by J. W. Croker in *Quarterly Review*. (September) Death of Hallam from cerebral haemorrhage whilst on holiday in Vienna.
1834	Falls in love with Rosa Baring, with whom he appears to have become disillusioned by the end of 1836 (she married Robert Shafto in 1838).
1836	(May) Marriage of Tennyson's brother Charles to Louisa Sellwood and start of Tennyson's love for her sister Emily.
1837	(May) The Tennysons leave Somersby for High Beech, Epping. Engagement to Emily Sellwood recognized by her family and his.
1840	Engagement to Emily broken off, partly because of Tennyson's financial insecurity. The Tennysons move to Tunbridge Wells (followed in 1841 by a move to Boxley). Beginning of almost a decade of depression and ill health for Tennyson.
1840–1	Invests his fortune (about £3000) in a wood-carving scheme which fails by 1843.
1842	(May) *Poems*. The first volume contains poems published in *1830* and *1832*, many of which are extensively revised. The second volume comprises new poems.
1845	(September) Granted a Civil List pension of £200 p.a.

1847 (December) *The Princess.*

1849 Renews relationship with Emily Sellwood.

1850 (May) *In Memoriam* published anonymously.
(June) Marries Emily.
(November) Appointed Poet Laureate.

1852 (August) Birth of Tennyson's son, Hallam.

1853 (November) Makes home at Farringford, Isle of Wight, which he buys in 1856.

1854 (March) Birth of Tennyson's second son, Lionel.

1855 (June) Hon. D. C. L. at Oxford.
(July) *Maud, and Other Poems.*

1859 (July) *Idylls of the King* ('Enid', 'Vivien', 'Elaine' and 'Guinevere'). The sequence of *Idylls* was gradually built up and completed with the publication of 'Balin and Balan' in *Tiresias and Other Poems*, 1885.

1861 (June) Tours the Pyrenees with his family.

1862 (April) First audience with Queen Victoria at Osborne, Isle of Wight.

1864 (August) *Enoch Arden.*

1865 (February) Death of Tennyson's mother.

1868 (April) Work starts on Tennyson's second home, Aldworth, at Blackdown, Haslemere.

1869 (December) *The Holy Grail and Other Poems* (title page dated 1870).

1872	(October) *Gareth and Lynette*. The Imperial Library edition of Tennyson's *Works* (1872–3) gathers together *Idylls of the King*, now complete except for 'Balin and Balan'.
1875	(June) *Queen Mary*. The first of Tennyson's plays, followed by *Harold*, 1876 ('1877'), *The Cup and the Falcon*, 1884, *Becket*, 1884, *The Promise of May*, 1886, and *The Foresters*, 1892.
1879	(May) Following piracies, publishes *The Lover's Tale*, which had been omitted from *1832*.
1880	(December) *Ballads and Other Poems*.
1883	(September) Visits Denmark with W. E. Gladstone. Tennyson accepts offer of a barony, taking his seat in the House of Lords in March 1884.
1885	(November) *Tiresias and Other Poems*.
1886	(April) Death of Lionel Tennyson, aged 32. (December) *Locksley Hall Sixty Years After*.
1889	(December) *Demeter and Other Poems*.
1892	(July) Last illness. (6 October) Dies at Aldworth. (28 October) Posthumous publication of *The Death of Oenone, Akbar's Dream and Other Poems*.

FURTHER READING

EDITIONS

Christopher Ricks, ed., *The Poems of Tennyson*, Longman, 1969; second edition in three volumes, incorporating the Trinity manuscripts, 1987.

and Aidan Day, eds., *The Tennyson Archive*, Vols. I–XXX, Garland Publishing, 1987–91. Reproduces Tennyson's poetical manuscripts in facsimile.

LETTERS

Cecil Y. Lang and Edgar F. Shannon, Jr., eds., *The Letters of Alfred Lord Tennyson*, Vol. I: *1821–1850*, 1982; Vol. II: *1851–1870*, 1987; Vol. III: *1871–1892*, 1990, Oxford: Clarendon Press.

BIOGRAPHY

Robert Bernard Martin, *Tennyson: The Unquiet Heart*, Oxford: Clarendon Press and Faber and Faber, 1980. The most recent biography. For an interesting dissent, see Jack Kolb, 'Portraits of Tennyson', in *Modern Philology*, 81, 1983–4, pp. 173–90.

Charles Tennyson, *Alfred Tennyson*, Macmillan, 1949; reissued with alterations, 1968.

GENERAL SCHOLARSHIP AND CRITICISM

Isobel Armstrong, ed., *The Major Victorian Poets: Reconsiderations*, Routledge and Kegan Paul, 1969. Includes four essays on Tennyson.

Isobel Armstrong, 'Tennyson, the collapse of object and subject: *In Memoriam*', *Language as Living Form in Nineteenth-Century Poetry*, Harvester Press, 1982, pp. 172–205.

Kirk H. Beetz, *Tennyson: A Bibliography, 1827–1982*, The Scarecrow Press, 1984.

Harold Bloom, 'Tennyson: In the Shadow of Keats', *Poetry and Repression*, Yale University Press, 1976, pp. 143–74.

Jerome Hamilton Buckley, *Tennyson: The Growth of a Poet*, Harvard University Press, 1960.

Aidan Day, 'The Archetype that Waits: *The Lover's Tale, In Memoriam*, and *Maud*', *Tennyson Society Lectures*, ed. Philip Collins, forthcoming Macmillian, 1991.

Terry Eagleton, 'Tennyson: Politics and Sexuality in *The Princess* and *In Memoriam*', *1848: The Sociology of Literature*, ed. Francis Barker *et al.*, University of Essex, 1978, pp. 77–106.

Eric Griffiths, 'Tennyson's Breath', *The Printed Voice of Victorian Poetry*, Oxford: Clarendon Press, 1989, pp. 97–170.

E. D. H. Johnson, *The Alien Vision of Victorian Poetry. Sources of the Poetic Imagination in Tennyson, Browning, and Arnold*, Princeton University Press, 1952.

John D. Jump, ed., *Tennyson: The Critical Heritage*, Routledge and Kegan Paul, 1967.

John Killham, *Tennyson and 'The Princess': Reflections of an Age*, Athlone Press, 1958.

— ed., *Critical Essays on the Poetry of Tennyson*, Routledge and Kegan Paul, 1960.

Harold Nicolson, *Tennyson: Aspects of his Life, Character and Poetry*, Constable, 1923.

D. J. Palmer, ed., *Tennyson* (Writers and their Background Series), George Bell and Sons, 1973.

F. B. Pinion, *A Tennyson Chronology*, Macmillan, 1990.

Ralph Wilson Rader, *Tennyson's 'Maud': The Biographical Genesis*, University of California Press, 1963.

Christopher Ricks, *Tennyson*, Macmillan, 1972; second revised edition, 1989.

Edgar F. Shannon, Jr., *Tennyson and the Reviewers: A Study of his Literary Reputation and the Influence of the Critics upon his Poetry, 1827–1851*, Harvard University Press, 1952.

Marion Shaw, *Alfred Lord Tennyson* (Feminist Readings Series), Harvester, 1988.

W. David Shaw, *Tennyson's Style*, Cornell University Press, 1976.

Alan Sinfield, *Alfred Tennyson* (Rereading Literature Series), Blackwell, 1986.

Ann Wordsworth, 'An Art That Will Not Abandon the Self to Language: Bloom, Tennyson and the Blind World of the Wish', *Untying the Text. A Post-Structuralist Reader*, ed. Robert Young, Routledge and Kegan Paul, 1981, pp. 207–22.

Timbuctoo

Deep in that lion-haunted inland lies
A mystick city, goal of high emprise.
Chapman

I stood upon the Mountain which o'erlooks
The narrow seas, whose rapid interval
Parts Afric from green Europe, when the Sun
Had fall'n below th' Atlantick, and above
The silent Heavens were blench'd with faery light,
Uncertain whether faery light or cloud,
Flowing Southward, and the chasms of deep, deep blue
Slumber'd unfathomable, and the stars
Were flooded over with clear glory and pale.
I gaz'd upon the sheeny coast beyond, 10
There where the Giant of old Time infixèd
The limits of his prowess, pillars high
Long time eras'd from Earth: even as the Sea
When weary of wild inroad buildeth up
Huge mounds whereby to stay his yeasty waves.
And much I mus'd on legends quaint and old
Which whilome won the hearts of all on Earth
Toward their brightness, ev'n as flame draws air;
But had their being in the heart of Man
As air is th' life of flame: and thou wert then 20
A center'd glory-circled Memory,
Divinest Atalantis, whom the waves
Have buried deep, and thou of later name
Imperial Eldorado roof'd with gold:
Shadows to which, despite all shocks of Change,
All on-set of capricious Accident,
Men clung with yearning Hope which would not die.
As when in some great City where the walls
Shake, and the streets with ghastly faces throng'd
Do utter forth a subterranean voice, 30

Among the inner columns far retir'd
At midnight, in the lone Acropolis,
Before the awful Genius of the place
Kneels the pale Priestess in deep faith, the while
Above her head the weak lamp dips and winks
Unto the fearful summoning without:
Nathless she ever clasps the marble knees,
Bathes the cold hand with tears, and gazeth on
Those eyes which wear no light but that wherewith
Her phantasy informs them.

40 Where are ye
Thrones of the Western wave, fair Islands green?
Where are your moonlight halls, your cedarn glooms,
The blossoming abysses of your hills?
Your flowering Capes, and your gold-sanded bays
Blown round with happy airs of odorous winds?
Where are the infinite ways, which, Seraph-trod,
Wound thro' your great Elysian solitudes,
Whose lowest deeps were, as with visible love,
Fill'd with Divine effulgence, circumfus'd,
50 Flowing between the clear and polish'd stems,
And ever circling round their emerald cones
In coronals and glories, such as gird
The unfading foreheads of the Saints in Heaven?
For nothing visible, they say, had birth
In that blest ground but it was play'd about
With its peculiar glory. Then I rais'd
My voice and cried, 'Wide Afric, doth thy Sun
Lighten, thy hills enfold a City as fair
As those which starr'd the night o' the elder World?
60 Or is the rumour of thy Timbuctoo
A dream as frail as those of ancient Time?'

A curve of whitening, flashing, ebbing light!
A rustling of white wings! the bright descent
Of a young Seraph! and he stood beside me
There on the ridge, and look'd into my face

With his unutterable, shining orbs.
So that with hasty motion I did veil
My vision with both hands, and saw before me
Such colour'd spots as dance athwart the eyes
Of those, that gaze upon the noonday Sun. 70
Girt with a Zone of flashing gold beneath
His breast, and compass'd round about his brow
With triple arch of everchanging bows,
And circled with the glory of living light
And alternation of all hues, he stood.

'O child of man, why muse you here alone
Upon the Mountain, on the dreams of old
Which fill'd the Earth with passing loveliness,
Which flung strange music on the howling winds,
And odours rapt from remote Paradise? 80
Thy sense is clogg'd with dull mortality,
Thy spirit fetter'd with the bond of clay:
Open thine eyes and see.'

I look'd, but not
Upon his face, for it was wonderful
With its exceeding brightness, and the light
Of the great Angel Mind which look'd from out
The starry glowing of his restless eyes.
I felt my soul grow mighty, and my Spirit
With supernatural excitation bound
Within me, and my mental eye grew large 90
With such a vast circumference of thought,
That in my vanity I seem'd to stand
Upon the outward verge and bound alone
Of full beatitude. Each failing sense
As with a momentary flash of light
Grew thrillingly distinct and keen. I saw
The smallest grain that dappled the dark Earth,
The indistinctest atom in deep air,
The Moon's white cities, and the opal width
Of her small glowing lakes, her silver heights 100

Unvisited with dew of vagrant cloud,
And the unsounded, undescended depth
Of her black hollows. The clear Galaxy
Shorn of its hoary lustre, wonderful,
Distinct and vivid with sharp points of light,
Blaze within blaze, an unimagin'd depth
And harmony of planet-girded Suns
And moon-encircled planets, wheel in wheel,
Arch'd the wan Sapphire. Nay – the hum of men,
110 Or other things talking in unknown tongues,
And notes of busy life in distant worlds
Beat like a far wave on my anxious ear.

A maze of piercing, trackless, thrilling thoughts,
Involving and embracing each with each,
Rapid as fire, inextricably link'd,
Expanding momently with every sight
And sound which struck the palpitating sense,
The issue of strong impulse, hurried through
The riv'n rapt brain; as when in some large lake
120 From pressure of descendant crags, which lapse
Disjointed, crumbling from their parent slope
At slender interval, the level calm
Is ridg'd with restless and increasing spheres
Which break upon each other, each th' effect
Of separate impulse, but more fleet and strong
Than its precursor, till the eye in vain
Amid the wild unrest of swimming shade
Dappled with hollow and alternate rise
Of interpenetrated arc, would scan
Definite round.

130 I know not if I shape
These things with accurate similitude
From visible objects, for but dimly now,
Less vivid than a half-forgotten dream,
The memory of that mental excellence
Comes o'er me, and it may be I entwine

The indecision of my present mind
With its past clearness, yet it seems to me
As even then the torrent of quick thought
Absorbed me from the nature of itself
With its own fleetness. Where is he that borne 140
Adown the sloping of an arrowy stream,
Could link his shallop to the fleeting edge,
And muse midway with philosophic calm
Upon the wondrous laws, which regulate
The fierceness of the bounding Element?

My thoughts which long had grovell'd in the slime
Of this dull world, like dusky worms which house
Beneath unshaken waters, but at once
Upon some Earth-awakening day of Spring
Do pass from gloom to glory, and aloft 150
Winnow the purple, bearing on both sides
Double display of starlit wings which burn,
Fanlike and fibred, with intensest bloom;
Ev'n so my thoughts, erewhile so low, now felt
Unutterable buoyancy and strength
To bear them upward through the trackless fields
Of undefin'd existence far and free.

Then first within the South methought I saw
A wilderness of spires, and chrystal pile
Of rampart upon rampart, dome on dome, 160
Illimitable range of battlement
On battlement, and the Imperial height
Of Canopy o'ercanopied.

Behind
In diamond light upsprung the dazzling cones
Of Pyramids as far surpassing Earth's
As Heaven than Earth is fairer. Each aloft
Upon his narrow'd Eminence bore globes
Of wheeling Suns, or Stars, or semblances
Of either, showering circular abyss

170 Of radiance. But the glory of the place
Stood out a pillar'd front of burnish'd gold,
Interminably high, if gold it were
Or metal more etherial, and beneath
Two doors of blinding brilliance, where no gaze
Might rest, stood open, and the eye could scan,
Through length of porch and valve and boundless hall,
Part of a throne of fiery flame, wherefrom
The snowy skirting of a garment hung,
And glimpse of multitudes of multitudes
180 That minister'd around it – if I saw
These things distinctly, for my human brain
Stagger'd beneath the vision, and thick night
Came down upon my eyelids, and I fell.

With ministering hand he rais'd me up:
Then with a mournful and ineffable smile,
Which but to look on for a moment fill'd
My eyes with irresistible sweet tears,
In accents of majestic melody,
Like a swoln river's gushings in still night
190 Mingled with floating music, thus he spake:

'There is no mightier Spirit than I to sway
The heart of man: and teach him to attain
By shadowing forth the Unattainable;
And step by step to scale that mighty stair
Whose landing-place is wrapt about with clouds
Of glory' of Heaven. With earliest light of Spring,
And in the glow of sallow Summertide,
And in red Autumn when the winds are wild
With gambols, and when full-voiced Winter roofs
200 The headland with inviolate white snow,
I play about his heart a thousand ways,
Visit his eyes with visions, and his ears
With harmonies of wind and wave and wood,
– Of winds which tell of waters, and of waters
Betraying the close kisses of the wind –

And win him unto me: and few there be
So gross of heart who have not felt and known
A higher than they see: They with dim eyes
Behold me darkling. Lo! I have given *thee*
To understand my presence, and to feel 210
My fullness; I have fill'd thy lips with power.
I have rais'd thee nigher to the spheres of Heaven
Man's first, last home: and thou with ravish'd sense
Listenest the lordly music flowing from
Th' illimitable years. I am the Spirit,
The permeating life which courseth through
All th' intricate and labyrinthine veins
Of the great vine of *Fable,* which, outspread
With growth of shadowing leaf and clusters rare,
Reacheth to every corner under Heaven, 220
Deep-rooted in the living soil of truth;
So that men's hopes and fears take refuge in
The fragrance of its complicated glooms,
And cool impleachèd twilights. Child of Man,
See'st thou yon river, whose translucent wave,
Forth issuing from the darkness, windeth through
The argent streets o' th' City, imaging
The soft inversion of her tremulous Domes,
Her gardens frequent with the stately Palm,
Her Pagods hung with music of sweet bells, 230
Her obelisks of rangèd Chrysolite,
Minarets and towers? Lo! how he passeth by,
And gulphs himself in sands, as not enduring
To carry through the world those waves, which bore
The reflex of my City in their depths.
Oh City! oh latest Throne! where I was rais'd
To be a mystery of loveliness
Unto all eyes, the time is well-nigh come
When I must render up this glorious home
To keen *Discovery*: soon yon brilliant towers 240
Shall darken with the waving of her wand;
Darken, and shrink and shiver into huts,

Black specks amid a waste of dreary sand,
Low-built, mud-wall'd, Barbarian settlements.
How chang'd from this fair City!'

Thus far the Spirit:
Then parted Heaven-ward on the wing: and I
Was left alone on Calpe, and the Moon
Had fallen from the night, and all was dark!

The Idealist

A mighty matter I rehearse,
A mighty matter undescried;
Come listen all who can.
I am the spirit of a man,
I weave the universe,
And indivisible divide,
Creating all I hear and see.
All souls are centres: I am one,
I am the earth, the stars, the sun,
10 I am the clouds, the sea.
I am the citadels and palaces
Of all great cities: I am Rome,
Tadmor and Cairo: I am Place
And Time, yet is my home
Eternity: (let no man think it odd,
For I am these,
And every other birth of every other race;)
I am all things, save souls of fellow men, and very God!

▲ ▲ ▲

From *Poems, Chiefly Lyrical* (1830)

Mariana

'Mariana in the moated grange'
Measure for Measure

With blackest moss the flower-plots
  Were thickly crusted, one and all:
The rusted nails fell from the knots
  That held the pear to the gable-wall.
The broken sheds look'd sad and strange:
  Unlifted was the clinking latch;
  Weeded and worn the ancient thatch
Upon the lonely moated grange.
    She only said, 'My life is dreary,
      He cometh not,' she said; 10
    She said, 'I am aweary, aweary,
      I would that I were dead!'

Her tears fell with the dews at even;
  Her tears fell ere the dews were dried;
She could not look on the sweet heaven,
  Either at morn or eventide.
After the flitting of the bats,
  When thickest dark did trance the sky,
  She drew her casement-curtain by,
And glanced athwart the glooming flats. 20
    She only said, 'The night is dreary,
      He cometh not,' she said;
    She said, 'I am aweary, aweary,
      I would that I were dead!'

Upon the middle of the night,
Waking she heard the night-fowl crow:
The cock sung out an hour ere light:
From the dark fen the oxen's low
Came to her: without hope of change,
30 In sleep she seem'd to walk forlorn,
Till cold winds woke the gray-eyed morn
About the lonely moated grange.
She only said, 'The day is dreary,
He cometh not,' she said;
She said, 'I am aweary, aweary,
I would that I were dead!'

About a stone-cast from the wall
A sluice with blacken'd waters slept,
And o'er it many, round and small,
40 The cluster'd marish-mosses crept.
Hard by a poplar shook alway,
All silver-green with gnarlèd bark:
For leagues no other tree did mark
The level waste, the rounding gray.
She only said, 'My life is dreary,
He cometh not,' she said;
She said, 'I am aweary, aweary,
I would that I were dead!'

And ever when the moon was low,
50 And the shrill winds were up and away,
In the white curtain, to and fro,
She saw the gusty shadow sway.
But when the moon was very low,
And wild winds bound within their cell,
The shadow of the poplar fell
Upon her bed, across her brow.
She only said, 'The night is dreary,
He cometh not,' she said;
She said, 'I am aweary, aweary,
60 I would that I were dead!'

All day within the dreamy house,
  The doors upon their hinges creak'd;
The blue fly sung in the pane; the mouse
  Behind the mouldering wainscot shriek'd,
Or from the crevice peer'd about.
  Old faces glimmer'd thro' the doors,
  Old footsteps trod the upper floors,
Old voices called her from without.
    She only said, 'My life is dreary,
      He cometh not,' she said; 70
    She said, 'I am aweary, aweary,
      I would that I were dead!'

The sparrow's chirrup on the roof,
  The slow clock ticking, and the sound
Which to the wooing wind aloof
  The poplar made, did all confound
Her sense; but most she loathed the hour
  When the thick-moted sunbeam lay
  Athwart the chambers, and the day
Was sloping toward his western bower. 80
    Then, said she, 'I am very dreary,
      He will not come,' she said;
    She wept, 'I am aweary, aweary,
      Oh God, that I were dead!'

Supposed Confessions of a Second-Rate Sensitive Mind

O God! my God! have mercy now.
I faint, I fall. Men say that Thou

Didst die for me, for such as *me*,
Patient of ill, and death, and scorn,
And that my sin was as a thorn
Among the thorns that girt Thy brow,
Wounding Thy soul. – That even now,
In this extremest misery
Of ignorance, I should require
10 A sign! and if a bolt of fire
Would rive the slumbrous summer noon
While I do pray to Thee alone,
Think my belief would stronger grow!
Is not my human pride brought low?
The boastings of my spirit still?
The joy I had in my freewill
All cold, and dead, and corpse-like grown?
And what is left to me, but Thou,
And faith in Thee? Men pass me by;
20 Christians with happy countenances –
And children all seem full of Thee!
And women smile with saint-like glances
Like Thine own mother's when she bow'd
Above Thee, on that happy morn
When angels spake to men aloud,
And Thou and peace to earth were born.
Goodwill to me as well as all –
I one of them: my brothers they:
Brothers in Christ – a world of peace
30 And confidence, day after day;
And trust and hope till things should cease,
And then one Heaven receive us all.

How sweet to have a common faith!
To hold a common scorn of death!
And at a burial to hear
The creaking cords which wound and eat
Into my human heart, whene'er
Earth goes to earth, with grief, not fear,
With hopeful grief, were passing sweet!

Thrice happy state again to be 40
The trustful infant on the knee!
Who lets his rosy fingers play
About his mother's neck, and knows
Nothing beyond his mother's eyes.
They comfort him by night and day;
They light his little life alway;
He hath no thought of coming woes;
He hath no care of life or death;
Scarce outward signs of joy arise,
Because the Spirit of happiness 50
And perfect rest so inward is;
And loveth so his innocent heart,
Her temple and her place of birth,
Where she would ever wish to dwell,
Life of the fountain there, beneath
Its salient springs, and far apart,
Hating to wander out on earth,
Or breathe into the hollow air,
Whose chillness would make visible
Her subtil, warm, and golden breath, 60
Which mixing with the infant's blood,
Fulfils him with beatitude.
Oh! sure it is a special care
Of God, to fortify from doubt,
To arm in proof, and guard about
With triple-mailèd trust, and clear
Delight, the infant's dawning year.

Would that my gloomèd fancy were
As thine, my mother, when with brows
Propt on thy knees, my hands upheld 70
In thine, I listen'd to thy vows,
For me outpour'd in holiest prayer –
For me unworthy! – and beheld
Thy mild deep eyes upraised, that knew
The beauty and repose of faith,

And the clear spirit shining thro'.
Oh! wherefore do we grow awry
From roots which strike so deep? why dare
Paths in the desert? Could not I
80 Bow myself down, where thou hast knelt,
To the earth – until the ice would melt
Here, and I feel as thou hast felt?
What Devil had the heart to scathe
Flowers thou hadst rear'd – to brush the dew
From thine own lily, when thy grave
Was deep, my mother, in the clay?
Myself? Is it thus? Myself? Had I
So little love for thee? But why
Prevail'd not thy pure prayers? Why pray
90 To one who heeds not, who can save
But will not? Great in faith, and strong
Against the grief of circumstance
Wert thou, and yet unheard. What if
Thou pleadest still, and seest me drive
Thro' utter dark a full-sail'd skiff,
Unpiloted i' the echoing dance
Of reboant whirlwinds, stooping low
Unto the death, not sunk! I know
At matins and at evensong,
100 That thou, if thou wert yet alive,
In deep and daily prayers would'st strive
To reconcile me with thy God.
Albeit, my hope is gray, and cold
At heart, thou wouldest murmur still –
'Bring this lamb back into Thy fold,
My Lord, if so it be Thy will.'
Would'st tell me I must brook the rod
And chastisement of human pride;
That pride, the sin of devils, stood
110 Betwixt me and the light of God!
That hitherto I had defied
And had rejected God – that grace

Would drop from his o'er-brimming love,
As manna on my wilderness,
If I would pray – that God would move
And strike the hard, hard rock, and thence,
Sweet in their utmost bitterness,
Would issue tears of penitence
Which would keep green hope's life. Alas!
I think that pride hath now no place 120
Nor sojourn in me. I am void,
Dark, formless, utterly destroyed.
Why not believe then? Why not yet
Anchor thy frailty there, where man
Hath moor'd and rested? Ask the sea
At midnight, when the crisp slope waves
After a tempest, rib and fret
The broad-imbasèd beach, why he
Slumbers not like a mountain tarn?
Wherefore his ridges are not curls 130
And ripples of an inland mere?
Wherefore he moaneth thus, nor can
Draw down into his vexèd pools
All that blue heaven which hues and paves
The other? I am too forlorn,
Too shaken: my own weakness fools
My judgment, and my spirit whirls,
Moved from beneath with doubt and fear.

'Yet,' said I, in my morn of youth,
The unsunn'd freshness of my strength, 140
When I went forth in quest of truth,
'It is man's privilege to doubt,
If so be that from doubt at length,
Truth may stand forth unmoved of change,
An image with profulgent brows,
And perfect limbs, as from the storm
Of running fires and fluid range
Of lawless airs, at last stood out

This excellence and solid form
150 Of constant beauty. For the Ox
Feeds in the herb, and sleeps, or fills
The hornèd valleys all about,
And hollows of the fringèd hills
In summer heats, with placid lows
Unfearing, till his own blood flows
About his hoof. And in the flocks
The lamb rejoiceth in the year,
And raceth freely with his fere,
And answers to his mother's calls
160 From the flower'd furrow. In a time,
Of which he wots not, run short pains
Thro' his warm heart; and then, from whence
He knows not, on his light there falls
A shadow; and his native slope,
Where he was wont to leap and climb,
Floats from his sick and filmèd eyes,
And something in the darkness draws
His forehead earthward, and he dies.
Shall man live thus, in joy and hope
170 As a young lamb, who cannot dream,
Living, but that he shall live on?
Shall we not look into the laws
Of life and death, and things that seem,
And things that be, and analyse
Our double nature, and compare
All creeds till we have found the one,
If one there be?' Ay me! I fear
All may not doubt, but everywhere
Some must clasp Idols. Yet, my God,
180 Whom call I Idol? Let Thy dove
Shadow me over, and my sins
Be unremember'd, and Thy love
Enlighten me. Oh teach me yet
Somewhat before the heavy clod

Weighs on me, and the busy fret
Of that sharp-headed worm begins
In the gross blackness underneath.

O weary life! O weary death!
O spirit and heart made desolate!
O damnèd vacillating state! 190

Song ['A Spirit haunts the year's last hours']

I

A spirit haunts the year's last hours
Dwelling amid these yellowing bowers:
        To himself he talks;
For at eventide, listening earnestly,
At his work you may hear him sob and sigh
        In the walks;
        Earthward he boweth the heavy stalks
Of the mouldering flowers:
    Heavily hangs the broad sunflower
        Over its grave i' the earth so chilly; 10
    Heavily hangs the hollyhock,
        Heavily hangs the tiger-lily.

II

The air is damp, and hush'd, and close,
As a sick man's room when he taketh repose
        An hour before death;
My very heart faints and my whole soul grieves
At the moist rich smell of the rotting leaves,
        And the breath
        Of the fading edges of box beneath,
And the year's last rose. 20

Heavily hangs the broad sunflower
Over its grave i' the earth so chilly;
Heavily hangs the hollyhock,
Heavily hangs the tiger-lily.

A Character

With a half-glance upon the sky
At night he said, 'The wanderings
Of this most intricate Universe
Teach me the nothingness of things.'
Yet could not all creation pierce
Beyond the bottom of his eye.

He spake of beauty: that the dull
Saw no divinity in grass,
Life in dead stones, or spirit in air;
10 Then looking as 'twere in a glass,
He smooth'd his chin and sleek'd his hair,
And said the earth was beautiful.

He spake of virtue: not the gods
More purely, when they wish to charm
Pallas and Juno sitting by:
And with a sweeping of the arm,
And a lack-lustre dead-blue eye,
Devolved his rounded periods.

Most delicately hour by hour
20 He canvass'd human mysteries,
And trod on silk, as if the winds
Blew his own praises in his eyes,

And stood aloof from other minds
In impotence of fancied power.

With lips depress'd as he were meek,
Himself unto himself he sold:
Upon himself himself did feed:
Quiet, dispassionate, and cold,
And other than his form of creed,
With chisell'd features clear and sleek. 30

The Poet's Mind

I

Vex not thou the poet's mind
With thy shallow wit:
Vex not thou the poet's mind;
For thou canst not fathom it.
Clear and bright it should be ever,
Flowing like a crystal river;
Bright as light, and clear as wind.

II

Dark-brow'd sophist, come not anear;
All the place is holy ground;
Hollow smile and frozen sneer 10
Come not here.
Holy water will I pour
Into every spicy flower
Of the laurel-shrubs that hedge it around.
The flowers would faint at your cruel cheer.
In your eye there is death,
There is frost in your breath

Which would blight the plants.
Where you stand you cannot hear
20 From the groves within
The wild-bird's din.
In the heart of the garden the merry bird chants.
It would fall to the ground if you came in.
In the middle leaps a fountain
Like sheet lightning,
Ever brightening
With a low melodious thunder;
All day and all night it is ever drawn
From the brain of the purple mountain
30 Which stands in the distance yonder:
It springs on a level of bowery lawn,
And the mountain draws it from Heaven above,
And it sings a song of undying love;
And yet, tho' its voice be so clear and full,
You never would hear it; your ears are so dull;
So keep where you are: you are foul with sin;
It would shrink to the earth if you came in.

Nothing Will Die

When will the stream be aweary of flowing
Under my eye?
When will the wind be aweary of blowing
Over the sky?
When will the clouds be aweary of fleeting?
When will the heart be aweary of beating?
And nature die?
Never, oh! never, nothing will die;

The stream flows,
The wind blows, 10
The cloud fleets,
The heart beats,
Nothing will die.

Nothing will die;
All things will change
Thro' eternity.
'Tis the world's winter;
Autumn and summer
Are gone long ago;
Earth is dry to the centre, 20
But spring, a new comer,
A spring rich and strange,
Shall make the winds blow
Round and round,
Thro' and thro',
Here and there,
Till the air
And the ground
Shall be fill'd with life anew.

The world was never made; 30
It will change, but it will not fade.
So let the wind range;
For even and morn
Ever will be
Thro' eternity.
Nothing was born;
Nothing will die;
All things will change.

All Things Will Die

Clearly the blue river chimes in its flowing
Under my eye;
Warmly and broadly the south winds are blowing
Over the sky.
One after another the white clouds are fleeting;
Every heart this May morning in joyance is beating
Full merrily;
Yet all things must die.
The stream will cease to flow;
10 The wind will cease to blow;
The clouds will cease to fleet;
The heart will cease to beat;
For all things must die.
All things must die.
Spring will come never more.
Oh! vanity!
Death waits at the door.
See! our friends are all forsaking
The wine and the merrymaking.
20 We are call'd – we must go.
Laid low, very low,
In the dark we must lie.
The merry glees are still;
The voice of the bird
Shall no more be heard,
Nor the wind on the hill.
Oh! misery!
Hark! death is calling
While I speak to ye,
30 The jaw is falling,
The red cheek paling,
The strong limbs failing;

Ice with the warm blood mixing;
The eyeballs fixing.
Nine times goes the passing bell:
Ye merry souls, farewell.
    The old earth
    Had a birth,
    As all men know,
    Long ago. 40
And the old earth must die.
So let the warm winds range,
And the blue wave beat the shore;
For even and morn
Ye will never see
Thro' eternity.
All things were born.
Ye will come never more,
For all things must die.

The Dying Swan

I

The plain was grassy, wild and bare,
Wide, wild, and open to the air,
Which had built up everywhere
  An under-roof of doleful gray.
With an inner voice the river ran,
Adown it floated a dying swan,
    And loudly did lament.
  It was the middle of the day.
Ever the weary wind went on,
    And took the reed-tops as it went. 10

II

Some blue peaks in the distance rose,
And white against the cold-white sky,
Shone out their crowning snows.
  One willow over the river wept,
And shook the wave as the wind did sigh;
Above in the wind was the swallow,
    Chasing itself at its own wild will,
    And far thro' the marish green and still
    The tangled water-courses slept,
20 Shot over with purple, and green, and yellow.

III

The wild swan's death-hymn took the soul
Of that waste place with joy
Hidden in sorrow: at first to the ear
The warble was low, and full and clear;
And floating about the under-sky,
Prevailing in weakness, the coronach stole
Sometimes afar, and sometimes anear;
But anon her awful jubilant voice,
With a music strange and manifold,
30 Flow'd forth on a carol free and bold;
As when a mighty people rejoice
With shawms, and with cymbals, and harps of gold,
And the tumult of their acclaim is roll'd
Thro' the open gates of the city afar,
To the shepherd who watcheth the evening star.
And the creeping mosses and clambering weeds,
And the willow-branches hoar and dank,
And the wavy swell of the soughing reeds,
And the wave-worn horns of the echoing bank,
40 And the silvery marish-flowers that throng
The desolate creeks and pools among,
Were flooded over with eddying song.

The Kraken

Below the thunders of the upper deep;
Far, far beneath in the abysmal sea,
His ancient, dreamless, uninvaded sleep
The Kraken sleepeth: faintest sunlights flee
About his shadowy sides: above him swell
Huge sponges of millennial growth and height;
And far away into the sickly light,
From many a wondrous grot and secret cell
Unnumber'd and enormous polypi
Winnow with giant arms the slumbering green. 10
There hath he lain for ages and will lie
Battening upon huge seaworms in his sleep,
Until the latter fire shall heat the deep;
Then once by man and angels to be seen,
In roaring he shall rise and on the surface die.

▲ ▲ ▲

From *Poems* (1832)

The Lady of Shalott

PART I

On either side the river lie
Long fields of barley and of rye,
That clothe the wold and meet the sky;
And thro' the field the road runs by
        To many-tower'd Camelot;
And up and down the people go,
Gazing where the lilies blow
Round an island there below,
        The island of Shalott.

10 Willows whiten, aspens quiver,
Little breezes dusk and shiver
Thro' the wave that runs for ever
By the island in the river
        Flowing down to Camelot.
Four gray walls, and four gray towers,
Overlook a space of flowers,
And the silent isle imbowers
        The Lady of Shalott.

By the margin, willow-veil'd,
20 Slide the heavy barges trail'd
By slow horses; and unhail'd
The shallop flitteth silken-sail'd
        Skimming down to Camelot:

But who hath seen her wave her hand?
Or at the casement seen her stand?
Or is she known in all the land,
    The Lady of Shalott?

Only reapers, reaping early
In among the bearded barley,
Hear a song that echoes cheerly 30
From the river winding clearly,
    Down to tower'd Camelot:
And by the moon the reaper weary,
Piling sheaves in uplands airy,
Listening, whispers ''Tis the fairy
    Lady of Shalott.'

PART II

There she weaves by night and day
A magic web with colours gay.
She has heard a whisper say,
A curse is on her if she stay 40
    To look down to Camelot.
She knows not what the curse may be,
And so she weaveth steadily,
And little other care hath she,
    The Lady of Shalott.

And moving thro' a mirror clear
That hangs before her all the year,
Shadows of the world appear.
There she sees the highway near
    Winding down to Camelot: 50
There the river eddy whirls,
And there the surly village-churls,
And the red cloaks of market girls,
    Pass onward from Shalott.

Sometimes a troop of damsels glad,
An abbot on an ambling pad,

Sometimes a curly shepherd-lad,
Or long-hair'd page in crimson clad,
Goes by to tower'd Camelot;
60 And sometimes thro' the mirror blue
The knights come riding two and two:
She hath no loyal knight and true,
The Lady of Shalott.

But in her web she still delights
To weave the mirror's magic sights,
For often thro' the silent nights
A funeral, with plumes and lights
And music, went to Camelot:
Or when the moon was overhead,
70 Came two young lovers lately wed;
'I am half sick of shadows,' said
The Lady of Shalott.

PART III

A bow-shot from her bower-eaves,
He rode between the barley-sheaves,
The sun came dazzling thro' the leaves,
And flamed upon the brazen greaves
Of bold Sir Lancelot.
A red-cross knight for ever kneel'd
To a lady in his shield,
80 That sparkled on the yellow field,
Beside remote Shalott.

The gemmy bridle glitter'd free,
Like to some branch of stars we see
Hung in the golden Galaxy.
The bridle bells rang merrily
As he rode down to Camelot:
And from his blazon'd baldric slung
A mighty silver bugle hung,
And as he rode his armour rung,
90 Beside remote Shalott.

All in the blue unclouded weather
Thick-jewell'd shone the saddle-leather,
The helmet and the helmet-feather
Burn'd like one burning flame together,
        As he rode down to Camelot.
As often thro' the purple night,
Below the starry clusters bright,
Some bearded meteor, trailing light,
        Moves over still Shalott.

His broad clear brow in sunlight glow'd; 100
On burnish'd hooves his war-horse trode;
From underneath his helmet flow'd
His coal-black curls as on he rode,
        As he rode down to Camelot.
From the bank and from the river
He flash'd into the crystal mirror,
'Tirra lirra,' by the river
        Sang Sir Lancelot.

She left the web, she left the loom,
She made three paces thro' the room, 110
She saw the water-lily bloom,
She saw the helmet and the plume,
        She look'd down to Camelot.
Out flew the web and floated wide;
The mirror crack'd from side to side;
'The curse is come upon me,' cried
        The Lady of Shalott.

PART IV

In the stormy east-wind straining,
The pale yellow woods were waning,
The broad stream in his banks complaining, 120
Heavily the low sky raining
        Over tower'd Camelot;
Down she came and found a boat

Beneath a willow left afloat,
And round about the prow she wrote
The Lady of Shalott.

And down the river's dim expanse
Like some bold seër in a trance,
Seeing all his own mischance –
130 With a glassy countenance
Did she look to Camelot.
And at the closing of the day
She loosed the chain, and down she lay;
The broad stream bore her far away,
The Lady of Shalott.

Lying, robed in snowy white
That loosely flew to left and right –
The leaves upon her falling light –
Thro' the noises of the night
140 She floated down to Camelot:
And as the boat-head wound along
The willowy hills and fields among,
They heard her singing her last song,
The Lady of Shalott.

Heard a carol, mournful, holy,
Chanted loudly, chanted lowly,
Till her blood was frozen slowly,
And her eyes were darken'd wholly,
Turn'd to tower'd Camelot.
150 For ere she reach'd upon the tide
The first house by the water-side,
Singing in her song she died,
The Lady of Shalott.

Under tower and balcony,
By garden-wall and gallery,
A gleaming shape she floated by,
Dead-pale between the houses high,
Silent into Camelot.

Out upon the wharfs they came,
Knight and burgher, lord and dame, 160
And round the prow they read her name,
The Lady of Shalott.

Who is this? and what is here?
And in the lighted palace near
Died the sound of royal cheer;
And they cross'd themselves for fear,
All the knights at Camelot:
But Lancelot mused a little space;
He said, 'She has a lovely face;
God in his mercy lend her grace, 170
The Lady of Shalott.'

Mariana in the South

With one black shadow at its feet,
The house thro' all the level shines,
Close-latticed to the brooding heat,
And silent in its dusty vines:
A faint-blue ridge upon the right,
An empty river-bed before,
And shallows on a distant shore,
In glaring sand and inlets bright.
But 'Ave Mary,' made she moan,
And 'Ave Mary,' night and morn, 10
And 'Ah,' she sang, 'to be all alone,
To live forgotten, and love forlorn.'

She, as her carol sadder grew,
From brow and bosom slowly down

Thro' rosy taper fingers drew
  Her streaming curls of deepest brown
To left and right, and made appear
  Still-lighted in a secret shrine,
  Her melancholy eyes divine,
20 The home of woe without a tear.
    And 'Ave Mary,' was her moan,
      'Madonna, sad is night and morn,'
    And 'Ah,' she sang, 'to be all alone,
      To live forgotten, and love forlorn.'

Till all the crimson changed, and past
  Into deep orange o'er the sea,
Low on her knees herself she cast,
  Before Our Lady murmur'd she;
Complaining, 'Mother, give me grace
30 To help me of my weary load.'
  And on the liquid mirror glow'd
The clear perfection of her face.
    'Is this the form,' she made her moan,
      'That won his praises night and morn?'
    And 'Ah,' she said, 'but I wake alone,
      I sleep forgotten, I wake forlorn.'

Nor bird would sing, nor lamb would bleat,
  Nor any cloud would cross the vault,
But day increased from heat to heat,
40 On stony drought and steaming salt;
Till now at noon she slept again,
  And seem'd knee-deep in mountain grass,
  And heard her native breezes pass,
And runlets babbling down the glen.
    She breathed in sleep a lower moan,
      And murmuring, as at night and morn,
    She thought, 'My spirit is here alone,
      Walks forgotten, and is forlorn.'

Dreaming, she knew it was a dream:
  She felt he was and was not there. 50
She woke: the babble of the stream
  Fell, and, without, the steady glare
Shrank one sick willow sere and small.
  The river-bed was dusty-white;
  And all the furnace of the light
Struck up against the blinding wall.
    She whisper'd, with a stifled moan
      More inward than at night or morn,
    'Sweet Mother, let me not here alone
      Live forgotten and die forlorn.' 60

And, rising, from her bosom drew
  Old letters, breathing of her worth,
For 'Love,' they said, 'must needs be true,
  To what is loveliest upon earth.'
An image seem'd to pass the door,
  To look at her with slight, and say
  'But now thy beauty flows away,
So be alone for evermore.'
    'O cruel heart,' she changed her tone,
      'And cruel love, whose end is scorn, 70
    Is this the end to be left alone,
      To live forgotten, and die forlorn?'

But sometimes in the falling day
  An image seem'd to pass the door,
To look into her eyes and say,
  'But thou shalt be alone no more.'
And flaming downward over all
  From heat to heat the day decreased,
  And slowly rounded to the east
The one black shadow from the wall. 80
    'The day to night,' she made her moan,
      'The day to night, the night to morn,
    And day and night I am left alone
      To live forgotten, and love forlorn.'

At eve a dry cicala sung,
There came a sound as of the sea;
Backward the lattice-blind she flung,
And lean'd upon the balcony.
There all in spaces rosy-bright
90 Large Hesper glitter'd on her tears,
And deepening thro' the silent spheres
Heaven over Heaven rose the night.
And weeping then she made her moan,
'The night comes on that knows not morn,
When I shall cease to be all alone,
To live forgotten, and love forlorn.'

Fatima

O Love, Love, Love! O withering might!
O sun, that from thy noonday height
Shudderest when I strain my sight,
Throbbing thro' all thy heat and light,
Lo, falling from my constant mind,
Lo, parch'd and wither'd, deaf and blind,
I whirl like leaves in roaring wind.

Last night I wasted hateful hours
Below the city's eastern towers:
10 I thirsted for the brooks, the showers:
I roll'd among the tender flowers:
I crush'd them on my breast, my mouth;
I look'd athwart the burning drouth
Of that long desert to the south.

Last night, when some one spoke his name,
From my swift blood that went and came
A thousand little shafts of flame
Were shiver'd in my narrow frame.
O Love, O fire! once he drew
With one long kiss my whole soul thro' 20
My lips, as sunlight drinketh dew.

Before he mounts the hill, I know
He cometh quickly: from below
Sweet gales, as from deep gardens, blow
Before him, striking on my brow.
In my dry brain my spirit soon,
Down-deepening from swoon to swoon,
Faints like a dazzled morning moon.

The wind sounds like a silver wire,
And from beyond the noon a fire 30
Is pour'd upon the hills, and nigher
The skies stoop down in their desire;
And, isled in sudden seas of light,
My heart, pierced thro' with fierce delight,
Bursts into blossom in his sight.

My whole soul waiting silently,
All naked in a sultry sky,
Droops blinded with his shining eye:
I *will* possess him or will die.
I will grow round him in his place, 40
Grow, live, die looking on his face,
Die, dying clasp'd in his embrace.

Oenone

There lies a vale in Ida, lovelier
Than all the valleys of Ionian hills.
The swimming vapour slopes athwart the glen,
Puts forth an arm, and creeps from pine to pine,
And loiters, slowly drawn. On either hand
The lawns and meadow-ledges midway down
Hang rich in flowers, and far below them roars
The long brook falling thro' the clov'n ravine
In cataract after cataract to the sea.
10 Behind the valley topmost Gargarus
Stands up and takes the morning: but in front
The gorges, opening wide apart, reveal
Troas and Ilion's column'd citadel,
The crown of Troas.
Hither came at noon
Mournful Oenone, wandering forlorn
Of Paris, once her playmate on the hills.
Her cheek had lost the rose, and round her neck
Floated her hair or seem'd to float in rest.
She, leaning on a fragment twined with vine,
20 Sang to the stillness, till the mountain-shade
Sloped downward to her seat from the upper cliff.

'O mother Ida, many-fountain'd Ida,
Dear mother Ida, harken ere I die.
For now the noonday quiet holds the hill:
The grasshopper is silent in the grass:
The lizard, with his shadow on the stone,
Rests like a shadow, and the winds are dead.
The purple flower droops: the golden bee
Is lily-cradled: I alone awake.
30 My eyes are full of tears, my heart of love,

My heart is breaking, and my eyes are dim,
And I am all aweary of my life.

'O mother Ida, many-fountain'd Ida,
Dear mother Ida, harken ere I die.
Hear me, O Earth, hear me, O Hills, O Caves
That house the cold crown'd snake! O mountain brooks,
I am the daughter of a River-God,
Hear me, for I will speak, and build up all
My sorrow with my song, as yonder walls
Rose slowly to a music slowly breathed, 40
A cloud that gather'd shape: for it may be
That, while I speak of it, a little while
My heart may wander from its deeper woe.

'O mother Ida, many-fountain'd Ida,
Dear mother Ida, harken ere I die.
I waited underneath the dawning hills,
Aloft the mountain lawn was dewy-dark,
And dewy dark aloft the mountain pine:
Beautiful Paris, evil-hearted Paris,
Leading a jet-black goat white-horn'd, white-hooved, 50
Came up from reedy Simois all alone.

'O mother Ida, harken ere I die.
Far-off the torrent call'd me from the cleft:
Far up the solitary morning smote
The streaks of virgin snow. With down-dropt eyes
I sat alone: white-breasted like a star
Fronting the dawn he moved; a leopard skin
Droop'd from his shoulder, but his sunny hair
Cluster'd about his temples like a God's:
And his cheek brighten'd as the foam-bow brightens 60
When the wind blows the foam, and all my heart
Went forth to embrace him coming ere he came.

'Dear mother Ida, harken ere I die.
He smiled, and opening out his milk-white palm
Disclosed a fruit of pure Hesperian gold,

That smelt ambrosially, and while I look'd
And listen'd, the full-flowing river of speech
Came down upon my heart.
'"My own Oenone,
Beautiful-brow'd Oenone, my own soul,
70 Behold this fruit, whose gleaming rind ingrav'n
'For the most fair,' would seem to award it thine,
As lovelier than whatever Oread haunt
The knolls of Ida, loveliest in all grace
Of movement, and the charm of married brows."

'Dear mother Ida, harken ere I die.
He prest the blossom of his lips to mine,
And added "This was cast upon the board,
When all the full-faced presence of the Gods
Ranged in the halls of Peleus; whereupon
80 Rose feud, with question unto whom 'twere due:
But light-foot Iris brought it yester-eve,
Delivering, that to me, by common voice
Elected umpire, Herè comes to-day,
Pallas and Aphroditè, claiming each
This meed of fairest. Thou, within the cave
Behind yon whispering tuft of oldest pine,
Mayst well behold them unbeheld, unheard
Hear all, and see thy Paris judge of Gods."

'Dear mother Ida, harken ere I die.
90 It was the deep midnoon: one silvery cloud
Had lost his way between the piney sides
Of this long glen. Then to the bower they came,
Naked they came to that smooth-swarded bower,
And at their feet the crocus brake like fire,
Violet, amaracus, and asphodel,
Lotos and lilies: and a wind arose,
And overhead the wandering ivy and vine,
This way and that, in many a wild festoon
Ran riot, garlanding the gnarlèd boughs
100 With bunch and berry and flower thro' and thro'.

'O mother Ida, harken ere I die.
On the tree-tops a crested peacock lit,
And o'er him flow'd a golden cloud, and lean'd
Upon him, slowly dropping fragrant dew.
Then first I heard the voice of her, to whom
Coming thro' Heaven, like a light that grows
Larger and clearer, with one mind the Gods
Rise up for reverence. She to Paris made
Proffer of royal power, ample rule
Unquestion'd, overflowing revenue 110
Wherewith to embellish state, "from many a vale
And river-sunder'd champaign clothed with corn,
Or labour'd mine undrainable of ore.
Honour," she said, "and homage, tax and toll,
From many an inland town and haven large,
Mast-throng'd beneath her shadowing citadel
In glassy bays among her tallest towers."

'O mother Ida, harken ere I die.
Still she spake on and still she spake of power,
"Which in all action is the end of all; 120
Power fitted to the season; wisdom-bred
And throned of wisdom – from all neighbour crowns
Alliance and allegiance, till thy hand
Fail from the sceptre-staff. Such boon from me,
From me, Heaven's Queen, Paris, to thee king-born,
A shepherd all thy life but yet king-born,
Should come most welcome, seeing men, in power
Only, are likest gods, who have attain'd
Rest in a happy place and quiet seats
Above the thunder, with undying bliss 130
In knowledge of their own supremacy."

'Dear mother Ida, harken ere I die.
She ceased, and Paris held the costly fruit
Out at arm's length, so much the thought of power
Flatter'd his spirit; but Pallas where she stood

Somewhat apart, her clear and bared limbs
O'erthwarted with the brazen-headed spear
Upon her pearly shoulder leaning cold,
The while, above, her full and earnest eye
140 Over her snow-cold breast and angry cheek
Kept watch, waiting decision, made reply.

'"Self-reverence, self-knowledge, self-control,
These three alone lead life to sovereign power.
Yet not for power (power of herself
Would come uncall'd for) but to live by law,
Acting the law we live by without fear;
And, because right is right, to follow right
Were wisdom in the scorn of consequence."

'Dear mother Ida, harken ere I die.
150 Again she said: "I woo thee not with gifts.
Sequel of guerdon could not alter me
To fairer. Judge thou me by what I am,
So shalt thou find me fairest.

Yet, indeed,
If gazing on divinity disrobed
Thy mortal eyes are frail to judge of fair,
Unbias'd by self-profit, oh! rest thee sure
That I shall love thee well and cleave to thee,
So that my vigour, wedded to thy blood,
Shall strike within thy pulses, like a God's,
160 To push thee forward thro' a life of shocks,
Dangers, and deeds, until endurance grow
Sinew'd with action, and the full-grown will,
Circled thro' all experiences, pure law,
Commeasure perfect freedom."

'Here she ceas'd,
And Paris ponder'd, and I cried, "O Paris,
Give it to Pallas!" but he heard me not,
Or hearing would not hear me, woe is me!

'O mother Ida, many-fountain'd Ida,
Dear mother Ida, harken ere I die.
Idalian Aphroditè beautiful, 170
Fresh as the foam, new-bathed in Paphian wells,
With rosy slender fingers backward drew
From her warm brows and bosom her deep hair
Ambrosial, golden round her lucid throat
And shoulder: from the violets her light foot
Shone rosy-white, and o'er her rounded form
Between the shadows of the vine-bunches
Floated the glowing sunlights, as she moved.

'Dear mother Ida, harken ere I die.
She with a subtle smile in her mild eyes, 180
The herald of her triumph, drawing nigh
Half-whisper'd in his ear, "I promise thee
The fairest and most loving wife in Greece,"
She spoke and laugh'd: I shut my sight for fear:
But when I look'd, Paris had raised his arm,
And I beheld great Herè's angry eyes,
As she withdrew into the golden cloud,
And I was left alone within the bower;
And from that time to this I am alone,
And I shall be alone until I die. 190

'Yet, mother Ida, harken ere I die.
Fairest – why fairest wife? am I not fair?
My love hath told me so a thousand times.
Methinks I must be fair, for yesterday,
When I past by, a wild and wanton pard,
Eyed like the evening star, with playful tail
Crouch'd fawning in the weed. Most loving is she?
Ah me, my mountain shepherd, that my arms
Were wound about thee, and my hot lips prest
Close, close to thine in that quick-falling dew 200
Of fruitful kisses, thick as Autumn rains
Flash in the pools of whirling Simois.

'O mother, hear me yet before I die.
They came, they cut away my tallest pines,
My tall dark pines, that plumed the craggy ledge
High over the blue gorge, and all between
The snowy peak and snow-white cataract
Foster'd the callow eaglet – from beneath
Whose thick mysterious boughs in the dark morn
210 The panther's roar came muffled, while I sat
Low in the valley. Never, never more
Shall lone Oenone see the morning mist
Sweep thro' them; never see them overlaid
With narrow moon-lit slips of silver cloud,
Between the loud stream and the trembling stars.

'O mother, hear me yet before I die.
I wish that somewhere in the ruin'd folds,
Among the fragments tumbled from the glens,
Or the dry thickets, I could meet with her
220 The Abominable, that uninvited came
Into the fair Peleïan banquet-hall,
And cast the golden fruit upon the board,
And bred this change; that I might speak my mind,
And tell her to her face how much I hate
Her presence, hated both of Gods and men.

'O mother, hear me yet before I die.
Hath he not sworn his love a thousand times,
In this green valley, under this green hill,
Ev'n on this hand, and sitting on this stone?
230 Seal'd it with kisses? water'd it with tears?
O happy tears, and how unlike to these!
O happy Heaven, how canst thou see my face?
O happy earth, how canst thou bear my weight?
O death, death, death, thou ever-floating cloud,
There are enough unhappy on this earth,
Pass by the happy souls, that love to live:
I pray thee, pass before my light of life,
And shadow all my soul, that I may die.

Thou weighest heavy on the heart within,
Weigh heavy on my eyelids: let me die. 240

'O mother, hear me yet before I die.
I will not die alone, for fiery thoughts
Do shape themselves within me, more and more,
Whereof I catch the issue, as I hear
Dead sounds at night come from the inmost hills,
Like footsteps upon wool. I dimly see
My far-off doubtful purpose, as a mother
Conjectures of the features of her child
Ere it is born: her child! – a shudder comes
Across me: never child be born of me, 250
Unblest, to vex me with his father's eyes!

'O mother, hear me yet before I die.
Hear me, O earth. I will not die alone,
Lest their shrill happy laughter come to me
Walking the cold and starless road of Death
Uncomforted, leaving my ancient love
With the Greek woman. I will rise and go
Down into Troy, and ere the stars come forth
Talk with the wild Cassandra, for she says
A fire dances before her, and a sound 260
Rings ever in her ears of armèd men.
What this may be I know not, but I know
That, wheresoe'er I am by night and day,
All earth and air seem only burning fire.'

The Palace of Art

I built my soul a lordly pleasure-house,
  Wherein at ease for aye to dwell.
I said, 'O Soul, make merry and carouse,
    Dear soul, for all is well.'

A huge crag-platform, smooth as burnish'd brass
  I chose. The rangèd ramparts bright
From level meadow-bases of deep grass
    Suddenly scaled the light.

Thereon I built it firm. Of ledge or shelf
10 The rock rose clear, or winding stair.
My soul would live alone unto herself
    In her high palace there.

And 'while the world runs round and round,' I said,
  'Reign thou apart, a quiet king,
Still as, while Saturn whirls, his stedfast shade
    Sleeps on his luminous ring.'

To which my soul made answer readily:
  'Trust me, in bliss I shall abide
In this great mansion, that is built for me,
20   So royal-rich and wide.'

*

Four courts I made, East, West and South and North,
  In each a squarèd lawn, wherefrom
The golden gorge of dragons spouted forth
    A flood of fountain-foam.

And round the cool green courts there ran a row
  Of cloisters, branch'd like mighty woods,

Echoing all night to that sonorous flow
    Of spouted fountain-floods.

And round the roofs a gilded gallery
  That lent broad verge to distant lands, 30
Far as the wild swan wings, to where the sky
    Dipt down to sea and sands.

From those four jets four currents in one swell
  Across the mountain stream'd below
In misty folds, that floating as they fell
    Lit up a torrent-bow.

And high on every peak a statue seem'd
  To hang on tiptoe, tossing up
A cloud of incense of all odour steam'd
    From out a golden cup. 40

So that she thought, 'And who shall gaze upon
  My palace with unblinded eyes,
While this great bow will waver in the sun,
    And that sweet incense rise?'

For that sweet incense rose and never fail'd,
  And, while day sank or mounted higher,
The light aërial gallery, golden-rail'd,
    Burnt like a fringe of fire.

Likewise the deep-set windows, stain'd and traced,
  Would seem slow-flaming crimson fires 50
From shadow'd grots of arches interlaced,
    And tipt with frost-like spires.

*

Full of long-sounding corridors it was,
  That over-vaulted grateful gloom,
Thro' which the livelong day my soul did pass,
    Well-pleased, from room to room.

Full of great rooms and small the palace stood,
  All various, each a perfect whole

From living Nature, fit for every mood
60 And change of my still soul.

For some were hung with arras green and blue,
Showing a gaudy summer-morn,
Where with puff'd cheek the belted hunter blew
His wreathèd bugle-horn.

One seem'd all dark and red – a tract of sand,
And some one pacing there alone,
Who paced for ever in a glimmering land,
Lit with a low large moon.

One show'd an iron coast and angry waves.
70 You seem'd to hear them climb and fall
And roar rock-thwarted under bellowing caves,
Beneath the windy wall.

And one, a full-fed river winding slow
By herds upon an endless plain,
The ragged rims of thunder brooding low,
With shadow-streaks of rain.

And one, the reapers at their sultry toil.
In front they bound the sheaves. Behind
Were realms of upland, prodigal in oil,
80 And hoary to the wind.

And one a foreground black with stones and slags,
Beyond, a line of heights, and higher
All barr'd with long white cloud the scornful crags,
And highest, snow and fire.

And one, an English home – gray twilight pour'd
On dewy pastures, dewy trees,
Softer than sleep – all things in order stored,
A haunt of ancient Peace.

Nor these alone, but every landscape fair,
90 As fit for every mood of mind,

Or gay, or grave, or sweet, or stern, was there
Not less than truth design'd.

*

Or the maid-mother by a crucifix,
In tracts of pasture sunny-warm,
Beneath branch-work of costly sardonyx
Sat smiling, babe in arm.

Or in a clear-wall'd city on the sea,
Near gilded organ-pipes, her hair
Wound with white roses, slept St Cecily;
An angel look'd at her. 100

Or thronging all one porch of Paradise
A group of Houris bow'd to see
The dying Islamite, with hands and eyes
That said, We wait for thee.

Or mythic Uther's deeply-wounded son
In some fair space of sloping greens
Lay, dozing in the vale of Avalon,
And watch'd by weeping queens.

Or hollowing one hand against his ear,
To list a foot-fall, ere he saw 110
The wood-nymph, stay'd the Ausonian king to hear
Of wisdom and of law.

Or over hills with peaky tops engrail'd,
And many a tract of palm and rice,
The throne of Indian Cama slowly sail'd
A summer fann'd with spice.

Or sweet Europa's mantle blew unclasp'd,
From off her shoulder backward borne:
From one hand droop'd a crocus: one hand grasp'd
The mild bull's golden horn. 120

Or else flush'd Ganymede, his rosy thigh
Half-buried in the Eagle's down,

Sole as a flying star shot thro' the sky
    Above the pillar'd town.

Nor these alone: but every legend fair
  Which the supreme Caucasian mind
Carved out of Nature for itself, was there,
    Not less than life, design'd.

*

Then in the towers I placed great bells that swung,
130 Moved of themselves, with silver sound;
And with choice paintings of wise men I hung
    The royal dais round.

For there was Milton like a seraph strong,
  Beside him Shakespeare bland and mild;
And there the world-worn Dante grasp'd his song,
    And somewhat grimly smiled.

And there the Ionian father of the rest;
  A million wrinkles carved his skin;
A hundred winters snow'd upon his breast,
140   From cheek and throat and chin.

Above, the fair hall-ceiling stately-set
  Many an arch high up did lift,
And angels rising and descending met
    With interchange of gift.

Below was all mosaic choicely plann'd
  With cycles of the human tale
Of this wide world, the times of every land
    So wrought, they will not fail.

The people here, a beast of burden slow,
150 Toil'd onward, prick'd with goads and stings;
Here play'd, a tiger, rolling to and fro
    The heads and crowns of kings;

Here rose, an athlete, strong to break or bind
  All force in bonds that might endure,
And here once more like some sick man declined,
    And trusted any cure.

But over these she trod: and those great bells
  Began to chime. She took her throne:
She sat betwixt the shining Oriels,
    To sing her songs alone. 160

And thro' the topmost Oriels' coloured flame
  Two godlike faces gazed below;
Plato the wise, and large-brow'd Verulam,
    The first of those who know.

And all those names, that in their motion were
  Full-welling fountain-heads of change,
Betwixt the slender shafts were blazon'd fair
    In diverse raiment strange:

Thro' which the lights, rose, amber, emerald, blue,
  Flush'd in her temples and her eyes, 170
And from her lips, as morn from Memnon, drew
    Rivers of melodies.

No nightingale delighteth to prolong
  Her low preamble all alone,
More than my soul to hear her echo'd song
    Throb thro' the ribbèd stone;

Singing and murmuring in her feastful mirth,
  Joying to feel herself alive,
Lord over Nature, Lord of the visible earth,
    Lord of the senses five; 180

Communing with herself: 'All these are mine,
  And let the world have peace or wars,
'Tis one to me.' She – when young night divine
    Crown'd dying day with stars,

Making sweet close of his delicious toils –
  Lit light in wreaths and anadems,
And pure quintessences of precious oils
    In hollow'd moons of gems,

To mimic heaven; and clapt her hands and cried,
190 'I marvel if my still delight
In this great house so royal-rich, and wide,
    Be flatter'd to the height.

'O all things fair to sate my various eyes!
  O shapes and hues that please me well!
O silent faces of the Great and Wise,
    My Gods, with whom I dwell!

'O God-like isolation which art mine,
  I can but count thee perfect gain,
What time I watch the darkening droves of swine
200   That range on yonder plain.

'In filthy sloughs they roll a prurient skin,
  They graze and wallow, breed and sleep;
And oft some brainless devil enters in,
    And drives them to the deep.'

Then of the moral instinct would she prate
  And of the rising from the dead,
As hers by right of full-accomplish'd Fate;
    And at the last she said:

'I take possession of man's mind and deed.
210 I care not what the sects may brawl.
I sit as God holding no form of creed,
    But contemplating all.'

*

Full oft the riddle of the painful earth
  Flash'd thro' her as she sat alone,
Yet not the less held she her solemn mirth,
    And intellectual throne.

And so she throve and prosper'd: so three years
She prosper'd: on the fourth she fell,
Like Herod, when the shout was in his ears,
Struck thro' with pangs of hell. 220

Lest she should fail and perish utterly,
God, before whom ever lie bare
The abysmal deeps of Personality,
Plagued her with sore despair.

When she would think, where'er she turn'd her sight
The airy hand confusion wrought,
Wrote, 'Mene, mene,' and divided quite
The kingdom of her thought.

Deep dread and loathing of her solitude
Fell on her, from which mood was born 230
Scorn of herself, again, from out that mood
Laughter at her self-scorn.

'What! is not this my place of strength,' she said,
'My spacious mansion built for me,
Whereof the strong foundation-stones were laid
Since my first memory?'

But in dark corners of her palace stood
Uncertain shapes; and unawares
On white-eyed phantasms weeping tears of blood,
And horrible nightmares, 240

And hollow shades enclosing hearts of flame,
And, with dim fretted foreheads all,
On corpses three-months-old at noon she came,
That stood against the wall.

A spot of dull stagnation, without light
Or power of movement, seem'd my soul,
'Mid onward-sloping motions infinite
Making for one sure goal.

A still salt pool, lock'd in with bars of sand,
250 Left on the shore; that hears all night
The plunging seas draw backward from the land
Their moon-led waters white.

A star that with the choral starry dance
Join'd not, but stood, and standing saw
The hollow orb of moving Circumstance
Roll'd round by one fix'd law.

Back on herself her serpent pride had curl'd.
'No voice,' she shriek'd in that lone hall,
'No voice breaks thro' the stillness of this world:
260 One deep, deep silence all!'

She, mouldering with the dull earth's mouldering sod,
Inwrapt tenfold in slothful shame,
Lay there exilèd from eternal God,
Lost to her place and name;

And death and life she hated equally,
And nothing saw, for her despair,
But dreadful time, dreadful eternity,
No comfort anywhere;

Remaining utterly confused with fears,
270 And ever worse with growing time,
And ever unrelieved by dismal tears,
And all alone in crime:

Shut up as in a crumbling tomb, girt round
With blackness as a solid wall,
Far off she seem'd to hear the dully sound
Of human footsteps fall.

As in strange lands a traveller walking slow,
In doubt and great perplexity,
A little before moon-rise hears the low
280 Moan of an unknown sea;

And knows not if it be thunder, or a sound
  Of rocks thrown down, or one deep cry
Of great wild beasts; then thinketh, 'I have found
    A new land, but I die.'

She howl'd aloud, 'I am on fire within.
  There comes no murmur of reply.
What is it that will take away my sin,
    And save me lest I die?'

So when four years were wholly finishèd
  She threw her royal robes away. 290
'Make me a cottage in the vale,' she said,
    'Where I may mourn and pray.

'Yet pull not down my palace towers, that are
  So lightly, beautifully built:
Perchance I may return with others there
    When I have purged my guilt.'

The Hesperides

Hesperus and his daughters three,
That sing about the golden tree.
Comus

The Northwind fall'n, in the newstarrèd night
Zidonian Hanno, voyaging beyond
The hoary promontory of Soloë
Past Thymiaterion, in calmèd bays,
Between the southern and the western Horn,
Heard neither warbling of the nightingale,
Nor melody o' the Lybian lotusflute
Blown seaward from the shore; but from a slope
That ran bloombright into the Atlantic blue,

10 Beneath a highland leaning down a weight
Of cliffs, and zoned below with cedarshade,
Came voices, like the voices in a dream,
Continuous, till he reached the outer sea.

SONG

I

The golden apple, the golden apple, the hallowed fruit,
Guard it well, guard it warily,
Singing airily,
Standing about the charmèd root.
Round about all is mute,
As the snowfield on the mountain-peaks,
20 As the sandfield at the mountain-foot.
Crocodiles in briny creeks
Sleep and stir not: all is mute.
If ye sing not, if ye make false measure,
We shall lose eternal pleasure,
Worth eternal want of rest.
Laugh not loudly: watch the treasure
Of the wisdom of the west.
In a corner wisdom whispers. Five and three
(Let it not be preached abroad) make an awful mystery.
30 For the blossom unto threefold music bloweth;
Evermore it is born anew;
And the sap to threefold music floweth,
From the root
Drawn in the dark,
Up to the fruit,
Creeping under the fragrant bark,
Liquid gold, honeysweet, thro' and thro'.
Keen-eyed Sisters, singing airily,
Looking warily
40 Every way,
Guard the apple night and day,
Lest one from the East come and take it away.

II

Father Hesper, Father Hesper, watch, watch, ever and aye,
Looking under silver hair with a silver eye.
Father, twinkle not thy stedfast sight;
Kingdoms lapse, and climates change, and races die;
Honour comes with mystery;
Hoarded wisdom brings delight.
Number, tell them over and number
How many the mystic fruittree holds, 50
Lest the redcombed dragon slumber
Rolled together in purple folds.
Look to him, father, lest he wink, and the golden apple be stol'n
away,
For his ancient heart is drunk with overwatchings night and day,
Round about the hallowed fruittree curled –
Sing away, sing aloud evermore in the wind, without stop,
Lest his scalèd eyelid drop,
For he is older than the world.
If he waken, we waken,
Rapidly levelling eager eyes. 60
If he sleep, we sleep,
Dropping the eyelid over the eyes.
If the golden apple be taken
The world will be overwise.
Five links, a golden chain, are we,
Hesper, the dragon, and sisters three,
Bound about the golden tree.

III

Father Hesper, Father Hesper, watch, watch, night and day,
Lest the old wound of the world be healèd,
The glory unsealèd, 70
The golden apple stol'n away,
And the ancient secret revealèd.
Look from west to east along:
Father, old Himala weakens, Caucasus is bold and strong.
Wandering waters unto wandering waters call;

Let them clash together, foam and fall.
Out of watchings, out of wiles,
Comes the bliss of secret smiles.
All things are not told to all.
80 Half-round the mantling night is drawn,
Purplefringèd with even and dawn.
Hesper hateth Phosphor, evening hateth morn.

IV

Every flower and every fruit the redolent breath
Of this warm seawind ripeneth,
Arching the billow in his sleep;
But the landwind wandereth,
Broken by the highland-steep,
Two streams upon the violet deep:
For the western sun and the western star,
90 And the low west wind, breathing afar,
The end of day and beginning of night
Make the apple holy and bright;
Holy and bright, round and full, bright and blest,
Mellowed in a land of rest;
Watch it warily day and night;
All good things are in the west.
Till midnoon the cool east light
Is shut out by the round of the tall hillbrow;
But when the fullfaced sunset yellowly
100 Stays on the flowering arch of the bough,
The luscious fruitage clustereth mellowly,
Goldenkernelled, goldencored,
Sunset-ripened above on the tree.
The world is wasted with fire and sword,
But the apple of gold hangs over the sea.
Five links, a golden chain, are we,
Hesper, the dragon, and sisters three,
Daughters three,
Bound about
110 All round about

The gnarlèd bole of the charmèd tree.
The golden apple, the golden apple, the hallowed fruit,
Guard it well, guard it warily,
Watch it warily,
Singing airily,
Standing about the charmèd root.

The Lotos-Eaters

'Courage!' he said, and pointed toward the land,
'This mounting wave will roll us shoreward soon.'
In the afternoon they came unto a land
In which it seemèd always afternoon.
All round the coast the languid air did swoon,
Breathing like one that hath a weary dream.
Full-faced above the valley stood the moon;
And like a downward smoke, the slender stream
Along the cliff to fall and pause and fall did seem.

A land of streams! some, like a downward smoke, 10
Slow-dropping veils of thinnest lawn, did go;
And some thro' wavering lights and shadows broke,
Rolling a slumbrous sheet of foam below.
They saw the gleaming river seaward flow
From the inner land: far off, three mountain-tops,
Three silent pinnacles of agèd snow,
Stood sunset-flush'd: and, dew'd with showery drops,
Up-clomb the shadowy pine above the woven copse.

The charmèd sunset linger'd low adown
In the red West: thro' mountain clefts the dale 20
Was seen far inland, and the yellow down

Border'd with palm, and many a winding vale
And meadow, set with slender galingale;
A land where all things always seem'd the same!
And round about the keel with faces pale,
Dark faces pale against that rosy flame,
The mild-eyed melancholy Lotos-eaters came.

Branches they bore of that enchanted stem,
Laden with flower and fruit, whereof they gave
30 To each, but whoso did receive of them,
And taste, to him the gushing of the wave
Far far away did seem to mourn and rave
On alien shores; and if his fellow spake,
His voice was thin, as voices from the grave;
And deep-asleep he seem'd, yet all awake,
And music in his ears his beating heart did make.

They sat them down upon the yellow sand,
Between the sun and moon upon the shore;
And sweet it was to dream of Fatherland,
40 Of child, and wife, and slave; but evermore
Most weary seem'd the sea, weary the oar,
Weary the wandering fields of barren foam.
Then some one said, 'We will return no more;'
And all at once they sang, 'Our island home
Is far beyond the wave; we will no longer roam.'

CHORIC SONG

I

There is sweet music here that softer falls
Than petals from blown roses on the grass,
Or night-dews on still waters between walls
Of shadowy granite, in a gleaming pass;
50 Music that gentlier on the spirit lies,
Than tir'd eyelids upon tir'd eyes;
Music that brings sweet sleep down from the blissful skies.
Here are cool mosses deep,

And thro' the moss the ivies creep,
And in the stream the long-leaved flowers weep,
And from the craggy ledge the poppy hangs in sleep.

II

Why are we weigh'd upon with heaviness,
And utterly consumed with sharp distress,
While all things else have rest from weariness?
All things have rest: why should we toil alone, 60
We only toil, who are the first of things,
And make perpetual moan,
Still from one sorrow to another thrown:
Nor ever fold our wings,
And cease from wanderings,
Nor steep our brows in slumber's holy balm;
Nor harken what the inner spirit sings,
'There is no joy but calm!'
Why should we only toil, the roof and crown of things?

III

Lo! in the middle of the wood, 70
The folded leaf is woo'd from out the bud
With winds upon the branch, and there
Grows green and broad, and takes no care,
Sun-steep'd at noon, and in the moon
Nightly dew-fed; and turning yellow
Falls, and floats adown the air.
Lo! sweeten'd with the summer light,
The full-juiced apple, waxing over-mellow,
Drops in a silent autumn night.
All its allotted length of days, 80
The flower ripens in its place,
Ripens and fades, and falls, and hath no toil,
Fast-rooted in the fruitful soil.

IV

Hateful is the dark-blue sky,
Vaulted o'er the dark-blue sea.
Death is the end of life; ah, why
Should life all labour be?
Let us alone. Time driveth onward fast,
And in a little while our lips are dumb.
90 Let us alone. What is it that will last?
All things are taken from us, and become
Portions and parcels of the dreadful Past.
Let us alone. What pleasure can we have
To war with evil? Is there any peace
In ever climbing up the climbing wave?
All things have rest, and ripen toward the grave
In silence; ripen, fall and cease:
Give us long rest or death, dark death, or dreamful ease.

V

How sweet it were, hearing the downward stream,
100 With half-shut eyes ever to seem
Falling asleep in a half-dream!
To dream and dream, like yonder amber light,
Which will not leave the myrrh-bush on the height;
To hear each other's whisper'd speech;
Eating the Lotos day by day,
To watch the crisping ripples on the beach,
And tender curving lines of creamy spray;
To lend our hearts and spirits wholly
To the influence of mild-minded melancholy;
110 To muse and brood and live again in memory,
With those old faces of our infancy
Heap'd over with a mound of grass,
Two handfuls of white dust, shut in an urn of brass!

VI

Dear is the memory of our wedded lives,
And dear the last embraces of our wives

And their warm tears: but all hath suffer'd change:
For surely now our household hearths are cold:
Our sons inherit us: our looks are strange:
And we should come like ghosts to trouble joy.
Or else the island princes over-bold 120
Have eat our substance, and the minstrel sings
Before them of the ten years' war in Troy,
And our great deeds, as half-forgotten things.
Is there confusion in the little isle?
Let what is broken so remain.
The Gods are hard to reconcile:
'Tis hard to settle order once again.
There *is* confusion worse than death,
Trouble on trouble, pain on pain,
Long labour unto agèd breath, 130
Sorc task to hearts worn out by many wars
And eyes grown dim with gazing on the pilot-stars.

VII

But, propt on beds of amaranth and moly,
How sweet (while warm airs lull us, blowing lowly)
With half-dropt eyelid still,
Beneath a heaven dark and holy,
To watch the long bright river drawing slowly
His waters from the purple hill –
To hear the dewy echoes calling
From cave to cave thro' the thick-twinèd vine – 140
To watch the emerald-colour'd water falling
Thro' many a wov'n acanthus-wreath divine!
Only to hear and see the far-off sparkling brine,
Only to hear were sweet, stretch'd out beneath the pine.

VIII

The Lotos blooms below the barren peak:
The Lotos blows by every winding creek:
All day the wind breathes low with mellower tone:
Thro' every hollow cave and alley lone

Round and round the spicy downs the yellow Lotos-dust is blown.
150 We have had enough of action, and of motion we,
Roll'd to starboard, roll'd to larboard, when the surge was seething
free,
Where the wallowing monster spouted his foam-fountains in the
sea.
Let us swear an oath, and keep it with an equal mind,
In the hollow Lotos-land to live and lie reclined
On the hills like Gods together, careless of mankind.
For they lie beside their nectar, and the bolts are hurl'd
Far below them in the valleys, and the clouds are lightly curl'd
Round their golden houses, girdled with the gleaming world:
Where they smile in secret, looking over wasted lands,
Blight and famine, plague and earthquake, roaring deeps and fiery
160 sands,
Clanging fights, and flaming towns, and sinking ships, and praying
hands.
But they smile, they find a music centred in a doleful song
Steaming up, a lamentation and an ancient tale of wrong,
Like a tale of little meaning tho' the words are strong;
Chanted from an ill-used race of men that cleave the soil,
Sow the seed, and reap the harvest with enduring toil,
Storing yearly little dues of wheat, and wine and oil;
Till they perish and they suffer – some, 'tis whisper'd – down in
hell
Suffer endless anguish, others in Elysian valleys dwell,
170 Resting weary limbs at last on beds of asphodel.
Surely, surely, slumber is more sweet than toil, the shore
Than labour in the deep mid-ocean, wind and wave and oar;
Oh rest ye, brother mariners, we will not wander more.

▲ ▲ ▲

'Hark! the dogs howl!'

Hark! the dogs howl! the sleetwinds blow,
The church-clocks knoll: the hours haste,
I leave the dreaming world below.
Blown o'er frore heads of hills I go,
Long narrowing friths and stripes of snow –
Time bears my soul into the waste.
I seek the voice I loved – ah where
Is that dear hand that I should press,
Those honoured brows that I would kiss?
Lo! the broad Heavens cold and bare, 10
The stars that know not my distress.
My sighs are wasted in the air,
My tears are dropt into the abyss.
Now riseth up a little cloud –
Divideth like a broken wave –
Shows Death a drooping youth pale-browed
And crowned with daisies of the grave.
The vapour labours up the sky,
Uncertain forms are darkly moved,
Larger than human passes by 20
The shadow of the man I loved.
I wind my arms for one embrace –
Can this be he? is that his face?
In my strait throat expires the cry.
He bends his eyes reproachfully
And clasps his hands, as one that prays.

'This Nature full of hints and mysteries'

This Nature full of hints and mysteries,
Untrackt conclusions, broken lights and shapes,
This world-reflecting mind, this complex life
Of checks and impulses and counterchecks,
Glimpses and aspirations, warnings, failings.

'Over the dark world flies the wind'

Over the dark world flies the wind
    And clatters in the sapless trees,
From cloud to cloud thro' darkness blind
    Quick stars scud o'er the sounding seas:
I look: the showery skirts unbind:
    Mars by the lonely Pleiades
Burns overhead: with brows declined
    I muse – I wander from my peace,
And still divide the rapid mind
10   This way and that in search of ease.

'Oh! that 'twere possible'

Oh! that 'twere possible,
After long grief and pain,
To find the arms of my true-love
Round me once again!

When I was wont to meet her
In the silent woody places
Of the land that gave me birth,
We stood tranced in long embraces,
Mixt with kisses sweeter, sweeter,
Than any thing on earth. 10

A shadow flits before me –
Not thou, but like to thee.
Ah God! that it were possible
For one short hour to see
The souls we loved, that they might tell us
What and where they be.

It leads me forth at Evening,
It lightly winds and steals
In a cold white robe before me,
When all my spirit reels 20
At the shouts, the leagues of lights,
And the roaring of the wheels.

Half the night I waste in sighs,
In a wakeful doze I sorrow
For the hand, the lips, the eyes –
For the meeting of tomorrow,
The delight of happy laughter,
The delight of low replies.

Do I hear the pleasant ditty,
That I heard her chant of old? 30

But I wake – my dream is fled.
Without knowledge, without pity –
In the shuddering dawn behold,
By the curtains of my bed,
That abiding phantom cold.

Then I rise: the eave-drops fall
And the yellow-vapours choke
The great city sounding wide;
The day comes – a dull red ball,
40 Wrapt in drifts of lurid smoke,
On the misty river-tide.

Thro' the hubbub of the market
I steal, a wasted frame;
It crosseth here, it crosseth there –
Thro' all that crowd, confused and loud,
The shadow still the same;
And on my heavy eyelids
My anguish hangs like shame.

Alas for her that met me,
50 That heard me softly call –
Came glimmering thro' the laurels
At the quiet even-fall,
In the garden by the turrets
Of the old Manorial Hall.

Then the broad light glares and beats,
And the sunk eye flits and fleets,
And will not let me be.
I loathe the squares and streets,
And the faces that one meets,
60 Hearts with no love for me;
Always I long to creep
To some still cavern deep,
And to weep, and weep and weep
My whole soul out to thee.

Get thee hence, nor come again
  Pass and cease to move about –
Pass, thou death-like type of pain,
  Mix not memory with doubt.
'Tis the blot upon the brain
  That *will* show itself without. 70

Would the happy Spirit descend
  In the chamber or the street
    As she looks among the blest;
Should I fear to greet my friend,
  Or to ask her, 'Take me, sweet,
    To the region of thy rest.'

But she tarries in her place,
And I paint the beauteous face
  Of the maiden, that I lost,
    In my inner eyes again, 80
Lest my heart be overborne
By the thing I hold in scorn,
  By a dull mechanic ghost
    And a juggle of the brain.

I can shadow forth my bride
  As I knew her fair and kind,
    As I woo'd her for my wife;
She is lovely by my side
    In the silence of my life –
  'Tis a phantom of the mind. 90

'Tis a phantom fair and good;
  I can call it to my side,
    So to guard my life from ill,
  Tho' its ghastly sister glide
    And be moved around me still
With the moving of the blood,
    That is moved not of the will.

Let it pass, the dreary brow,
  Let the dismal face go by.
Will it lead me to the grave? 100
  Then I lose it: it will fly:
Can it overlast the nerves?
  Can it overlive the eye?
But the other, like a star,
Thro' the channel windeth far
  Till it fade and fail and die,
To its Archetype that waits,
Clad in light by golden gates –
Clad in light the Spirit waits
  To embrace me in the sky. 110

▲ ▲ ▲

From *Poems* (1842)

The Epic [*Morte d' Arthur*]

At Francis Allen's on the Christmas-eve, –
The game of forfeits done – the girls all kiss'd
Beneath the sacred bush and past away –
The parson Holmes, the poet Everard Hall,
The host, and I sat round the wassail-bowl,
Then half-way ebb'd: and there we held a talk,
How all the old honour had from Christmas gone,
Or gone, or dwindled down to some odd games
In some odd nooks like this; till I, tired out
With cutting eights that day upon the pond, 10
Where, three times slipping from the outer edge,
I bump'd the ice into three several stars,
Fell in a doze; and half-awake I heard
The parson taking wide and wider sweeps,
Now harping on the church-commissioners,
Now hawking at Geology and schism;
Until I woke, and found him settled down
Upon the general decay of faith
Right thro' the world, 'at home was little left,
And none abroad: there was no anchor, none, 20
To hold by.' Francis, laughing, clapt his hand
On Everard's shoulder, with 'I hold by him.'
'And I,' quoth Everard, 'by the wassail-bowl.'
'Why yes,' I said, 'we knew your gift that way
At college: but another which you had,
I mean of verse (for so we held it then),

What came of that?' 'You know,' said Frank, 'he burnt
His epic, his King Arthur, some twelve books' –
And then to me demanding why? 'Oh, sir,
30 He thought that nothing new was said, or else
Something so said 'twas nothing – that a truth
Looks freshest in the fashion of the day:
God knows: he has a mint of reasons: ask.
It pleased *me* well enough.' 'Nay, nay,' said Hall,
'Why take the style of those heroic times?
For nature brings not back the Mastodon,
Nor we those times; and why should any man
Remodel models? these twelve books of mine
Were faint Homeric echoes, nothing-worth,
40 Mere chaff and draff, much better burnt.' 'But I,'
Said Francis, 'pick'd the eleventh from this hearth
And have it: keep a thing, its use will come.
I hoard it as a sugar-plum for Holmes.'
He laugh'd, and I, tho' sleepy, like a horse
That hears the corn-bin open, prick'd my ears;
For I remember'd Everard's college fame
When we were Freshmen: then at my request
He brought it; and the poet little urged,
But with some prelude of disparagement,
50 Read, mouthing out his hollow oes and aes,
Deep-chested music, and to this result.

Morte d'Arthur

So all day long the noise of battle roll'd
Among the mountains by the winter sea;
Until King Arthur's table, man by man,

Had fallen in Lyonnesse about their Lord,
King Arthur: then, because his wound was deep,
The bold Sir Bedivere uplifted him,
Sir Bedivere, the last of all his knights,
And bore him to a chapel nigh the field,
A broken chancel with a broken cross,
That stood on a dark strait of barren land. 10
On one side lay the Ocean, and on one
Lay a great water, and the moon was full.

Then spake King Arthur to Sir Bedivere:
'The sequel of to-day unsolders all
The goodliest fellowship of famous knights
Whereof this world holds record. Such a sleep
They sleep – the men I loved. I think that we
Shall never more, at any future time,
Delight our souls with talk of knightly deeds,
Walking about the gardens and the halls 20
Of Camelot, as in the days that were.
I perish by this people which I made, –
Tho' Merlin sware that I should come again
To rule once more – but let what will be, be,
I am so deeply smitten thro' the helm
That without help I cannot last till morn.
Thou therefore take my brand Excalibur,
Which was my pride: for thou rememberest how
In those old days, one summer noon, an arm
Rose up from out the bosom of the lake, 30
Clothed in white samite, mystic, wonderful,
Holding the sword – and how I row'd across
And took it, and have worn it, like a king:
And, wheresoever I am sung or told
In aftertime, this also shall be known:
But now delay not: take Excalibur,
And fling him far into the middle mere:
Watch what thou seëst, and lightly bring me word.'

To him replied the bold Sir Bedivere:
40 'It is not meet, Sir King, to leave thee thus,
Aidless, alone, and smitten thro' the helm.
A little thing may harm a wounded man.
Yet I thy hest will all perform at full,
Watch what I see, and lightly bring thee word.'

So saying, from the ruin'd shrine he stept
And in the moon athwart the place of tombs,
Where lay the mighty bones of ancient men,
Old knights, and over them the sea-wind sang
Shrill, chill, with flakes of foam. He, stepping down
50 By zig-zag paths, and juts of pointed rock,
Came on the shining levels of the lake.

There drew he forth the brand Excalibur,
And o'er him, drawing it, the winter moon,
Brightening the skirts of a long cloud, ran forth
And sparkled keen with frost against the hilt:
For all the haft twinkled with diamond sparks,
Myriads of topaz-lights, and jacinth-work
Of subtlest jewellery. He gazed so long
That both his eyes were dazzled, as he stood,
60 This way and that dividing the swift mind,
In act to throw: but at the last it seem'd
Better to leave Excalibur conceal'd
There in the many-knotted waterflags,
That whistled stiff and dry about the marge.
So strode he back slow to the wounded King.

Then spake King Arthur to Sir Bedivere:
'Hast thou perform'd my mission which I gave?
What is it thou hast seen? or what hast heard?'

And answer made the bold Sir Bedivere:
70 'I heard the ripple washing in the reeds,
And the wild water lapping on the crag.'

To whom replied King Arthur, faint and pale:
'Thou hast betray'd thy nature and thy name,
Not rendering true answer, as beseem'd
Thy fëalty, nor like a noble knight:
For surer sign had follow'd, either hand,
Or voice, or else a motion of the mere.
This is a shameful thing for men to lie.
Yet now, I charge thee, quickly go again
As thou art lief and dear, and do the thing 80
I bad thee, watch, and lightly bring me word.'

Then went Sir Bedivere the second time
Across the ridge, and paced beside the mere,
Counting the dewy pebbles, fix'd in thought;
But when he saw the wonder of the hilt,
How curiously and strangely chased, he smote
His palms together, and he cried aloud,

'And if indeed I cast the brand away,
Surely a precious thing, one worthy note,
Should thus be lost for ever from the earth, 90
Which might have pleased the eyes of many men.
What good should follow this, if this were done?
What harm, undone? deep harm to disobey,
Seeing obedience is the bond of rule.
Were it well to obey then, if a king demand
An act unprofitable, against himself?
The King is sick, and knows not what he does.
What record, or what relic of my lord
Should be to aftertime, but empty breath
And rumours of a doubt? but were this kept, 100
Stored in some treasure-house of mighty kings,
Some one might show it at a joust of arms,
Saying, "King Arthur's sword, Excalibur,
Wrought by the lonely maiden of the Lake.
Nine years she wrought it, sitting in the deeps
Upon the hidden bases of the hills."
So might some old man speak in the aftertime

To all the people, winning reverence.
But now much honour and much fame were lost.'

10 So spake he, clouded with his own conceit,
And hid Excalibur the second time,
And so strode back slow to the wounded King.

Then spoke King Arthur, breathing heavily:
'What is it thou hast seen? or what hast heard?'

And answer made the bold Sir Bedivere:
'I heard the water lapping on the crag,
And the long ripple washing in the reeds.'

To whom replied King Arthur, much in wrath:
'Ah, miserable and unkind, untrue,
20 Unknightly, traitor-hearted! Woe is me!
Authority forgets a dying king,
Laid widow'd of the power in his eye
That bow'd the will. I see thee what thou art,
For thou, the latest-left of all my knights,
In whom should meet the offices of all,
Thou wouldst betray me for the precious hilt;
Either from lust of gold, or like a girl
Valuing the giddy pleasure of the eyes.
Yet, for a man may fail in duty twice,
130 And the third time may prosper, get thee hence:
But, if thou spare to fling Excalibur,
I will arise and slay thee with my hands.'

Then quickly rose Sir Bedivere, and ran,
And, leaping down the ridges lightly, plunged
Among the bulrush-beds, and clutch'd the sword,
And strongly wheel'd and threw it. The great brand
Made lightnings in the splendour of the moon,
And flashing round and round, and whirl'd in an arch,
Shot like a streamer of the northern morn,
140 Seen where the moving isles of winter shock
By night, with noises of the northern sea.

So flash'd and fell the brand Excalibur:
But ere he dipt the surface, rose an arm
Clothed in white samite, mystic, wonderful,
And caught him by the hilt, and brandish'd him
Three times, and drew him under in the mere.
And lightly went the other to the King.

Then spoke King Arthur, drawing thicker breath:
'Now see I by thine eyes that this is done.
Speak out: what is it thou hast heard, or seen?' 150

And answer made the bold Sir Bedivere:
'Sir King, I closed mine eyelids, lest the gems
Should blind my purpose, for I never saw,
Nor shall see, here or elsewhere, till I die,
Not tho' I live three lives of mortal men,
So great a miracle as yonder hilt.
Then with both hands I flung him, wheeling him;
But when I look'd again, behold an arm,
Clothed in white samite, mystic, wonderful,
That caught him by the hilt, and brandish'd him 160
Three times, and drew him under in the mere.'

And answer made King Arthur, breathing hard:
'My end draws nigh; 'tis time that I were gone.
Make broad thy shoulders to receive my weight,
And bear me to the margin; yet I fear
My wound hath taken cold, and I shall die.'

So saying, from the pavement he half rose,
Slowly, with pain, reclining on his arm,
And looking wistfully with wide blue eyes
As in a picture. Him Sir Bedivere 170
Remorsefully regarded thro' his tears,
And would have spoken, but he found not words,
Then took with care, and kneeling on one knee,
O'er both his shoulders drew the languid hands,
And rising bore him thro' the place of tombs.

But, as he walk'd, King Arthur panted hard,
Like one that feels a nightmare on his bed
When all the house is mute. So sigh'd the King,
Muttering and murmuring at his ear, 'Quick, quick!
180 I fear it is too late, and I shall die.'
But the other swiftly strode from ridge to ridge,
Clothed with his breath, and looking, as he walk'd,
Larger than human on the frozen hills.
He heard the deep behind him, and a cry
Before. His own thought drove him, like a goad.
Dry clash'd his harness in the icy caves
And barren chasms, and all to left and right
The bare black cliff clang'd round him, as he based
His feet on juts of slippery crag that rang
190 Sharp-smitten with the dint of armèd heels –
And on a sudden, lo! the level lake,
And the long glories of the winter moon.

Then saw they how there hove a dusky barge,
Dark as a funeral scarf from stem to stern,
Beneath them; and descending they were ware
That all the decks were dense with stately forms
Black-stoled, black-hooded, like a dream – by these
Three Queens with crowns of gold – and from them rose
A cry that shiver'd to the tingling stars,
200 And, as it were one voice, an agony
Of lamentation, like a wind, that shrills
All night in a waste land, where no one comes,
Or hath come, since the making of the world.

Then murmur'd Arthur, 'Place me in the barge,'
And to the barge they came. There those three Queens
Put forth their hands, and took the King, and wept.
But she, that rose the tallest of them all
And fairest, laid his head upon her lap,
And loosed the shatter'd casque, and chafed his hands,
210 And call'd him by his name, complaining loud,
And dropping bitter tears against his brow

Striped with dark blood: for all his face was white
And colourless, and like the wither'd moon
Smote by the fresh beam of the springing east;
And all his greaves and cuisses dash'd with drops
Of onset; and the light and lustrous curls –
That made his forehead like a rising sun
High from the daïs-throne – were parch'd with dust;
Or, clotted into points and hanging loose,
Mix'd with the knightly growth that fringed his lips. 220
So like a shatter'd column lay the King;
Not like that Arthur who, with lance in rest,
From spur to plume a star of tournament,
Shot thro' the lists at Camelot, and charged
Before the eyes of ladies and of kings.

Then loudly cried the bold Sir Bedivere,
'Ah! my Lord Arthur, whither shall I go?
Where shall I hide my forehead and my eyes?
For now I see the true old times are dead,
When every morning brought a noble chance, 230
And every chance brought out a noble knight.
Such times have been not since the light that led
The holy Elders with the gift of myrrh.
But now the whole ROUND TABLE is dissolved
Which was an image of the mighty world;
And I, the last, go forth companionless,
And the days darken round me, and the years,
Among new men, strange faces, other minds.'

And slowly answered Arthur from the barge:
'The old order changeth, yielding place to new, 240
And God fulfils Himself in many ways,
Lest one good custom should corrupt the world.
Comfort thyself: what comfort is in me?
I have lived my life, and that which I have done
May He within Himself make pure! but thou,
If thou shouldst never see my face again,
Pray for my soul. More things are wrought by prayer

Than this world dreams of. Wherefore, let thy voice
Rise like a fountain for me night and day.
250 For what are men better than sheep or goats
That nourish a blind life within the brain,
If, knowing God, they lift not hands of prayer
Both for themselves and those who call them friend?
For so the whole round earth is every way
Bound by gold chains about the feet of God.
But now farewell. I am going a long way
With these thou seëst – if indeed I go –
(For all my mind is clouded with a doubt)
To the island-valley of Avilion;
260 Where falls not hail, or rain, or any snow,
Nor ever wind blows loudly; but it lies
Deep-meadow'd, happy, fair with orchard-lawns
And bowery hollows crown'd with summer sea,
Where I will heal me of my grievous wound.'

So said he, and the barge with oar and sail
Moved from the brink, like some full-breasted swan
That, fluting a wild carol ere her death,
Ruffles her pure cold plume, and takes the flood
With swarthy webs. Long stood Sir Bedivere
270 Revolving many memories, till the hull
Look'd one black dot against the verge of dawn,
And on the mere the wailing died away.

[THE EPIC]

Here ended Hall, and our last light, that long
Had wink'd and threaten'd darkness, flared and fell:
At which the Parson, sent to sleep with sound,
And waked with silence, grunted 'Good!' but we
Sat rapt: it was the tone with which he read –
Perhaps some modern touches here and there
Redeem'd it from the charge of nothingness –

Or else we loved the man, and prized his work; 280
I know not: but we sitting, as I said,
The cock crew loud; as at that time of year
The lusty bird takes every hour for dawn:
Then Francis, muttering, like a man ill-used,
'There now – that's nothing!' drew a little back,
And drove his heel into the smoulder'd log,
That sent a blast of sparkles up the flue:
And so to bed; where yet in sleep I seem'd
To sail with Arthur under looming shores,
Point after point; till on to dawn, when dreams 290
Begin to feel the truth and stir of day,
To me, methought, who waited with a crowd,
There came a bark that, blowing forward, bore
King Arthur, like a modern gentleman
Of stateliest port; and all the people cried,
'Arthur is come again: he cannot die.'
Then those that stood upon the hills behind
Repeated – 'Come again, and thrice as fair;'
And, further inland, voices echo'd – 'Come
With all good things, and war shall be no more.' 300
At this a hundred bells began to peal,
That with the sound I woke, and heard indeed
The clear church-bells ring in the Christmas-morn.

The Gardener's Daughter

Or, the Pictures

This morning is the morning of the day,
When I and Eustace from the city went

To see the Gardener's Daughter; I and he,
Brothers in Art; a friendship so complete
Portion'd in halves between us, that we grew
The fable of the city where we dwelt.

My Eustace might have sat for Hercules;
So muscular he spread, so broad of breast.
He, by some law that holds in love, and draws
10 The greater to the lesser, long desired
A certain miracle of symmetry,
A miniature of loveliness, all grace
Summ'd up and closed in little; – Juliet, she
So light of foot, so light of spirit – oh, she
To me myself, for some three careless moons,
The summer pilot of an empty heart
Unto the shores of nothing! Know you not
Such touches are but embassies of love,
To tamper with the feelings, ere he found
20 Empire for life? but Eustace painted her,
And said to me, she sitting with us then,
'When will *you* paint like this?' and I replied,
(My words were half in earnest, half in jest,)
' 'Tis not your work, but Love's. Love, unperceived,
A more ideal Artist he than all,
Came, drew your pencil from you, made those eyes
Darker than darkest pansies, and that hair
More black than ashbuds in the front of March.'
And Juliet answer'd laughing, 'Go and see
30 The Gardener's daughter: trust me, after that,
You scarce can fail to match his masterpiece.'
And up we rose, and on the spur we went.

Not wholly in the busy world, nor quite
Beyond it, blooms the garden that I love.
News from the humming city comes to it
In sound of funeral or of marriage bells;
And, sitting muffled in dark leaves, you hear
The windy clanging of the minster clock;

Although between it and the garden lies
A league of grass, wash'd by a slow broad stream, 40
That, stirr'd with languid pulses of the oar,
Waves all its lazy lilies, and creeps on,
Barge-laden, to three arches of a bridge
Crown'd with the minster-towers.

The fields between
Are dewy-fresh, browsed by deep-udder'd kine,
And all about the large lime feathers low,
The lime a summer home of murmurous wings.

In that still place she, hoarded in herself,
Grew, seldom seen; not less among us lived
Her fame from lip to lip. Who had not heard 50
Of Rose, the Gardener's daughter? Where was he,
So blunt in memory, so old at heart,
At such a distance from his youth in grief,
That, having seen, forgot? The common mouth,
So gross to express delight, in praise of her
Grew oratory. Such a lord is Love,
And Beauty such a mistress of the world.

And if I said that Fancy, led by Love,
Would play with flying forms and images,
Yet this is also true, that, long before 60
I look'd upon her, when I heard her name
My heart was like a prophet to my heart,
And told me I should love. A crowd of hopes,
That sought to sow themselves like wingèd seeds,
Born out of everything I heard and saw,
Flutter'd about my senses and my soul;
And vague desires, like fitful blasts of balm
To one that travels quickly, made the air
Of Life delicious, and all kinds of thought,
That verged upon them, sweeter than the dream 70
Dreamed by a happy man, when the dark East,
Unseen, is brightening to his bridal morn.

And sure this orbit of the memory folds
For ever in itself the day we went
To see her. All the land in flowery squares,
Beneath a broad and equal-blowing wind,
Smelt of the coming summer, as one large cloud
Drew downward: but all else of heaven was pure
Up to the Sun, and May from verge to verge,
80 And May with me from head to heel. And now,
As tho' 'twere yesterday, as tho' it were
The hour just flown, that morn with all its sound,
(For those old Mays had thrice the life of these,)
Rings in mine ears. The steer forgot to graze,
And, where the hedge-row cuts the pathway, stood,
Leaning his horns into the neighbour field,
And lowing to his fellows. From the woods
Came voices of the well-contented doves.
The lark could scarce get out his notes for joy,
90 But shook his song together as he near'd
His happy home, the ground. To left and right,
The cuckoo told his name to all the hills;
The mellow ouzel fluted in the elm;
The redcap whistled; and the nightingale
Sang loud, as tho' he were the bird of day.

And Eustace turn'd, and smiling said to me,
'Hear how the bushes echo! by my life,
These birds have joyful thoughts. Think you they sing
Like poets, from the vanity of song?
100 Or have they any sense of why they sing?
And would they praise the heavens for what they have?'
And I made answer, 'Were there nothing else
For which to praise the heavens but only love,
That only love were cause enough for praise.'

Lightly he laugh'd, as one that read my thought,
And on we went; but ere an hour had pass'd,
We reach'd a meadow slanting to the North;
Down which a well-worn pathway courted us

To one green wicket in a privet hedge;
This, yielding, gave into a grassy walk 110
Thro' crowded lilac-ambush trimly pruned;
And one warm gust, full-fed with perfume, blew
Beyond us, as we enter'd in the cool.
The garden stretches southward. In the midst
A cedar spread his dark-green layers of shade.
The garden-glasses glanced, and momently
The twinkling laurel scatter'd silver lights.

'Eustace,' I said, 'this wonder keeps the house.'
He nodded, but a moment afterwards
He cried, 'Look! look!' Before he ceased I turn'd, 120
And, ere a star can wink, beheld her there.

For up the porch there grew an Eastern rose,
That, flowering high, the last night's gale had caught,
And blown across the walk. One arm aloft –
Gown'd in pure white, that fitted to the shape –
Holding the bush, to fix it back, she stood,
A single stream of all her soft brown hair
Pour'd on one side: the shadow of the flowers
Stole all the golden gloss, and, wavering
Lovingly lower, trembled on her waist – 130
Ah, happy shade – and still went wavering down,
But, ere it touch'd a foot, that might have danced
The greensward into greener circles, dipt,
And mix'd with shadows of the common ground!
But the full day dwelt on her brows, and sunn'd
Her violet eyes, and all her Hebe bloom,
And doubled his own warmth against her lips,
And on the bounteous wave of such a breast
As never pencil drew. Half light, half shade,
She stood, a sight to make an old man young. 140

So rapt, we near'd the house; but she, a Rose
In roses, mingled with her fragrant toil,
Nor heard us come, nor from her tendance turn'd

Into the world without; till close at hand,
And almost ere I knew mine own intent,
This murmur broke the stillness of that air
Which brooded round about her:
'Ah, one rose,
One rose, but one, by those fair fingers cull'd,
Were worth a hundred kisses press'd on lips
Less exquisite than thine.'
150 She look'd: but all
Suffused with blushes – neither self-possess'd
Nor startled, but betwixt this mood and that,
Divided in a graceful quiet – paused,
And dropt the branch she held, and turning, wound
Her looser hair in braid, and stirr'd her lips
For some sweet answer, tho' no answer came,
Nor yet refused the rose, but granted it,
And moved away, and left me, statue-like,
In act to render thanks.
I, that whole day,
160 Saw her no more, altho' I linger'd there
Till every daisy slept, and Love's white star
Beam'd thro' the thicken'd cedar in the dusk.

So home we went, and all the livelong way
With solemn gibe did Eustace banter me.
'Now,' said he, 'will you climb the top of Art.
You cannot fail but work in hues to dim
The Titianic Flora. Will you match
My Juliet? you, not you, – the Master, Love,
A more ideal Artist he than all.'

170 So home I went, but could not sleep for joy,
Reading her perfect features in the gloom,
Kissing the rose she gave me o'er and o'er,
And shaping faithful record of the glance
That graced the giving – such a noise of life
Swarm'd in the golden present, such a voice
Call'd to me from the years to come, and such

A length of bright horizon rimm'd the dark.
And all that night I heard the watchman peal
The sliding season: all that night I heard
The heavy clocks knolling the drowsy hours. 180
The drowsy hours, dispensers of all good,
O'er the mute city stole with folded wings,
Distilling odours on me as they went
To greet their fairer sisters of the East.

Love at first sight, first-born, and heir to all,
Made this night thus. Henceforward squall nor storm
Could keep me from that Eden where she dwelt.
Light pretexts drew me; sometimes a Dutch love
For tulips; then for roses, moss or musk,
To grace my city rooms; or fruits and cream 190
Served in the weeping elm; and more and more
A word could bring the colour to my cheek;
A thought would fill my eyes with happy dew;
Love trebled life within me, and with each
The year increased.
The daughters of the year,
One after one, thro' that still garden pass'd;
Each garlanded with her peculiar flower
Danced into light, and died into the shade;
And each in passing touch'd with some new grace
Or seem'd to touch her, so that day by day, 200
Like one that never can be wholly known,
Her beauty grew; till Autumn brought an hour
For Eustace, when I heard his deep 'I will,'
Breathed, like the covenant of a God, to hold
From thence thro' all the worlds: but I rose up
Full of his bliss, and following her dark eyes
Felt earth as air beneath me, till I reach'd
The wicket-gate, and found her standing there.

There sat we down upon a garden mound,
Two mutually enfolded; Love, the third, 210
Between us, in the circle of his arms

Enwound us both; and over many a range
Of waning lime the gray cathedral towers,
Across a hazy glimmer of the west,
Reveal'd their shining windows: from them clash'd
The bells; we listen'd; with the time we play'd,
We spoke of other things; we coursed about
The subject most at heart, more near and near,
Like doves about a dovecote, wheeling round
220 The central wish, until we settled there.

Then, in that time and place, I spoke to her,
Requiring, tho' I knew it was mine own,
Yet for the pleasure that I took to hear,
Requiring at her hand the greatest gift,
A woman's heart, the heart of her I loved;
And in that time and place she answer'd me,
And in the compass of three little words,
More musical than ever came in one,
The silver fragments of a broken voice,
230 Made me most happy, faltering, 'I am thine.'

Shall I cease here? Is this enough to say
That my desire, like all strongest hopes,
By its own energy fulfill'd itself,
Merged in completion? Would you learn at full
How passion rose thro' circumstantial grades
Beyond all grades develop'd? and indeed
I had not staid so long to tell you all,
But while I mused came Memory with sad eyes,
Holding the folded annals of my youth;
240 And while I mused, Love with knit brows went by,
And with a flying finger swept my lips,
And spake, 'Be wise: not easily forgiven
Are those, who setting wide the doors that bar
The secret bridal-chambers of the heart,
Let in the day.' Here, then, my words have end.

Yet might I tell of meetings, of farewells –
Of that which came between, more sweet than each,

In whispers, like the whispers of the leaves
That tremble round a nightingale – in sighs
Which perfect Joy, perplex'd for utterance, 250
Stole from her sister Sorrow. Might I not tell
Of difference, reconcilement, pledges given,
And vows, where there was never need of vows,
And kisses, where the heart on one wild leap
Hung tranced from all pulsation, as above
The heavens between their fairy fleeces pale
Sow'd all their mystic gulfs with fleeting stars;
Or while the balmy glooming, crescent-lit,
Spread the light haze along the river-shores,
And in the hollows; or as once we met 260
Unheedful, tho' beneath a whispering rain
Night slid down one long stream of sighing wind,
And in her bosom bore the baby, Sleep.

But this whole hour your eyes have been intent
On that veil'd picture – veil'd, for what it holds
May not be dwelt on by the common day.
This prelude has prepared thee. Raise thy soul;
Make thine heart ready with thine eyes: the time
Is come to raise the veil.

Behold her there,
As I beheld her ere she knew my heart, 270
My first, last love; the idol of my youth,
The darling of my manhood, and, alas!
Now the most blessèd memory of mine age.

St Simeon Stylites

Altho' I be the basest of mankind,
From scalp to sole one slough and crust of sin,
Unfit for earth, unfit for heaven, scarce meet
For troops of devils, mad with blasphemy,
I will not cease to grasp the hope I hold
Of saintdom, and to clamour, mourn and sob,
Battering the gates of heaven with storms of prayer,
Have mercy, Lord, and take away my sin.

Let this avail, just, dreadful, mighty God,
This not be all in vain, that thrice ten years,
Thrice multiplied by superhuman pangs,
In hungers and in thirsts, fevers and cold,
In coughs, aches, stitches, ulcerous throes and cramps,
A sign betwixt the meadow and the cloud,
Patient on this tall pillar I have borne
Rain, wind, frost, heat, hail, damp, and sleet, and snow;
And I had hoped that ere this period closed
Thou wouldst have caught me up into thy rest,
Denying not these weather-beaten limbs
The meed of saints, the white robe and the palm.

O take the meaning, Lord: I do not breathe,
Not whisper, any murmur of complaint.
Pain heap'd ten-hundred-fold to this, were still
Less burthen, by ten-hundred-fold, to bear,
Than were those lead-like tons of sin that crush'd
My spirit flat before thee.

O Lord, Lord,

Thou knowest I bore this better at the first,
For I was strong and hale of body then;
And tho' my teeth, which now are dropt away,
Would chatter with the cold, and all my beard

Was tagg'd with icy fringes in the moon,
I drown'd the whoopings of the owl with sound
Of pious hymns and psalms, and sometimes saw
An angel stand and watch me, as I sang.
Now am I feeble grown; my end draws nigh;
I hope my end draws nigh: half deaf I am,
So that I scarce can hear the people hum
About the column's base, and almost blind,
And scarce can recognise the fields I know;
And both my thighs are rotted with the dew; 40
Yet cease I not to clamour and to cry,
While my stiff spine can hold my weary head,
Till all my limbs drop piecemeal from the stone,
Have mercy, mercy: take away my sin.

O Jesus, if thou wilt not save my soul,
Who may be saved? who is it may be saved?
Who may be made a saint, if I fail here?
Show me the man hath suffer'd more than I.
For did not all thy martyrs die one death?
For either they were stoned, or crucified, 50
Or burn'd in fire, or boil'd in oil, or sawn
In twain beneath the ribs; but I die here
To-day, and whole years long, a life of death.
Bear witness, if I could have found a way
(And heedfully I sifted all my thought)
More slowly-painful to subdue this home
Of sin, my flesh, which I despise and hate,
I had not stinted practice, O my God.

For not alone this pillar-punishment,
Not this alone I bore: but while I lived 60
In the white convent down the valley there,
For many weeks about my loins I wore
The rope that haled the buckets from the well,
Twisted as tight as I could knot the noose;
And spake not of it to a single soul,
Until the ulcer, eating thro' my skin,

Betray'd my secret penance, so that all
My brethren marvell'd greatly. More than this
I bore, whereof, O God, thou knowest all.

70 Three winters, that my soul might grow to thee,
I lived up there on yonder mountain side.
My right leg chain'd into the crag, I lay
Pent in a roofless close of ragged stones;
Inswathed sometimes in wandering mist, and twice
Black'd with thy branding thunder, and sometimes
Sucking the damps for drink, and eating not,
Except the spare chance-gift of those that came
To touch my body and be heal'd, and live:
And they say then that I work'd miracles,
80 Whereof my fame is loud amongst mankind,
Cured lameness, palsies, cancers. Thou, O God,
Knowest alone whether this was or no.
Have mercy, mercy! cover all my sin.

Then, that I might be more alone with thee,
Three years I lived upon a pillar, high
Six cubits, and three years on one of twelve;
And twice three years I crouch'd on one that rose
Twenty by measure; last of all, I grew
Twice ten long weary weary years to this,
90 That numbers forty cubits from the soil.

I think that I have borne as much as this –
Or else I dream – and for so long a time,
If I may measure time by yon slow light,
And this high dial, which my sorrow crowns –
So much – even so.

And yet I know not well,
For that the evil ones come here, and say,
'Fall down, O Simeon: thou hast suffer'd long
For ages and for ages!' then they prate
Of penances I cannot have gone thro',
100 Perplexing me with lies; and oft I fall,

Maybe for months, in such blind lethargies
That Heaven, and Earth, and Time are choked.
But yet
Bethink thee, Lord, while thou and all the saints
Enjoy themselves in heaven, and men on earth
House in the shade of comfortable roofs,
Sit with their wives by fires, eat wholesome food,
And wear warm clothes, and even beasts have stalls,
I, 'tween the spring and downfall of the light,
Bow down one thousand and two hundred times,
To Christ, the Virgin Mother, and the saints; 110
Or in the night, after a little sleep,
I wake: the chill stars sparkle; I am wet
With drenching dews, or stiff with crackling frost.
I wear an undress'd goatskin on my back;
A grazing iron collar grinds my neck;
And in my weak, lean arms I lift the cross,
And strive and wrestle with thee till I die:
O mercy, mercy! wash away my sin.

O Lord, thou knowest what a man I am;
A sinful man, conceived and born in sin: 120
'Tis their own doing; this is none of mine;
Lay it not to me. Am I to blame for this,
That here come those that worship me? Ha! ha!
They think that I am somewhat. What am I?
The silly people take me for a saint,
And bring me offerings of fruit and flowers:
And I, in truth (thou wilt bear witness here)
Have all in all endured as much, and more
Than many just and holy men, whose names
Are register'd and calendar'd for saints. 130

Good people, you do ill to kneel to me.
What is it I can have done to merit this?
I am a sinner viler than you all.
It may be I have wrought some miracles,
And cured some halt and maim'd; but what of that?

It may be, no one, even among the saints,
May match his pains with mine; but what of that?
Yet do not rise; for you may look on me,
And in your looking you may kneel to God.
140 Speak! is there any of you halt or maim'd?
I think you know I have some power with Heaven
From my long penance: let him speak his wish.

Yes, I can heal him. Power goes forth from me.
They say that they are heal'd. Ah, hark! they shout
'St Simeon Stylites.' Why, if so,
God reaps a harvest in me. O my soul,
God reaps a harvest in thee. If this be,
Can I work miracles and not be saved?
This is not told of any. They were saints.
150 It cannot be but that I shall be saved;
Yea, crown'd a saint. They shout, 'Behold a saint!'
And lower voices saint me from above.
Courage, St Simeon! This dull chrysalis
Cracks into shining wings, and hope ere death
Spreads more and morc and more, that God hath nov
Sponged and made blank of crimeful record all
My mortal archives.

O my sons, my sons,
I, Simeon of the pillar, by surname
160 Stylites, among men; I, Simeon,
The watcher on the column till the end;
I, Simeon, whose brain the sunshine bakes;
I, whose bald brows in silent hours become
Unnaturally hoar with rime, do now
From my high nest of penance here proclaim
That Pontius and Iscariot by my side
Show'd like fair seraphs. On the coals I lay,
A vessel full of sin: all hell beneath
Made me boil over. Devils pluck'd my sleeve,
170 Abaddon and Asmodeus caught at me.
I smote them with the cross; they swarm'd again.

In bed like monstrous apes they crush'd my chest:
They flapp'd my light out as I read: I saw
Their faces grow between me and my book;
With colt-like whinny and with hoggish whine
They burst my prayer. Yet this way was left,
And by this way I 'scaped them. Mortify
Your flesh, like me, with scourges and with thorns;
Smite, shrink not, spare not. If it may be, fast
Whole Lents, and pray. I hardly, with slow steps, 180
With slow, faint steps, and much exceeding pain,
Have scrambled past those pits of fire, that still
Sing in mine ears. But yield not me the praise:
God only thro' his bounty hath thought fit,
Among the powers and princes of this world,
To make me an example to mankind,
Which few can reach to. Yet I do not say
But that a time may come – yea, even now,
Now, now, his footsteps smite the threshold stairs
Of life – I say, that time is at the doors 190
When you may worship me without reproach;
For I will leave my relics in your land,
And you may carve a shrine about my dust,
And burn a fragrant lamp before my bones,
When I am gather'd to the glorious saints.

While I spake then, a sting of shrewdest pain
Ran shrivelling thro' me, and a cloudlike change,
In passing, with a grosser film made thick
These heavy, horny eyes. The end! the end!
Surely the end! What's here? a shape, a shade,
A flash of light. Is that the angel there 200
That holds a crown? Come, blessèd brother, come.
I know thy glittering face. I waited long;
My brows are ready. What! deny it now?
Nay, draw, draw, draw nigh. So I clutch it. Christ!
'Tis gone: 'tis here again; the crown! the crown!
So now 'tis fitted on and grows to me,

And from it melt the dews of Paradise,
Sweet! sweet! spikenard, and balm, and frankincense.
210 Ah! let me not be fool'd, sweet saints: I trust
That I am whole, and clean, and meet for Heaven.

Speak, if there be a priest, a man of God,
Among you there, and let him presently
Approach, and lean a ladder on the shaft,
And climbing up into my airy home,
Deliver me the blessèd sacrament;
For by the warning of the Holy Ghost,
I prophesy that I shall die to-night,
A quarter before twelve.
But thou, O Lord,
220 Aid all this foolish people; let them take
Example, pattern: lead them to thy light.

Ulysses

It little profits that an idle king,
By this still hearth, among these barren crags,
Match'd with an agèd wife, I mete and dole
Unequal laws unto a savage race,
That hoard, and sleep, and feed, and know not me.

I cannot rest from travel: I will drink
Life to the lees: all times I have enjoy'd
Greatly, have suffer'd greatly, both with those
That loved me, and alone; on shore, and when
10 Thro' scudding drifts the rainy Hyades
Vext the dim sea: I am become a name;
For always roaming with a hungry heart
Much have I seen and known; cities of men

And manners, climates, councils, governments,
Myself not least, but honour'd of them all;
And drunk delight of battle with my peers,
Far on the ringing plains of windy Troy.
I am a part of all that I have met;
Yet all experience is an arch wherethro'
Gleams that untravell'd world, whose margin fades 20
For ever and for ever when I move.
How dull it is to pause, to make an end,
To rust unburnish'd, not to shine in use!
As tho' to breathe were life. Life piled on life
Were all too little, and of one to me
Little remains: but every hour is saved
From that eternal silence, something more,
A bringer of new things; and vile it were
For some three suns to store and hoard myself,
And this gray spirit yearning in desire 30
To follow knowledge like a sinking star,
Beyond the utmost bound of human thought.

This is my son, mine own Telemachus,
To whom I leave the sceptre and the isle –
Well-loved of me, discerning to fulfil
This labour, by slow prudence to make mild
A rugged people, and thro' soft degrees
Subdue them to the useful and the good.
Most blameless is he, centred in the sphere
Of common duties, decent not to fail 40
In offices of tenderness, and pay
Meet adoration to my household gods,
When I am gone. He works his work, I mine.

There lies the port; the vessel puffs her sail:
There gloom the dark broad seas. My mariners,
Souls that have toil'd, and wrought, and thought with me –
That ever with a frolic welcome took
The thunder and the sunshine, and opposed
Free hearts, free foreheads – you and I are old;

50 Old age hath yet his honour and his toil;
Death closes all: but something ere the end,
Some work of noble note, may yet be done,
Not unbecoming men that strove with Gods.
The lights begin to twinkle from the rocks:
The long day wanes: the slow moon climbs: the deep
Moans round with many voices. Come, my friends,
'Tis not too late to seek a newer world.
Push off, and sitting well in order smite
The sounding furrows; for my purpose holds
60 To sail beyond the sunset, and the baths
Of all the western stars, until I die.
It may be that the gulfs will wash us down:
It may be we shall touch the Happy Isles,
And see the great Achilles, whom we knew.
Tho' much is taken, much abides; and tho'
We are not now that strength which in old days
Moved earth and heaven; that which we are, we are;
One equal temper of heroic hearts,
Made weak by time and fate, but strong in will
70 To strive, to seek, to find, and not to yield.

Locksley Hall

Comrades, leave me here a little, while as yet 'tis early morn:
Leave me here, and when you want me, sound upon the bugle-horn.

'Tis the place, and all around it, as of old, the curlews call,
Dreary gleams about the moorland flying over Locksley Hall;

Locksley Hall, that in the distance overlooks the sandy tracts,
And the hollow ocean-ridges roaring into cataracts.

Many a night from yonder ivied casement, ere I went to rest,
Did I look on great Orion sloping slowly to the West.

Many a night I saw the Pleiads, rising thro' the mellow shade,
Glitter like a swarm of fire-flies tangled in a silver braid. 10

Here about the beach I wander'd, nourishing a youth sublime
With the fairy tales of science, and the long result of Time;

When the centuries behind me like a fruitful land reposed;
When I clung to all the present for the promise that it closed:

When I dipt into the future far as human eye could see;
Saw the Vision of the world, and all the wonder that would be.—

In the Spring a fuller crimson comes upon the robin's breast;
In the Spring the wanton lapwing gets himself another crest;

In the Spring a livelier iris changes on the burnish'd dove;
In the Spring a young man's fancy lightly turns to thoughts of
love. 20

Then her cheek was pale and thinner than should be for one so
young,
And her eyes on all my motions with a mute observance hung.

And I said, 'My cousin Amy, speak, and speak the truth to me,
Trust me, cousin, all the current of my being sets to thee.'

On her pallid cheek and forehead came a colour and a light,
As I have seen the rosy red flushing in the northern night.

And she turn'd – her bosom shaken with a sudden storm of
sighs –
All the spirit deeply dawning in the dark of hazel eyes –

Saying, 'I have hid my feelings, fearing they should do me wrong;'
Saying, 'Dost thou love me, cousin?' weeping, 'I have loved thee
long.' 30

Love took up the glass of Time, and turn'd it in his glowing
hands;
Every moment, lightly shaken, ran itself in golden sands.

Love took up the harp of Life, and smote on all the chords with might;
Smote the chord of Self, that, trembling, pass'd in music out of sight.

Many a morning on the moorland did we hear the copses ring,
And her whisper throng'd my pulses with the fulness of the Spring.

Many an evening by the waters did we watch the stately ships,
And our spirits rush'd together at the touching of the lips.

O my cousin, shallow-hearted! O my Amy, mine no more!
40 O the dreary, dreary moorland! O the barren, barren shore!

Falser than all fancy fathoms, falser than all songs have sung,
Puppet to a father's threat, and servile to a shrewish tongue!

Is it well to wish thee happy? – having known me – to decline
On a range of lower feelings and a narrower heart than mine!

Yet it shall be: thou shalt lower to his level day by day,
What is fine within thee growing coarse to sympathise with clay.

As the husband is, the wife is: thou art mated with a clown,
And the grossness of his nature will have weight to drag thee down.

He will hold thee, when his passion shall have spent its novel force,
50 Something better than his dog, a little dearer than his horse.

What is this? his eyes are heavy: think not they are glazed with wine.
Go to him: it is thy duty: kiss him: take his hand in thine.

It may be my lord is weary, that his brain is overwrought:
Soothe him with thy finer fancies, touch him with thy lighter thought.

He will answer to the purpose, easy things to understand –
Better thou wert dead before me, tho' I slew thee with my hand!

Better thou and I were lying, hidden from the heart's disgrace,
Roll'd in one another's arms, and silent in a last embrace.

Cursèd be the social wants that sin against the strength of youth!
Cursèd be the social lies that warp us from the living truth! 60

Cursèd be the sickly forms that err from honest Nature's rule!
Cursèd be the gold that gilds the straiten'd forehead of the fool!

Well – 'tis well that I should bluster! – Hadst thou less unworthy
 proved –
Would to God – for I had loved thee more than ever wife was
 loved.

Am I mad, that I should cherish that which bears but bitter fruit?
I will pluck it from my bosom, tho' my heart be at the root.

Never, tho' my mortal summers to such length of years should
 come
As the many-winter'd crow that leads the clanging rookery home.

Where is comfort? in division of the records of the mind?
Can I part her from herself, and love her, as I knew her, kind? 70

I remember one that perish'd: sweetly did she speak and move:
Such a one do I remember, whom to look at was to love.

Can I think of her as dead, and love her for the love she bore?
No – she never loved me truly: love is love for evermore.

Comfort? comfort scorn'd of devils! this is truth the poet sings,
That a sorrow's crown of sorrow is remembering happier things.

Drug thy memories, lest thou learn it, lest thy heart be put to
 proof,
In the dead unhappy night, and when the rain is on the roof.

Like a dog, he hunts in dreams, and thou art staring at the wall,
Where the dying night-lamp flickers, and the shadows rise and
 fall. 80

Then a hand shall pass before thee, pointing to his drunken sleep,
To thy widow'd marriage-pillows, to the tears that thou wilt weep.

Thou shalt hear the 'Never, never,' whisper'd by the phantom
years,
And a song from out the distance in the ringing of thine ears;

And an eye shall vex thee, looking ancient kindness on thy pain.
Turn thee, turn thee on thy pillow: get thee to thy rest again.

Nay, but Nature brings thee solace; for a tender voice will cry.
'Tis a purer life than thine; a lip to drain thy trouble dry.

Baby lips will laugh me down: my latest rival brings thee rest.
90 Baby fingers, waxen touches, press me from the mother's breast.

O, the child too clothes the father with a dearness not his due.
Half is thine and half is his: it will be worthy of the two.

O, I see thee old and formal, fitted to thy petty part,
With a little hoard of maxims preaching down a daughter's heart.

'They were dangerous guides the feelings – she herself was not
exempt –
Truly, she herself had suffer'd' – Perish in thy self-contempt!

Overlive it – lower yet – be happy! wherefore should I care?
I myself must mix with action, lest I wither by despair.

What is that which I should turn to, lighting upon days like
these?
100 Every door is barr'd with gold, and opens but to golden keys.

Every gate is throng'd with suitors, all the markets overflow.
I have but an angry fancy: what is that which I should do?

I had been content to perish, falling on the foeman's ground,
When the ranks are roll'd in vapour, and the winds are laid with
sound.

But the jingling of the guinea helps the hurt that Honour feels,
And the nations do but murmur, snarling at each other's heels.

Can I but relive in sadness? I will turn that earlier page.
Hide me from my deep emotion, O thou wondrous Mother-Age!

Make me feel the wild pulsation that I felt before the strife,
When I heard my days before me, and the tumult of my life; 110

Yearning for the large excitement that the coming years would
yield,
Eager-hearted as a boy when first he leaves his father's field,

And at night along the dusky highway near and nearer drawn,
Sees in heaven the light of London flaring like a dreary dawn;

And his spirit leaps within him to be gone before him then,
Underneath the light he looks at, in among the throngs of men:

Men, my brothers, men the workers, ever reaping something new:
That which they have done but earnest of the things that they
shall do:

For I dipt into the future, far as human eye could see,
Saw the Vision of the world, and all the wonder that would be; 120

Saw the heavens fill with commerce, argosies of magic sails,
Pilots of the purple twilight, dropping down with costly bales;

Heard the heavens fill with shouting, and there rain'd a ghastly dew
From the nations' airy navies grappling in the central blue;

Far along the world-wide whisper of the south-wind rushing
warm,
With the standards of the peoples plunging thro' the thunder-
storm;

Till the war-drum throbb'd no longer, and the battle-flags were furl'd
In the Parliament of man, the Federation of the world.

There the common sense of most shall hold a fretful realm in awe,
And the kindly earth shall slumber, lapt in universal law. 130

So I triumph'd ere my passion sweeping thro' me left me dry,
Left me with the palsied heart, and left me with the jaundiced
eye;

Eye, to which all order festers, all things here are out of joint:
Science moves, but slowly slowly, creeping on from point to point:

Slowly comes a hungry people, as a lion creeping nigher,
Glares at one that nods and winks behind a slowly-dying fire.

Yet I doubt not thro' the ages one increasing purpose runs,
And the thoughts of men are widen'd with the process of the suns.

What is that to him that reaps not harvest of his youthful joys,
140 Tho' the deep heart of existence beat for ever like a boy's?

Knowledge comes, but wisdom lingers, and I linger on the shore,
And the individual withers, and the world is more and more.

Knowledge comes, but wisdom lingers, and he bears a laden
 breast,
Full of sad experience, moving toward the stillness of his rest.

Hark, my merry comrades call me, sounding on the bugle-horn,
They to whom my foolish passion were a target for their scorn:

Shall it not be scorn to me to harp on such a moulder'd string?
I am shamed thro' all my nature to have loved so slight a thing.

Weakness to be wroth with weakness! woman's pleasure, woman's
 pain –
150 Nature made them blinder motions bounded in a shallower brain:

Woman is the lesser man, and all thy passions, match'd with
 mine,
Are as moonlight unto sunlight, and as water unto wine –

Here at least, where nature sickens, nothing. Ah, for some retreat
Deep in yonder shining Orient, where my life began to beat;

Where in wild Mahratta-battle fell my father evil-starr'd; –
I was left a trampled orphan, and a selfish uncle's ward.

Or to burst all links of habit – there to wander far away,
On from island unto island at the gateways of the day.

Larger constellations burning, mellow moons and happy skies,
160 Breadths of tropic shade and palms in cluster, knots of Paradise.

Never comes the trader, never floats an European flag,

Slides the bird o'er lustrous woodland, swings the trailer from the
crag;

Droops the heavy-blossom'd bower, hangs the heavy-fruited tree –
Summer isles of Eden lying in dark-purple spheres of sea.

There methinks would be enjoyment more than in this march of
mind,
In the steamship, in the railway, in the thoughts that shake
mankind.

There the passions cramp'd no longer shall have scope and
breathing space;
I will take some savage woman, she shall rear my dusky race.

Iron jointed, supple-sinew'd, they shall dive, and they shall run,
Catch the wild goat by the hair, and hurl their lances in the sun; 170

Whistle back the parrot's call, and leap the rainbows of the brooks,
Not with blinded eyesight poring over miserable books –

Fool, again the dream, the fancy! but I *know* my words are wild,
But I count the gray barbarian lower than the Christian child.

I, to herd with narrow foreheads, vacant of our glorious gains,
Like a beast with lower pleasures, like a beast with lower pains!

Mated with a squalid savage – what to me were sun or clime?
I the heir of all the ages, in the foremost files of time –

I that rather held it better men should perish one by one,
Than that earth should stand at gaze like Joshua's moon in Ajalon! 180

Not in vain the distance beacons. Forward, forward let us range,
Let the great world spin for ever down the ringing grooves of
change.

Thro' the shadow of the globe we sweep into the younger day:
Better fifty years of Europe than a cycle of Cathay.

Mother-Age (for mine I knew not) help me as when life begun:
Rift the hills, and roll the waters, flash the lightnings, weigh the
Sun.

O, I see the crescent promise of my spirit hath not set.
Ancient founts of inspiration well thro' all my fancy yet.

Howsoever these things be, a long farewell to Locksley Hall!
190 Now for me the woods may wither, now for me the roof-tree fall.

Comes a vapour from the margin, blackening over heath and holt,
Cramming all the blast before it, in its breast a thunderbolt.

Let it fall on Locksley Hall, with rain or hail, or fire or snow;
For the mighty wind arises, roaring seaward, and I go.

The Two Voices

A still small voice spake unto me,
'Thou art so full of misery,
Were it not better not to be?'

Then to the still small voice I said;
'Let me not cast in endless shade
What is so wonderfully made.'

To which the voice did urge reply;
'To-day I saw the dragon-fly
Come from the wells where he did lie.

10 'An inner impulse rent the veil
Of his old husk: from head to tail
Came out clear plates of sapphire mail.

'He dried his wings: like gauze they grew;
Thro' crofts and pastures wet with dew
A living flash of light he flew.'

I said, 'When first the world began,
Young Nature thro' five cycles ran,
And in the sixth she moulded man.

'She gave him mind, the lordliest
Proportion, and, above the rest, 20
Dominion in the head and breast.'

Thereto the silent voice replied;
'Self-blinded are you by your pride:
Look up thro' night: the world is wide.

'This truth within thy mind rehearse,
That in a boundless universe
Is boundless better, boundless worse.

'Think you this mould of hopes and fears
Could find no statelier than his peers
In yonder hundred million spheres?' 30

It spake, moreover, in my mind:
'Tho' thou wert scatter'd to the wind,
Yet is there plenty of the kind.'

Then did my response clearer fall:
'No compound of this earthly ball
Is like another, all in all.'

To which he answer'd scoffingly;
'Good soul! suppose I grant it thee,
Who'll weep for thy deficiency?

'Or will one beam be less intense, 40
When thy peculiar difference
Is cancell'd in the world of sense?'

I would have said, 'Thou canst not know,'
But my full heart, that work'd below,
Rain'd thro' my sight its overflow.

Again the voice spake unto me:
'Thou art so steep'd in misery,
Surely 'twere better not to be.

'Thine anguish will not let thee sleep,
50 Nor any train of reason keep:
Thou canst not think, but thou wilt weep.'

I said, 'The years with change advance:
If I make dark my countenance,
I shut my life from happier chance.

'Some turn this sickness yet might take,
Ev'n yet.' But he: 'What drug can make
A wither'd palsy cease to shake?'

I wept, 'Tho' I should die, I know
That all about the thorn will blow
60 In tufts of rosy-tinted snow;

'And men, thro' novel spheres of thought
Still moving after truth long sought,
Will learn new things when I am not.'

'Yet,' said the secret voice, 'some time,
Sooner or later, will gray prime
Make thy grass hoar with early rime.

'Not less swift souls that yearn for light,
Rapt after heaven's starry flight,
Would sweep the tracts of day and night.

70 'Not less the bee would range her cells,
The furzy prickle fire the dells,
The foxglove cluster dappled bells.'

I said that 'all the years invent;
Each month is various to present
The world with some development.

'Were this not well, to bide mine hour,
Tho' watching from a ruin'd tower
How grows the day of human power?'

'The highest-mounted mind,' he said,
80 'Still sees the sacred morning spread
The silent summit overhead.

'Will thirty seasons render plain
Those lonely lights that still remain,
Just breaking over land and main?

'Or make that morn, from his cold crown
And crystal silence creeping down,
Flood with full daylight glebe and town?

Forerun thy peers, thy time, and let
Thy feet, millenniums hence, be set
In midst of knowledge, dream'd not yet. 90

'Thou hast not gain'd a real height,
Nor art thou nearer to the light,
Because the scale is infinite.

''Twere better not to breathe or speak,
Than cry for strength, remaining weak,
And seem to find, but still to seek.

'Moreover, but to seem to find
Asks what thou lackest, thought resign'd,
A healthy frame, a quiet mind.'

I said, 'When I am gone away, 100
"He dared not tarry," men will say,
Doing dishonour to my clay.'

'This is more vile,' he made reply,
'To breathe and loathe, to live and sigh,
Than once from dread of pain to die.

'Sick art thou – a divided will
Still heaping on the fear of ill
The fear of men, a coward still.

'Do men love thee? Art thou so bound
To men, that how thy name may sound 110
Will vex thee lying underground?

'The memory of the wither'd leaf
In endless time is scarce more brief
Than of the garner'd Autumn-sheaf.

'Go, vexèd Spirit, sleep in trust;
The right ear, that is fill'd with dust,
Hears little of the false or just.'

'Hard task, to pluck resolve,' I cried,
'From emptiness and the waste wide
120 Of that abyss, or scornful pride!

'Nay – rather yet that I could raise
One hope that warm'd me in the days
While still I yearn'd for human praise.

'When, wide in soul and bold of tongue,
Among the tents I paused and sung,
The distant battle flash'd and rung.

'I sung the joyful Pæan clear,
And, sitting, burnish'd without fear
The brand, the buckler, and the spear –

130 'Waiting to strive a happy strife,
To war with falsehood to the knife,
And not to lose the good of life –

'Some hidden principle to move,
To put together, part and prove,
And mete the bounds of hate and love –

'As far as might be, to carve out
Free space for every human doubt,
That the whole mind might orb about –

'To search thro' all I felt or saw,
140 The springs of life, the depths of awe,
And reach the law within the law:

'At least, not rotting like a weed,
But, having sown some generous seed,
Fruitful of further thought and deed,

'To pass, when Life her light withdraws,
Not void of righteous self-applause,
Nor in a merely selfish cause –

'In some good cause, not in mine own,
To perish, wept for, honour'd, known,
And like a warrior overthrown; 150

'Whose eyes are dim with glorious tears,
When, soil'd with noble dust, he hears
His country's war-song thrill his ears:

'Then dying of a mortal stroke,
What time the foeman's line is broke,
And all the war is roll'd in smoke.'

'Yea!' said the voice, 'thy dream was good,
While thou abodest in the bud.
It was the stirring of the blood.

'If Nature put not forth her power 160
About the opening of the flower,
Who is it that could live an hour?

'Then comes the check, the change, the fall,
Pain rises up, old pleasures pall.
There is one remedy for all.

'Yet hadst thou, thro' enduring pain,
Link'd month to month with such a chain
Of knitted purport, all were vain.

'Thou hadst not between death and birth
Dissolved the riddle of the earth. 170
So were thy labour little-worth.

'That men with knowledge merely play'd,
I told thee – hardly nigher made,
Tho' scaling slow from grade to grade;

'Much less this dreamer, deaf and blind,
Named man, may hope some truth to find,
That bears relation to the mind.

'For every worm beneath the moon
Draws different threads, and late and soon
Spins, toiling out his own cocoon. 180

'Cry, faint not: either Truth is born
Beyond the polar gleam forlorn,
Or in the gateways of the morn.

'Cry, faint not, climb: the summits slope
Beyond the furthest flights of hope,
Wrapt in dense cloud from base to cope.

'Sometimes a little corner shines,
As over rainy mist inclines
A gleaming crag with belts of pines.

190 'I will go forward, sayest thou,
I shall not fail to find her now.
Look up, the fold is on her brow.

'If straight thy track, or if oblique,
Thou know'st not. Shadows thou dost strike,
Embracing cloud, Ixion-like;

'And owning but a little more
Than beasts, abidest lame and poor,
Calling thyself a little lower

'Than angels. Cease to wail and brawl!
200 Why inch by inch to darkness crawl?
There is one remedy for all.'

'O dull, one-sided voice,' said I,
'Wilt thou make everything a lie,
To flatter me that I may die?

'I know that age to age succeeds,
Blowing a noise of tongues and deeds,
A dust of systems and of creeds.

'I cannot hide that some have striven,
Achieving calm, to whom was given
210 The joy that mixes man with Heaven:

'Who, rowing hard against the stream,
Saw distant gates of Eden gleam,
And did not dream it was a dream;

'But heard, by secret transport led,
Ev'n in the charnels of the dead,
The murmur of the fountain-head –

'Which did accomplish their desire,
Bore and forbore, and did not tire,
Like Stephen, an unquenchèd fire.

'He heeded not reviling tones, 220
Nor sold his heart to idle moans,
Tho' cursed and scorn'd, and bruised with stones:

'But looking upward, full of grace,
He pray'd, and from a happy place
God's glory smote him on the face.'

The sullen answer slid betwixt:
'Not that the grounds of hope were fix'd,
The elements were kindlier mix'd.'

I said, 'I toil beneath the curse,
But, knowing not the universe, 230
I fear to slide from bad to worse.

'And that, in seeking to undo
One riddle, and to find the true,
I knit a hundred others new:

'Or that this anguish fleeting hence,
Unmanacled from bonds of sense,
Be fix'd and froz'n to permanence:

'For I go, weak from suffering here:
Naked I go, and void of cheer:
What is it that I may not fear?' 240

'Consider well,' the voice replied,
'His face, that two hours since hath died;
Wilt thou find passion, pain or pride?

'Will he obey when one commands?
Or answer should one press his hands?
He answers not, nor understands.

'His palms are folded on his breast:
There is no other thing express'd
But long disquiet merged in rest.

250 'His lips are very mild and meek:
Tho' one should smite him on the cheek,
And on the mouth, he will not speak.

'His little daughter, whose sweet face
He kiss'd, taking his last embrace,
Becomes dishonour to her race –

'His sons grow up that bear his name,
Some grow to honour, some to shame, –
But he is chill to praise or blame.

'He will not hear the north-wind rave,
260 Nor, moaning, household shelter crave
From winter rains that beat his grave.

'High up the vapours fold and swim:
About him broods the twilight dim:
The place he knew forgetteth him.'

'If all be dark, vague voice,' I said,
'These things are wrapt in doubt and dread,
Nor canst thou show the dead are dead.

'The sap dries up: the plant declines.
A deeper tale my heart divines.

270 Know I not Death? the outward signs?

'I found him when my years were few;
A shadow on the graves I knew,
And darkness in the village yew.

'From grave to grave the shadow crept:
In her still place the morning wept:
Touch'd by his feet the daisy slept.

'The simple senses crown'd his head:
"Omega! thou art Lord," they said,
"We find no motion in the dead."

'Why, if man rot in dreamless ease, 280
Should that plain fact, as taught by these,
Not make him sure that he shall cease?

'Who forged that other influence,
That heat of inward evidence,
By which he doubts against the sense?

'He owns the fatal gift of eyes,
That read his spirit blindly wise,
Not simple as a thing that dies.

'Here sits he shaping wings to fly:
His heart forebodes a mystery: 290
He names the name Eternity.

'That type of Perfect in his mind
In Nature can he nowhere find.
He sows himself on every wind.

'He seems to hear a Heavenly Friend,
And thro' thick veils to apprehend
A labour working to an end.

'The end and the beginning vex
His reason: many things perplex,
With motions, checks, and counterchecks. 300

'He knows a baseness in his blood
At such strange war with something good,
He may not do the thing he would.

'Heaven opens inward, chasms yawn,
Vast images in glimmering dawn,
Half shown, are broken and withdrawn.

'Ah! sure within him and without,
Could his dark wisdom find it out,
There must be answer to his doubt,

'But thou canst answer not again. 310
With thine own weapon art thou slain,
Or thou wilt answer but in vain.

'The doubt would rest, I dare not solve
In the same circle we revolve.
Assurance only breeds resolve.'

As when a billow, blown against,
Falls back, the voice with which I fenced
A little ceased, but recommenced.

'Where wert thou when thy father play'd
320 In his free field, and pastime made,
A merry boy in sun and shade?

'A merry boy they call'd him then,
He sat upon the knees of men
In days that never come again.

'Before the little ducts began
To feed thy bones with lime, and ran
Their course, till thou wert also man:

'Who took a wife, who rear'd his race,
Whose wrinkles gather'd on his face,
330 Whose troubles number with his days:

'A life of nothings, nothing-worth,
From that first nothing ere his birth
To that last nothing under earth!'

'These words,' I said, 'are like the rest;
No certain clearness, but at best
A vague suspicion of the breast:

'But if I grant, thou mightst defend
The thesis which thy words intend –
That to begin implies to end;

340 'Yet how should I for certain hold,
Because my memory is so cold,
That I first was in human mould?

'I cannot make this matter plain,
But I would shoot, howe'er in vain,
A random arrow from the brain.

'It may be that no life is found,
Which only to one engine bound
Falls off, but cycles always round.

'As old mythologies relate,
Some draught of Lethe might await 350
The slipping thro' from state to state.

'As here we find in trances, men
Forget the dream that happens then,
Until they fall in trance again.

'So might we, if our state were such
As one before, remember much,
For those two likes might meet and touch.

'But, if I lapsed from nobler place,
Some legend of a fallen race
Alone might hint of my disgrace; 360

'Some vague emotion of delight
In gazing up an Alpine height,
Some yearning toward the lamps of night;

'Or if thro' lower lives I came –
Tho' all experience past became
Consolidate in mind and frame –

'I might forget my weaker lot;
For is not our first year forgot?
The haunts of memory echo not.

'And men, whose reason long was blind, 370
From cells of madness unconfined,
Oft lose whole years of darker mind.

'Much more, if first I floated free,
As naked essence, must I be
Incompetent of memory:

'For memory dealing but with time,
And he with matter, could she climb
Beyond her own material prime?

'Moreover, something is or seems,
380 That touches me with mystic gleams,
Like glimpses of forgotten dreams –

'Of something felt, like something here;
Of something done, I know not where;
Such as no language may declare.'

The still voice laugh'd. 'I talk,' said he,
'Not with thy dreams. Suffice it thee
Thy pain is a reality.'

'But thou,' said I, 'hast missed thy mark,
Who sought'st to wreck my mortal ark,
390 By making all the horizon dark.

'Why not set forth, if I should do
This rashness, that which might ensue
With this old soul in organs new?

'Whatever crazy sorrow saith,
No life that breathes with human breath
Has ever truly long'd for death.

' 'Tis life, whereof our nerves are scant,
Oh life, not death, for which we pant;
More life, and fuller, that I want.'

400 I ceased, and sat as one forlorn.
Then said the voice, in quiet scorn,
'Behold, it is the Sabbath morn.'

And I arose, and I released
The casement, and the light increased
With freshness in the dawning east.

Like soften'd airs that blowing steal,
When meres begin to uncongeal,
The sweet church bells began to peal.

On to God's house the people prest:
410 Passing the place where each must rest,
Each enter'd like a welcome guest.

One walk'd between his wife and child,
With measured footfall firm and mild,
And now and then he gravely smiled.

The prudent partner of his blood
Lean'd on him, faithful, gentle, good,
Wearing the rose of womanhood.

And in their double love secure,
The little maiden walk'd demure,
Pacing with downward eyelids pure. 420

These three made unity so sweet,
My frozen heart began to beat,
Remembering its ancient heat.

I blest them, and they wander'd on:
I spoke, but answer came there none:
The dull and bitter voice was gone.

A second voice was at mine ear,
A little whisper silver-clear,
A murmur, 'Be of better cheer.'

As from some blissful neighbourhood, 430
A notice faintly understood,
'I see the end, and know the good.'

A little hint to solace woe,
A hint, a whisper breathing low,
'I may not speak of what I know.'

Like an Æolian harp that wakes
No certain air, but overtakes
Far thought with music that it makes:

Such seem'd the whisper at my side:
'What is it thou knowest, sweet voice?' I cried. 440
'A hidden hope,' the voice replied:

So heavenly-toned, that in that hour
From out my sullen heart a power
Broke, like the rainbow from the shower,

To feel, altho' no tongue can prove,
That every cloud, that spreads above
And veileth love, itself is love.

And forth into the fields I went,
And Nature's living motion lent
450 The pulse of hope to discontent.

I wonder'd at the bounteous hours,
The slow result of winter showers:
You scarce could see the grass for flowers.

I wonder'd, while I paced along:
The woods were fill'd so full with song,
There seem'd no room for sense of wrong;

And all so variously wrought,
I marvell'd how the mind was brought
To anchor by one gloomy thought;

460 And wherefore rather I made choice
To commune with that barren voice,
Than him that said, 'Rejoice! Rejoice!'

'Move eastward, happy earth, and leave'

Move eastward, happy earth, and leave
  Yon orange sunset waning slow:
From fringes of the faded eve,
  O, happy planet, eastward go;
Till over thy dark shoulder glow
  Thy silver sister-world, and rise
  To glass herself in dewy eyes
That watch me from the glen below.

Ah, bear me with thee, smoothly borne,
Dip forward under starry light, 10
And move me to my marriage-morn,
And round again to happy night.

'Break, break, break'

Break, break, break,
On thy cold gray stones, O Sea!
And I would that my tongue could utter
The thoughts that arise in me.

O well for the fisherman's boy,
That he shouts with his sister at play!
O well for the sailor lad,
That he sings in his boat on the bay!

And the stately ships go on
To their haven under the hill; 10
But O for the touch of a vanish'd hand,
And the sound of a voice that is still!

Break, break, break
At the foot of thy crags, O Sea!
But the tender grace of a day that is dead
Will never come back to me.

▲ ▲ ▲

From *Poems* (1846)

The Golden Year

Well, you shall have that song which Leonard wrote:
It was last summer on a tour in Wales:
Old James was with me: we that day had been
Up Snowdon; and I wish'd for Leonard there,
And found him in Llanberis: then we crost
Between the lakes, and clamber'd half way up
The counter side; and that same song of his
He told me; for I banter'd him, and swore
They said he lived shut up within himself,
10 A tongue-tied Poet in the feverous days,
That, setting the *how much* before the *how*,
Cry, like the daughters of the horseleech, 'Give,
Cram us with all,' but count not me the herd!

To which 'They call me what they will,' he said:
'But I was born too late: the fair new forms,
That float about the threshold of an age,
Like truths of Science waiting to be caught –
Catch me who can, and make the catcher crown'd –
Are taken by the forelock. Let it be.
20 But if you care indeed to listen, hear
These measured words, my work of yestermorn.

'We sleep and wake and sleep, but all things move;
The Sun flies forward to his brother Sun;
The dark Earth follows wheel'd in her ellipse;
And human things returning on themselves
Move onward, leading up the golden year.

'Ah, tho' the times, when some new thought can bud,
Are but as poets' seasons when they flower,
Yet oceans daily gaining on the land,
Have ebb and flow conditioning their march, 30
And slow and sure comes up the golden year.
'When wealth no more shall rest in mounded heaps,
But smit with freër light shall slowly melt
In many streams to fatten lower lands,
And light shall spread, and man be liker man
Thro' all the season of the golden year.
'Shall eagles not be eagles? wrens be wrens?
If all the world were falcons, what of that?
The wonder of the eagle were the less,
But he not less the eagle. Happy days 40
Roll onward, leading up the golden year.

'Fly, happy happy sails, and bear the Press;
Fly happy with the mission of the Cross;
Knit land to land, and blowing havenward
With silks, and fruits, and spices, clear of toll,
Enrich the markets of the golden year.
'But we grow old. Ah! when shall all men's good
Be each man's rule, and universal Peace
Lie like a shaft of light across the land,
And like a lane of beams athwart the sea, 50
Thro' all the circle of the golden year?'

Thus far he flow'd, and ended; whereupon
'Ah, folly!' in mimic cadence answer'd James –
'Ah, folly! for it lies so far away,
Not in our time, nor in our children's time,
'Tis like the second world to us that live;
'Twere all as one to fix our hopes on Heaven
As on this vision of the golden year.'

With that he struck his staff against the rocks
And broke it, – James, – you know him, – old, but full 60
Of force and choler, and firm upon his feet,

And like an oaken stock in winter woods,
O'erflourish'd with the hoary clematis:
Then added, all in heat:

'What stuff is this!
Old writers push'd the happy season back, –
The more fools they, – we forward: dreamers both:
You most, that in an age, when every hour
Must sweat her sixty minutes to the death,
Live on, God love us, as if the seedsman, rapt
70 Upon the teeming harvest, should not plunge
His hand into the bag: but well I know
That unto him who works, and feels he works,
This same grand year is ever at the doors.'

He spoke; and, high above, I heard them blast
The steep slate-quarry, and the great echo flap
And buffet round the hills, from bluff to bluff.

▲ ▲ ▲

From *The Princess* (1847)

'*As thro' the land at eve we went*'

As thro' the land at eve we went,
  And pluck'd the ripen'd ears,
We fell out, my wife and I,
O we fell out I know not why,
  And kiss'd again with tears.
And blessings on the falling out
  That all the more endears,
When we fall out with those we love
  And kiss again with tears!
For when we came where lies the child 10
  We lost in other years,
There above the little grave,
O there above the little grave,
  We kiss'd again with tears.

'*Sweet and low, sweet and low*'

Sweet and low, sweet and low,
  Wind of the western sea,
Low, low, breathe and blow,
  Wind of the western sea!

Over the rolling waters go,
Come from the dying moon, and blow,
  Blow him again to me;
While my little one, while my pretty one, sleeps.

Sleep and rest, sleep and rest,
10 Father will come to thee soon;
Rest, rest, on mother's breast,
  Father will come to thee soon;
Father will come to his babe in the nest,
Silver sails all out of the west
  Under the silver moon:
Sleep, my little one, sleep, my pretty one, sleep.

'The splendour falls on castle walls'

The splendour falls on castle walls
  And snowy summits old in story:
The long light shakes across the lakes,
  And the wild cataract leaps in glory.
Blow, bugle, blow, set the wild echoes flying,
Blow, bugle; answer, echoes, dying, dying, dying.

O hark, O hear! how thin and clear,
  And thinner, clearer, farther going!
O sweet and far from cliff and scar
10 The horns of Elfland faintly blowing!
Blow, let us hear the purple glens replying:
Blow, bugle; answer, echoes, dying, dying, dying.

O love, they die in yon rich sky,
They faint on hill or field or river:
Our echoes roll from soul to soul,
And grow for ever and for ever.
Blow, bugle, blow, set the wild echoes flying,
And answer, echoes, answer, dying, dying, dying.

'Tears, idle tears, I know not what they mean'

'Tears, idle tears, I know not what they mean,
Tears from the depth of some divine despair
Rise in the heart, and gather to the eyes,
In looking on the happy Autumn-fields,
And thinking of the days that are no more.

'Fresh as the first beam glittering on a sail,
That brings our friends up from the underworld,
Sad as the last which reddens over one
That sinks with all we love below the verge;
So sad, so fresh, the days that are no more. 10

'Ah, sad and strange as in dark summer dawns
The earliest pipe of half-awaken'd birds
To dying ears, when unto dying eyes
The casement slowly grows a glimmering square;
So sad, so strange, the days that are no more.

'Dear as remember'd kisses after death,
And sweet as those by hopeless fancy feign'd
On lips that are for others; deep as love,
Deep as first love, and wild with all regret;
O Death in Life, the days that are no more.' 20

'Ask me no more: the moon may draw the sea'

Ask me no more: the moon may draw the sea;
The cloud may stoop from heaven and take the shape
With fold to fold, of mountain or of cape;
But O too fond, when have I answer'd thee?
Ask me no more.

Ask me no more: what answer should I give?
I love not hollow cheek or faded eye:
Yet, O my friend, I will not have thee die!
Ask me no more, lest I should bid thee live;
10 Ask me no more.

Ask me no more: thy fate and mine are seal'd:
I strove against the stream and all in vain:
Let the great river take me to the main:
No more, dear love, for at a touch I yield;
Ask me no more.

'Now sleeps the crimson petal, now the white'

'Now sleeps the crimson petal, now the white;
Nor waves the cypress in the palace walk;
Nor winks the gold fin in the porphyry font:
The fire-fly wakens: waken thou with me.

Now droops the milkwhite peacock like a ghost,
And like a ghost she glimmers on to me.

Now lies the Earth all Danaë to the stars,
And all thy heart lies open unto me.

Now slides the silent meteor on, and leaves
A shining furrow, as thy thoughts in me. 10

Now folds the lily all her sweetness up,
And slips into the bosom of the lake:
So fold thyself, my dearest, thou, and slip
Into my bosom and be lost in me.'

'Come down, O maid, from yonder mountain height'

'Come down, O maid, from yonder mountain height:
What pleasure lives in height (the shepherd sang)
In height and cold, the splendour of the hills?
But cease to move so near the Heavens, and cease
To glide a sunbeam by the blasted Pine,
To sit a star upon the sparkling spire;
And come, for Love is of the valley, come,
For Love is of the valley, come thou down
And find him; by the happy threshold, he,
Or hand in hand with Plenty in the maize, 10
Or red with spirted purple of the vats,
Or foxlike in the vine; nor cares to walk
With Death and Morning on the silver horns,
Nor wilt thou snare him in the white ravine,
Nor find him dropt upon the firths of ice,
That huddling slant in furrow-cloven falls
To roll the torrent out of dusky doors:

But follow; let the torrent dance thee down
To find him in the valley; let the wild
20 Lean-headed Eagles yelp alone, and leave
The monstrous ledges there to slope, and spill
Their thousand wreaths of dangling water-smoke,
That like a broken purpose waste in air:
So waste not thou; but come; for all the vales
Await thee; azure pillars of the hearth
Arise to thee; the children call, and I
Thy shepherd pipe, and sweet is every sound,
Sweeter thy voice, but every sound is sweet;
Myriads of rivulets hurrying thro' the lawn,
30 The moan of doves in immemorial elms,
And murmuring of innumerable bees.'

▲ ▲ ▲

Lines [*'Here often, when a child, I lay reclined'*]

Here often, when a child, I lay reclined:
  I took delight in this fair strand and free:
Here stood the infant Ilion of my mind,
  And here the Grecian ships did seem to be.
And here again I come and only find
  The drain-cut levels of the marshy lea,
Gray sandbanks and pale sunsets, dreary wind,
  Dim shores, dense rains and heavy-clouded sea.

Yet tho' perchance no tract of earth have more
  Unlikeness to the fair Ionian plain, 10
I love the place that I have loved before,
  I love the rolling cloud, the flying rain,
The brown sea lapsing back with sullen roar
  To travel leagues before he comes again,
The misty desert of the houseless shore,
  The phantom-circle of the moaning main.

▲ ▲ ▲

In Memoriam A. H. H. (1850)

OBIIT MDCCCXXXIII

[PROLOGUE]

Strong Son of God, immortal Love,
    Whom we, that have not seen thy face,
    By faith, and faith alone, embrace,
Believing where we cannot prove;

Thine are these orbs of light and shade;
    Thou madest Life in man and brute;
    Thou madest Death; and lo, thy foot
Is on the skull which thou hast made.

Thou wilt not leave us in the dust:
10   Thou madest man, he knows not why,
    He thinks he was not made to die;
And thou hast made him: thou art just.

Thou seemest human and divine,
    The highest, holiest manhood, thou:
    Our wills are ours, we know not how;
Our wills are ours, to make them thine.

Our little systems have their day;
    They have their day and cease to be:
    They are but broken lights of thee,
20 And thou, O Lord, art more than they.

We have but faith: we cannot know;
    For knowledge is of things we see;

And yet we trust it comes from thee,
A beam in darkness: let it grow.

Let knowledge grow from more to more,
But more of reverence in us dwell;
That mind and soul, according well,
May make one music as before,

But vaster. We are fools and slight;
We mock thee when we do not fear: 30
But help thy foolish ones to bear;
Help thy vain worlds to bear thy light.

Forgive what seem'd my sin in me;
What seem'd my worth since I began;
For merit lives from man to man,
And not from man, O Lord, to thee.

Forgive my grief for one removed,
Thy creature, whom I found so fair.
I trust he lives in thee, and there
I find him worthier to be loved. 40

Forgive these wild and wandering cries,
Confusions of a wasted youth;
Forgive them where they fail in truth,
And in thy wisdom make me wise.

1849

I

I held it truth, with him who sings
To one clear harp in divers tones,
That men may rise on stepping-stones
Of their dead selves to higher things.

But who shall so forecast the years
And find in loss a gain to match?
Or reach a hand thro' time to catch
The far-off interest of tears?

Let Love clasp Grief lest both be drown'd,
10 Let darkness keep her raven gloss:
Ah, sweeter to be drunk with loss,
To dance with death, to beat the ground,

Than that the victor Hours should scorn
The long result of love, and boast,
'Behold the man that loved and lost,
But all he was is overworn.'

II

Old Yew, which graspest at the stones
That name the under-lying dead,
Thy fibres net the dreamless head,
Thy roots are wrapt about the bones.

The seasons bring the flower again,
And bring the firstling to the flock;
And in the dusk of thee, the clock
Beats out the little lives of men.

O not for thee the glow, the bloom,
10 Who changest not in any gale,
Nor branding summer suns avail
To touch thy thousand years of gloom:

And gazing on thee, sullen tree,
Sick for thy stubborn hardihood,
I seem to fail from out my blood
And grow incorporate into thee.

III

O Sorrow, cruel fellowship,
O Priestess in the vaults of Death,
O sweet and bitter in a breath,
What whispers from thy lying lip?

'The stars,' she whispers, 'blindly run;
A web is wov'n across the sky;

From out waste places comes a cry,
And murmurs from the dying sun:

'And all the phantom, Nature, stands –
With all the music in her tone, 10
A hollow echo of my own, –
A hollow form with empty hands.'

And shall I take a thing so blind,
Embrace her as my natural good;
Or crush her, like a vice of blood,
Upon the threshold of the mind?

IV

To Sleep I give my powers away;
My will is bondsman to the dark;
I sit within a helmless bark,
And with my heart I muse and say:

O heart, how fares it with thee now,
That thou should'st fail from thy desire,
Who scarcely darest to inquire,
'What is it makes me beat so low?'

Something it is which thou hast lost,
Some pleasure from thine early years. 10
Break, thou deep vase of chilling tears,
That grief hath shaken into frost!

Such clouds of nameless trouble cross
All night below the darken'd eyes;
With morning wakes the will, and cries,
'Thou shalt not be the fool of loss.'

V

I sometimes hold it half a sin
To put in words the grief I feel;
For words, like Nature, half reveal
And half conceal the Soul within.

But, for the unquiet heart and brain,
A use in measured language lies;
The sad mechanic exercise,
Like dull narcotics, numbing pain.

In words, like weeds, I'll wrap me o'er,
10 Like coarsest clothes against the cold:
But that large grief which these enfold
Is given in outline and no more.

VI

One writes, that 'Other friends remain,'
That 'Loss is common to the race' –
And common is the commonplace,
And vacant chaff well meant for grain.

That loss is common would not make
My own less bitter, rather more:
Too common! Never morning wore
To evening, but some heart did break.

O father, wheresoe'er thou be,
10 Who pledgest now thy gallant son;
A shot, ere half thy draught be done,
Hath still'd the life that beat from thee.

O mother, praying God will save
Thy sailor, – while thy head is bow'd,
His heavy-shotted hammock-shroud
Drops in his vast and wandering grave.

Ye know no more than I who wrought
At that last hour to please him well;
Who mused on all I had to tell,
20 And something written, something thought;

Expecting still his advent home;
And ever met him on his way
With wishes, thinking, 'here to-day,'
Or 'here to-morrow will he come.'

O somewhere, meek, unconscious dove,
That sittest ranging golden hair;
And glad to find thyself so fair,
Poor child, that waitest for thy love!

For now her father's chimney glows
In expectation of a guest; 30
And thinking 'this will please him best,'
She takes a riband or a rose;

For he will see them on to-night;
And with the thought her colour burns;
And, having left the glass, she turns
Once more to set a ringlet right;

And, even when she turn'd, the curse
Had fallen, and her future Lord
Was drown'd in passing thro' the ford,
Or kill'd in falling from his horse. 40

O what to her shall be the end?
And what to me remains of good?
To her, perpetual maidenhood,
And unto me no second friend.

VII

Dark house, by which once more I stand
Here in the long unlovely street,
Doors, where my heart was used to beat
So quickly, waiting for a hand,

A hand that can be clasp'd no more –
Behold me, for I cannot sleep,
And like a guilty thing I creep
At earliest morning to the door.

He is not here; but far away
The noise of life begins again, 10
And ghastly thro' the drizzling rain
On the bald street breaks the blank day.

VIII

A happy lover who has come
To look on her that loves him well,
Who 'lights and rings the gateway bell,
And learns her gone and far from home;

He saddens, all the magic light
Dies off at once from bower and hall,
And all the place is dark, and all
The chambers emptied of delight:

So find I every pleasant spot
10 In which we two were wont to meet,
The field, the chamber and the street,
For all is dark where thou art not.

Yet as that other, wandering there
In those deserted walks, may find
A flower beat with rain and wind,
Which once she foster'd up with care;

So seems it in my deep regret,
O my forsaken heart, with thee
And this poor flower of poesy
20 Which little cared for fades not yet.

But since it pleased a vanish'd eye,
I go to plant it on his tomb,
That if it can it there may bloom,
Or dying, there at least may die.

IX

Fair ship, that from the Italian shore
Sailest the placid ocean-plains
With my lost Arthur's loved remains,
Spread thy full wings, and waft him o'er.

So draw him home to those that mourn
In vain; a favourable speed

Ruffle thy mirror'd mast, and lead
Thro' prosperous floods his holy urn.

All night no ruder air perplex
Thy sliding keel, till Phosphor, bright 10
As our pure love, thro' early light
Shall glimmer on the dewy decks.

Sphere all your lights around, above;
Sleep, gentle heavens, before the prow;
Sleep, gentle winds, as he sleeps now,
My friend, the brother of my love;

My Arthur, whom I shall not see
Till all my widow'd race be run;
Dear as the mother to the son,
More than my brothers are to me. 20

X

I hear the noise about thy keel;
I hear the bell struck in the night:
I see the cabin-window bright;
I see the sailor at the wheel.

Thou bring'st the sailor to his wife,
And travell'd men from foreign lands;
And letters unto trembling hands;
And, thy dark freight, a vanish'd life.

So bring him: we have idle dreams:
This look of quiet flatters thus 10
Our home-bred fancies: O to us,
The fools of habit, sweeter seems

To rest beneath the clover sod,
That takes the sunshine and the rains,
Or where the kneeling hamlet drains
The chalice of the grapes of God;

Than if with thee the roaring wells
    Should gulf him fathom-deep in brine;
    And hands so often clasp'd in mine,
20 Should toss with tangle and with shells.

XI

Calm is the morn without a sound,
    Calm as to suit a calmer grief,
    And only thro' the faded leaf
The chestnut pattering to the ground:

Calm and deep peace on this high wold,
    And on these dews that drench the furze,
    And all the silvery gossamers
That twinkle into green and gold:

Calm and still light on yon great plain
10 That sweeps with all its autumn bowers,
    And crowded farms and lessening towers,
To mingle with the bounding main:

Calm and deep peace in this wide air,
    These leaves that redden to the fall;
    And in my heart, if calm at all,
If any calm, a calm despair:

Calm on the seas, and silver sleep,
    And waves that sway themselves in rest,
    And dead calm in that noble breast
20 Which heaves but with the heaving deep.

XII

Lo, as a dove when up she springs
    To bear thro' Heaven a tale of woe,
    Some dolorous message knit below
The wild pulsation of her wings;

Like her I go; I cannot stay;
    I leave this mortal ark behind,

A weight of nerves without a mind,
And leave the cliffs, and haste away

O'er ocean-mirrors rounded large,
And reach the glow of southern skies, 10
And see the sails at distance rise,
And linger weeping on the marge,

And saying; 'Comes he thus, my friend?
Is this the end of all my care?'
And circle moaning in the air:
'Is this the end? Is this the end?'

And forward dart again, and play
About the prow, and back return
To where the body sits, and learn
That I have been an hour away. 20

XIII

Tears of the widower, when he sees
A late-lost form that sleep reveals,
And moves his doubtful arms, and feels
Her place is empty, fall like these;

Which weep a loss for ever new,
A void where heart on heart reposed;
And, where warm hands have prest and closed,
Silence, till I be silent too.

Which weep the comrade of my choice,
An awful thought, a life removed, 10
The human-hearted man I loved,
A Spirit, not a breathing voice.

Come Time, and teach me, many years,
I do not suffer in a dream;
For now so strange do these things seem,
Mine eyes have leisure for their tears;

My fancies time to rise on wing,
  And glance about the approaching sails,
  As tho' they brought but merchants' bales,
20 And not the burthen that they bring.

XIV

If one should bring me this report,
  That thou hadst touch'd the land to-day,
  And I went down unto the quay,
And found thee lying in the port;

And standing, muffled round with woe,
  Should see thy passengers in rank
  Come stepping lightly down the plank,
And beckoning unto those they know;

And if along with these should come
10 The man I held as half-divine;
  Should strike a sudden hand in mine,
And ask a thousand things of home;

And I should tell him all my pain,
  And how my life had droop'd of late,
  And he should sorrow o'er my state
And marvel what possess'd my brain;

And I perceived no touch of change,
  No hint of death in all his frame,
  But found him all in all the same,
20 I should not feel it to be strange.

XV

To-night the winds begin to rise
  And roar from yonder dropping day:
  The last red leaf is whirl'd away,
The rooks are blown about the skies;

The forest crack'd, the waters curl'd,
  The cattle huddled on the lea;

And wildly dash'd on tower and tree
The sunbeam strikes along the world:

And but for fancies, which aver
That all thy motions gently pass 10
Athwart a plane of molten glass,
I scarce could brook the strain and stir

That makes the barren branches loud;
And but for fear it is not so,
The wild unrest that lives in woe
Would dote and pore on yonder cloud

That rises upward always higher,
And onward drags a labouring breast,
And topples round the dreary west,
A looming bastion fringed with fire. 20

XVI

What words are these have fall'n from me?
Can calm despair and wild unrest
Be tenants of a single breast,
Or sorrow such a changeling be?

Or doth she only seem to take
The touch of change in calm or storm;
But knows no more of transient form
In her deep self, than some dead lake

That holds the shadow of a lark
Hung in the shadow of a heaven? 10
Or has the shock, so harshly given,
Confused me like the unhappy bark

That strikes by night a craggy shelf,
And staggers blindly ere she sink?
And stunn'd me from my power to think
And all my knowledge of myself;

And made me that delirious man
Whose fancy fuses old and new,
And flashes into false and true,
20 And mingles all without a plan?

XVII

Thou comest, much wept for: such a breeze
Compell'd thy canvas, and my prayer
Was as the whisper of an air
To breathe thee over lonely seas.

For I in spirit saw thee move
Thro' circles of the bounding sky,
Week after week: the days go by:
Come quick, thou bringest all I love.

Henceforth, wherever thou may'st roam,
10 My blessing, like a line of light,
Is on the waters day and night,
And like a beacon guards thee home.

So may whatever tempest mars
Mid-ocean, spare thee, sacred bark;
And balmy drops in summer dark
Slide from the bosom of the stars.

So kind an office hath been done,
Such precious relics brought by thee;
The dust of him I shall not see
20 Till all my widow'd race be run.

XVIII

'Tis well; 'tis something; we may stand
Where he in English earth is laid,
And from his ashes may be made
The violet of his native land.

'Tis little; but it looks in truth
As if the quiet bones were blest

Among familiar names to rest
And in the places of his youth.

Come then, pure hands, and bear the head
That sleeps or wears the mask of sleep, 10
And come, whatever loves to weep,
And hear the ritual of the dead.

Ah, yet, ev'n yet, if this might be,
I, falling on his faithful heart,
Would breathing thro' his lips impart
The life that almost dies in me;

That dies not, but endures with pain,
And slowly forms the firmer mind,
Treasuring the look it cannot find,
The words that are not heard again. 20

XIX

The Danube to the Severn gave
The darken'd heart that beat no more;
They laid him by the pleasant shore,
And in the hearing of the wave.

There twice a day the Severn fills;
The salt sea-water passes by,
And hushes half the babbling Wye,
And makes a silence in the hills.

The Wye is hush'd nor moved along,
And hush'd my deepest grief of all, 10
When fill'd with tears that cannot fall,
I brim with sorrow drowning song.

The tide flows down, the wave again
Is vocal in its wooded walls;
My deeper anguish also falls,
And I can speak a little then.

XX

The lesser griefs that may be said,
  That breathe a thousand tender vows,
  Are but as servants in a house
Where lies the master newly dead;

Who speak their feeling as it is,
  And weep the fulness from the mind:
  'It will be hard,' they say, 'to find
Another service such as this.'

My lighter moods are like to these,
10 That out of words a comfort win;
  But there are other griefs within,
And tears that at their fountain freeze;

For by the hearth the children sit
  Cold in that atmosphere of Death,
  And scarce endure to draw the breath,
Or like to noiseless phantoms flit:

But open converse is there none,
  So much the vital spirits sink
  To see the vacant chair, and think,
20 'How good! how kind! and he is gone.'

XXI

I sing to him that rests below,
  And, since the grasses round me wave,
  I take the grasses of the grave,
And make them pipes whereon to blow.

The traveller hears me now and then,
  And sometimes harshly will he speak:
  'This fellow would make weakness weak,
And melt the waxen hearts of men.'

Another answers, 'Let him be,
10 He loves to make parade of pain,

That with his piping he may gain
The praise that comes to constancy.'

A third is wroth: 'Is this an hour
For private sorrow's barren song,
When more and more the people throng
The chairs and thrones of civil power?

'A time to sicken and to swoon,
When Science reaches forth her arms
To feel from world to world, and charms
Her secret from thc latest moon?' 20

Behold, ye speak an idle thing:
Ye never knew the sacred dust:
I do but sing because I must,
And pipe but as the linnets sing:

And one is glad; her note is gay,
For now her little ones have ranged;
And one is sad; her note is changed,
Because her brood is stol'n away.

XXII

The path by which we twain did go,
Which led by tracts that pleased us well,
Thro' four sweet years arose and fell,
From flower to flower, from snow to snow:

And we with singing cheer'd the way,
And, crown'd with all the season lent,
From April on to April went,
And glad at heart from May to May:

But where the path we walk'd began
To slant the fifth autumnal slope, 10
As we descended following Hope,
There sat the Shadow fear'd of man;

Who broke our fair companionship,
And spread his mantle dark and cold,
And wrapt thee formless in the fold,
And dull'd the murmur on thy lip,

And bore thee where I could not see
Nor follow, tho' I walk in haste,
And think, that somewhere in the waste
20 The Shadow sits and waits for me.

XXIII

Now, sometimes in my sorrow shut,
Or breaking into song by fits,
Alone, alone, to where he sits,
The Shadow cloak'd from head to foot,

Who keeps the keys of all the creeds,
I wander, often falling lame,
And looking back to whence I came,
Or on to where the pathway leads;

And crying, How changed from where it ran
10 Thro' lands where not a leaf was dumb;
But all the lavish hills would hum
The murmur of a happy Pan:

When each by turns was guide to each,
And Fancy light from Fancy caught,
And Thought leapt out to wed with Thought
Ere Thought could wed itself with Speech;

And all we met was fair and good,
And all was good that Time could bring,
And all the secret of the Spring
20 Moved in the chambers of the blood;

And many an old philosophy
On Argive heights divinely sang,
And round us all the thicket rang
To many a flute of Arcady.

XXIV

And was the day of my delight
As pure and perfect as I say?
The very source and fount of Day
Is dash'd with wandering isles of night.

If all was good and fair we met,
This earth had been the Paradise
It never look'd to human eyes
Since our first Sun arose and set.

And is it that the haze of grief
Makes former gladness loom so great? 10
The lowness of the present state,
That sets the past in this relief?

Or that the past will always win
A glory from its being far;
And orb into the perfect star
We saw not, when we moved therein?

XXV

I know that this was Life, – the track
Whereon with equal feet we fared;
And then, as now, the day prepared
The daily burden for the back.

But this it was that made me move
As light as carrier-birds in air;
I loved the weight I had to bear,
Because it needed help of Love:

Nor could I weary, heart or limb,
When mighty Love would cleave in twain 10
The lading of a single pain,
And part it, giving half to him.

XXVI

Still onward winds the dreary way;
I with it; for I long to prove

No lapse of moons can canker Love,
Whatever fickle tongues may say.

And if that eye which watches guilt
And goodness, and hath power to see
Within the green the moulder'd tree,
And towers fall'n as soon as built –

Oh, if indeed that eye foresee
10 Or see (in Him is no before)
In more of life true life no more
And Love the indifference to be,

Then might I find, ere yet the morn
Breaks hither over Indian seas,
That Shadow waiting with the keys,
To shroud me from my proper scorn.

XXVII

I envy not in any moods
The captive void of noble rage,
The linnet born within the cage,
That never knew the summer woods:

I envy not the beast that takes
His license in the field of time,
Unfetter'd by the sense of crime,
To whom a conscience never wakes;

Nor, what may count itself as blest,
10 The heart that never plighted troth
But stagnates in the weeds of sloth;
Nor any want-begotten rest.

I hold it true, whate'er befall;
I feel it, when I sorrow most;
'Tis better to have loved and lost
Than never to have loved at all.

XXVIII

The time draws near the birth of Christ:
The moon is hid; the night is still;
The Christmas bells from hill to hill
Answer each other in the mist.

Four voices of four hamlets round,
From far and near, on mead and moor,
Swell out and fail, as if a door
Were shut between me and the sound:

Each voice four changes on the wind,
That now dilate, and now decrease, 10
Peace and goodwill, goodwill and peace,
Peace and goodwill, to all mankind.

This year I slept and woke with pain,
I almost wish'd no more to wake,
And that my hold on life would break
Before I heard those bells again:

But they my troubled spirit rule,
For they controll'd me when a boy;
They bring me sorrow touch'd with joy,
The merry merry bells of Yule. 20

XXIX

With such compelling cause to grieve
As daily vexes household peace,
And chains regret to his decease,
How dare we keep our Christmas-eve;

Which brings no more a welcome guest
To enrich the threshold of the night
With shower'd largess of delight
In dance and song and game and jest?

Yet go, and while the holly boughs
Entwine the cold baptismal font, 10

Make one wreath more for Use and Wont,
That guard the portals of the house;

Old sisters of a day gone by,
Gray nurses, loving nothing new;
Why should they miss their yearly due
Before their time? They too will die.

XXX

With trembling fingers did we weave
The holly round the Christmas hearth;
A rainy cloud possess'd the earth,
And sadly fell our Christmas-eve.

At our old pastimes in the hall
We gambol'd, making vain pretence
Of gladness, with an awful sense
Of one mute Shadow watching all.

We paused: the winds were in the beech:
10 We heard them sweep the winter land;
And in a circle hand-in-hand
Sat silent, looking each at each.

Then echo-like our voices rang;
We sung, tho' every eye was dim,
A merry song we sang with him
Last year: impetuously we sang:

We ceased: a gentler feeling crept
Upon us: surely rest is meet:
'They rest,' we said, 'their sleep is sweet,'
20 And silence follow'd, and we wept.

Our voices took a higher range;
Once more we sang: 'They do not die
Nor lose their mortal sympathy,
Nor change to us, although they change;

'Rapt from the fickle and the frail
With gather'd power, yet the same,

Pierces the keen seraphic flame
From orb to orb, from veil to veil.'

Rise, happy morn, rise, holy morn,
Draw forth the cheerful day from night: 30
O Father, touch the east, and light
The light that shone when Hope was born.

XXXI

When Lazarus left his charnel-cave,
And home to Mary's house return'd,
Was this demanded – if he yearn'd
To hear her weeping by his grave?

'Where wert thou, brother, those four days?'
There lives no record of reply,
Which telling what it is to die
Had surely added praise to praise.

From every house the neighbours met,
The streets were fill'd with joyful sound, 10
A solemn gladness even crown'd
The purple brows of Olivet.

Behold a man raised up by Christ!
The rest remaineth unreveal'd;
He told it not; or something seal'd
The lips of that Evangelist.

XXXII

Her eyes are homes of silent prayer,
Nor other thought her mind admits
But, he was dead, and there he sits,
And he that brought him back is there.

Then one deep love doth supersede
All other, when her ardent gaze
Roves from the living brother's face,
And rests upon the Life indeed.

All subtle thought, all curious fears,
10 Borne down by gladness so complete,
She bows, she bathes the Saviour's feet
With costly spikenard and with tears.

Thrice blest whose lives are faithful prayers,
Whose loves in higher love endure;
What souls possess themselves so pure,
Or is there blessedness like theirs?

XXXIII

O thou that after toil and storm
Mayst seem to have reach'd a purer air,
Whose faith has centre everywhere,
Nor cares to fix itself to form,

Leave thou thy sister when she prays,
Her early Heaven, her happy views;
Nor thou with shadow'd hint confuse
A life that leads melodious days.

Her faith thro' form is pure as thine,
10 Her hands are quicker unto good:
Oh, sacred be the flesh and blood
To which she links a truth divine!

See thou, that countest reason ripe
In holding by the law within,
Thou fail not in a world of sin,
And ev'n for want of such a type.

XXXIV

My own dim life should teach me this,
That life shall live for evermore,
Else earth is darkness at the core,
And dust and ashes all that is;

This round of green, this orb of flame,
Fantastic beauty; such as lurks

In some wild Poet, when he works
Without a conscience or an aim.

What then were God to such as I?
'Twere hardly worth my while to choose 10
Of things all mortal, or to use
A little patience ere I die;

'Twere best at once to sink to peace,
Like birds the charming serpent draws,
To drop head-foremost in the jaws
Of vacant darkness and to cease.

XXXV

Yet if some voice that man could trust
Should murmur from the narrow house,
'The cheeks drop in; the body bows;
Man dies: nor is there hope in dust:'

Might I not say? 'Yet even here,
But for one hour, O Love, I strive
To keep so sweet a thing alive:'
But I should turn mine ears and hear

The moanings of the homeless sea,
The sound of streams that swift or slow 10
Draw down Æonian hills, and sow
The dust of continents to be;

And Love would answer with a sigh,
'The sound of that forgetful shore
Will change my sweetness more and more,
Half-dead to know that I shall die.'

O me, what profits it to put
An idle case? If Death were seen
At first as Death, Love had not been,
Or been in narrowest working shut, 20

Mere fellowship of sluggish moods,
Or in his coarsest Satyr-shape

Had bruised the herb and crush'd the grape,
And bask'd and batten'd in the woods.

XXXVI

Tho' truths in manhood darkly join,
Deep-seated in our mystic frame,
We yield all blessing to the name
Of Him that made them current coin;

For Wisdom dealt with mortal powers,
Where truth in closest words shall fail,
When truth embodied in a tale
Shall enter in at lowly doors.

And so the Word had breath, and wrought
o With human hands the creed of creeds
In loveliness of perfect deeds,
More strong than all poetic thought;

Which he may read that binds the sheaf,
Or builds the house, or digs the grave,
And those wild eyes that watch the wave
In roarings round the coral reef.

XXXVII

Urania speaks with darken'd brow:
'Thou pratest here where thou art least;
This faith has many a purer priest,
And many an abler voice than thou.

'Go down beside thy native rill,
On thy Parnassus set thy feet,
And hear thy laurel whisper sweet
About the ledges of the hill.'

And my Melpomene replies,
10 A touch of shame upon her cheek:
'I am not worthy ev'n to speak
Of thy prevailing mysteries;

'For I am but an earthly Muse,
And owning but a little art
To lull with song an aching heart,
And render human love his dues;

'But brooding on the dear one dead,
And all he said of things divine,
(And dear to me as sacred wine
To dying lips is all he said), 20

'I murmur'd, as I came along,
Of comfort clasp'd in truth reveal'd;
And loiter'd in the master's field,
And darken'd sanctities with song.'

XXXVIII

With weary steps I loiter on,
Tho' always under alter'd skies
The purple from the distance dies,
My prospect and horizon gone.

No joy the blowing season gives,
The herald melodies of spring,
But in the songs I love to sing
A doubtful gleam of solace lives.

If any care for what is here
Survive in spirits render'd free, 10
Then are these songs I sing of thee
Not all ungrateful to thine ear.

XXXIX

Old warder of these buried bones,
And answering now my random stroke
With fruitful cloud and living smoke,
Dark yew, that graspest at the stones

And dippest toward the dreamless head,
To thee too comes the golden hour

When flower is feeling after flower;
But Sorrow – fixt upon the dead,

And darkening the dark graves of men, –
10 What whisper'd from her lying lips?
Thy gloom is kindled at the tips,
And passes into gloom again.

XL

Could we forget the widow'd hour
And look on Spirits breathed away,
As on a maiden in the day
When first she wears her orange-flower!

When crown'd with blessing she doth rise
To take her latest leave of home,
And hopes and light regrets that come
Make April of her tender eyes;

And doubtful joys the father move,
10 And tears are on the mother's face,
As parting with a long embrace
She enters other realms of love;

Her office there to rear, to teach,
Becoming as is meet and fit
A link among the days, to knit
The generations each with each;

And, doubtless, unto thee is given
A life that bears immortal fruit
In those great offices that suit
20 The full-grown energies of heaven.

Ay me, the difference I discern!
How often shall her old fireside
Be cheer'd with tidings of the bride,
How often she herself return,

And tell them all they would have told,
    And bring her babe, and make her boast,
    Till even those that miss'd her most
Shall count new things as dear as old:

But thou and I have shaken hands,
    Till growing winters lay me low; 30
    My paths are in the fields I know,
And thine in undiscover'd lands.

XLI

Thy spirit ere our fatal loss
    Did ever rise from high to higher;
    As mounts the heavenward altar-fire,
As flies the lighter thro' the gross.

But thou art turn'd to something strange,
    And I have lost the links that bound
    Thy changes; here upon the ground,
No more partaker of thy change.

Deep folly! yet that this could be –
    That I could wing my will with might 10
    To leap the grades of life and light,
And flash at once, my friend, to thee.

For tho' my nature rarely yields
    To that vague fear implied in death;
    Nor shudders at the gulfs beneath,
The howlings from forgotten fields;

Yet oft when sundown skirts the moor
    An inner trouble I behold,
    A spectral doubt which makes me cold,
That I shall be thy mate no more, 20

Tho' following with an upward mind
    The wonders that have come to thee,
    Thro' all the secular to-be,
But evermore a life behind.

XLII

I vex my heart with fancies dim:
He still outstript me in the race;
It was but unity of place
That made me dream I rank'd with him.

And so may Place retain us still,
And he the much-beloved again,
A lord of large experience, train
To riper growth the mind and will:

And what delights can equal those
10 That stir the spirit's inner deeps,
When one that loves but knows not, reaps
A truth from one that loves and knows?

XLIII

If Sleep and Death be truly one,
And every spirit's folded bloom
Thro' all its intervital gloom
In some long trance should slumber on;

Unconscious of the sliding hour,
Bare of the body, might it last,
And silent traces of the past
Be all the colour of the flower:

So then were nothing lost to man;
10 So that still garden of the souls
In many a figured leaf enrolls
The total world since life began;

And love will last as pure and whole
As when he loved me here in Time,
And at the spiritual prime
Rewaken with the dawning soul.

XLIV

How fares it with the happy dead?
For here the man is more and more;

But he forgets the days before
God shut the doorways of his head.

The days have vanish'd, tone and tint,
And yet perhaps the hoarding sense
Gives out at times (he knows not whence)
A little flash, a mystic hint;

And in the long harmonious years
(If Death so taste Lethean springs), 10
May some dim touch of earthly things
Surprise thee ranging with thy peers.

If such a dreamy touch should fall,
O turn thee round, resolve the doubt;
My guardian angel will speak out
In that high place, and tell thee all.

XLV

The baby new to earth and sky,
What time his tender palm is prest
Against the circle of the breast,
Has never thought that 'this is I:'

But as he grows he gathers much,
And learns the use of 'I,' and 'me,'
And finds 'I am not what I see,
And other than the things I touch.'

So rounds he to a separate mind
From whence clear memory may begin, 10
As thro' the frame that binds him in
His isolation grows defined.

This use may lie in blood and breath,
Which else were fruitless of their due,
Had man to learn himself anew
Beyond the second birth of Death.

XLVI

We ranging down this lower track,
The path we came by, thorn and flower,
Is shadow'd by the growing hour,
Lest life should fail in looking back.

So be it: there no shade can last
In that deep dawn behind the tomb,
But clear from marge to marge shall bloom
The eternal landscape of the past;

A lifelong tract of time reveal'd;
10 The fruitful hours of still increase;
Days order'd in a wealthy peace,
And those five years its richest field.

O Love, thy province were not large,
A bounded field, nor stretching far;
Look also, Love, a brooding star,
A rosy warmth from marge to marge.

XLVII

That each, who seems a separate whole,
Should move his rounds, and fusing all
The skirts of self again, should fall
Remerging in the general Soul,

Is faith as vague as all unsweet:
Eternal form shall still divide
The eternal soul from all beside;
And I shall know him when we meet:

And we shall sit at endless feast,
10 Enjoying each the other's good:
What vaster dream can hit the mood
Of Love on earth? He seeks at least

Upon the last and sharpest height,
Before the spirits fade away,

Some landing-place, to clasp and say,
'Farewell! We lose ourselves in light.'

XLVIII

If these brief lays, of Sorrow born,
Were taken to be such as closed
Grave doubts and answers here proposed,
Then these were such as men might scorn:

Her care is not to part and prove;
She takes, when harsher moods remit,
What slender shade of doubt may flit,
And makes it vassal unto love:

And hence, indeed, she sports with words,
But better serves a wholesome law, 10
And holds it sin and shame to draw
The deepest measure from the chords:

Nor dare she trust a larger lay,
But rather loosens from the lip
Short swallow-flights of song, that dip
Their wings in tears, and skim away.

XLIX

From art, from nature, from the schools,
Let random influences glance,
Like light in many a shiver'd lance
That breaks about the dappled pools:

The lightest wave of thought shall lisp,
The fancy's tenderest eddy wreathe,
The slightest air of song shall breathe
To make the sullen surface crisp.

And look thy look, and go thy way,
But blame not thou the winds that make 10
The seeming-wanton ripple break,
The tender-pencil'd shadow play.

Beneath all fancied hopes and fears
Ay me, the sorrow deepens down,
Whose muffled motions blindly drown
The bases of my life in tears.

L

Be near me when my light is low,
When the blood creeps, and the nerves prick
And tingle; and the heart is sick,
And all the wheels of Being slow.

Be near me when the sensuous frame
Is rack'd with pangs that conquer trust;
And Time, a maniac scattering dust,
And Life, a Fury slinging flame.

Be near me when my faith is dry,
10 And men the flies of latter spring,
That lay their eggs, and sting and sing
And weave their petty cells and die.

Be near me when I fade away,
To point the term of human strife,
And on the low dark verge of life
The twilight of eternal day.

LI

Do we indeed desire the dead
Should still be near us at our side?
Is there no baseness we would hide?
No inner vileness that we dread?

Shall he for whose applause I strove,
I had such reverence for his blame,
See with clear eye some hidden shame
And I be lessen'd in his love?

I wrong the grave with fears untrue:
10 Shall love be blamed for want of faith?

There must be wisdom with great Death:
The dead shall look me thro' and thro'.

Be near us when we climb or fall:
Ye watch, like God, the rolling hours
With larger other eyes than ours,
To make allowance for us all.

LII

I cannot love thee as I ought,
For love reflects the thing beloved;
My words are only words, and moved
Upon the topmost froth of thought.

'Yet blame not thou thy plaintive song,'
The Spirit of true love replied;
'Thou canst not move me from thy side,
Nor human frailty do me wrong.

'What keeps a spirit wholly true
To that ideal which he bears? 10
What record? not the sinless years
That breathed beneath the Syrian blue:

'So fret not, like an idle girl,
That life is dash'd with flecks of sin.
Abide: thy wealth is gather'd in,
When Time hath sunder'd shell from pearl.'

LIII

How many a father have I seen,
A sober man, among his boys,
Whose youth was full of foolish noise,
Who wears his manhood hale and green:

And dare we to this fancy give,
That had the wild oat not been sown,
The soil, left barren, scarce had grown
The grain by which a man may live?

Or, if we held the doctrine sound
10 For life outliving heats of youth,
Yet who would preach it as a truth
To those that eddy round and round?

Hold thou the good: define it well:
For fear divine Philosophy
Should push beyond her mark, and be
Procuress to the Lords of Hell.

LIV

Oh yet we trust that somehow good
Will be the final goal of ill,
To pangs of nature, sins of will,
Defects of doubt, and taints of blood;

That nothing walks with aimless feet;
That not one life shall be destroy'd,
Or cast as rubbish to the void,
When God hath made the pile complete;

That not a worm is cloven in vain;
10 That not a moth with vain desire
Is shrivell'd in a fruitless fire,
Or but subserves another's gain.

Behold, we know not anything;
I can but trust that good shall fall
At last – far off – at last, to all,
And every winter change to spring.

So runs my dream: but what am I?
An infant crying in the night:
An infant crying for the light:
20 And with no language but a cry.

LV

The wish, that of the living whole
No life may fail beyond the grave,

Derives it not from what we have
The likest God within the soul?

Are God and Nature then at strife,
That Nature lends such evil dreams?
So careful of the type she seems,
So careless of the single life;

That I, considering everywhere
Her secret meaning in her deeds, 10
And finding that of fifty seeds
She often brings but one to bear,

I falter where I firmly trod,
And falling with my weight of cares
Upon the great world's altar-stairs
That slope thro' darkness up to God,

I stretch lame hands of faith, and grope,
And gather dust and chaff, and call
To what I feel is Lord of all,
And faintly trust the larger hope. 20

LVI

'So careful of the type?' but no.
From scarpèd cliff and quarried stone
She cries, 'A thousand types are gone:
I care for nothing, all shall go.

'Thou makest thine appeal to me:
I bring to life, I bring to death:
The spirit does but mean the breath:
I know no more.' And he, shall he,

Man, her last work, who seem'd so fair,
Such splendid purpose in his eyes, 10
Who roll'd the psalm to wintry skies,
Who built him fanes of fruitless prayer,

Who trusted God was love indeed
And love Creation's final law –

Tho' Nature, red in tooth and claw
With ravine, shriek'd against his creed –

Who loved, who suffer'd countless ills,
Who battled for the True, the Just,
Be blown about the desert dust,
20 Or seal'd within the iron hills?

No more? A monster then, a dream,
A discord. Dragons of the prime,
That tare each other in their slime,
Were mellow music match'd with him.

O life as futile, then, as frail!
O for thy voice to soothe and bless!
What hope of answer, or redress?
Behind the veil, behind the veil.

LVII

Peace; come away: the song of woe
Is after all an earthly song:
Peace; come away: we do him wrong
To sing so wildly: let us go.

Come; let us go: your cheeks are pale;
But half my life I leave behind:
Methinks my friend is richly shrined;
But I shall pass; my work will fail.

Yet in these ears, till hearing dies,
10 One set slow bell will seem to toll
The passing of the sweetest soul
That ever look'd with human eyes.

I hear it now, and o'er and o'er,
Eternal greetings to the dead;
And 'Ave, Ave, Ave,' said,
'Adieu, adieu' for evermore.

LVIII

In those sad words I took farewell:
Like echoes in sepulchral halls,
As drop by drop the water falls
In vaults and catacombs, they fell;

And, falling, idly broke the peace
Of hearts that beat from day to day,
Half-conscious of their dying clay,
And those cold crypts where they shall cease.

The high Muse answer'd: 'Wherefore grieve
Thy brethren with a fruitless tear? 10
Abide a little longer here,
And thou shalt take a nobler leave.'

LIX

O Sorrow, wilt thou live with me
No casual mistress, but a wife,
My bosom-friend and half of life;
As I confess it needs must be;

O Sorrow, wilt thou rule my blood,
Be sometimes lovely like a bride,
And put thy harsher moods aside,
If thou wilt have me wise and good.

My centred passion cannot move,
Nor will it lessen from to-day; 10
But I'll have leave at times to play
As with the creature of my love;

And set thee forth, for thou art mine,
With so much hope for years to come,
That, howsoe'er I know thee, some
Could hardly tell what name were thine.

LX

He past; a soul of nobler tone:
My spirit loved and loves him yet,

Like some poor girl whose heart is set
On one whose rank exceeds her own.

He mixing with his proper sphere,
She finds the baseness of her lot,
Half jealous of she knows not what,
And envying all that meet him there.

The little village looks forlorn;
10 She sighs amid her narrow days,
Moving about the household ways,
In that dark house where she was born.

The foolish neighbours come and go,
And tease her till the day draws by:
At night she weeps, 'How vain am I!
How should he love a thing so low?'

LXI

If, in thy second state sublime,
Thy ransom'd reason change replies
With all the circle of the wise,
The perfect flower of human time;

And if thou cast thine eyes below,
How dimly character'd and slight,
How dwarf'd a growth of cold and night,
How blanch'd with darkness must I grow!

Yet turn thee to the doubtful shore,
10 Where thy first form was made a man;
I loved thee, Spirit, and love, nor can
The soul of Shakspeare love thee more.

LXII

Tho' if an eye that's downward cast
Could make thee somewhat blench or fail,
Then be my love an idle tale,
And fading legend of the past;

And thou, as one that once declined,
When he was little more than boy,
On some unworthy heart with joy,
But lives to wed an equal mind;

And breathes a novel world, the while
His other passion wholly dies, 10
Or in the light of deeper eyes
Is matter for a flying smile.

LXIII

Yet pity for a horsc o'er-driven,
And love in which my hound has part,
Can hang no weight upon my heart
In its assumptions up to heaven;

And I am so much more than these,
As thou, perchance, art more than I,
And yet I spare them sympathy,
And I would set their pains at ease.

So mayst thou watch me where I weep,
As, unto vaster motions bound, 10
The circuits of thine orbit round
A higher height, a deeper deep.

LXIV

Dost thou look back on what hath been,
As some divinely gifted man,
Whose life in low estate began
And on a simple village green;

Who breaks his birth's invidious bar,
And grasps the skirts of happy chance,
And breasts the blows of circumstance,
And grapples with his evil star;

Who makes by force his merit known
And lives to clutch the golden keys, 10

To mould a mighty state's decrees,
And shape the whisper of the throne;

And moving up from high to higher,
Becomes on Fortune's crowning slope
The pillar of a people's hope,
The centre of a world's desire;

Yet feels, as in a pensive dream,
When all his active powers are still,
A distant dearness in the hill,
20 A secret sweetness in the stream,

The limit of his narrower fate,
While yet beside its vocal springs
He play'd at counsellors and kings,
With one that was his earliest mate;

Who ploughs with pain his native lea
And reaps the labour of his hands,
Or in the furrow musing stands;
'Does my old friend remember me?'

LXV

Sweet soul, do with me as thou wilt;
I lull a fancy trouble-tost
With 'Love's too precious to be lost,
A little grain shall not be spilt.'

And in that solace can I sing,
Till out of painful phases wrought
There flutters up a happy thought,
Self-balanced on a lightsome wing:

Since we deserved the name of friends,
10 And thine effect so lives in me,
A part of mine may live in thee
And move thee on to noble ends.

LXVI

You thought my heart too far diseased;
You wonder when my fancies play
To find me gay among the gay,
Like one with any trifle pleased.

The shade by which my life was crost,
Which makes a desert in the mind,
Has made me kindly with my kind,
And like to him whose sight is lost;

Whose feet are guided thro' the land,
Whose jest among his friends is free, 10
Who takes the children on his knee,
And winds their curls about his hand:

He plays with threads, he beats his chair
For pastime, dreaming of the sky;
His inner day can never die,
His night of loss is always there.

LXVII

When on my bed the moonlight falls,
I know that in thy place of rest
By that broad water of the west,
There comes a glory on the walls;

Thy marble bright in dark appears,
As slowly steals a silver flame
Along the letters of thy name,
And o'er the number of thy years.

The mystic glory swims away;
From off my bed the moonlight dies; 10
And closing eaves of wearied eyes
I sleep till dusk is dipt in gray:

And then I know the mist is drawn
A lucid veil from coast to coast,

And in the dark church like a ghost
Thy tablet glimmers to the dawn.

LXVIII

When in the down I sink my head,
Sleep, Death's twin-brother, times my breath;
Sleep, Death's twin-brother, knows not Death,
Nor can I dream of thee as dead:

I walk as ere I walk'd forlorn,
When all our path was fresh with dew,
And all the bugle breezes blew
Reveillée to the breaking morn.

But what is this? I turn about,
10 I find a trouble in thine eye,
Which makes me sad I know not why,
Nor can my dream resolve the doubt:

But ere the lark hath left the lea
I wake, and I discern the truth;
It is the trouble of my youth
That foolish sleep transfers to thee.

LXIX

I dream'd there would be Spring no more,
That Nature's ancient power was lost:
The streets were black with smoke and frost,
They chatter'd trifles at the door:

I wander'd from the noisy town,
I found a wood with thorny boughs:
I took the thorns to bind my brows,
I wore them like a civic crown:

I met with scoffs, I met with scorns
10 From youth and babe and hoary hairs:
They call'd me in the public squares
The fool that wears a crown of thorns:

They call'd me fool, they call'd me child:
I found an angel of the night;
The voice was low, the look was bright;
He look'd upon my crown and smiled:

He reach'd the glory of a hand,
That seem'd to touch it into leaf:
The voice was not the voice of grief,
The words were hard to understand. 20

LXX

I cannot see the features right,
When on the gloom I strive to paint
The face I know; the hues are faint
And mix with hollow masks of night;

Cloud-towers by ghostly masons wrought,
A gulf that ever shuts and gapes,
A hand that points, and pallèd shapes
In shadowy thoroughfares of thought;

And crowds that stream from yawning doors,
And shoals of pucker'd faces drive; 10
Dark bulks that tumble half alive,
And lazy lengths on boundless shores;

Till all at once beyond the will
I hear a wizard music roll,
And thro' a lattice on the soul
Looks thy fair face and makes it still.

LXXI

Sleep, kinsman thou to death and trance
And madness, thou hast forged at last
A night-long Present of the Past
In which we went thro' summer France.

Hadst thou such credit with the soul?
Then bring an opiate trebly strong,

Drug down the blindfold sense of wrong
That so my pleasure may be whole;

While now we talk as once we talk'd
10 Of men and minds, the dust of change,
The days that grow to something strange,
In walking as of old we walk'd

Beside the river's wooded reach,
The fortress, and the mountain ridge,
The cataract flashing from the bridge,
The breaker breaking on the beach.

LXXII

Risest thou thus, dim dawn, again,
And howlest, issuing out of night,
With blasts that blow the poplar white,
And lash with storm the streaming pane?

Day, when my crown'd estate begun
To pine in that reverse of doom,
Which sicken'd every living bloom,
And blurr'd the splendour of the sun;

Who usherest in the dolorous hour
10 With thy quick tears that make the rose
Pull sideways, and the daisy close
Her crimson fringes to the shower;

Who might'st have heaved a windless flame
Up the deep East, or, whispering, play'd
A chequer-work of beam and shade
Along the hills, yet look'd the same,

As wan, as chill, as wild as now;
Day, mark'd as with some hideous crime,
When the dark hand struck down thro' time,
20 And cancell'd nature's best: but thou,

Lift as thou may'st thy burthen'd brows
Thro' clouds that drench the morning star,

And whirl the ungarner'd sheaf afar,
And sow the sky with flying boughs,

And up thy vault with roaring sound
Climb thy thick noon, disastrous day;
Touch thy dull goal of joyless gray,
And hide thy shame beneath the ground.

LXXIII

So many worlds, so much to do,
So little done, such things to be,
How know I what had need of thee,
For thou wert strong as thou wert true?

The fame is quench'd that I foresaw,
The head hath miss'd an earthly wreath:
I curse not nature, no, nor death;
For nothing is that errs from law.

We pass; the path that each man trod
Is dim, or will be dim, with weeds: 10
What fame is left for human deeds
In endless age? It rests with God.

O hollow wraith of dying fame,
Fade wholly, while the soul exults,
And self-infolds the large results
Of force that would have forged a name.

LXXIV

As sometimes in a dead man's face,
To those that watch it more and more,
A likeness, hardly seen before,
Comes out – to some one of his race:

So, dearest, now thy brows are cold,
I see thee what thou art, and know
Thy likeness to the wise below,
Thy kindred with the great of old.

But there is more than I can see,
10 And what I see I leave unsaid,
Nor speak it, knowing Death has made
His darkness beautiful with thee.

LXXV

I leave thy praises unexpress'd
In verse that brings myself relief,
And by the measure of my grief
I leave thy greatness to be guess'd;

What practice howsoe'er expert
In fitting aptest words to things,
Or voice the richest-toned that sings,
Hath power to give thee as thou wert?

I care not in these fading days
10 To raise a cry that lasts not long,
And round thee with the breeze of song
To stir a little dust of praise.

Thy leaf has perish'd in the green,
And, while we breathe beneath the sun,
The world which credits what is done
Is cold to all that might have been.

So here shall silence guard thy fame;
But somewhere, out of human view,
Whate'er thy hands are set to do
20 Is wrought with tumult of acclaim.

LXXVI

Take wings of fancy, and ascend,
And in a moment set thy face
Where all the starry heavens of space
Are sharpen'd to a needle's end;

Take wings of foresight; lighten thro'
The secular abyss to come,

And lo, thy deepest lays are dumb
Before the mouldering of a yew;

And if the matin songs, that woke
The darkness of our planet, last, 10
Thine own shall wither in the vast,
Ere half the lifetime of an oak.

Ere these have clothed their branchy bowers
With fifty Mays, thy songs are vain;
And what are they when these remain
The ruin'd shells of hollow towers?

LXXVII

What hope is here for modern rhyme
To him, who turns a musing eye
On songs, and deeds, and lives, that lie
Foreshorten'd in the tract of time?

These mortal lullabies of pain
May bind a book, may line a box,
May serve to curl a maiden's locks;
Or when a thousand moons shall wane

A man upon a stall may find,
And, passing, turn the page that tells 10
A grief, then changed to something else,
Sung by a long-forgotten mind.

But what of that? My darken'd ways
Shall ring with music all the same;
To breathe my loss is more than fame,
To utter love more sweet than praise.

LXXVIII

Again at Christmas did we weave
The holly round the Christmas hearth;
The silent snow possess'd the earth,
And calmly fell our Christmas-eve:

The yule-clog sparkled keen with frost,
No wing of wind the region swept,
But over all things brooding slept
The quiet sense of something lost.

As in the winters left behind,
10 Again our ancient games had place,
The mimic picture's breathing grace,
And dance and song and hoodman-blind.

Who show'd a token of distress?
No single tear, no mark of pain:
O sorrow, then can sorrow wane?
O grief, can grief be changed to less?

O last regret, regret can die!
No – mixt with all this mystic frame,
Her deep relations are the same,
20 But with long use her tears are dry.

LXXIX

'More than my brothers are to me,' –
Let this not vex thee, noble heart!
I know thee of what force thou art
To hold the costliest love in fee.

But thou and I are one in kind,
As moulded like in Nature's mint;
And hill and wood and field did print
The same sweet forms in either mind.

For us the same cold streamlet curl'd
10 Thro' all his eddying coves; the same
All winds that roam the twilight came
In whispers of the beauteous world.

At one dear knee we proffer'd vows,
One lesson from one book we learn'd,
Ere childhood's flaxen ringlet turn'd
To black and brown on kindred brows.

And so my wealth resembles thine,
But he was rich where I was poor,
And he supplied my want the more
As his unlikeness fitted mine. 20

LXXX

If any vague desire should rise,
That holy Death ere Arthur died
Had moved me kindly from his side,
And dropt the dust on tearless eyes;

Then fancy shapes, as fancy can,
The grief my loss in him had wrought,
A grief as deep as life or thought,
But stay'd in peace with God and man.

I make a picture in the brain;
I hear the sentence that he speaks; 10
He bears the burthen of the weeks
But turns his burthen into gain.

His credit thus shall set me free;
And, influence rich to soothe and save,
Unused example from the grave
Reach out dead hands to comfort me.

LXXXI

Could I have said while he was here,
'My love shall now no further range;
There cannot come a mellower change,
For now is love mature in ear.'

Love, then, had hope of richer store:
What end is here to my complaint?
This haunting whisper makes me faint,
'More years had made me love thee more.'

But Death returns an answer sweet:
'My sudden frost was sudden gain, 10

And gave all ripeness to the grain,
It might have drawn from after-heat.'

LXXXII

I wage not any feud with Death
For changes wrought on form and face;
No lower life that earth's embrace
May breed with him, can fright my faith.

Eternal process moving on,
From state to state the spirit walks;
And these are but the shatter'd stalks,
Or ruin'd chrysalis of one.

Nor blame I Death, because he bare
10 The use of virtue out of earth:
I know transplanted human worth
Will bloom to profit, otherwhere.

For this alone on Death I wreak
The wrath that garners in my heart;
He put our lives so far apart
We cannot hear each other speak.

LXXXIII

Dip down upon the northern shore,
O sweet new-year delaying long;
Thou doest expectant nature wrong;
Delaying long, delay no more.

What stays thee from the clouded noons,
Thy sweetness from its proper place?
Can trouble live with April days,
Or sadness in the summer moons?

Bring orchis, bring the foxglove spire,
10 The little speedwell's darling blue,
Deep tulips dash'd with fiery dew,
Laburnums, dropping-wells of fire.

O thou, new-year, delaying long,
Delayest the sorrow in my blood,
That longs to burst a frozen bud
And flood a fresher throat with song.

LXXXIV

When I contemplate all alone
The life that had been thine below,
And fix my thoughts on all the glow
To which thy crescent would have grown;

I see thee sitting crown'd with good,
A central warmth diffusing bliss
In glance and smile, and clasp and kiss,
On all the branches of thy blood;

Thy blood, my friend, and partly mine;
For now the day was drawing on, 10
When thou should'st link thy life with one
Of mine own house, and boys of thine

Had babbled 'Uncle' on my knee;
But that remorseless iron hour
Made cypress of her orange flower,
Despair of Hope, and earth of thee.

I seem to meet their least desire,
To clap their cheeks, to call them mine.
I see their unborn faces shine
Beside the never-lighted fire. 20

I see myself an honour'd guest,
Thy partner in the flowery walk
Of letters, genial table-talk,
Or deep dispute, and graceful jest;

While now thy prosperous labour fills
The lips of men with honest praise,
And sun by sun the happy days
Descend below the golden hills

With promise of a morn as fair;
30 And all the train of bounteous hours
Conduct by paths of growing powers,
To reverence and the silver hair;

Till slowly worn her earthly robe,
Her lavish mission richly wrought,
Leaving great legacies of thought,
Thy spirit should fail from off the globe;

What time mine own might also flee,
As link'd with thine in love and fate,
And, hovering o'er the dolorous strait
40 To the other shore, involved in thee,

Arrive at last the blessèd goal,
And He that died in Holy Land
Would reach us out the shining hand,
And take us as a single soul.

What reed was that on which I leant?
Ah, backward fancy, wherefore wake
The old bitterness again, and break
The low beginnings of content.

LXXXV

This truth came borne with bier and pall,
I felt it, when I sorrow'd most,
'Tis better to have loved and lost,
Than never to have loved at all —

O true in word, and tried in deed,
Demanding, so to bring relief
To this which is our common grief,
What kind of life is that I lead;

And whether trust in things above
10 Be dimm'd of sorrow, or sustain'd;
And whether love for him have drain'd
My capabilities of love;

Your words have virtue such as draws
A faithful answer from the breast,
Thro' light reproaches, half exprest,
And loyal unto kindly laws.

My blood an even tenor kept,
Till on mine ear this message falls,
That in Vienna's fatal walls
God's finger touch'd him, and he slept. 20

The great Intelligences fair
That range above our mortal state,
In circle round the blessèd gate,
Received and gave him welcome there;

And led him thro' the blissful climes,
And show'd him in the fountain fresh
All knowledge that the sons of flesh
Shall gather in the cycled times.

But I remain'd, whose hopes were dim,
Whose life, whose thoughts were little worth, 30
To wander on a darken'd earth,
Where all things round me breathed of him.

O friendship, equal-poised control,
O heart, with kindliest motion warm,
O sacred essence, other form,
O solemn ghost, O crownèd soul!

Yet none could better know than I,
How much of act at human hands
The sense of human will demands
By which we dare to live or die. 40

Whatever way my days decline,
I felt and feel, tho' left alone,
His being working in mine own,
The footsteps of his life in mine;

A life that all the Muses deck'd
With gifts of grace, that might express
All-comprehensive tenderness,
All-subtilising intellect:

And so my passion hath not swerved
50 To works of weakness, but I find
An image comforting the mind,
And in my grief a strength reserved.

Likewise the imaginative woe,
That loved to handle spiritual strife
Diffused the shock thro' all my life,
But in the present broke the blow.

My pulses therefore beat again
For other friends that once I met;
Nor can it suit me to forget
60 The mighty hopes that make us men.

I woo your love: I count it crime
To mourn for any overmuch;
I, the divided half of such
A friendship as had master'd Time;

Which masters Time indeed, and is
Eternal, separate from fears:
The all-assuming months and years
Can take no part away from this:

But Summer on the steaming floods,
70 And Spring that swells the narrow brooks,
And Autumn, with a noise of rooks,
That gather in the waning woods,

And every pulse of wind and wave
Recalls, in change of light or gloom,
My old affection of the tomb,
And my prime passion in the grave:

My old affection of the tomb,
A part of stillness, yearns to speak:
'Arise, and get thee forth and seek
A friendship for the years to come. 80

'I watch thee from the quiet shore;
Thy spirit up to mine can reach;
But in dear words of human speech
We two communicate no more.'

And I, 'Can clouds of nature stain
The starry clearness of the free?
How is it? Canst thou feel for me
Some painless sympathy with pain?'

And lightly does the whisper fall;
''Tis hard for thee to fathom this; 90
I triumph in conclusive bliss,
And that serene result of all.'

So hold I commerce with the dead;
Or so methinks the dead would say;
Or so shall grief with symbols play
And pining life be fancy-fed.

Now looking to some settled end,
That these things pass, and I shall prove
A meeting somewhere, love with love,
I crave your pardon, O my friend; 100

If not so fresh, with love as truc,
I, clasping brother-hands, aver
I could not, if I would, transfer
The whole I felt for him to you.

For which be they that hold apart
The promise of the golden hours?
First love, first friendship, equal powers,
That marry with the virgin heart.

Still mine, that cannot but deplore,
110 That beats within a lonely place,
That yet remembers his embrace,
But at his footstep leaps no more,

My heart, tho' widow'd, may not rest
Quite in the love of what is gone,
But seeks to beat in time with one
That warms another living breast.

Ah, take the imperfect gift I bring,
Knowing the primrose yet is dear,
The primrose of the later year,
120 As not unlike to that of Spring.

LXXXVI

Sweet after showers, ambrosial air,
That rollest from the gorgeous gloom
Of evening over brake and bloom
And meadow, slowly breathing bare

The round of space, and rapt below
Thro' all the dewy-tassell'd wood,
And shadowing down the hornèd flood
In ripples, fan my brows and blow

The fever from my cheek, and sigh
10 The full new life that feeds thy breath
Throughout my frame, till Doubt and Death,
Ill brethren, let the fancy fly

From belt to belt of crimson seas
On leagues of odour streaming far,
To where in yonder orient star
A hundred spirits whisper 'Peace.'

LXXXVII

I past beside the reverend walls
In which of old I wore the gown;

I roved at random thro' the town,
And saw the tumult of the halls;

And heard once more in college fanes
The storm their high-built organs make,
And thunder-music, rolling, shake
The prophet blazon'd on the panes;

And caught once more the distant shout,
The measured pulse of racing oars 10
Among the willows; paced the shores
And many a bridge, and all about

The same gray flats again, and felt
The same, but not the same; and last
Up that long walk of limes I past
To see the rooms in which he dwelt.

Another name was on the door:
I linger'd; all within was noise
Of songs, and clapping hands, and boys
That crash'd the glass and beat the floor; 20

Where once we held debate, a band
Of youthful friends, on mind and art,
And labour, and the changing mart,
And all the framework of the land;

When one would aim an arrow fair,
But send it slackly from the string;
And one would pierce an outer ring,
And one an inner, here and there;

And last the master-bowman, he,
Would cleave the mark. A willing ear 30
We lent him. Who, but hung to hear
The rapt oration flowing free

From point to point, with power and grace
And music in the bounds of law,

To those conclusions when we saw
The God within him light his face,

And seem to lift the form, and glow
In azure orbits heavenly-wise;
And over those ethereal eyes
40 The bar of Michael Angelo.

LXXXVIII

Wild bird, whose warble, liquid sweet,
Rings Eden thro' the budded quicks,
O tell me where the senses mix,
O tell me where the passions meet,

Whence radiate: fierce extremes employ
Thy spirits in the darkening leaf,
And in the midmost heart of grief
Thy passion clasps a secret joy:

And I – my harp would prelude woe –
10 I cannot all command the strings;
The glory of the sum of things
Will flash along the chords and go.

LXXXIX

Witch-elms that counterchange the floor
Of this flat lawn with dusk and bright;
And thou, with all thy breadth and height
Of foliage, towering sycamore;

How often, hither wandering down,
My Arthur found your shadows fair,
And shook to all the liberal air
The dust and din and steam of town:

He brought an eye for all he saw;
10 He mixt in all our simple sports;
They pleased him, fresh from brawling courts
And dusty purlieus of the law.

O joy to him in this retreat,
Immantled in ambrosial dark,
To drink the cooler air, and mark
The landscape winking thro' the heat:

O sound to rout the brood of cares,
The sweep of scythe in morning dew,
The gust that round the garden flew,
And tumbled half the mellowing pears! 20

O bliss, when all in circle drawn
About him, heart and ear were fed
To hear him, as he lay and read
The Tuscan poets on the lawn:

Or in the all-golden afternoon
A guest, or happy sister, sung,
Or here she brought the harp and flung
A ballad to the brightening moon:

Nor less it pleased in livelier moods,
Beyond the bounding hill to stray, 30
And break the livelong summer day
With banquet in the distant woods;

Whereat we glanced from theme to theme,
Discuss'd the books to love or hate,
Or touch'd the changes of the state,
Or threaded some Socratic dream;

But if I praised the busy town,
He loved to rail against it still,
For 'ground in yonder social mill
We rub each other's angles down, 40

'And merge' he said 'in form and gloss
The picturesque of man and man.'
We talk'd: the stream beneath us ran,
The wine-flask lying couch'd in moss,

Or cool'd within the glooming wave;
  And last, returning from afar,
  Before the crimson-circled star
Had fall'n into her father's grave,

And brushing ankle-deep in flowers,
50 We heard behind the woodbine veil
  The milk that bubbled in the pail,
And buzzings of the honied hours.

XC

He tasted love with half his mind,
  Nor ever drank the inviolate spring
  Where nighest heaven, who first could fling
This bitter seed among mankind;

That could the dead, whose dying eyes
  Were closed with wail, resume their life,
  They would but find in child and wife
An iron welcome when they rise:

'Twas well, indeed, when warm with wine,
10 To pledge them with a kindly tear,
  To talk them o'er, to wish them here,
To count their memories half divine;

But if they came who past away,
  Behold their brides in other hands;
  The hard heir strides about their lands,
And will not yield them for a day.

Yea, tho' their sons were none of these,
  Not less the yet-loved sire would make
  Confusion worse than death, and shake
20 The pillars of domestic peace.

Ah dear, but come thou back to me:
  Whatever change the years have wrought,
  I find not yet one lonely thought
That cries against my wish for thee.

XCI

When rosy plumelets tuft the larch,
And rarely pipes the mounted thrush;
Or underneath the barren bush
Flits by the sea-blue bird of March;

Come, wear the form by which I know
Thy spirit in time among thy peers;
The hope of unaccomplish'd years
Be large and lucid round thy brow.

When summer's hourly-mellowing change 10
May breathe, with many roses sweet,
Upon the thousand waves of wheat,
That ripple round the lonely grange;

Come: not in watches of the night,
But where the sunbeam broodeth warm,
Come, beauteous in thine after form,
And like a finer light in light.

XCII

If any vision should reveal
Thy likeness, I might count it vain
As but the canker of the brain;
Yea, tho' it spake and made appeal

To chances where our lots were cast
Together in the days behind,
I might but say, I hear a wind
Of memory murmuring the past.

Yea, tho' it spake and bared to view
A fact within the coming year; 10
And tho' the months, revolving near,
Should prove the phantom-warning true,

They might not seem thy prophecies,
But spiritual presentiments,

And such refraction of events
As often rises ere they rise.

XCIII

I shall not see thee. Dare I say
No spirit ever brake the band
That stays him from the native land
Where first he walk'd when claspt in clay?

No visual shade of some one lost,
But he, the Spirit himself, may come
Where all the nerve of sense is numb;
Spirit to Spirit, Ghost to Ghost.

O, therefore from thy sightless range
10 With gods in unconjectured bliss,
O, from the distance of the abyss
Of tenfold-complicated change,

Descend, and touch, and enter; hear
The wish too strong for words to name;
That in this blindness of the frame
My Ghost may feel that thine is near.

XCIV

How pure at heart and sound in head,
With what divine affections bold
Should be the man whose thought would hold
An hour's communion with the dead.

In vain shalt thou, or any, call
The spirits from their golden day,
Except, like them, thou too canst say,
My spirit is at peace with all.

They haunt the silence of the breast,
10 Imaginations calm and fair,
The memory like a cloudless air,
The conscience as a sea at rest:

But when the heart is full of din,
And doubt beside the portal waits,
They can but listen at the gates,
And hear the household jar within.

XCV

By night we linger'd on the lawn,
For underfoot the herb was dry;
And genial warmth; and o'er the sky
The silvery haze of summer drawn;

And calm that let the tapers burn
Unwavering: not a cricket chirr'd:
The brook alone far-off was heard,
And on the board the fluttering urn:

And bats went round in fragrant skies,
And wheel'd or lit the filmy shapes 10
That haunt the dusk, with ermine capes
And woolly breasts and beaded eyes;

While now we sang old songs that peal'd
From knoll to knoll, where, couch'd at ease,
The white kine glimmer'd, and the trees
Laid their dark arms about the field.

But when those others, one by one,
Withdrew themselves from me and night,
And in the house light after light
Went out, and I was all alone, 20

A hunger seized my heart; I read
Of that glad year which once had been,
In those fall'n leaves which kept their green,
The noble letters of the dead:

And strangely on the silence broke
The silent-speaking words, and strange
Was love's dumb cry defying change
To test his worth; and strangely spoke

The faith, the vigour, bold to dwell
30 On doubts that drive the coward back,
And keen thro' wordy snares to track
Suggestion to her inmost cell.

So word by word, and line by line,
The dead man touch'd me from the past,
And all at once it seem'd at last
The living soul was flash'd on mine,

And mine in this was wound, and whirl'd
About empyreal heights of thought,
And came on that which is, and caught
40 The deep pulsations of the world,

Aeonian music measuring out
The steps of Time – the shocks of Chance –
The blows of Death. At length my trance
Was cancell'd, stricken thro' with doubt.

Vague words! but ah, how hard to frame
In matter-moulded forms of speech,
Or ev'n for intellect to reach
Thro' memory that which I became:

Till now the doubtful dusk reveal'd
50 The knolls once more where, couch'd at ease,
The white kine glimmer'd, and the trees
Laid their dark arms about the field:

And suck'd from out the distant gloom
A breeze began to tremble o'er
The large leaves of the sycamore,
And fluctuate all the still perfume,

And gathering freshlier overhead,
Rock'd the full-foliaged elms, and swung
The heavy-folded rose, and flung
60 The lilies to and fro, and said

'The dawn, the dawn,' and died away;
And East and West, without a breath,
Mixt their dim lights, like life and death,
To broaden into boundless day.

XCVI

You say, but with no touch of scorn,
Sweet-hearted, you, whose light-blue eyes
Are tender over drowning flies,
You tell me, doubt is Devil-born.

I know not: one indeed I knew
In many a subtle question versed,
Who touch'd a jarring lyre at first,
But ever strove to make it true:

Perplext in faith, but pure in deeds,
At last he beat his music out. 10
There lives more faith in honest doubt,
Believe me, than in half the creeds.

He fought his doubts and gather'd strength,
He would not make his judgment blind,
He faced the spectres of the mind
And laid them: thus he came at length

To find a stronger faith his own;
And Power was with him in the night,
Which makes the darkness and the light,
And dwells not in the light alone, 20

But in the darkness and the cloud,
As over Sinaï's peaks of old,
While Israel made their gods of gold,
Altho' the trumpet blew so loud.

XCVII

My love has talk'd with rocks and trees;
He finds on misty mountain-ground

His own vast shadow glory-crown'd;
He sees himself in all he sees.

Two partners of a married life –
I look'd on these and thought of thee
In vastness and in mystery,
And of my spirit as of a wife.

These two – they dwelt with eye on eye,
10 Their hearts of old have beat in tune,
Their meetings made December June,
Their every parting was to die.

Their love has never past away;
The days she never can forget
Are earnest that he loves her yet,
Whate'er the faithless people say.

Her life is lone, he sits apart,
He loves her yet, she will not weep,
Tho' rapt in matters dark and deep
20 He seems to slight her simple heart.

He thrids the labyrinth of the mind,
He reads the secret of the star,
He seems so near and yet so far,
He looks so cold: she thinks him kind.

She keeps the gift of years before,
A wither'd violet is her bliss:
She knows not what his greatness is,
For that, for all, she loves him more.

For him she plays, to him she sings
30 Of early faith and plighted vows;
She knows but matters of the house,
And he, he knows a thousand things.

Her faith is fixt and cannot move,
She darkly feels him great and wise,

She dwells on him with faithful eyes,
'I cannot understand: I love.'

XCVIII

You leave us: you will see the Rhine,
And those fair hills I sail'd below,
When I was there with him; and go
By summer belts of wheat and vine

To where he breathed his latest breath,
That City. All her splendour seems
No livelier than the wisp that gleams
On Lethe in the eyes of Death.

Let her great Danube rolling fair
Enwind her isles, unmark'd of me: 10
I have not seen, I will not see
Vienna; rather dream that there,

A treble darkness, Evil haunts
The birth, the bridal; friend from friend
Is oftener parted, fathers bend
Above more graves, a thousand wants

Gnarr at the heels of men, and prey
By each cold hearth, and sadness flings
Her shadow on the blaze of kings:
And yet myself have heard him say, 20

That not in any mother town
With statelier progress to and fro
The double tides of chariots flow
By park and suburb under brown

Of lustier leaves; nor more content,
He told me, lives in any crowd,
When all is gay with lamps, and loud
With sport and song, in booth and tent,

Imperial halls, or open plain;
30 And wheels the circled dance, and breaks
The rocket molten into flakes
Of crimson or in emerald rain.

XCIX

Risest thou thus, dim dawn, again,
So loud with voices of the birds,
So thick with lowings of the herds,
Day, when I lost the flower of men;

Who tremblest thro' thy darkling red
On yon swoll'n brook that bubbles fast
By meadows breathing of the past,
And woodlands holy to the dead;

Who murmurest in the foliaged eaves
10 A song that slights the coming care,
And Autumn laying here and there
A fiery finger on the leaves;

Who wakenest with thy balmy breath
To myriads on the genial earth,
Memories of bridal, or of birth,
And unto myriads more, of death.

O wheresoever those may be,
Betwixt the slumber of the poles,
To-day they count as kindred souls;
20 They know me not, but mourn with me.

C

I climb the hill: from end to end
Of all the landscape underneath,
I find no place that does not breathe
Some gracious memory of my friend;

No gray old grange, or lonely fold,
Or low morass and whispering reed,

Or simple stile from mead to mead,
Or sheepwalk up the windy wold;

Nor hoary knoll of ash and haw
That hears the latest linnet trill, 10
Nor quarry trench'd along the hill
And haunted by the wrangling daw;

Nor runlet tinkling from the rock;
Nor pastoral rivulet that swerves
To left and right thro' meadowy curves,
That feed the mothers of the flock;

But each has pleased a kindred eye,
And each reflects a kindlier day;
And, leaving these, to pass away,
I think once more he seems to die. 20

CI

Unwatch'd, the garden bough shall sway,
The tender blossom flutter down,
Unloved, that beech will gather brown,
This maple burn itself away;

Unloved, the sun-flower, shining fair,
Ray round with flames her disk of seed,
And many a rose-carnation feed
With summer spice the humming air;

Unloved, by many a sandy bar,
The brook shall babble down the plain, 10
At noon or when the lesser wain
Is twisting round the polar star;

Uncared for, gird the windy grove,
And flood the haunts of hern and crake;
Or into silver arrows break
The sailing moon in creek and cove;

Till from the garden and the wild
A fresh association blow,
And year by year the landscape grow
20 Familiar to the stranger's child;

As year by year the labourer tills
His wonted glebe, or lops the glades;
And year by year our memory fades
From all the circle of the hills.

CII

We leave the well-belovèd place
Where first we gazed upon the sky;
The roofs, that heard our earliest cry,
Will shelter one of stranger race.

We go, but ere we go from home,
As down the garden-walks I move,
Two spirits of a diverse love
Contend for loving masterdom.

One whispers, 'Here thy boyhood sung
10 Long since its matin song, and heard
The low love-language of the bird
In native hazels tassel-hung.'

The other answers, 'Yea, but here
Thy feet have stray'd in after hours
With thy lost friend among the bowers,
And this hath made them trebly dear.'

These two have striven half the day,
And each prefers his separate claim,
Poor rivals in a losing game,
20 That will not yield each other way.

I turn to go: my feet are set
To leave the pleasant fields and farms;
They mix in one another's arms
To one pure image of regret.

CIII

On that last night before we went
From out the doors where I was bred,
I dream'd a vision of the dead,
Which left my after-morn content.

Methought I dwelt within a hall,
And maidens with me: distant hills
From hidden summits fed with rills
A river sliding by the wall.

The hall with harp and carol rang.
They sang of what is wise and good 10
And graceful. In the centre stood
A statue veil'd, to which they sang;

And which, tho' veil'd, was known to me,
The shape of him I loved, and love
For ever: then flew in a dove
And brought a summons from the sea:

And when they learnt that I must go
They wept and wail'd, but led the way
To where a little shallop lay
At anchor in the flood below; 20

And on by many a level mead,
And shadowing bluff that made the banks,
We glided winding under ranks
Of iris, and the golden reed;

And still as vaster grew the shore
And roll'd the floods in grander space,
The maidens gather'd strength and grace
And presence, lordlier than before;

And I myself, who sat apart
And watch'd them, wax'd in every limb; 30
I felt the thews of Anakim,
The pulses of a Titan's heart;

As one would sing the death of war,
And one would chant the history
Of that great race, which is to be,
And one the shaping of a star;

Until the forward-creeping tides
Began to foam, and we to draw
From deep to deep, to where we saw
40 A great ship lift her shining sides.

The man we loved was there on deck,
But thrice as large as man he bent
To greet us. Up the side I went,
And fell in silence on his neck:

Whereat those maidens with one mind
Bewail'd their lot; I did them wrong:
'We served thee here,' they said, 'so long,
And wilt thou leave us now behind?'

So rapt I was, they could not win
50 An answer from my lips, but he
Replying, 'Enter likewise ye
And go with us:' they enter'd in.

And while the wind began to sweep
A music out of sheet and shroud,
We steer'd her toward a crimson cloud
That landlike slept along the deep.

CIV

The time draws near the birth of Christ;
The moon is hid, the night is still;
A single church below the hill
Is pealing, folded in the mist.

A single peal of bells below,
That wakens at this hour of rest

A single murmur in the breast,
That these are not the bells I know.

Like strangers' voices here they sound,
In lands where not a memory strays, 10
Nor landmark breathes of other days,
But all is new unhallow'd ground.

CV

To-night ungather'd let us leave
This laurel, let this holly stand:
We live within the stranger's land,
And strangely falls our Christmas-eve.

Our father's dust is left alone
And silent under other snows:
There in due time the woodbine blows,
The violet comes, but we are gone.

No more shall wayward grief abuse
The genial hour with mask and mime; 10
For change of place, like growth of time,
Has broke the bond of dying use.

Let cares that petty shadows cast,
By which our lives are chiefly proved,
A little spare the night I loved,
And hold it solemn to the past.

But let no footstep beat the floor,
Nor bowl of wassail mantle warm;
For who would keep an ancient form
Thro' which the spirit breathes no more? 20

Be neither song, nor game, nor feast;
Nor harp be touch'd, nor flute be blown;
No dance, no motion, save alone
What lightens in the lucid east

Of rising worlds by yonder wood.
Long sleeps the summer in the seed;
Run out your measured arcs, and lead
The closing cycle rich in good.

CVI

Ring out, wild bells, to the wild sky,
The flying cloud, the frosty light:
The year is dying in the night;
Ring out, wild bells, and let him die.

Ring out the old, ring in the new,
Ring, happy bells, across the snow:
The year is going, let him go;
Ring out the false, ring in the true.

Ring out the grief that saps the mind,
10 For those that here we see no more;
Ring out the feud of rich and poor,
Ring in redress to all mankind.

Ring out a slowly dying cause,
And ancient forms of party strife;
Ring in the nobler modes of life,
With sweeter manners, purer laws.

Ring out the want, the care, the sin,
The faithless coldness of the times;
Ring out, ring out my mournful rhymes,
20 But ring the fuller minstrel in.

Ring out false pride in place and blood,
The civic slander and the spite;
Ring in the love of truth and right,
Ring in the common love of good.

Ring out old shapes of foul disease;
Ring out the narrowing lust of gold;
Ring out the thousand wars of old,
Ring in the thousand years of peace.

Ring in the valiant man and free,
The larger heart, the kindlier hand; 30
Ring out the darkness of the land,
Ring in the Christ that is to be.

CVII

It is the day when he was born,
A bitter day that early sank
Behind a purple-frosty bank
Of vapour, leaving night forlorn.

The time admits not flowers or leaves
To deck the banquet. Fiercely flies
The blast of North and East, and ice
Makes daggers at the sharpen'd eaves,

And bristles all the brakes and thorns
To yon hard crescent, as she hangs 10
Above the wood which grides and clangs
Its leafless ribs and iron horns

Together, in the drifts that pass
To darken on the rolling brine
That breaks the coast. But fetch the wine,
Arrange the board and brim the glass;

Bring in great logs and let them lie,
To make a solid core of heat;
Be cheerful-minded, talk and treat
Of all things ev'n as he were by; 20

We keep the day. With festal cheer,
With books and music, surely we
Will drink to him, whate'er he be,
And sing the songs he loved to hear.

CVIII

I will not shut me from my kind,
And, lest I stiffen into stone,

I will not eat my heart alone,
Nor feed with sighs a passing wind:

What profit lies in barren faith,
And vacant yearning, tho' with might
To scale the heaven's highest height,
Or dive below the wells of Death?

What find I in the highest place,
10 But mine own phantom chanting hymns?
And on the depths of death there swims
The reflex of a human face.

I'll rather take what fruit may be
Of sorrow under human skies:
'Tis held that sorrow makes us wise,
Whatever wisdom sleep with thee.

CIX

Heart-affluence in discursive talk
From household fountains never dry;
The critic clearness of an eye,
That saw thro' all the Muses' walk;

Seraphic intellect and force
To seize and throw the doubts of man;
Impassion'd logic, which outran
The hearer in its fiery course;

High nature amorous of the good,
10 But touch'd with no ascetic gloom;
And passion pure in snowy bloom
Thro' all the years of April blood;

A love of freedom rarely felt,
Of freedom in her regal seat
Of England; not the schoolboy heat,
The blind hysterics of the Celt;

And manhood fused with female grace
In such a sort, the child would twine
A trustful hand, unask'd, in thine,
And find his comfort in thy face; 20

All these have been, and thee mine eyes
Have look'd on: if they look'd in vain,
My shame is greater who remain,
Nor let thy wisdom make me wise.

CX

Thy converse drew us with delight,
The men of rathe and riper years:
The feeble soul, a haunt of fears,
Forgot his weakness in thy sight.

On thee the loyal-hearted hung,
The proud was half disarm'd of pride,
Nor cared the serpent at thy side
To flicker with his double tongue.

The stern were mild when thou wert by,
The flippant put himself to school 10
And heard thee, and the brazen fool
Was soften'd, and he knew not why;

While I, thy nearest, sat apart,
And felt thy triumph was as mine;
And loved them more, that they were thine,
The graceful tact, the Christian art;

Nor mine the sweetness or the skill,
But mine the love that will not tire,
And, born of love, the vague desire
That spurs an imitative will. 20

CXI

The churl in spirit, up or down
Along the scale of ranks, thro' all,

To him who grasps a golden ball,
By blood a king, at heart a clown;

The churl in spirit, howe'er he veil
His want in forms for fashion's sake,
Will let his coltish nature break
At seasons thro' the gilded pale:

For who can always act? but he,
10 To whom a thousand memories call,
Not being less but more than all
The gentleness he seem'd to be,

Best seem'd the thing he was, and join'd
Each office of the social hour
To noble manners, as the flower
And native growth of noble mind;

Nor ever narrowness or spite,
Or villain fancy fleeting by,
Drew in the expression of an eye,
20 Where God and Nature met in light;

And thus he bore without abuse
The grand old name of gentleman,
Defamed by every charlatan,
And soil'd with all ignoble use.

CXII

High wisdom holds my wisdom less,
That I, who gaze with temperate eyes
On glorious insufficiencies,
Set light by narrower perfectness.

But thou, that fillest all the room
Of all my love, art reason why
I seem to cast a careless eye
On souls, the lesser lords of doom.

For what wert thou? some novel power
Sprang up for ever at a touch, 10
And hope could never hope too much,
In watching thee from hour to hour,

Large elements in order brought,
And tracts of calm from tempest made,
And world-wide fluctuation sway'd
In vassal tides that follow'd thought.

CXIII

'Tis held that sorrow makes us wise;
Yet how much wisdom sleeps with thee
Which not alone had guided me,
But served the seasons that may rise;

For can I doubt, who knew thee keen
In intellect, with force and skill
To strive, to fashion, to fulfil –
I doubt not what thou wouldst have been:

A life in civic action warm,
A soul on highest mission sent, 10
A potent voice of Parliament,
A pillar steadfast in the storm,

Should licensed boldness gather force,
Becoming, when the time has birth,
A lever to uplift the earth
And roll it in another course,

With thousand shocks that come and go,
With agonies, with energies,
With overthrowings, and with cries,
And undulations to and fro. 20

CXIV

Who loves not Knowledge? Who shall rail
Against her beauty? May she mix

With men and prosper! Who shall fix
Her pillars? Let her work prevail.

But on her forehead sits a fire:
She sets her forward countenance
And leaps into the future chance,
Submitting all things to desire.

Half-grown as yet, a child, and vain –
10 She cannot fight the fear of death.
What is she, cut from love and faith,
But some wild Pallas from the brain

Of Demons? fiery-hot to burst
All barriers in her onward race
For power. Let her know her place;
She is the second, not the first.

A higher hand must make her mild,
If all be not in vain; and guide
Her footsteps, moving side by side
20 With wisdom, like the younger child:

For she is earthly of the mind,
But Wisdom heavenly of the soul.
O, friend, who camest to thy goal
So early, leaving me behind,

I would the great world grew like thee,
Who grewest not alone in power
And knowledge, but by year and hour
In reverence and in charity.

CXV

Now fades the last long streak of snow,
Now burgeons every maze of quick
About the flowering squares, and thick
By ashen roots the violets blow.

Now rings the woodland loud and long,
The distance takes a lovelier hue,

And drown'd in yonder living blue
The lark becomes a sightless song.

Now dance the lights on lawn and lea,
The flocks are whiter down the vale, 10
And milkier every milky sail
On winding stream or distant sea;

Where now the seamew pipes, or dives
In yonder greening gleam, and fly
The happy birds, that change their sky
To build and brood; that live their lives

From land to land; and in my breast
Spring wakens too; and my regret
Becomes an April violet,
And buds and blossoms like the rest. 20

CXVI

Is it, then, regret for buried time
That keenlier in sweet April wakes,
And meets the year, and gives and takes
The colours of the crescent prime?

Not all: the songs, the stirring air,
The life re-orient out of dust,
Cry thro' the sense to hearten trust
In that which made the world so fair.

Not all regret: the face will shine
Upon me, while I muse alone; 10
And that dear voice, I once have known,
Still speak to me of me and mine:

Yet less of sorrow lives in me
For days of happy commune dead;
Less yearning for the friendship fled,
Than some strong bond which is to be.

CXVII

O days and hours, your work is this
To hold me from my proper place,
A little while from his embrace,
For fuller gain of after bliss:

That out of distance might ensue
Desire of nearness doubly sweet;
And unto meeting when we meet,
Delight a hundredfold accrue,

For every grain of sand that runs,
o And every span of shade that steals,
And every kiss of toothèd wheels,
And all the courses of the suns.

CXVIII

Contemplate all this work of Time,
The giant labouring in his youth;
Nor dream of human love and truth,
As dying Nature's earth and lime;

But trust that those we call the dead
Are breathers of an ampler day
For ever nobler ends. They say,
The solid earth whereon we tread

In tracts of fluent heat began,
10 And grew to seeming-random forms,
The seeming prey of cyclic storms,
Till at the last arose the man;

Who throve and branch'd from clime to clime,
The herald of a higher race,
And of himself in higher place,
If so he type this work of time

Within himself, from more to more;
Or, crown'd with attributes of woe
Like glories, move his course, and show
20 That life is not as idle ore,

But iron dug from central gloom,
    And heated hot with burning fears,
    And dipt in baths of hissing tears,
And batter'd with the shocks of doom

To shape and usc. Arise and fly
    The reeling Faun, the sensual feast;
    Move upward, working out the beast,
And let the ape and tiger die.

CXIX

Doors, where my heart was used to beat
    So quickly, not as one that weeps
    I come once more; the city sleeps;
I smell the meadow in the street;

I hear a chirp of birds; I see
    Betwixt the black fronts long-withdrawn
    A light-blue lane of early dawn,
And think of early days and thee,

And bless thee, for thy lips are bland,
    And bright the friendship of thine eye; 10
    And in my thoughts with scarce a sigh
I take the pressure of thine hand.

CXX

I trust I have not wasted breath:
    I think we are not wholly brain,
    Magnetic mockeries; not in vain,
Like Paul with beasts, I fought with Death;

Not only cunning casts in clay:
    Let Science prove we are, and then
    What matters Science unto men,
At least to me? I would not stay.

Let him, the wiser man who springs
    Hereafter, up from childhood shape 10

His action like the greater ape,
But I was *born* to other things.

CXXI

Sad Hesper o'er the buried sun
And ready, thou, to die with him,
Thou watchest all things ever dim
And dimmer, and a glory done:

The team is loosen'd from the wain,
The boat is drawn upon the shore;
Thou listenest to the closing door,
And life is darken'd in the brain.

Bright Phosphor, fresher for the night,
10 By thee the world's great work is heard
Beginning, and the wakeful bird;
Behind thee comes the greater light:

The market boat is on the stream,
And voices hail it from the brink;
Thou hear'st the village hammer clink,
And see'st the moving of the team.

Sweet Hesper-Phosphor, double name
For what is one, the first, the last,
Thou, like my present and my past,
20 Thy place is changed; thou art the same.

CXXII

Oh, wast thou with me, dearest, then,
While I rose up against my doom,
And yearn'd to burst the folded gloom,
To bare the eternal Heavens again,

To feel once more, in placid awe,
The strong imagination roll
A sphere of stars about my soul,
In all her motion one with law;

If thou wert with me, and the grave
    Divide us not, be with me now, 10
    And enter in at breast and brow,
Till all my blood, a fuller wave,

Be quicken'd with a livelier breath,
    And like an inconsiderate boy,
    As in the former flash of joy,
I slip the thoughts of life and death;

And all the breeze of Fancy blows,
    And every dew-drop paints a bow,
    The wizard lightnings deeply glow,
And every thought breaks out a rose. 20

CXXIII

There rolls the deep where grew the tree.
    O earth, what changes hast thou seen!
    There where the long street roars, hath been
The stillness of the central sea.

The hills are shadows, and they flow
    From form to form, and nothing stands;
    They melt like mist, the solid lands,
Like clouds they shape themselves and go.

But in my spirit will I dwell,
    And dream my dream, and hold it true; 10
    For tho' my lips may breathe adieu,
I cannot think the thing farewell.

CXXIV

That which we dare invoke to bless;
    Our dearest faith; our ghastliest doubt;
    He, They, One, All; within, without;
The Power in darkness whom we guess;

I found Him not in world or sun,
    Or eagle's wing, or insect's eye;

Nor thro' the questions men may try,
The petty cobwebs we have spun:

If e'er when faith had fall'n asleep,
10 I heard a voice 'believe no more'
And heard an ever-breaking shore
That tumbled in the Godless deep;

A warmth within the breast would melt
The freezing reason's colder part,
And like a man in wrath the heart
Stood up and answer'd 'I have felt.'

No, like a child in doubt and fear:
But that blind clamour made me wise;
Then was I as a child that cries,
20 But, crying, knows his father near;

And what I am beheld again
What is, and no man understands;
And out of darkness came the hands
That reach thro' nature, moulding men.

CXXV

Whatever I have said or sung,
Some bitter notes my harp would give,
Yea, tho' there often seem'd to live
A contradiction on the tongue,

Yet Hope had never lost her youth;
She did but look through dimmer eyes;
Or Love but play'd with gracious lies,
Because he felt so fix'd in truth:

And if the song were full of care,
10 He breathed the spirit of the song;
And if the words were sweet and strong
He set his royal signet there;

Abiding with me till I sail
　　To seek thee on the mystic deeps,
　　And this electric force, that keeps
A thousand pulses dancing, fail.

CXXVI

Love is and was my Lord and King,
　　And in his presence I attend
　　To hear the tidings of my friend,
Which every hour his couriers bring.

Love is and was my King and Lord,
　　And will be, tho' as yet I keep
　　Within his court on earth, and sleep
Encompass'd by his faithful guard,

And hear at times a sentinel
　　Who moves about from place to place, 10
　　And whispers to the worlds of space,
In the deep night, that all is well.

CXXVII

And all is well, tho' faith and form
　　Be sunder'd in the night of fear;
　　Well roars the storm to those that hear
A deeper voice across the storm,

Proclaiming social truth shall spread,
　　And justice, ev'n tho' thrice again
　　The red fool-fury of the Seine
Should pile her barricades with dead.

But ill for him that wears a crown,
　　And him, the lazar, in his rags: 10
　　They tremble, the sustaining crags;
The spires of ice are toppled down,

And molten up, and roar in flood;
　　The fortress crashes from on high,

The brute earth lightens to the sky,
And the great Aeon sinks in blood,

And compass'd by the fires of Hell;
While thou, dear spirit, happy star,
O'erlook'st the tumult from afar,
20 And smilest, knowing all is well.

CXXVIII

The love that rose on stronger wings,
Unpalsied when he met with Death,
Is comrade of the lesser faith
That sees the course of human things.

No doubt vast eddies in the flood
Of onward time shall yet be made,
And thronèd races may degrade;
Yet O ye mysteries of good,

Wild Hours that fly with Hope and Fear,
10 If all your office had to do
With old results that look like new;
If this were all your mission here,

To draw, to sheathe a useless sword,
To fool the crowd with glorious lies,
To cleave a creed in sects and cries,
To change the bearing of a word,

To shift an arbitrary power,
To cramp the student at his desk,
To make old bareness picturesque
20 And tuft with grass a feudal tower;

Why then my scorn might well descend
On you and yours. I see in part
That all, as in some piece of art,
Is toil cöoperant to an end.

CXXIX

Dear friend, far off, my lost desire,
 So far, so near in woe and weal;
 O loved the most, when most I feel
There is a lower and a higher;

Known and unknown; human, divine;
 Sweet human hand and lips and eye;
 Dear heavenly friend that canst not die,
Mine, mine, for ever, ever mine;

Strange friend, past, present, and to be;
 Loved deeplier, darklier understood; 10
 Behold, I dream a dream of good,
And mingle all the world with thee.

CXXX

Thy voice is on the rolling air;
 I hear thee where the waters run;
 Thou standest in the rising sun,
And in the setting thou art fair.

What art thou then? I cannot guess;
 But tho' I seem in star and flower
 To feel thee some diffusive power,
I do not therefore love thee less:

My love involves the love before;
 My love is vaster passion now; 10
 Tho' mix'd with God and Nature thou,
I seem to love thee more and more.

Far off thou art, but ever nigh;
 I have thee still, and I rejoice;
 I prosper, circled with thy voice;
I shall not lose thee tho' I die.

CXXXI

O living will that shalt endure
 When all that seems shall suffer shock,

Rise in the spiritual rock,
Flow thro' our deeds and make them pure,

That we may lift from out of dust
A voice as unto him that hears,
A cry above the conquer'd years
To one that with us works, and trust,

With faith that comes of self-control,
10 The truths that never can be proved
Until we close with all we loved,
And all we flow from, soul in soul.

*

[EPILOGUE]

O true and tried, so well and long,
Demand not thou a marriage lay;
In that it is thy marriage day
Is music more than any song.

Nor have I felt so much of bliss
Since first he told me that he loved
A daughter of our house; nor proved
Since that dark day a day like this;

Tho' I since then have number'd o'er
10 Some thrice three years: they went and came,
Remade the blood and changed the frame,
And yet is love not less, but more;

No longer caring to embalm
In dying songs a dead regret,
But like a statue solid-set,
And moulded in colossal calm.

Regret is dead, but love is more
Than in the summers that are flown,
For I myself with these have grown
20 To something greater than before;

Which makes appear the songs I made
    As echoes out of weaker times,
    As half but idle brawling rhymes,
The sport of random sun and shade.

But where is she, the bridal flower,
    That must be made a wife ere noon?
    She enters, glowing like the moon
Of Eden on its bridal bower:

On me she bends her blissful eyes
    And then on thee; they meet thy look 30
    And brighten like the star that shook
Betwixt the palms of paradise.

O when her life was yet in bud,
    He too foretold the perfect rose.
    For thee she grew, for thee she grows
For ever, and as fair as good.

And thou art worthy; full of power;
    As gentle; liberal-minded, great,
    Consistent; wearing all that weight
Of learning lightly like a flower. 40

But now set out: the noon is near,
    And I must give away the bride;
    She fears not, or with thee beside
And me behind her, will not fear.

For I that danced her on my knee,
    That watch'd her on her nurse's arm,
    That shielded all her life from harm
At last must part with her to thee;

Now waiting to be made a wife,
    Her feet, my darling, on the dead; 50
    Their pensive tablets round her head,
And the most living words of life

Breathed in her ear. The ring is on,
The 'wilt thou' answer'd, and again
The 'wilt thou' ask'd, till out of twain
Her sweet 'I will' has made you one.

Now sign your names, which shall be read,
Mute symbols of a joyful morn,
By village eyes as yet unborn;
60 The names are sign'd, and overhead

Begins the clash and clang that tells
The joy to every wandering breeze;
The blind wall rocks, and on the trees
The dead leaf trembles to the bells.

O happy hour, and happier hours
Await them. Many a merry face
Salutes them – maidens of the place,
That pelt us in the porch with flowers.

O happy hour, behold the bride
70 With him to whom her hand I gave.
They leave the porch, they pass the grave
That has to-day its sunny side.

To-day the grave is bright for me,
For them the light of life increased,
Who stay to share the morning feast,
Who rest to-night beside the sea.

Let all my genial spirits advance
To meet and greet a whiter sun;
My drooping memory will not shun
80 The foaming grape of eastern France.

It circles round, and fancy plays,
And hearts are warm'd and faces bloom,
As drinking health to bride and groom
We wish them store of happy days.

Nor count me all to blame if I
Conjecture of a stiller guest,
Perchance, perchance, among the rest,
And, tho' in silence, wishing joy.

But they must go, the time draws on,
And those white-favour'd horses wait; 90
They rise, but linger; it is late;
Farewell, we kiss, and they are gone.

A shade falls on us like the dark
From little cloudlets on the grass,
But sweeps away as out we pass
To range the woods, to roam the park,

Discussing how their courtship grew,
And talk of others that are wed,
And how she look'd, and what he said,
And back we come at fall of dew. 100

Again the feast, the speech, the glee,
The shade of passing thought, the wealth
Of words and wit, the double health,
The crowning cup, the three-times-three,

And last the dance; – till I retire:
Dumb is that tower which spake so loud,
And high in heaven the streaming cloud,
And on the downs a rising fire:

And rise, O moon, from yonder down,
Till over down and over dale 110
All night the shining vapour sail
And pass the silent-lighted town,

The white-faced halls, the glancing rills,
And catch at every mountain head,
And o'er the friths that branch and spread
Their sleeping silver thro' the hills;

And touch with shade the bridal doors,
With tender gloom the roof, the wall;
And breaking let the splendour fall
120 To spangle all the happy shores

By which they rest, and ocean sounds,
And, star and system rolling past,
A soul shall draw from out the vast
And strike his being into bounds,

And, moved thro' life of lower phase,
Result in man, be born and think,
And act and love, a closer link
Betwixt us and the crowning race

Of those that, eye to eye, shall look
130 On knowledge; under whose command
Is Earth and Earth's, and in their hand
Is Nature like an open book;

No longer half-akin to brute,
For all we thought and loved and did,
And hoped, and suffer'd, is but seed
Of what in them is flower and fruit;

Whereof the man, that with me trod
This planet, was a noble type
Appearing ere the times were ripe,
140 That friend of mine who lives in God,

That God, which ever lives and loves,
One God, one law, one element,
And one far-off divine event,
To which the whole creation moves.

▲ ▲ ▲

From *Poems* (1851)

Edwin Morris

Or, the Lake

O me, my pleasant rambles by the lake,
My sweet, wild, fresh three quarters of a year,
My one Oasis in the dust and drouth
Of city life! I was a sketcher then:
See here, my doing: curves of mountain, bridge,
Boat, island, ruins of a castle, built
When men knew how to build, upon a rock
With turrets lichen-gilded like a rock:
And here, new-comers in an ancient hold,
New-comers from the Mersey, millionaires, 10
Here lived the Hills – a Tudor-chimnied bulk
Of mellow brickwork on an isle of bowers.

O me, my pleasant rambles by the lake
With Edwin Morris and with Edward Bull
The curate; he was fatter than his cure.

But Edwin Morris, he that knew the names,
Long learnèd names of agaric, moss and fern,
Who forged a thousand theories of the rocks,
Who taught me how to skate, to row, to swim,
Who read me rhymes elaborately good, 20
His own – I call'd him Crichton, for he seem'd
All-perfect, finish'd to the finger nail.

And once I ask'd him of his early life,
And his first passion; and he answer'd me;
And well his words became him: was he not
A full-cell'd honeycomb of eloquence
Stored from all flowers? Poet-like he spoke.

'My love for Nature is as old as I;
But thirty moons, one honeymoon to that,
30 And three rich sennights more, my love for her.
My love for Nature and my love for her,
Of different ages, like twin-sisters grew,
Twin-sisters differently beautiful.
To some full music rose and sank the sun,
And some full music seem'd to move and change
With all the varied changes of the dark,
And either twilight and the day between;
For daily hope fulfill'd, to rise again
Revolving toward fulfilment, made it sweet
40 To walk, to sit, to sleep, to wake, to breathe.'

Or this or something like to this he spoke.
Then said the fat-faced curate Edward Bull,

'I take it, God made the woman for the man,
And for the good and increase of the world.
A pretty face is well, and this is well,
To have a dame indoors, that trims us up,
And keeps us tight; but these unreal ways
Seem but the theme of writers, and indeed
Worn threadbare. Man is made of solid stuff.
50 I say, God made the woman for the man,
And for the good and increase of the world.'

'Parson,' said I, 'you pitch the pipe too low:
But I have sudden touches, and can run
My faith beyond my practice into his:
Tho' if, in dancing after Letty Hill,
I do not hear the bells upon my cap,
I scarce have other music: yet say on.

What should one give to light on such a dream?'
I ask'd him half-sardonically.
'Give?
Give all thou art,' he answer'd, and a light 60
Of laughter dimpled in his swarthy cheek;
'I would have hid her needle in my heart,
To save her little finger from a scratch
No deeper than the skin: my ears could hear
Her lightest breath; her least remark was worth
The experience of the wise. I went and came;
Her voice fled always thro' the summer land;
I spoke her name alone. Thrice-happy days!
The flower of each, those moments when we met,
The crown of all, we met to part no more.' 70

Were not his words delicious, I a beast
To take them as I did? but something jarr'd;
Whether he spoke too largely; that there seem'd
A touch of something false, some self-conceit,
Or over-smoothness: howsoe'er it was,
He scarcely hit my humour, and I said:

'Friend Edwin, do not think yourself alone
Of all men happy. Shall not Love to me,
As in the Latin song I learnt at school,
Sneeze out a full God-bless-you right and left? 80
But you can talk: yours is a kindly vein:
I have, I think, – Heaven knows – as much within;
Have, or should have, but for a thought or two,
That like a purple beech among the greens
Looks out of place: 'tis from no want in her:
It is my shyness, or my self-distrust,
Or something of a wayward modern mind
Dissecting passion. Time will set me right.'

So spoke I knowing not the things that were.
Then said the fat-faced curate, Edward Bull: 90
'God made the woman for the use of man,

And for the good and increase of the world.'
And I and Edwin laughed; and now we paused
About the windings of the marge to hear
The soft wind blowing over meadowy holms
And alders, garden-isles; and now we left
The clerk behind us, I and he, and ran
By ripply shallows of the lisping lake,
Delighted with the freshness and the sound.

100 But, when the bracken rusted on their crags,
My suit had wither'd, nipt to death by him
That was a God, and is a lawyer's clerk,
The rentroll Cupid of our rainy isles.
'Tis true, we met; one hour I had, no more:
She sent a note, the seal an *Elle vous suit*,
The close, 'Your Letty, only yours;' and this
Thrice underscored. The friendly mist of morn
Clung to the lake. I boated over, ran
My craft aground, and heard with beating heart
110 The Sweet-Gale rustle round the shelving keel;
And out I stept, and up I crept: she moved,
Like Proserpine in Enna, gathering flowers:
Then low and sweet I whistled thrice; and she,
She turn'd, we closed, we kiss'd, swore faith, I breathed
In some new planet: a silent cousin stole
Upon us and departed: 'Leave,' she cried,
'O leave me!' 'Never, dearest, never: here
I brave the worst:' and while we stood like fools
Embracing, all at once a score of pugs
120 And poodles yell'd within, and out they came
Trustees and Aunts and Uncles. 'What, with him!
Go' (shrill'd the cotton-spinning chorus); 'him!'
I choked. Again they shriek'd the burthen – 'Him!'
Again with hands of wild rejection 'Go! –
Girl, get you in!' She went – and in one month
They wedded her to sixty thousand pounds,
To lands in Kent and messuages in York,

And slight Sir Robert with his watery smile
And educated whisker. But for me,
They set an ancient creditor to work: 130
It seems I broke a close with force and arms:
There came a mystic token from the king
To greet the sheriff, needless courtesy!
I read, and fled by night, and flying turn'd:
Her taper glimmer'd in the lake below:
I turn'd once more, close-button'd to the storm;
So left the place, left Edwin, nor have seen
Him since, nor heard of her, nor cared to hear.

Nor cared to hear? perhaps: yet long ago
I have pardon'd little Letty; not indeed, 140
It may be, for her own dear sake but this,
She seems a part of those fresh days to me;
For in the dust and drouth of London life
She moves among my visions of the lake,
While the prime swallow dips his wing, or then
While the gold-lily blows, and overhead
The light cloud smoulders on the summer crag.

The Eagle

FRAGMENT

He clasps the crag with crookèd hands;
Close to the sun in lonely lands,
Ring'd with the azure world, he stands.

The wrinkled sea beneath him crawls;
He watches from his mountain walls,
And like a thunderbolt he falls.

▲ ▲ ▲

From *Maud, and Other Poems* (1855)

Maud

A Monodrama

PART I

I

I

I hate the dreadful hollow behind the little wood,
Its lips in the field above are dabbled with blood-red heath,
The red-ribb'd ledges drip with a silent horror of blood,
And Echo there, whatever is ask'd her, answers 'Death.'

II

For there in the ghastly pit long since a body was found,
His who had given me life – O father! O God! was it well? –
Mangled, and flatten'd, and crush'd, and dinted into the ground:
There yet lies the rock that fell with him when he fell.

III

Did he fling himself down? who knows? for a vast speculation had
    fail'd,
And ever he mutter'd and madden'd, and ever wann'd with
    despair, 10
And out he walk'd when the wind like a broken worldling wail'd,
And the flying gold of the ruin'd woodlands drove thro' the air.

IV

I remember the time, for the roots of my hair were stirr'd
By a shuffled step, by a dead weight trail'd, by a whisper'd fright.
And my pulses closed their gates with a shock on my heart as I
heard
The shrill-edged shriek of a mother divide the shuddering night.

V

Villainy somewhere! whose? One says, we are villains all.
Not he: his honest fame should at least by me be maintained:
But that old man, now lord of the broad estate and the Hall,
Dropt off gorged from a scheme that had left us flaccid and
20 drain'd.

VI

Why do they prate of the blessings of Peace? we have made them
a curse,
Pickpockets, each hand lusting for all that is not its own;
And lust of gain, in the spirit of Cain, is it better or worse
Than the heart of the citizen hissing in war on his own
hearthstone?

VII

But these are the days of advance, the works of the men of mind,
When who but a fool would have faith in a tradesman's ware or
his word?
Is it peace or war? Civil war, as I think, and that of a kind
The viler, as underhand, not openly bearing the sword.

VIII

Sooner or later I too may passively take the print
30 Of the golden age – why not? I have neither hope nor trust;
May make my heart as a millstone, set my face as a flint,
Cheat and be cheated, and die: who knows? we are ashes and dust.

IX

Peace sitting under her olive, and slurring the days gone by,
When the poor are hovell'd and hustled together, each sex, like
    swine,
When only the ledger lives, and when only not all men lie;
Peace in her vineyard – yes! – but a company forges the wine.

X

And the vitriol madness flushes up in the ruffian's head,
Till the filthy by-lane rings to the yell of the trampled wife,
And chalk and alum and plaster are sold to the poor for bread,
And the spirit of murder works in the very means of life, 40

XI

And Sleep must lie down arm'd, for the villainous centre-bits
Grind on the wakeful ear in the hush of the moonless nights,
While another is cheating the sick of a few last gasps, as he sits
To pestle a poison'd poison behind his crimson lights.

XII

When a Mammonite mother kills her babe for a burial fee,
And Timour-Mammon grins on a pile of children's bones,
Is it peace or war? better, war! loud war by land and by sea,
War with a thousand battles, and shaking a hundred thrones.

XIII

For I trust if an enemy's fleet came yonder round by the hill,
And the rushing battle-bolt sang from the three-decker out of the
    foam, 50
That the smooth-faced snubnosed rogue would leap from his
    counter and till,
And strike, if he could, were it but with his cheating yardwand,
    home.—

XIV

What! am I raging alone as my father raged in his mood?
Must *I* too creep to the hollow and dash myself down and die

Rather than hold by the law that I made, nevermore to brood
On a horror of shatter'd limbs and a wretched swindler's lie?

XV

Would there be sorrow for *me*? there was *love* in the passionate
 shriek,
Love for the silent thing that had made false haste to the grave –
Wrapt in a cloak, as I saw him, and thought he would rise and
 speak
60 And rave at the lie and the liar, ah God, as he used to rave.

XVI

I am sick of the Hall and the hill, I am sick of the moor and the
 main.
Why should I stay? can a sweeter chance ever come to me here?
O, having the nerves of motion as well as the nerves of pain,
Were it not wise if I fled from the place and the pit and the
 fear?

XVII

Workmen up at the Hall! – they are coming back from abroad;
The dark old place will be gilt by the touch of a millionaire:
I have heard, I know not whence, of the singular beauty of Maud;
I play'd with the girl when a child; she promised then to be fair.

XVIII

Maud with her venturous climbings and tumbles and childish
 escapes,
70 Maud the delight of the village, the ringing joy of the Hall,
Maud with her sweet purse-mouth when my father dangled the
 grapes,
Maud the beloved of my mother, the moon-faced darling of all, –

XIX

What is she now? My dreams are bad. She may bring me a curse.
No, there is fatter game on the moor; she will let me alone.

Thanks, for the fiend best knows whether woman or man be the
worse.
I will bury myself in myself, and the Devil may pipe to his own.

II

Long have I sigh'd for a calm: God grant I may find it at last!
It will never be broken by Maud, she has neither savour nor salt,
But a cold and clear-cut face, as I found when her carriage past,
Perfectly beautiful: let it be granted her: where is the fault? 80
All that I saw (for her eyes were downcast, not to be seen)
Faultily faultless, icily regular, splendidly null,
Dead perfection, no more; nothing more, if it had not been
For a chance of travel, a paleness, an hour's defect of the rose,
Or an underlip, you may call it a little too ripe, too full,
Or the least little delicate aquiline curve in a sensitive nose,
From which I escaped heart-free, with the least little touch of
spleen.

III

Cold and clear-cut face, why come you so cruelly meek,
Breaking a slumber in which all spleenful folly was drown'd,
Pale with the golden beam of an eyelash dead on the cheek, 90
Passionless, pale, cold face, star-sweet on a gloom profound;
Womanlike, taking revenge too deep for a transient wrong
Done but in thought to your beauty, and ever as pale as before
Growing and fading and growing upon me without a sound,
Luminous, gemlike, ghostlike, deathlike, half the night long
Growing and fading and growing, till I could bear it no more,
But arose, and all by myself in my own dark garden ground,
Listening now to the tide in its broad-flung ship-wrecking roar,
Now to the scream of a madden'd beach dragg'd down by the
wave,
Walk'd in a wintry wind by a ghastly glimmer, and found 100
The shining daffodil dead, and Orion low in his grave.

IV

I

A million emeralds break from the ruby-budded lime
In the little grove where I sit – ah, wherefore cannot I be
Like things of the season gay, like the bountiful season bland,
When the far-off sail is blown by the breeze of a softer clime,
Half-lost in the liquid azure bloom of a crescent of sea,
The silent sapphire-spangled marriage ring of the land?

II

Below me, there, is the village, and looks how quiet and small!
And yet bubbles o'er like a city, with gossip, scandal, and spite;
10 And Jack on his ale-house bench has as many lies as a Czar;
And here on the landward side, by a red rock, glimmers the Hall;
And up in the high Hall-garden I see her pass like a light;
But sorrow seize me if ever that light be my leading star!

III

When have I bow'd to her father, the wrinkled head of the race?
I met her to-day with her brother, but not to her brother I bow'd:
I bow'd to his lady-sister as she rode by on the moor;
But the fire of a foolish pride flash'd over her beautiful face.
O child, you wrong your beauty, believe it, in being so proud;
Your father has wealth well-gotten, and I am nameless and poor.

IV

120 I keep but a man and a maid, ever ready to slander and steal;
I know it, and smile a hard-set smile, like a stoic, or like
A wiser epicurean, and let the world have its way:
For nature is one with rapine, a harm no preacher can heal;
The Mayfly is torn by the swallow, the sparrow spear'd by the shrike,
And the whole little wood where I sit is a world of plunder and prey.

V

We are puppets, Man in his pride, and Beauty fair in her flower;
Do we move ourselves, or are moved by an unseen hand at a game

That pushes us off from the board, and others ever succeed?
Ah yet, we cannot be kind to each other here for an hour;
We whisper, and hint, and chuckle, and grin at a brother's shame; 130
However we brave it out, we men are a little breed.

VI

A monstrous eft was of old the Lord and Master of Earth,
For him did his high sun flame, and his river billowing ran,
And he felt himself in his force to be Nature's crowning race.
As nine months go to the shaping an infant ripe for his birth,
So many a million of ages have gone to the making of man:
He now is first, but is he the last? is he not too base?

VII

The man of science himself is fonder of glory, and vain,
An eye well-practised in nature, a spirit bounded and poor;
The passionate heart of the poet is whirl'd into folly and vice. 140
I would not marvel at either, but keep a temperate brain;
For not to desire or admire, if a man could learn it, were more
Than to walk all day like the sultan of old in a garden of spice.

VIII

For the drift of the Maker is dark, an Isis hid by the veil.
Who knows the ways of the world, how God will bring them
about?
Our planet is one, the suns are many, the world is wide.
Shall I weep if a Poland fall? shall I shriek if a Hungary fail?
Or an infant civilisation be ruled with rod or with knout?
I have not made the world, and He that made it will guide.

IX

Be mine a philosopher's life in the quiet woodland ways, 150
Where if I cannot be gay let a passionless peace be my lot,
Far-off from the clamour of liars belied in the hubbub of
lies;
From the long-neck'd geese of the world that are ever hissing
dispraise

Because their natures are little, and, whether he heed it or not,
Where each man walks with his head in a cloud of poisonous flies.

X

And most of all would I flee from the cruel madness of love,
The honey of poison-flowers and all the measureless ill.
Ah Maud, you milkwhite fawn, you are all unmeet for a wife.
Your mother is mute in her grave as her image in marble above;
160 Your father is ever in London, you wander about at your will;
You have but fed on the roses and lain in the lilies of life.

V

I

A voice by the cedar tree
In the meadow under the Hall!
She is singing an air that is known to me,
A passionate ballad gallant and gay,
A martial song like a trumpet's call!
Singing alone in the morning of life,
In the happy morning of life and of May,
Singing of men that in battle array,
170 Ready in heart and ready in hand,
March with banner and bugle and fife
To the death, for their native land.

II

Maud with her exquisite face,
And wild voice pealing up to the sunny sky,
And feet like sunny gems on an English green,
Maud in the light of her youth and her grace,
Singing of Death, and of Honour that cannot die,
Till I well could weep for a time so sordid and mean,
And myself so languid and base.

III

Silence, beautiful voice! 180
Be still, for you only trouble the mind
With a joy in which I cannot rejoice,
A glory I shall not find.
Still! I will hear you no more,
For your sweetness hardly leaves me a choice
But to move to the meadow and fall before
Her feet on the meadow grass, and adore,
Not her, who is neither courtly nor kind,
Not her, not her, but a voice.

VI

I

Morning arises stormy and pale, 190
No sun, but a wannish glare
In fold upon fold of hueless cloud,
And the budded peaks of the wood are bow'd
Caught and cuff'd by the gale:
I had fancied it would be fair.

II

Whom but Maud should I meet
Last night, when the sunset burn'd
On the blossom'd gable-ends
At the head of the village street,
Whom but Maud should I meet? 200
And she touch'd my hand with a smile so sweet,
She made me divine amends
For a courtesy not return'd.

III

And thus a delicate spark
Of glowing and growing light
Thro' the livelong hours of the dark
Kept itself warm in the heart of my dreams,

Ready to burst in a colour'd flame;
Till at last when the morning came
210 In a cloud, it faded, and seems
But an ashen-gray delight.

IV

What if with her sunny hair,
And smile as sunny as cold,
She meant to weave me a snare
Of some coquettish deceit,
Cleopatra-like as of old
To entangle me when we met,
To have her lion roll in a silken net
And fawn at a victor's feet.

V

220 Ah, what shall I be at fifty
Should Nature keep me alive,
If I find the world so bitter
When I am but twenty-five?
Yet, if she were not a cheat,
If Maud were all that she seem'd,
And her smile were all that I dream'd,
Then the world were not so bitter
But a smile could make it sweet.

VI

What if tho' her eye seem'd full
230 Of a kind intent to me,
What if that dandy-despot, he,
That jewell'd mass of millinery,
That oil'd and curl'd Assyrian Bull
Smelling of musk and of insolence,
Her brother, from whom I keep aloof,
Who wants the finer politic sense
To mask, tho' but in his own behoof,
With a glassy smile his brutal scorn –

What if he had told her yestermorn
How prettily for his own sweet sake 240
A face of tenderness might be feign'd,
And a moist mirage in desert eyes,
That so, when the rotten hustings shake
In another month to his brazen lies,
A wretched vote may be gain'd.

VII

For a raven ever croaks, at my side,
Keep watch and ward, keep watch and ward,
Or thou wilt prove their tool.
Yea, too, myself from myself I guard,
For often a man's own angry pride 250
Is cap and bells for a fool.

VIII

Perhaps the smile and tender tone
Came out of her pitying womanhood,
For am I not, am I not, here alone
So many a summer since she died,
My mother, who was so gentle and good?
Living alone in an empty house,
Here half-hid in the gleaming wood,
Where I hear the dead at midday moan,
And the shrieking rush of the wainscot mouse, 260
And my own sad name in corners cried,
When the shiver of dancing leaves is thrown
About its echoing chambers wide,
Till a morbid hate and horror have grown
Of a world in which I have hardly mixt,
And a morbid eating lichen fixt
On a heart half-turn'd to stone.

IX

O heart of stone, are you flesh, and caught
By that you swore to withstand?

270 For what was it else within me wrought
But, I fear, the new strong wine of love,
That made my tongue so stammer and trip
When I saw the treasured splendour, her hand,
Come sliding out of her sacred glove,
And the sunlight broke from her lip?

X

I have play'd with her when a child;
She remembers it now we meet.
Ah well, well, well, I *may* be beguiled
By some coquettish deceit.
280 Yet, if she were not a cheat,
If Maud were all that she seem'd,
And her smile had all that I dream'd,
Then the world were not so bitter
But a smile could make it sweet.

VII

I

Did I hear it half in a doze
Long since, I know not where?
Did I dream it an hour ago,
When asleep in this arm-chair?

II

Men were drinking together,
290 Drinking and talking of me;
'Well, if it prove a girl, the boy
Will have plenty: so let it be.'

III

Is it an echo of something
Read with a boy's delight,
Viziers nodding together
In some Arabian night?

IV

Strange, that I hear two men,
  Somewhere, talking of me;
'Well, if it prove a girl, my boy
  Will have plenty: so let it be.' 300

VIII

She came to the village church,
And sat by a pillar alone;
An angel watching an urn
Wept over her, carved in stone;
And once, but once, she lifted her eyes,
And suddenly, sweetly, strangely blush'd
To find they were met by my own;
And suddenly, sweetly, my heart beat stronger
And thicker, until I heard no longer
The snowy-banded, dilettante, 310
Delicate-handed priest intone;
And thought, is it pride, and mused and sigh'd
'No surely, now it cannot be pride.'

IX

I was walking a mile,
More than a mile from the shore,
The sun look'd out with a smile
Betwixt the cloud and the moor,
And riding at set of day
Over the dark moor land,
Rapidly riding far away, 320
She waved to me with her hand.
There were two at her side,
Something flash'd in the sun,
Down by the hill I saw them ride,
In a moment they were gone:
Like a sudden spark

Struck vainly in the night,
Then returns the dark
With no more hope of light.

X

I

330 Sick, am I sick of a jealous dread?
Was not one of the two at her side
This new-made lord, whose splendour plucks
The slavish hat from the villager's head?
Whose old grandfather has lately died,
Gone to a blacker pit, for whom
Grimy nakedness dragging his trucks
And laying his trams in a poison'd gloom
Wrought, till he crept from a gutted mine
Master of half a servile shire,
340 And left his coal all turn'd into gold
To a grandson, first of his noble line,
Rich in the grace all women desire,
Strong in the power that all men adore,
And simper and set their voices lower,
And soften as if to a girl, and hold
Awe-stricken breaths at a work divine,
Seeing his gewgaw castle shine,
New as his title, built last year,
There amid perky larches and pine,
350 And over the sullen-purple moor
(Look at it) pricking a cockney ear.

II

What, has he found my jewel out?
For one of the two that rode at her side
Bound for the Hall, I am sure was he:
Bound for the Hall, and I think for a bride.
Blithe would her brother's acceptance be.
Maud could be gracious too, no doubt

To a lord, a captain, a padded shape,
A bought commission, a waxen face,
A rabbit mouth that is ever agape – 360
Bought? what is it he cannot buy?
And therefore splenetic, personal, base,
A wounded thing with a rancorous cry,
At war with myself and a wretched race,
Sick, sick to the heart of life, am I.

III

Last week came one to the county town,
To preach our poor little army down,
And play the game of the despot kings,
Tho' the state has done it and thrice as well:
This broad-brimm'd hawker of holy things, 370
Whose ear is cramm'd with his cotton, and rings
Even in dreams to the chink of his pence,
This huckster put down war! can he tell
Whether war be a cause or a consequence?
Put down the passions that make earth Hell!
Down with ambition, avarice, pride,
Jealousy, down! cut off from the mind
The bitter springs of anger and fear;
Down too, down at your own fireside,
With the evil tongue and the evil ear, 380
For each is at war with mankind.

IV

I wish I could hear again
The chivalrous battle-song
That she warbled alone in her joy!
I might persuade myself then
She would not do herself this great wrong,
To take a wanton dissolute boy
For a man and leader of men.

V

Ah God, for a man with heart, head, hand,
390 Like some of the simple great ones gone
For ever and ever by,
One still strong man in a blatant land,
Whatever they call him, what care I,
Aristocrat, democrat, autocrat – one
Who can rule and dare not lie.

VI

And ah for a man to arise in me,
That the man I am may cease to be!

XI

I

O let the solid ground
 Not fail beneath my feet
400 Before my life has found
 What some have found so sweet;
Then let come what come may,
What matter if I go mad,
I shall have had my day.

II

Let the sweet heavens endure,
 Not close and darken above me
Before I am quite quite sure
 That there is one to love me;
Then let come what come may
410 To a life that has been so sad,
I shall have had my day.

XII

I

Birds in the high Hall-garden
  When twilight was falling,
Maud, Maud, Maud, Maud,
  They were crying and calling.

II

Where was Maud? in our wood;
  And I, who else, was with her,
Gathering woodland lilies,
  Myriads blow together.

III

Birds in our wood sang 420
  Ringing thro' the valleys,
Maud is here, here, here
  In among the lilies.

IV

I kiss'd her slender hand,
  She took the kiss sedately;
Maud is not seventeen,
  But she is tall and stately.

V

I to cry out on pride
  Who have won her favour!
O Maud were sure of Heaven 430
  If lowliness could save her.

VI

I know the way she went
  Home with her maiden posy,
For her feet have touch'd the meadows
  And left the daisies rosy.

VII

Birds in the high Hall-garden
  Were crying and calling to her,
Where is Maud, Maud, Maud?
  One is come to woo her.

VIII

440 Look, a horse at the door,
  And little King Charley snarling,
Go back, my lord, across the moor,
  You are not her darling.

XIII

I

Scorn'd, to be scorn'd by one that I scorn,
Is that a matter to make me fret?
That a calamity hard to be borne?
Well, he may live to hate me yet.
Fool that I am to be vext with his pride!
I past him, I was crossing his lands;
450 He stood on the path a little aside;
His face, as I grant, in spite of spite,
Has a broad-blown comeliness, red and white,
And six feet two, as I think, he stands;
But his essences turn'd the live air sick,
And barbarous opulence jewel-thick
Sunn'd itself on his breast and his hands.

II

Who shall call me ungentle, unfair,
I long'd so heartily then and there
To give him the grasp of fellowship;
460 But while I past he was humming an air,
Stopt, and then with a riding-whip
Leisurely tapping a glossy boot,
And curving a contumelious lip,

Gorgonised me from head to foot
With a stony British stare.

III

Why sits he here in his father's chair?
That old man never comes to his place:
Shall I believe him ashamed to be seen?
For only once, in the village street,
Last year, I caught a glimpse of his face, 470
A gray old wolf and a lean.
Scarcely, now, would I call him a cheat;
For then, perhaps, as a child of deceit,
She might by a true descent be untrue;
And Maud is as true as Maud is sweet:
Tho' I fancy her sweetness only due
To the sweeter blood by the other side;
Her mother has been a thing complete,
However she came to be so allied.
And fair without, faithful within, 480
Maud to him is nothing akin:
Some peculiar mystic grace
Made her only the child of her mother,
And heap'd the whole inherited sin
On that huge scapegoat of the race,
All, all upon the brother.

IV

Peace, angry spirit, and let him be!
Has not his sister smiled on me?

XIV

I

Maud has a garden of roses
And lilies fair on a lawn; 490
There she walks in her state
And tends upon bed and bower,

And thither I climb'd at dawn
And stood by her garden-gate;
A lion ramps at the top,
He is claspt by a passion-flower.

II

Maud's own little oak-room
(Which Maud, like a precious stone
Set in the heart of the carven gloom,
500 Lights with herself, when alone
She sits by her music and books
And her brother lingers late
With a roystering company) looks
Upon Maud's own garden-gate:
And I thought as I stood, if a hand, as white
As ocean-foam in the moon, were laid
On the hasp of the window, and my Delight
Had a sudden desire, like a glorious ghost, to glide,
Like a beam of the seventh Heaven, down to my side,
510 There were but a step to be made.

III

The fancy flatter'd my mind,
And again seem'd overbold;
Now I thought that she cared for me,
Now I thought she was kind
Only because she was cold.

IV

I heard no sound where I stood
But the rivulet on from the lawn
Running down to my own dark wood;
Or the voice of the long sea-wave as it swell'd
520 Now and then in the dim-gray dawn;
But I look'd, and round, all round the house I beheld
The death-white curtain drawn;

Felt a horror over me creep,
Prickle my skin and catch my breath,
Knew that the death-white curtain meant but sleep,
Yet I shudder'd and thought like a fool of the sleep of death.

XV

So dark a mind within me dwells,
  And I make myself such evil cheer,
That if *I* be dear to some one else,
  Then some one else may have much to fear; 530
But if *I* be dear to some one else,
  Then I should be to myself more dear.
Shall I not take care of all that I think,
Yea ev'n of wretched meat and drink,
If I be dear,
If I be dear to some one else.

XVI

I

This lump of earth has left his estate
The lighter by the loss of his weight;
And so that he find what he went to seek,
And fulsome Pleasure clog him, and drown 540
His heart in the gross mud-honey of town,
He may stay for a year who has gone for a week:
But this is the day when I must speak,
And I see my Oread coming down,
O this is the day!
O beautiful creature, what am I
That I dare to look her way;
Think I may hold dominion sweet,
Lord of the pulse that is lord of her breast,
And dream of her beauty with tender dread, 550
From the delicate Arab arch of her feet
To the grace that, bright and light as the crest

Of a peacock, sits on her shining head,
And she knows it not: O, if she knew it,
To know her beauty might half undo it.
I know it the one bright thing to save
My yet young life in the wilds of Time,
Perhaps from madness, perhaps from crime,
Perhaps from a selfish grave.

II

560 What, if she be fasten'd to this fool lord,
Dare I bid her abide by her word?
Should I love her so well if she
Had given her word to a thing so low?
Shall I love her as well if she
Can break her word were it even for me?
I trust that it is not so.

III

Catch not my breath, O clamorous heart,
Let not my tongue be a thrall to my eye,
For I must tell her before we part,
570 I must tell her, or die.

XVII

Go not, happy day,
From the shining fields,
Go not, happy day,
Till the maiden yields.
Rosy is the West,
Rosy is the South,
Roses are her cheeks,
And a rose her mouth.
When the happy Yes
580 Falters from her lips,
Pass and blush the news
Over glowing ships;

Over blowing seas,
  Over seas at rest,
Pass the happy news,
  Blush it thro' the West;
Till the red man dance
  By his red cedar-tree,
And the red man's babe
  Leap, beyond the sea. 590
Blush from West to East,
  Blush from East to West,
Till the West is East,
  Blush it thro' the West.
Rosy is the West,
  Rosy is the South,
Roses are her cheeks,
  And a rose her mouth.

XVIII

I

I have led her home, my love, my only friend.
There is none like her, none. 600
And never yet so warmly ran my blood
And sweetly, on and on
Calming itself to the long-wish'd-for end,
Full to the banks, close on the promised good.

II

None like her, none.
Just now the dry-tongued laurels' pattering talk
Seem'd her light foot along the garden walk,
And shook my heart to think she comes once more;
But even then I heard her close the door,
The gates of Heaven are closed, and she is gone. 610

III

There is none like her, none.
Nor will be when our summers have deceased.
O, art thou sighing for Lebanon
In the long breeze that streams to thy delicious East,
Sighing for Lebanon,
Dark cedar, tho' thy limbs have here increased,
Upon a pastoral slope as fair,
And looking to the South, and fed
With honey'd rain and delicate air,
620 And haunted by the starry head
Of her whose gentle will has changed my fate,
And made my life a perfumed altar-flame;
And over whom thy darkness must have spread
With such delight as theirs of old, thy great
Forefathers of the thornless garden, there
Shadowing the snow-limb'd Eve from whom she came.

IV

Here will I lie, while these long branches sway,
And you fair stars that crown a happy day
Go in and out as if at merry play,
630 Who am no more so all forlorn,
As when it seem'd far better to be born
To labour and the mattock-harden'd hand,
Than nursed at ease and brought to understand
A sad astrology, the boundless plan
That makes you tyrants in your iron skies,
Innumerable, pitiless, passionless eyes,
Cold fires, yet with power to burn and brand
His nothingness into man.

V

But now shine on, and what care I,
640 Who in this stormy gulf have found a pearl
The countercharm of space and hollow sky,

And do accept my madness, and would die
To save from some slight shame one simple girl.

VI

Would die; for sullen-seeming Death may give
More life to Love than is or ever was
In our low world, where yet 'tis sweet to live.
Let no one ask me how it came to pass;
It seems that I am happy, that to me
A livelier emerald twinkles in the grass,
A purer sapphire melts into the sea. 650

VII

Not die; but live a life of truest breath,
And teach true life to fight with mortal wrongs.
O, why should Love, like men in drinking-songs,
Spice his fair banquet with the dust of death?
Make answer, Maud my bliss,
Maud made my Maud by that long loving kiss,
Life of my life, wilt thou not answer this?
'The dusky strand of Death inwoven here
With dear Love's tie, makes Love himself more dear.'

VIII

Is that enchanted moan only the swell 660
Of the long waves that roll in yonder bay?
And hark the clock within, the silver knell
Of twelve sweet hours that past in bridal white,
And died to live, long as my pulses play;
But now by this my love has closed her sight
And given false death her hand, and stol'n away
To dreamful wastes where footless fancies dwell
Among the fragments of the golden day.
May nothing there her maiden grace affright!
Dear heart, I feel with thee the drowsy spell. 670
My bride to be, my evermore delight,
My own heart's heart, my ownest own, farewell;

It is but for a little space I go:
And ye meanwhile far over moor and fell
Beat to the noiseless music of the night!
Has our whole earth gone nearer to the glow
Of your soft splendours that you look so bright?
I have climb'd nearer out of lonely Hell.
Beat, happy stars, timing with things below,
680 Beat with my heart more blest than heart can tell,
Blest, but for some dark undercurrent woe
That seems to draw – but it shall not be so:
Let all be well, be well.

XIX

I

Her brother is coming back to-night,
Breaking up my dream of delight.

II

My dream? do I dream of bliss?
I have walk'd awake with Truth.
O when did a morning shine
So rich in atonement as this
690 For my dark-dawning youth,
Darken'd watching a mother decline
And that dead man at her heart and mine:
For who was left to watch her but I?
Yet so did I let my freshness die.

III

I trust that I did not talk
To gentle Maud in our walk
(For often in lonely wanderings
I have cursed him even to lifeless things)
But I trust that I did not talk,
700 Not touch on her father's sin:
I am sure I did but speak

Of my mother's faded cheek
When it slowly grew so thin,
That I felt she was slowly dying
Vext with lawyers and harass'd with debt:
For how often I caught her with eyes all wet,
Shaking her head at her son and sighing
A world of trouble within!

IV

And Maud too, Maud was moved
To speak of the mother she loved 710
As one scarce less forlorn,
Dying abroad and it seems apart
From him who had ceased to share her heart,
And ever mourning over the feud,
The household Fury sprinkled with blood
By which our houses are torn:
How strange was what she said,
When only Maud and the brother
Hung over her dying bed –
That Maud's dark father and mine 720
Had bound us one to the other,
Betrothed us over their wine,
On the day when Maud was born;
Seal'd her mine from her first sweet breath.
Mine, mine by a right, from birth till death.
Mine, mine – our fathers have sworn.

V

But the true blood spilt had in it a heat
To dissolve the precious seal on a bond,
That, if left uncancell'd, had been so sweet:
And none of us thought of a something beyond, 730
A desire that awoke in the heart of the child,
As it were a duty done to the tomb,
To be friends for her sake, to be reconciled;
And I was cursing them and my doom,

And letting a dangerous thought run wild
While often abroad in the fragrant gloom
Of foreign churches – I see her there,
Bright English lily, breathing a prayer
To be friends, to be reconciled!

VI

740 But then what a flint is he!
Abroad, at Florence, at Rome,
I find whenever she touch'd on me
This brother had laugh'd her down,
And at last, when each came home,
He had darken'd into a frown,
Chid her, and forbid her to speak
To me, her friend of the years before;
And this was what had redden'd her cheek
When I bow'd to her on the moor.

VII

750 Yet Maud, altho' not blind
To the faults of his heart and mind,
I see she cannot but love him,
And says he is rough but kind,
And wishes me to approve him,
And tells me, when she lay
Sick once, with a fear of worse,
That he left his wine and horses and play,
Sat with her, read to her, night and day,
And tended her like a nurse.

VIII

760 Kind? but the deathbed desire
Spurn'd by this heir of the liar –
Rough but kind? yet I know
He has plotted against me in this,
That he plots against me still.
Kind to Maud? that were not amiss.

Well, rough but kind; why let it be so:
For shall not Maud have her will?

IX

For, Maud, so tender and true,
As long as my life endures
I feel I shall owe you a debt, 770
That I never can hope to pay;
And if ever I should forget
That I owe this debt to you
And for your sweet sake to yours;
O then, what then shall I say? –
If ever I *should* forget,
May God make me more wretched
Than ever I have been yet!

X

So now I have sworn to bury
All this dead body of hate, 780
I feel so free and so clear
By the loss of that dead weight,
That I should grow light-headed, I fear,
Fantastically merry;
But that her brother comes, like a blight
On my fresh hope, to the Hall to-night.

XX

I

Strange, that I felt so gay,
Strange, that *I* tried to-day
To beguile her melancholy;
The Sultan, as we name him, – 790
She did not wish to blame him –
But he vext her and perplext her
With his worldly talk and folly:
Was it gentle to reprove her

For stealing out of view
From a little lazy lover
Who but claims her as his due?
Or for chilling his caresses
By the coldness of her manners,
800 Nay, the plainness of her dresses?
Now I know her but in two,
Nor can pronounce upon it
If one should ask me whether
The habit, hat, and feather,
Or the frock and gipsy bonnet
Be the neater and completer;
For nothing can be sweeter
Than maiden Maud in either.

II

But to-morrow, if we live,
810 Our ponderous squire will give
A grand political dinner
To half the squirelings near;
And Maud will wear her jewels,
And the bird of prey will hover,
And the titmouse hope to win her
With his chirrup at her ear.

III

A grand political dinner
To the men of many acres,
A gathering of the Tory,
820 A dinner and then a dance
For the maids and marriage-makers,
And every eye but mine will glance
At Maud in all her glory.

IV

For I am not invited,
But, with the Sultan's pardon,

I am all as well delighted,
For I know her own rose-garden,
And mean to linger in it
Till the dancing will be over;
And then, oh then, come out to me 830
For a minute, but for a minute,
Come out to your own true lover,
That your true lover may see
Your glory also, and render
All homage to his own darling,
Queen Maud in all her splendour.

XXI

Rivulet crossing my ground,
And bringing me down from the Hall
This garden-rose that I found,
Forgetful of Maud and me, 840
And lost in trouble and moving round
Here at the head of a tinkling fall,
And trying to pass to the sea;
O Rivulet, born at the Hall,
My Maud has sent it by thee
(If I read her sweet will right)
On a blushing mission to me,
Saying in odour and colour, 'Ah, be
Among the roses to-night.'

XXII

I

Come into the garden, Maud, 850
For the black bat, night, has flown,
Come into the garden, Maud,
I am here at the gate alone;
And the woodbine spices are wafted abroad,
And the musk of the rose is blown.

II

For a breeze of morning moves,
  And the planet of Love is on high,
Beginning to faint in the light that she loves
  On a bed of daffodil sky,
860 To faint in the light of the sun she loves,
  To faint in his light, and to die.

III

All night have the roses heard
  The flute, violin, bassoon;
All night has the casement jessamine stirr'd
  To the dancers dancing in tune;
Till a silence fell with the waking bird,
  And a hush with the setting moon.

IV

I said to the lily, 'There is but one
  With whom she has heart to be gay.
870 When will the dancers leave her alone?
  She is weary of dance and play.'
Now half to the setting moon are gone,
  And half to the rising day;
Low on the sand and loud on the stone
  The last wheel echoes away.

V

I said to the rose, 'The brief night goes
  In babble and revel and wine.
O young lord-lover, what sighs are those,
  For one that will never be thine?
880 But mine, but mine,' so I sware to the rose,
  'For ever and ever, mine.'

VI

And the soul of the rose went into my blood,
  As the music clash'd in the hall;

And long by the garden lake I stood,
For I heard your rivulet fall
From the lake to the meadow and on to the wood,
Our wood, that is dearer than all;

VII

From the meadow your walks have left so sweet
That whenever a March-wind sighs
He sets the jewel-print of your feet 890
In violets blue as your eyes,
To the woody hollows in which we meet
And the valleys of Paradise.

VIII

The slender acacia would not shake
One long milk-bloom on the tree;
The white lake-blossom fell into the lake
As the pimpernel dozed on the lea;
But the rose was awake all night for your sake,
Knowing your promise to me;
The lilies and roses were all awake, 900
They sigh'd for the dawn and thee.

IX

Queen rose of the rosebud garden of girls,
Come hither, the dances are done,
In gloss of satin and glimmer of pearls,
Queen lily and rose in one;
Shine out, little head, sunning over with curls,
To the flowers, and be their sun.

X

There has fallen a splendid tear
From the passion-flower at the gate.
She is coming, my dove, my dear; 910
She is coming, my life, my fate;
…d rose cries, 'She is near, she is near;'

And the white rose weeps, 'She is late;'
The larkspur listens, 'I hear, I hear;'
And the lily whispers, 'I wait.'

XI

She is coming, my own, my sweet;
Were it ever so airy a tread,
My heart would hear her and beat,
Were it earth in an earthy bed;
920 My dust would hear her and beat,
Had I lain for a century dead;
Would start and tremble under her feet,
And blossom in purple and red.

PART II

I

I

'The fault was mine, the fault was mine' –
Why am I sitting here so stunn'd and still,
Plucking the harmless wild-flower on the hill? –
It is this guilty hand! –
And there rises ever a passionate cry
From underneath in the darkening land –
What is it, that has been done?
O dawn of Eden bright over earth and sky,
The fires of Hell brake out of thy rising sun,
10 The fires of Hell and of Hate;
For she, sweet soul, had hardly spoken a word,
When her brother ran in his rage to the gate,
He came with the babe-faced lord;
Heap'd on her terms of disgrace,
And while she wept, and I strove to be cool,
He fiercely gave me the lie,
Till I with as fierce an anger spoke,

And he struck me, madman, over the face,
Struck me before the languid fool,
Who was gaping and grinning by: 20
Struck for himself an evil stroke;
Wrought for his house an irredeemable woe;
For front to front in an hour we stood,
And a million horrible bellowing echoes broke
From the red-ribb'd hollow behind the wood,
And thunder'd up into Heaven the Christless code,
That must have life for a blow.
Ever and ever afresh they seem'd to grow.
Was it he lay there with a fading eye?
'The fault was mine,' he whisper'd, 'fly!' 30
Then glided out of the joyous wood
The ghastly Wraith of one that I know;
And there rang on a sudden a passionate cry,
A cry for a brother's blood:
It will ring in my heart and my ears, till I die, till I die.

II

Is it gone? my pulses beat –
What was it? a lying trick of the brain?
Yet I thought I saw her stand,
A shadow there at my feet,
High over the shadowy land. 40
It is gone; and the heavens fall in a gentle rain,
When they should burst and drown with deluging storms
The feeble vassals of wine and anger and lust,
The little hearts that know not how to forgive:
Arise, my God, and strike, for we hold Thee just,
Strike dead the whole weak race of venomous worms,
That sting each other here in the dust;
We are not worthy to live.

II

I

See what a lovely shell,
50 Small and pure as a pearl,
Lying close to my foot,
Frail, but a work divine,
Made so fairily well
With delicate spire and whorl,
How exquisitely minute,
A miracle of design!

II

What is it? a learned man
Could give it a clumsy name.
Let him name it who can,
60 The beauty would be the same.

III

The tiny cell is forlorn,
Void of the little living will
That made it stir on the shore.
Did he stand at the diamond door
Of his house in a rainbow frill?
Did he push, when he was uncurl'd,
A golden foot or a fairy horn
Thro' his dim water-world?

IV

Slight, to be crush'd with a tap
70 Of my finger-nail on the sand,
Small, but a work divine,
Frail, but of force to withstand,
Year upon year, the shock
Of cataract seas that snap
The three decker's oaken spine

Athwart the ledges of rock,
Here on the Breton strand!

V

Breton, not Briton; here
Like a shipwreck'd man on a coast
Of ancient fable and fear – 80
Plagued with a flitting to and fro,
A disease, a hard mechanic ghost
That never came from on high
Nor ever arose from below,
But only moves with the moving eye,
Flying along the land and the main –
Why should it look like Maud?
Am I to be overawed
By what I cannot but know
Is a juggle born of the brain? 90

VI

Back from the Breton coast,
Sick of a nameless fear,
Back to the dark sea-line
Looking, thinking of all I have lost;
An old song vexes my ear;
But that of Lamech is mine.

VII

For years, a measureless ill,
For years, for ever, to part –
But she, she would love me still;
And as long, O God, as she 100
Have a grain of love for me,
So long, no doubt, no doubt,
Shall I nurse in my dark heart,
However weary, a spark of will
Not to be trampled out.

VIII

Strange, that the mind, when fraught
With a passion so intense
One would think that it well
Might drown all life in the eye, –
110 That it should, by being so overwrought,
Suddenly strike on a sharper sense
For a shell, or a flower, little things
Which else would have been past by!
And now I remember, I,
When he lay dying there,
I noticed one of his many rings
(For he had many, poor worm) and thought
It is his mother's hair.

IX

Who knows if he be dead?
120 Whether I need have fled?
Am I guilty of blood?
However this may be,
Comfort her, comfort her, all things good,
While I am over the sea!
Let me and my passionate love go by,
But speak to her all things holy and high,
Whatever happen to me!
Me and my harmful love go by;
But come to her waking, find her asleep,
130 Powers of the height, Powers of the deep,
And comfort her tho' I die.

III

Courage, poor heart of stone!
I will not ask thee why
Thou canst not understand
That thou art left for ever alone:
Courage, poor stupid heart of stone. –

Or if I ask thee why,
Care not thou to reply:
She is but dead, and the time is at hand
When thou shalt more than die. 140

IV

I

O that 'twere possible
After long grief and pain
To find the arms of my true love
Round me once again!

II

When I was wont to meet her
In the silent woody places
By the home that gave me birth,
We stood tranced in long embraces
Mixt with kisses sweeter sweeter
Than anything on earth. 150

III

A shadow flits before me,
Not thou, but like to thee:
Ah Christ, that it were possible
For one short hour to see
The souls we loved, that they might tell us
What and where they be.

IV

It leads me forth at evening,
It lightly winds and steals
In a cold white robe before me,
When all my spirit reels 160
At the shouts, the leagues of lights,
And the roaring of the wheels.

V

Half the night I waste in sighs,
Half in dreams I sorrow after
The delight of early skies;
In a wakeful doze I sorrow
For the hand, the lips, the eyes,
For the meeting of the morrow,
The delight of happy laughter,
170 The delight of low replies.

VI

'Tis a morning pure and sweet,
And a dewy splendour falls
On the little flower that clings
To the turrets and the walls;
'Tis a morning pure and sweet,
And the light and shadow fleet;
She is walking in the meadow,
And the woodland echo rings;
In a moment we shall meet;
180 She is singing in the meadow
And the rivulet at her feet
Ripples on in light and shadow
To the ballad that she sings.

VII

Do I hear her sing as of old,
My bird with the shining head,
My own dove with the tender eye?
But there rings on a sudden a passionate cry,
There is some one dying or dead,
And a sullen thunder is roll'd;
190 For a tumult shakes the city,
And I wake, my dream is fled;
In the shuddering dawn, behold,
Without knowledge, without pity,

By the curtains of my bed
That abiding phantom cold.

VIII

Get thee hence, nor come again,
Mix not memory with doubt,
Pass, thou deathlike type of pain,
Pass and cease to move about!
'Tis the blot upon the brain 200
That *will* show itself without.

IX

Then I rise, the eavedrops fall,
And the yellow vapours choke
The great city sounding wide;
The day comes, a dull red ball
Wrapt in drifts of lurid smoke
On the misty river-tide.

X

Thro' the hubbub of the market
I steal, a wasted frame,
It crosses here, it crosses there, 210
Thro' all that crowd confused and loud,
The shadow still the same;
And on my heavy eyelids
My anguish hangs like shame.

XI

Alas for her that met me,
That heard me softly call,
Came glimmering thro' the laurels
At the quiet evenfall,
In the garden by the turrets
Of the old manorial hall. 220

XII

Would the happy spirit descend,
From the realms of light and song,
In the chamber or the street,
As she looks among the blest,
Should I fear to greet my friend
Or to say 'Forgive the wrong,'
Or to ask her, 'Take me, sweet,
To the regions of thy rest'?

XIII

But the broad light glares and beats,
230 And the shadow flits and fleets
And will not let me be;
And I loathe the squares and streets,
And the faces that one meets,
Hearts with no love for me:
Always I long to creep
Into some still cavern deep,
There to weep, and weep, and weep
My whole soul out to thee.

V

I

Dead, long dead,
240 Long dead!
And my heart is a handful of dust,
And the wheels go over my head,
And my bones are shaken with pain,
For into a shallow grave they are thrust,
Only a yard beneath the street,
And the hoofs of the horses beat, beat,
The hoofs of the horses beat,
Beat into my scalp and my brain,
With never an end to the stream of passing feet,
250 Driving, hurrying, marrying, burying,

Clamour and rumble, and ringing and clatter,
And here beneath it is all as bad,
For I thought the dead had peace, but it is not so;
To have no peace in the grave, is that not sad?
But up and down and to and fro,
Ever about me the dead men go;
And then to hear a dead man chatter
Is enough to drive one mad.

II

Wretchedest age, since Time began,
They cannot even bury a man; 260
And tho' we paid our tithes in the days that are gone,
Not a bell was rung, not a prayer was read;
It is that which makes us loud in the world of the dead;
There is none that does his work, not one;
A touch of their office might have sufficed,
But the churchmen fain would kill their church,
As the churches have kill'd their Christ.

III

See, there is one of us sobbing,
No limit to his distress;
And another, a lord of all things, praying 270
To his own great self, as I guess;
And another, a statesman there, betraying
His party-secret, fool, to the press;
And yonder a vile physician, blabbing
The case of his patient – all for what?
To tickle the maggot born in an empty head,
And wheedle a world that loves him not,
For it is but a world of the dead.

IV

Nothing but idiot gabble!
For the prophecy given of old 280
And then not understood,

Has come to pass as foretold;
Not let any man think for the public good,
But babble, merely for babble.
For I never whisper'd a private affair
Within the hearing of cat or mouse,
No, not to myself in the closet alone,
But I heard it shouted at once from the top of the house;
Everything came to be known.
,90 Who told *him* we were there?

V

Not that gray old wolf, for he came not back
From the wilderness, full of wolves, where he used to lie;
He has gather'd the bones for his o'ergrown whelp to crack;
Crack them now for yourself, and howl, and die.

VI

Prophet, curse me the blabbing lip,
And curse me the British vermin, the rat;
I know not whether he came in the Hanover ship,
But I know that he lies and listens mute
In an ancient mansion's crannies and holes:
oo Arsenic, arsenic, sure, would do it,
Except that now we poison our babes, poor souls!
It is all used up for that.

VII

Tell him now: she is standing here at my head;
Not beautiful now, not even kind;
He may take her now; for she never speaks her mind,
But is ever the one thing silent here.
She is not *of* us, as I divine;
She comes from another stiller world of the dead,
Stiller, not fairer than mine.

VIII

But I know where a garden grows, 310
Fairer than aught in the world beside,
All made up of the lily and rose
That blow by night, when the season is good,
To the sound of dancing music and flutes:
It is only flowers, they had no fruits,
And I almost fear they are not roses, but blood;
For the keeper was one, so full of pride,
He linkt a dead man there to a spectral bride;
For he, if he had not been a Sultan of brutes,
Would he have that hole in his side? 320

IX

But what will the old man say?
He laid a cruel snare in a pit
To catch a friend of mine one stormy day;
Yet now I could even weep to think of it;
For what will the old man say
When he comes to the second corpse in the pit?

X

Friend, to be struck by the public foe,
Then to strike him and lay him low,
That were a public merit, far,
Whatever the Quaker holds, from sin; 330
But the red life spilt for a private blow –
I swear to you, lawful and lawless war
Are scarcely even akin.

XI

O me, why have they not buried me deep enough?
Is it kind to have made me a grave so rough,
Me, that was never a quiet sleeper?
Maybe still I am but half-dead;
Then I cannot be wholly dumb;
I will cry to the steps above my head

340 And somebody, surely, some kind heart will come
To bury me, bury me
Deeper, ever so little deeper.

PART III

VI

I

My life has crept so long on a broken wing
Thro' cells of madness, haunts of horror and fear,
That I come to be grateful at last for a little thing:
My mood is changed, for it fell at a time of year
When the face of night is fair on the dewy downs,
And the shining daffodil dies, and the Charioteer
And starry Gemini hang like glorious crowns
Over Orion's grave low down in the west,
That like a silent lightning under the stars
10 She seem'd to divide in a dream from a band of the blest,
And spoke of a hope for the world in the coming wars –
'And in that hope, dear soul, let trouble have rest,
Knowing I tarry for thee,' and pointed to Mars
As he glow'd like a ruddy shield on the Lion's breast.

II

And it was but a dream, yet it yielded a dear delight
To have look'd, tho' but in a dream, upon eyes so fair,
That had been in a weary world my one thing bright;
And it was but a dream, yet it lighten'd my despair
When I thought that a war would arise in defence of the right,
20 That an iron tyranny now should bend or cease,
The glory of manhood stand on his ancient height,
Nor Britain's one sole God be the millionaire:
No more shall commerce be all in all, and Peace
Pipe on her pastoral hillock a languid note,
And watch her harvest ripen, her herd increase,

Nor the cannon-bullet rust on a slothful shore,
And the cobweb woven across the cannon's throat
Shall shake its threaded tears in the wind no more.

III

And as months ran on and rumour of battle grew,
'It is time, it is time, O passionate heart,' said I 30
(For I cleaved to a cause that I felt to be pure and true),
'It is time, O passionate heart and morbid eye,
That old hysterical mock-disease should die.'
And I stood on a giant deck and mix'd my breath
With a loyal people shouting a battle cry,
Till I saw the dreary phantom arise and fly
Far into the North, and battle, and seas of death.

IV

Let it go or stay, so I wake to the higher aims
Of a land that has lost for a little her lust of gold,
And love of a peace that was full of wrongs and shames, 40
Horrible, hateful, monstrous, not to be told;
And hail once more to the banner of battle unroll'd!
Tho' many a light shall darken, and many shall weep
For those that are crush'd in the clash of jarring claims,
Yet God's just wrath shall be wreak'd on a giant liar;
And many a darkness into the light shall leap,
And shine in the sudden making of splendid names,
And noble thought be freër under the sun,
And the heart of a people beat with one desire;
For the peace, that I deem'd no peace, is over and done, 50
And now by the side of the Black and the Baltic deep,
And deathful-grinning mouths of the fortress, flames
The blood-red blossom of war with a heart of fire.

V

Let it flame or fade, and the war roll down like a wind,
We have proved we have hearts in a cause, we are noble still,
And myself have awaked, as it seems, to the better mind;

It is better to fight for the good than to rail at the ill;
I have felt with my native land, I am one with my kind,
I embrace the purpose of God, and the doom assign'd.

Ode on the Death of the Duke of Wellington

PUBLISHED IN 1852

I

Bury the Great Duke
With an empire's lamentation,
Let us bury the Great Duke
To the noise of the mourning of a mighty nation,
Mourning when their leaders fall,
Warriors carry the warrior's pall,
And sorrow darkens hamlet and hall.

II

Where shall we lay the man whom we deplore?
Here, in streaming London's central roar.
10 Let the sound of those he wrought for,
And the feet of those he fought for,
Echo round his bones for evermore.

III

Lead out the pageant: sad and slow,
As fits an universal woe,
Let the long long procession go,
And let the sorrowing crowd about it grow,
And let the mournful martial music blow;
The last great Englishman is low.

IV

Mourn, for to us he seems the last,
Remembering all his greatness in the Past. 20
No more in soldier fashion will he greet
With lifted hand the gazer in the street.
O friends, our chief state-oracle is mute:
Mourn for the man of long-enduring blood,
The statesman-warrior, moderate, resolute,
Whole in himself, a common good.
Mourn for the man of amplest influence,
Yet clearest of ambitious crime,
Our greatest yet with least pretence,
Great in council and great in war, 30
Foremost captain of his time,
Rich in saving common-sense,
And, as the greatest only are,
In his simplicity sublime.
O good gray head which all men knew,
O voice from which their omens all men drew,
O iron nerve to true occasion true,
O fall'n at length that tower of strength
Which stood four-square to all the winds that blew!
Such was he whom we deplore. 40
The long self-sacrifice of life is o'er.
The great World-victor's victor will be seen no more.

V

All is over and done:
Render thanks to the Giver,
England, for thy son.
Let the bell be toll'd.
Render thanks to the Giver,
And render him to the mould.
Under the cross of gold
That shines over city and river, 50
There he shall rest for ever
Among the wise and the bold.

Let the bell be toll'd:
And a reverent people behold
The towering car, the sable steeds:
Bright let it be with its blazon'd deeds,
Dark in its funeral fold.
Let the bell be toll'd:
And a deeper knell in the heart be knoll'd;
60 And the sound of the sorrowing anthem roll'd
Thro' the dome of the golden cross;
And the volleying cannon thunder his loss;
He knew their voices of old.
For many a time in many a clime
His captain's-ear has heard them boom
Bellowing victory, bellowing doom:
When he with those deep voices wrought,
Guarding realms and kings from shame;
With those deep voices our dead captain taught
70 The tyrant, and asserts his claim
In that dread sound to the great name,
Which he has worn so pure of blame,
In praise and in dispraise the same,
A man of well-attemper'd frame.
O civic muse, to such a name,
To such a name for ages long,
To such a name,
Preserve a broad approach of fame,
And ever-echoing avenues of song.

VI

80 Who is he that cometh, like an honour'd guest,
With banner and with music, with soldier and with priest,
With a nation weeping, and breaking on my rest?
Mighty Seaman, this is he
Was great by land as thou by sea.
Thine island loves thee well, thou famous man,
The greatest sailor since our world began.
Now, to the roll of muffled drums,

To thee the greatest soldier comes;
For this is he
Was great by land as thou by sea; 90
His foes were thine; he kept us free;
O give him welcome, this is he
Worthy of our gorgeous rites,
And worthy to be laid by thee;
For this is England's greatest son,
He that gain'd a hundred fights,
Nor ever lost an English gun;
This is he that far away
Against the myriads of Assaye
Clash'd with his fiery few and won; 100
And underneath another sun,
Warring on a later day,
Round affrighted Lisbon drew
The treble works, the vast designs
Of his labour'd rampart-lines,
Where he greatly stood at bay,
Whence he issued forth anew,
And ever great and greater grew,
Beating from the wasted vines
Back to France her banded swarms, 110
Back to France with countless blows,
Till o'er the hills her eagles flew
Beyond the Pyrenean pines,
Follow'd up in valley and glen
With blare of bugle, clamour of men,
Roll of cannon and clash of arms,
And England pouring on her foes.
Such a war had such a close.
Again their ravening eagle rose
In anger, wheel'd on Europe-shadowing wings, 120
And barking for the thrones of kings;
Till one that sought but Duty's iron crown
On that loud sabbath shook the spoiler down;
A day of onsets of despair!

Dash'd on every rocky square
Their surging charges foam'd themselves away;
Last, the Prussian trumpet blew;
Thro' the long-tormented air
Heaven flash'd a sudden jubilant ray,
130 And down we swept and charged and overthrew.
So great a soldier taught us there,
What long-enduring hearts could do
In that world-earthquake, Waterloo!
Mighty Seaman, tender and true,
And pure as he from taint of craven guile,
O saviour of the silver-coasted isle,
O shaker of the Baltic and the Nile,
If aught of things that here befall
Touch a spirit among things divine,
140 If love of country move thee there at all,
Be glad, because his bones are laid by thine!
And thro' the centuries let a people's voice
In full acclaim,
A people's voice,
The proof and echo of all human fame,
A people's voice, when they rejoice
At civic revel and pomp and game,
Attest their great commander's claim
With honour, honour, honour, honour to him,
150 Eternal honour to his name.

VII

A people's voice! we are a people yet.
Tho' all men else their nobler dreams forget,
Confused by brainless mobs and lawless Powers;
Thank Him who isled us here, and roughly set
His Briton in blown seas and storming showers,
We have a voice, with which to pay the debt,
Of boundless love and reverence and regret
To those great men who fought, and kept it ours.
And keep it ours, O God, from brute control;

O Statesmen, guard us, guard the eye, the soul 160
Of Europe, keep our noble England whole,
And save the one true seed of freedom sown
Betwixt a people and their ancient throne,
That sober freedom out of which there springs
Our loyal passion for our temperate kings;
For, saving that, ye help to save mankind
Till public wrong be crumbled into dust,
And drill the raw world for the march of mind,
Till crowds at length be sane and crowns be just.
But wink no more in slothful overtrust. 170
Remember him who led your hosts;
He bad you guard the sacred coasts.
Your cannons moulder on the seaward wall;
His voice is silent in your council-hall
For ever; and whatever tempests lour
For ever silent; even if they broke
In thunder, silent; yet remember all
He spoke among you, and the Man who spoke;
Who never sold the truth to serve the hour,
Nor palter'd with Eternal God for power; 180
Who let the turbid streams of rumour flow
Thro' either babbling world of high and low;
Whose life was work, whose language rife
With rugged maxims hewn from life;
Who never spoke against a foe;
Whose eighty winters freeze with one rebuke
All great self-seekers trampling on the right:
Truth-teller was our England's Alfred named;
Truth-lover was our English Duke;
Whatever record leap to light 190
He never shall be shamed.

VIII

Lo, the leader in these glorious wars
Now to glorious burial slowly borne,
Follow'd by the brave of other lands,

He, on whom from both her open hands
Lavish Honour shower'd all her stars,
And affluent Fortune emptied all her horn.
Yea, let all good things await
Him who cares not to be great,
200 But as he saves or serves the state.
Not once or twice in our rough island-story,
The path of duty was the way to glory:
He that walks it, only thirsting
For the right, and learns to deaden
Love of self, before his journey closes,
He shall find the stubborn thistle bursting
Into glossy purples, which outredden
All voluptuous garden-roses.
Not once or twice in our fair island-story,
210 The path of duty was the way to glory:
He, that ever following her commands,
On with toil of heart and knees and hands,
Thro' the long gorge to the far light has won
His path upward, and prevail'd,
Shall find the toppling crags of Duty scaled
Are close upon the shining table-lands
To which our God Himself is moon and sun.
Such was he: his work is done.
But while the races of mankind endure,
220 Let his great example stand
Colossal, seen of every land,
And keep the soldier firm, the statesman pure:
Till in all lands and thro' all human story
The path of duty be the way to glory:
And let the land whose hearths he saved from shame
For many and many an age proclaim
At civic revel and pomp and game,
And when the long-illumined cities flame,
Their ever-loyal iron leader's fame,
230 With honour, honour, honour, honour to him,
Eternal honour to his name.

IX

Peace, his triumph will be sung
By some yet unmoulded tongue
Far on in summers that we shall not see:
Peace, it is a day of pain
For one about whose patriarchal knee
Late the little children clung:
O peace, it is a day of pain
For one, upon whose hand and heart and brain
Once the weight and fate of Europe hung. 240
Ours the pain, be his the gain!
More than is of man's degree
Must be with us, watching here
At this, our great solemnity.
Whom we see not we revere;
We revere, and we refrain
From talk of battles loud and vain,
And brawling memories all too free
For such a wise humility
As befits a solemn fane: 250
We revere, and while we hear
The tides of Music's golden sea
Setting toward eternity,
Uplifted high in heart and hope are we,
Until we doubt not that for one so true
There must be other nobler work to do
Than when he fought at Waterloo,
And Victor he must ever be.
For tho' the Giant Ages heave the hill
And break the shore, and evermore 260
Make and break, and work their will;
Tho' world on world in myriad myriads roll
Round us, each with different powers,
And other forms of life than ours,
What know we greater than the soul?
On God and Godlike men we build our trust.
Hush, the Dead March wails in the people's ears:

The dark crowd moves, and there are sobs and tears:
The black earth yawns: the mortal disappears;
270 Ashes to ashes, dust to dust;
He is gone who seem'd so great. –
Gone; but nothing can bereave him
Of the force he made his own
Being here, and we believe him
Something far advanced in State,
And that he wears a truer crown
Than any wreath that man can weave him.
Speak no more of his renown,
Lay your earthly fancies down,
280 And in the vast cathedral leave him.
God accept him, Christ receive him.

1852

To the Rev. F. D. Maurice

Come, when no graver cares employ,
Godfather, come and see your boy:
  Your presence will be sun in winter,
Making the little one leap for joy.

For, being of that honest few,
Who give the Fiend himself his due,
  Should eighty-thousand college-councils
Thunder 'Anathema,' friend, at you;

Should all our churchmen foam in spite
10 At you, so careful of the right,
  Yet one lay-hearth would give you welcome
(Take it and come) to the Isle of Wight;

Where, far from noise and smoke of town,
I watch the twilight falling brown
  All round a careless-order'd garden
Close to the ridge of a noble down.

You'll have no scandal while you dine,
But honest talk and wholesome wine,
  And only hear the magpie gossip
Garrulous under a roof of pine: 20

For groves of pine on either hand,
To break the blast of winter, stand;
  And further on, the hoary Channel
Tumbles a billow on chalk and sand;

Where, if below the milky steep
Some ship of battle slowly creep,
  And on thro' zones of light and shadow
Glimmer away to the lonely deep,

We might discuss the Northern sin
Which made a selfish war begin; 30
  Dispute the claims, arrange the chances;
Emperor, Ottoman, which shall win:

Or whether war's avenging rod
Shall lash all Europe into blood;
  Till you should turn to dearer matters,
Dear to the man that is dear to God;

How best to help the slender store,
How mend the dwellings, of the poor;
  How gain in life, as life advances,
Valour and charity more and more. 40

Come, Maurice, come: the lawn as yet
Is hoar with rime, or spongy-wet;
  But when the wreath of March has blossom'd,
Crocus, anemone, violet,

Or later, pay one visit here,
For those are few we hold as dear;
Nor pay but one, but come for many,
Many and many a happy year.

January, 1854

Will

I

O well for him whose will is strong!
He suffers, but he will not suffer long;
He suffers, but he cannot suffer wrong:
For him nor moves the loud world's random mock,
Nor all Calamity's hugest waves confound,
Who seems a promontory of rock,
That, compass'd round with turbulent sound,
In middle ocean meets the surging shock,
Tempest-buffeted, citadel-crown'd.

II

10 But ill for him who, bettering not with time,
Corrupts the strength of heaven-descended Will,
And ever weaker grows thro' acted crime,
Or seeming-genial venial fault,
Recurring and suggesting still!
He seems as one whose footsteps halt,
Toiling in immeasurable sand,
And o'er a weary sultry land,
Far beneath a blazing vault,
Sown in a wrinkle of the monstrous hill,
20 The city sparkles like a grain of salt.

The Charge of the Light Brigade

I

Half a league, half a league,
  Half a league onward,
All in the valley of Death
  Rode the six hundred.
'Forward, the Light Brigade!
Charge for the guns!' he said:
Into the valley of Death
  Rode the six hundred.

II

'Forward, the Light Brigade!'
Was there a man dismay'd? 10
Not tho' the soldier knew
  Some one had blunder'd:
Their's not to make reply,
Their's not to reason why,
Their's but to do and die:
Into the valley of Death
  Rode the six hundred.

III

Cannon to right of them,
Cannon to left of them,
Cannon in front of them 20
  Volley'd and thunder'd;
Storm'd at with shot and shell,
Boldly they rode and well,
Into the jaws of Death,
Into the mouth of Hell
  Rode the six hundred.

IV

Flash'd all their sabres bare,
Flash'd as they turn'd in air
Sabring the gunners there,
30 Charging an army, while
All the world wonder'd:
Plunged in the battery-smoke
Right thro' the line they broke;
Cossack and Russian
Reel'd from the sabre-stroke
Shatter'd and sunder'd.
Then they rode back, but not
Not the six hundred.

V

Cannon to right of them,
40 Cannon to left of them,
Cannon behind them
Volley'd and thunder'd;
Storm'd at with shot and shell,
While horse and hero fell,
They that had fought so well
Came thro' the jaws of Death,
Back from the mouth of Hell,
All that was left of them,
Left of six hundred.

VI

50 When can their glory fade?
O the wild charge they made!
All the world wonder'd.
Honour the charge they made!
Honour the Light Brigade,
Noble six hundred!

▲ ▲ ▲

From *Enoch Arden* (1864)

The Grandmother

I

And Willy, my eldest-born, is gone, you say, little Anne?
Ruddy and white, and strong on his legs, he looks like a man.
And Willy's wife has written: she never was over-wise,
Never the wife for Willy: he wouldn't take my advice.

II

For, Annie, you see, her father was not the man to save,
Hadn't a head to manage, and drank himself into his grave.
Pretty enough, very pretty! but I was against it for one.
Eh! – but he wouldn't hear me – and Willy, you say, is gone.

III

Willy, my beauty, my eldest-born, the flower of the flock;
Never a man could fling him: for Willy stood like a rock. 10
'Here's a leg for a babe of a week!' says doctor; and he would be
bound,
There was not his like that year in twenty parishes round.

IV

Strong of his hands, and strong on his legs, but still of his tongue!
I ought to have gone before him: I wonder he went so young.
I cannot cry for him, Annie: I have not long to stay;
Perhaps I shall see him the sooner, for he lived far away.

V

Why do you look at me, Annie? you think I am hard and cold;
But all my children have gone before me, I am so old:
I cannot weep for Willy, nor can I weep for the rest;
20 Only at your age, Annie, I could have wept with the best.

VI

For I remember a quarrel I had with your father, my dear,
All for a slanderous story, that cost me many a tear.
I mean your grandfather, Annie: it cost me a world of woe,
Seventy years ago, my darling, seventy years ago.

VII

For Jenny, my cousin, had come to the place, and I knew right
well
That Jenny had tript in her time: I knew, but I would not tell.
And she to be coming and slandering me, the base little liar!
But the tongue is a fire as you know, my dear, the tongue is a
fire.

VIII

And the parson made it his text that week, and he said likewise,
30 That a lie which is half a truth is ever the blackest of lies,
That a lie which is all a lie may be met and fought with outright,
But a lie which is part a truth is a harder matter to fight.

IX

And Willy had not been down to the farm for a week and a day;
And all things look'd half-dead, tho' it was the middle of May.
Jenny, to slander me, who knew what Jenny had been!
But soiling another, Annie, will never make oneself clean.

X

And I cried myself well-nigh blind, and all of an evening late
I climb'd to the top of the garth, and stood by the road at the
gate.

The moon like a rick on fire was rising over the dale,
And whit, whit, whit, in the bush beside me chirrupt the
nightingale. 40

XI

All of a sudden he stopt: there past by the gate of the farm,
Willy, – he didn't see me, – and Jenny hung on his arm.
Out into the road I started, and spoke I scarce knew how;
Ah, there's no fool like the old one – it makes me angry now.

XII

Willy stood up like a man, and look'd the thing that he meant;
Jenny, the viper, made me a mocking curtsey and went.
And I said, 'Let us part: in a hundred years it'll all be the same,
You cannot love me at all, if you love not my good name.'

XIII

And he turn'd, and I saw his eyes all wet, in the sweet moonshine:
'Sweetheart, I love you so well that your good name is mine. 50
And what do I care for Jane, let her speak of you well or ill;
But marry me out of hand: we two shall be happy still.'

XIV

'Marry you, Willy!' said I, 'but I needs must speak my mind,
And I fear you'll listen to tales, be jealous and hard and unkind.'
But he turn'd and claspt me in his arms, and answer'd, 'No, love,
no;'
Seventy years ago, my darling, seventy years ago.

XV

So Willy and I were wedded: I wore a lilac gown;
And the ringers rang with a will, and he gave the ringers a crown.
But the first that ever I bare was dead before he was born,
Shadow and shine is life, little Annie, flower and thorn. 60

XVI

That was the first time, too, that ever I thought of death.
There lay the sweet little body that never had drawn a breath.
I had not wept, little Annie, not since I had been a wife;
But I wept like a child that day, for the babe had fought for his life.

XVII

His dear little face was troubled, as if with anger or pain:
I look'd at the still little body – his trouble had all been in vain.
For Willy I cannot weep, I shall see him another morn:
But I wept like a child for the child that was dead before he was born.

XVIII

But he cheer'd me, my good man, for he seldom said me nay:
70 Kind, like a man, was he; like a man, too, would have his way:
Never jealous – not he: we had many a happy year;
And he died, and I could not weep – my own time seem'd so near.

XIX

But I wish'd it had been God's will that I, too, then could have died:
I began to be tired a little, and fain had slept at his side.
And that was ten years back, or more, if I don't forget:
But as to the children, Annie, they're all about me yet.

XX

Pattering over the boards, my Annie who left me at two,
Patter she goes, my own little Annie, an Annie like you:
Pattering over the boards, she comes and goes at her will,
80 While Harry is in the five-acre and Charlie ploughing the hill.

XXI

And Harry and Charlie, I hear them too – they sing to their team:
Often they come to the door in a pleasant kind of a dream.

They come and sit by my chair, they hover about my bed –
I am not always certain if they be alive or dead.

XXII

And yet I know for a truth, there's none of them left alive;
For Harry went at sixty, your father at sixty-five:
And Willy, my eldest-born, at nigh threescore and ten;
I knew them all as babies, and now they're elderly men.

XXIII

For mine is a time of peace, it is not often I grieve;
I am oftener sitting at home in my father's farm at eve: 90
And the neighbours come and laugh and gossip, and so do I;
I find myself often laughing at things that have long gone by.

XXIV

To be sure the preacher says, our sins should make us sad:
But mine is a time of peace, and there is Grace to be had;
And God, not man, is the Judge of us all when life shall cease;
And in this Book, little Annie, the message is one of Peace.

XXV

And age is a time of peace, so it be free from pain,
And happy has been my life; but I would not live it again.
I seem to be tired a little, that's all, and long for rest;
Only at your age, Annie, I could have wept with the best. 100

XXVI

So Willy has gone, my beauty, my eldest-born, my flower;
But how can I weep for Willy, he has but gone for an hour, –
Gone for a minute, my son, from this room into the next;
I, too, shall go in a minute. What time have I to be vext?

XXVII

And Willy's wife has written, she never was over-wise.
Get me my glasses, Annie: thank God that I keep my eyes.

There is but a trifle left you, when I shall have past away.
But stay with the old woman now: you cannot have long to stay.

Tithonus

The woods decay, the woods decay and fall,
The vapours weep their burthen to the ground,
Man comes and tills the field and lies beneath,
And after many a summer dies the swan.
Me only cruel immortality
Consumes: I wither slowly in thine arms,
Here at the quiet limit of the world,
A white-hair'd shadow roaming like a dream
The ever-silent spaces of the East,
10 Far-folded mists, and gleaming halls of morn.

Alas! for this gray shadow, once a man –
So glorious in his beauty and thy choice,
Who madest him thy chosen, that he seem'd
To his great heart none other than a God!
I ask'd thee, 'Give me immortality.'
Then didst thou grant mine asking with a smile,
Like wealthy men who care not how they give.
But thy strong Hours indignant work'd their wills,
And beat me down and marr'd and wasted me,
20 And tho' they could not end me, left me maim'd
To dwell in presence of immortal youth,
Immortal age beside immortal youth,
And all I was, in ashes. Can thy love,
Thy beauty, make amends, tho' even now,
Close over us, the silver star, thy guide,
Shines in those tremulous eyes that fill with tears

To hear me? Let me go: take back thy gift:
Why should a man desire in any way
To vary from the kindly race of men,
Or pass beyond the goal of ordinance 30
Where all should pause, as is most meet for all?

A soft air fans the cloud apart; there comes
A glimpse of that dark world where I was born.
Once more the old mysterious glimmer steals
From thy pure brows, and from thy shoulders pure,
And bosom beating with a heart renew'd.
Thy cheek begins to redden thro' the gloom,
Thy sweet eyes brighten slowly close to mine,
Ere yet they blind the stars, and the wild team
Which love thee, yearning for thy yoke, arise, 40
And shake the darkness from their loosen'd manes,
And beat the twilight into flakes of fire.

Lo! ever thus thou growest beautiful
In silence, then before thine answer given
Departest, and thy tears are on my cheek.

Why wilt thou ever scare me with thy tears,
And make me tremble lest a saying learnt,
In days far-off, on that dark earth, be true?
'The Gods themselves cannot recall their gifts.'

Ay me! ay me! with what another heart 50
In days far-off, and with what other eyes
I used to watch – if I be he that watch'd –
The lucid outline forming round thee; saw
The dim curls kindle into sunny rings;
Changed with thy mystic change, and felt my blood
Glow with the glow that slowly crimson'd all
Thy presence and thy portals, while I lay,
Mouth, forehead, eyelids, growing dewy-warm
With kisses balmier than half-opening buds
Of April, and could hear the lips that kiss'd 60
Whispering I knew not what of wild and sweet,

Like that strange song I heard Apollo sing,
While Ilion like a mist rose into towers.

Yet hold me not for ever in thine East:
How can my nature longer mix with thine?
Coldly thy rosy shadows bathe me, cold
Are all thy lights, and cold my wrinkled feet
Upon thy glimmering thresholds, when the steam
Floats up from those dim fields about the homes
70 Of happy men that have the power to die,
And grassy barrows of the happier dead.
Release me, and restore me to the ground;
Thou seëst all things, thou wilt see my grave:
Thou wilt renew thy beauty morn by morn;
I earth in earth forget these empty courts,
And thee returning on thy silver wheels.

In the Valley of Cauteretz

All along the valley, stream that flashest white,
Deepening thy voice with the deepening of the night,
All along the valley, where thy waters flow,
I walk'd with one I loved two and thirty years ago.
All along the valley, while I walk'd to-day,
The two and thirty years were a mist that rolls away;
For all along the valley, down thy rocky bed,
Thy living voice to me was as the voice of the dead,
And all along the valley, by rock and cave and tree,
10 The voice of the dead was a living voice to me.

▲ ▲ ▲

On a Mourner

I

Nature, so far as in her lies,
Imitates God, and turns her face
To every land beneath the skies,
Counts nothing that she meets with base,
But lives and loves in every place;

II

Fills out the homely quickset-screens,
And makes the purple lilac ripe,
Steps from her airy hill, and greens
The swamp, where humm'd the dropping snipe,
With moss and braided marish-pipe; 10

III

And on thy heart a finger lays,
Saying, 'Beat quicker, for the time
Is pleasant, and the woods and ways
Are pleasant, and the beech and lime
Put forth and feel a gladder clime.'

IV

And murmurs of a deeper voice,
Going before to some far shrine,
Teach that sick heart the stronger choice,
Till all thy life one way incline
With one wide Will that closes thine. 20

V

And when the zoning eve has died
Where yon dark valleys wind forlorn,
Come Hope and Memory, spouse and bride,

From out the borders of the morn,
With that fair child betwixt them born.

VI

And when no mortal motion jars
The blackness round the tombing sod,
Thro' silence and the trembling stars
Comes Faith from tracts no feet have trod,
30 And Virtue, like a household god

VII

Promising empire; such as those
Once heard at dead of night to greet
Troy's wandering prince, so that he rose
With sacrifice, while all the fleet
Had rest by stony hills of Crete.

▲ ▲ ▲

From *The Holy Grail and Other Poems* (1869)

Northern Farmer,

New Style

I

Dosn't thou 'ear my 'erse's legs, as they canters awaäy?
Proputty, proputty, proputty – that's what I 'ears 'em saäy.
Proputty, proputty, proputty – Sam, thou's an ass for thy paaïns:
Theer's moor sense i' one o' 'is legs nor in all thy braaïns.

II

Woä – theer's a craw to pluck wi' tha, Sam: yon's parson's 'ouse –
Dosn't thou knaw that a man mun be eäther a man or a mouse?
Time to think on it then; for thou'll be twenty to weeäk.[1]
Proputty, proputty – woä then woä – let ma 'ear mysén speäk.

III

Me an' thy muther, Sammy, 'as beän a-talkin' o' thee;
Thou's beän talkin' to muther, an' she beän a tellin' it me. 10
Thou'll not marry for munny – thou's sweet upo' parson's lass –
Noä – thou'll marry for luvv – an' we boäth on us thinks tha an ass.

1 This week

IV

Seeä'd her todaäy goä by – Saäint's-daäy – they was ringing the
bells.
She's a beauty thou thinks – an' soä is scoors o' gells,
Them as 'as munny an' all – wot's a beauty? – the flower as
blaws.
But proputty, proputty sticks, an' proputty, proputty graws.

V

Do'ant be stunt:[2] taäke time: I knaws what maäkes tha sa mad.
Warn't I craäzed fur the lasses mysén when I wur a lad?
But I knaw'd a Quaäker feller as often 'as towd ma this:
20 'Doänt thou marry for munny, but goä wheer munny is!'

VI

An' I went wheer munny war: an' thy muther coom to 'and,
Wi' lots o' munny laaïd by, an' a nicetish bit o' land.
Maäybe she warn't a beauty: – I niver giv it a thowt –
But warn't she as good to cuddle an' kiss as a lass as 'ant nowt?

VII

Parson's lass 'ant nowt, an' she weänt 'a nowt when 'e's deäd,
Mun be a guvness, lad, or summut, and addle[3] her breäd:
Why? fur 'e's nobbut a curate, an' weänt niver git hissen clear,
An' 'e maäde the bed as 'e ligs on afoor 'e coom'd to the shere.

VIII

An' thin 'e coom'd to the parish wi' lots o' Varsity debt,
30 Stook to his taaïl they did, an' 'e 'ant got shut on 'em yet.
An' 'e ligs on 'is back i' the grip, wi' noän to lend 'im a shuvv,
Woorse nor a far-welter'd[4] yowe: fur, Sammy, 'e married for luvv.

2 Obstinate
3 Earn
4 Or fow-welter'd, – said of a sheep lying on its back

IX

Luvv? what's luvv? thou can luvv thy lass an' 'er munny too,
Maakin' 'em goä togither as they've good right to do.
Could'n I luvv thy muther by cause o' 'er munny laaïd by?
Naäy – fur I luvv'd 'er a vast sight moor fur it: reäson why.

X

Ay an' thy muther says thou wants to marry the lass,
Cooms of a gentleman burn: an' we boäth on us thinks tha an ass.
Woä then, proputty, wiltha? – an ass as near as mays nowt[5] –
Woä then, wiltha? dangtha! – the bees is as fell as owt.[6] 40

XI

Breäk me a bit o' the esh for his 'eäd lad, out o' the fence!
Gentleman burn! what's gentleman burn? is it shillins an' pence?
Proputty, proputty's ivrything 'ere, an', Sammy, I'm blest
If it isn't the saäme oop yonder, fur them as 'as it's the best.

XII

Tis'n them as 'as munny as breäks into 'ouses an' steäls,
Them as 'as coäts to their backs an' taäkes their regular meäls.
Noä, but it's them as niver knaws wheer a meäl's to be 'ad.
Taäke my word for it, Sammy, the poor in a loomp is bad.

XIII

Them or thir feythers, tha sees, mun 'a beän a laäzy lot,
Fur work mun 'a gone to the gittin' whiniver munny was got. 50
Feyther 'ad ammost nowt; leästways 'is munny was 'id.
But 'e tued an' moil'd 'issén deäd, an 'e died a good un, 'e did.

XIV

Loook thou theer wheer Wrigglesby beck cooms out by the 'ill!
Feyther run oop to the farm, an' I runs oop to the mill;

5 Makes nothing
6 The flies are as fierce as anything

An' I'll run oop to the brig, an' that thou'll live to see;
And if thou marries a good un I'll leäve the land to thee.

XV

Thim's my noätions, Sammy, wheerby I means to stick;
But if thou marries a bad un, I'll leäve the land to Dick. –
Coom oop, proputty, proputty – that's what I 'ears 'im saäy –
60 Proputty, proputty, proputty – canter an' canter awaäy.

'Flower in the crannied wall'

Flower in the crannied wall,
I pluck you out of the crannies,
I hold you here, root and all, in my hand,
Little flower – but *if* I could understand
What you are, root and all, and all in all,
I should know what God and man is.

Lucretius

Lucilia, wedded to Lucretius, found
Her master cold; for when the morning flush
Of passion and the first embrace had died
Between them, tho' he lov'd her none the less,

Yet often when the woman heard his foot
Return from pacings in the field, and ran
To greet him with a kiss, the master took
Small notice, or austerely, for – his mind
Half buried in some weightier argument,
Or fancy-borne perhaps upon the rise 10
And long roll of the Hexameter – he past
To turn and ponder those three hundred scrolls
Left by the Teacher, whom he held divine.
She brook'd it not; but wrathful, petulant,
Dreaming some rival, sought and found a witch
Who brew'd the philtre which had power, they said,
To lead an errant passion home again.
And this, at times, she mingled with his drink,
And this destroy'd him; for the wicked broth
Confused the chemic labour of the blood, 20
And tickling the brute brain within the man's
Made havock among those tender cells, and check'd
His power to shape: he loathed himself; and once
After a tempest woke upon a morn
That mock'd him with returning calm, and cried:

'Storm in the night! for thrice I heard the rain
Rushing; and once the flash of a thunderbolt –
Methought I never saw so fierce a fork –
Struck out the streaming mountain-side, and show'd
A riotous confluence of watercourses 30
Blanching and billowing in a hollow of it,
Where all but yester-eve was dusty-dry.

'Storm, and what dreams, ye holy Gods, what dreams!
For thrice I waken'd after dreams. Perchance
We do but recollect the dreams that come
Just ere the waking: terrible! for it seem'd
A void was made in Nature; all her bonds
Crack'd; and I saw the flaring atom-streams
And torrents of her myriad universe,
Ruining along the illimitable inane, 40

Fly on to clash together again, and make
Another and another frame of things
For ever: that was mine, my dream, I knew it –
Of and belonging to me, as the dog
With inward yelp and restless forefoot plies
His function of the woodland: but the next!
I thought that all the blood by Sylla shed
Came driving rainlike down again on earth,
And where it dash'd the reddening meadow, sprang
50 No dragon warriors from Cadmean teeth,
For these I thought my dream would show to me,
But girls, Hetairai, curious in their art,
Hired animalisms, vile as those that made
The mulberry-faced Dictator's orgies worse
Than aught they fable of the quiet Gods.
And hands they mixt, and yell'd and round me drove
In narrowing circles till I yell'd again
Half-suffocated, and sprang up, and saw –
Was it the first beam of my latest day?

60 'Then, then, from utter gloom stood out the breasts,
The breasts of Helen, and hoveringly a sword
Now over and now under, now direct,
Pointed itself to pierce, but sank down shamed
At all that beauty; and as I stared, a fire,
The fire that left a roofless Ilion,
Shot out of them, and scorch'd me that I woke.

'Is this thy vengeance, holy Venus, thine,
Because I would not one of thine own doves,
Not ev'n a rose, were offer'd to thee? thine,
70 Forgetful how my rich prooemion makes
Thy glory fly along the Italian field,
In lays that will outlast thy Deity?

'Deity? nay, thy worshippers. My tongue
Trips, or I speak profanely. Which of these
Angers thee most, or angers thee at all?

Not if thou be'st of those who, far aloof
From envy, hate and pity, and spite and scorn,
Live the great life which all our greatest fain
Would follow, center'd in eternal calm.

'Nay, if thou canst, O Goddess, like ourselves 80
Touch, and be touch'd, then would I cry to thee
To kiss thy Mavors, roll thy tender arms
Round him, and keep him from the lust of blood
That makes a steaming slaughter-house of Rome.

'Ay, but I meant not thee; I meant not her,
Whom all the pines of Ida shook to see
Slide from that quiet heaven of hers, and tempt
The Trojan, while his neat-herds were abroad;
Nor her that o'er her wounded hunter wept
Her Deity false in human-amorous tears; 90
Nor whom her beardless apple-arbiter
Decided fairest. Rather, O ye Gods,
Poet-like, as the great Sicilian called
Calliope to grace his golden verse –
Ay, and this Kypris also – did I take
That popular name of thine to shadow forth
The all-generating powers and genial heat
Of Nature, when she strikes thro' the thick blood
Of cattle, and light is large, and lambs are glad
Nosing the mother's udder, and the bird 100
Makes his heart voice amid the blaze of flowers:
Which things appear the work of mighty Gods.

'The Gods! and if I go *my* work is left
Unfinish'd – *if* I go. The Gods, who haunt
The lucid interspace of world and world,
Where never creeps a cloud, or moves a wind,
Nor ever falls the least white star of snow,
Nor ever lowest roll of thunder moans,
Nor sound of human sorrow mounts to mar
Their sacred everlasting calm! and such, 110

Not all so fine, nor so divine a calm,
Not such, nor all unlike it, man may gain
Letting his own life go. The Gods, the Gods!
If all be atoms, how then should the Gods
Being atomic not be dissoluble,
Not follow the great law? My master held
That Gods there are, for all men so believe.
I prest my footsteps into his, and meant
Surely to lead my Memmius in a train
120 Of flowery clauses onward to the proof
That Gods there are, and deathless. Meant? I meant?
I have forgotten what I meant: my mind
Stumbles, and all my faculties are lamed.

'Look where another of our Gods, the Sun,
Apollo, Delius, or of older use
All-seeing Hyperion – what you will –
Has mounted yonder; since he never sware,
Except his wrath were wreak'd on wretched man,
That he would only shine among the dead
130 Hereafter; tales! for never yet on earth
Could dead flesh creep, or bits of roasting ox
Moan round the spit – nor knows he what he sees;
King of the East altho' he seem, and girt
With song and flame and fragrance, slowly lifts
His golden feet on those empurpled stairs
That climb into the windy halls of heaven:
And here he glances on an eye new-born,
And gets for greeting but a wail of pain;
And here he stays upon a freezing orb
140 That fain would gaze upon him to the last;
And here upon a yellow eyelid fall'n
And closed by those who mourn a friend in vain,
Not thankful that his troubles are no more.
And me, altho' his fire is on my face
Blinding, he sees not, nor at all can tell
Whether I mean this day to end myself,

Or lend an ear to Plato where he says,
That men like soldiers may not quit the post
Allotted by the Gods: but he that holds
The Gods are careless, wherefore need he care 150
Greatly for them, nor rather plunge at once,
Being troubled, wholly out of sight, and sink
Past earthquake – ay, and gout and stone, that break
Body toward death, and palsy, death-in-life,
And wretched age – and worst disease of all,
These prodigies of myriad nakednesses,
And twisted shapes of lust, unspeakable,
Abominable, strangers at my hearth
Not welcome, harpies miring every dish,
The phantom husks of something foully done, 160
And fleeting thro' the boundless universe,
And blasting the long quiet of my breast
With animal heat and dire insanity?

'How should the mind, except it loved them, clasp
These idols to herself? or do they fly
Now thinner, and now thicker, like the flakes
In a fall of snow, and so press in, perforce
Of multitude, as crowds that in an hour
Of civic tumult jam the doors, and bear
The keepers down, and throng, their rags and they 170
The basest, far into that council-hall
Where sit the best and stateliest of the land?

'Can I not fling this horror off me again,
Seeing with how great ease Nature can smile,
Balmier and nobler from her bath of storm,
At random ravage? and how easily
The mountain there has cast his cloudy slough,
Now towering o'er him in serenest air,
A mountain o'er a mountain, – ay, and within
All hollow as the hopes and fears of men? 180

'But who was he, that in the garden snared
Picus and Faunus, rustic Gods? a tale
To laugh at – more to laugh at in myself –
For look! what is it? there? yon arbutus
Totters; a noiseless riot underneath
Strikes through the wood, sets all the tops quivering –
The mountain quickens into Nymph and Faun;
And here an Oread – how the sun delights
To glance and shift about her slippery sides,
190 And rosy knees and supple roundedness,
And budded bosom-peaks – who this way runs
Before the rest – A satyr, a satyr, see,
Follows; but him I proved impossible;
Twy-natured is no nature: yet he draws
Nearer and nearer, and I scan him now
Beastlier than any phantom of his kind
That ever butted his rough brother-brute
For lust or lusty blood or provender:
I hate, abhor, spit, sicken at him; and she
200 Loathes him as well; such a precipitate heel,
Fledged as it were with Mercury's ankle-wing,
Whirls her to me: but will she fling herself,
Shameless upon me? Catch her, goat-foot: nay,
Hide, hide them, million-myrtled wilderness,
And cavern-shadowing laurels, hide! do I wish –
What? – that the bush were leafless? or to whelm
All of them in one massacre? O ye Gods,
I know you careless, yet, behold, to you
From childly wont and ancient use I call –
210 I thought I lived securely as yourselves –
No lewdness, narrowing envy, monkey-spite,
No madness of ambition, avarice, none:
No larger feast than under plane or pine
With neighbours laid along the grass, to take
Only such cups as left us friendly-warm,
Affirming each his own philosophy –
Nothing to mar the sober majesties

Of settled, sweet, Epicurean life.
But now it seems some unseen monster lays
His vast and filthy hands upon my will, 220
Wrenching it backward into his; and spoils
My bliss in being; and it was not great;
For save when shutting reasons up in rhythm,
Or Heliconian honey in living words,
To make a truth less harsh, I often grew
Tired of so much within our little life,
Or of so little in our little life –
Poor little life that toddles half an hour
Crown'd with a flower or two, and there an end –
And since the nobler pleasure seems to fade, 230
Why should I, beastlike as I find myself,
Not manlike end myself? – our privilege –
What beast has heart to do it? And what man,
What Roman would be dragg'd in triumph thus?
Not I; not he, who bears one name with her
Whose death-blow struck the dateless doom of kings,
When, brooking not the Tarquin in her veins,
She made her blood in sight of Collatine
And all his peers, flushing the guiltless air,
Spout from the maiden fountain in her heart. 240
And from it sprang the Commonwealth, which breaks
As I am breaking now!

'And therefore now
Let her, that is the womb and tomb of all,
Great Nature, take, and forcing far apart
Those blind beginnings that have made me man,
Dash them anew together at her will
Thro' all her cycles – into man once more,
Or beast or bird or fish, or opulent flower:
But till this cosmic order everywhere
Shatter'd into one earthquake in one day 250
Cracks all to pieces, – and that hour perhaps
Is not so far when momentary man

Shall seem no more a something to himself,
But he, his hopes and hates, his homes and fanes,
And even his bones long laid within the grave,
The very sides of the grave itself shall pass,
Vanishing, atom and void, atom and void,
Into the unseen for ever, – till that hour,
My golden work in which I told a truth
260 That stays the rolling Ixionian wheel,
That numbs the Fury's ringlet-snake, and plucks
The mortal soul from out immortal hell,
Shall stand: ay, surely: then it fails at last
And perishes as I must; for O Thou,
Passionless bride, divine Tranquillity,
Yearn'd after by the wisest of the wise,
Who fail to find thee, being as thou art
Without one pleasure and without one pain,
Howbeit I know thou surely must be mine
270 Or soon or late, yet out of season, thus
I woo thee roughly, for thou carest not
How roughly men may woo thee so they win –
Thus – thus: the soul flies out and dies in the air.'

With that he drove the knife into his side:
She heard him raging, heard him fall; ran in,
Beat breast, tore hair, cried out upon herself
As having fail'd in duty to him, shriek'd
That she but meant to win him back, fell on him,
Clasp'd, kiss'd him, wail'd: he answer'd, 'Care not thou!
280 Thy duty? What is duty? Fare thee well!'

▲ ▲ ▲

From *Tiresias and Other Poems* (1885)

To E. FitzGerald

Old Fitz, who from your suburb grange,
  Where once I tarried for a while,
Glance at the wheeling Orb of change,
  And greet it with a kindly smile;
Whom yet I see as there you sit
  Beneath your sheltering garden-tree,
And while your doves about you flit,
  And plant on shoulder, hand and knee,
Or on your head their rosy feet,
  As if they knew your diet spares 10
Whatever moved in that full sheet
  Let down to Peter at his prayers;
Who live on milk and meal and grass;
  And once for ten long weeks I tried
Your table of Pythagoras,
  And seem'd at first 'a thing enskied'
(As Shakespeare has it) airy-light
  To float above the ways of men,
Then fell from that half-spiritual height
  Chill'd, till I tasted flesh again 20
One night when earth was winter-black,
  And all the heavens flash'd in frost;
And on me, half-asleep, came back
  That wholesome heat the blood had lost,
And set me climbing icy capes
  And glaciers, over which there roll'd
To meet me long-arm'd vines with grapes

Of Eshcol hugeness; for the cold
Without, and warmth within me, wrought
30 To mould the dream; but none can say
That Lenten fare makes Lenten thought,
Who reads your golden Eastern lay,
Than which I know no version done
In English more divinely well;
A planet equal to the sun
Which cast it, that large infidel
Your Omar; and your Omar drew
Full-handed plaudits from our best
In modern letters, and from two,
40 Old friends outvaluing all the rest,
Two voices heard on earth no more;
But we old friends are still alive,
And I am nearing seventy-four,
While you have touch'd at seventy-five,
And so I send a birthday line
Of greeting; and my son, who dipt
In some forgotten book of mine
With sallow scraps of manuscript,
And dating many a year ago,
50 Has hit on this, which you will take
My Fitz, and welcome, as I know
Less for its own than for the sake
Of one recalling gracious times,
When, in our younger London days,
You found some merit in my rhymes,
And I more pleasure in your praise.

*

'One height and one far-shining fire'
And while I fancied that my friend
For this brief idyll would require
60 A less diffuse and opulent end,
And would defend his judgment well,
If I should deem it over nice –

The tolling of his funeral bell
  Broke on my Pagan Paradise,
And mixt the dream of classic times,
  And all the phantoms of the dream,
With present grief, and made the rhymes,
  That miss'd his living welcome, seem
Like would-be guests an hour too late,
  Who down the highway moving on 70
With easy laughter find the gate
  Is bolted, and the master gone.
Gone into darkness, that full light
  Of friendship! past, in sleep, away
By night, into the deeper night!
  The deeper night? A clearer day
Than our poor twilight dawn on earth –
  If night, what barren toil to be!
What life, so maim'd by night, were worth
  Our living out? Not mine to me 80
Remembering all the golden hours
  Now silent, and so many dead,
And him the last; and laying flowers,
  This wreath, above his honour'd head,
And praying that, when I from hence
  Shall fade with him into the unknown,
My close of earth's experience
  May prove as peaceful as his own.

Tiresias

I wish I were as in the years of old,
While yet the blessèd daylight made itself
Ruddy thro' both the roofs of sight, and woke
These eyes, now dull, but then so keen to seek
The meanings ambush'd under all they saw,
The flight of birds, the flame of sacrifice,
What omens may foreshadow fate to man
And woman, and the secret of the Gods.
My son, the Gods, despite of human prayer,
10 Are slower to forgive than human kings.
The great God, Arês, burns in anger still
Against the guiltless heirs of him from Tyre,
Our Cadmus, out of whom thou art, who found
Beside the springs of Dircê, smote, and still'd
Thro' all its folds the multitudinous beast,
The dragon, which our trembling fathers call'd
The God's own son.
A tale, that told to me,
When but thine age, by age as winter-white
As mine is now, amazed, but made me yearn
20 For larger glimpses of that more than man
Which rolls the heavens, and lifts, and lays the deep,
Yet loves and hates with mortal hates and loves,
And moves unseen among the ways of men.
Then, in my wanderings all the lands that lie
Subjected to the Heliconian ridge
Have heard this footstep fall, altho' my wont
Was more to scale the highest of the heights
With some strange hope to see the nearer God.
One naked peak – the sister of the sun
30 Would climb from out the dark, and linger there
To silver all the valleys with her shafts –

There once, but long ago, five-fold thy term
Of years, I lay; the winds were dead for heat;
The noonday crag made the hand burn; and sick
For shadow – not one bush was near – I rose
Following a torrent till its myriad falls
Found silence in the hollows underneath.
  There in a secret olive-glade I saw
Pallas Athene climbing from the bath
In anger; yet one glittering foot disturb'd 40
The lucid well; one snowy knee was prest
Against the margin flowers; a dreadful light
Came from her golden hair, her golden helm
And all her golden armour on the grass,
And from her virgin breast, and virgin eyes
Remaining fixt on mine, till mine grew dark
For ever, and I heard a voice that said
'Henceforth be blind, for thou hast seen too much,
And speak the truth that no man may believe.'
  Son, in the hidden world of sight, that lives 50
Behind this darkness, I behold her still,
Beyond all work of those who carve the stone,
Beyond all dreams of Godlike womanhood,
Ineffable beauty, out of whom, at a glance,
And as it were, perforce, upon me flash'd
The power of prophesying – but to me
No power – so chain'd and coupled with the curse
Of blindness and their unbelief, who heard
And heard not, when I spake of famine, plague,
Shrine-shattering earthquake, fire, flood, thunderbolt, 60
And angers of the Gods for evil done
And expiation lack'd – no power on Fate,
Theirs, or mine own! for when the crowd would roar
For blood, for war, whose issue was their doom,
To cast wise words among the multitude
Was flinging fruit to lions; nor, in hours
Of civil outbreak, when I knew the twain
Would each waste each, and bring on both the yoke

Of stronger states, was mine the voice to curb
70 The madness of our cities and their kings.
  Who ever turn'd upon his heel to hear
My warning that the tyranny of one
Was prelude to the tyranny of all?
My counsel that the tyranny of all
Led backward to the tyranny of one?
  This power hath work'd no good to aught that lives,
And these blind hands were useless in their wars.
O therefore that the unfulfill'd desire,
The grief for ever born from griefs to be,
80 The boundless yearning of the Prophet's heart –
Could *that* stand forth, and like a statue, rear'd
To some great citizen, win all praise from all
Who past it, saying, 'That was he!'
                                        In vain!
Virtue must shape itself in deed, and those
Whom weakness or necessity have cramp'd
Within themselves, immerging, each, his urn
In his own well, draw solace as he may.
  Menœceus, thou hast eyes, and I can hear
Too plainly what full tides of onset sap
90 Our seven high gates, and what a weight of war
Rides on those ringing axles! jingle of bits,
Shouts, arrows, tramp of the hornfooted horse
That grind the glebe to powder! Stony showers
Of that ear-stunning hail of Arês crash
Along the sounding walls. Above, below,
Shock after shock, the song-built towers and gates
Reel, bruised and butted with the shuddering
War-thunder of iron rams; and from within
The city comes a murmur void of joy,
100 Lest she be taken captive – maidens, wives,
And mothers with their babblers of the dawn,
And oldest age in shadow from the night,
Falling about their shrines before their Gods,
And wailing 'Save us.'
                                        And they wail to thee!

These eyeless eyes, that cannot see thine own,
See this, that only in thy virtue lies
The saving of our Thebes; for, yesternight,
To me, the great God Arês, whose one bliss
Is war, and human sacrifice – himself
Blood-red from battle, spear and helmet tipt 110
With stormy light as on a mast at sea,
Stood out before a darkness, crying 'Thebes,
Thy Thebes shall fall and perish, for I loathe
The seed of Cadmus – yet if one of these
By his own hand – if one of these—'

My son,

No sound is breathed so potent to coerce,
And to conciliate, as their names who dare
For that sweet mother land which gave them birth
Nobly to do, nobly to die. Their names,
Graven on memorial columns, are a song 120
Heard in the future; few, but more than wall
And rampart, their examples reach a hand
Far thro' all years, and everywhere they meet
And kindle generous purpose, and the strength
To mould it into action pure as theirs.

Fairer thy fate than mine, if life's best end
Be to end well! and thou refusing this,
Unvenerable will thy memory be
While men shall move the lips: but if thou dare –
Thou, one of these, the race of Cadmus – then 130
No stone is fitted in yon marble girth
Whose echo shall not tongue thy glorious doom,
Nor in this pavement but shall ring thy name
To every hoof that clangs it, and the springs
Of Dircê laving yonder battle-plain,
Heard from the roofs by night, will murmur thee
To thine own Thebes, while Thebes thro' thee shall stand
Firm-based with all her Gods.

The Dragon's cave

Half hid, they tell me, now in flowing vines –
140 Where once he dwelt and whence he roll'd himself
At dead of night – thou knowest, and that smooth rock
Before it, altar-fashion'd, where of late
The woman-breasted Sphinx, with wings drawn back,
Folded her lion paws, and look'd to Thebes.
There blanch the bones of whom she slew, and these
Mixt with her own, because the fierce beast found
A wiser than herself, and dash'd herself
Dead in her rage: but thou art wise enough,
Tho' young, to love thy wiser, blunt the curse
150 Of Pallas, hear, and tho' I speak the truth
Believe I speak it, let thine own hand strike
Thy youthful pulses into rest and quench
The red God's anger, fearing not to plunge
Thy torch of life in darkness, rather – thou
Rejoicing that the sun, the moon, the stars
Send no such light upon the ways of men
As one great deed.
Thither, my son, and there
Thou, that hast never known the embrace of love,
Offer thy maiden life.
This useless hand!
160 I felt one warm tear fall upon it. Gone!
He will achieve his greatness.
But for me,
I would that I were gather'd to my rest,
And mingled with the famous kings of old,
On whom about their ocean-islets flash
The faces of the Gods – the wise man's word,
Here trampled by the populace underfoot,
There crown'd with worship – and these eyes will find
The men I knew, and watch the chariot whirl
About the goal again, and hunters race
170 The shadowy lion, and the warrior-kings,
In height and prowess more than human, strive
Again for glory, while the golden lyre

Is ever sounding in heroic ears
Heroic hymns, and every way the vales
Wind, clouded with the grateful incense-fume
Of those who mix all odour to the Gods
On one far height in one far-shining fire.

The Ancient Sage

A thousand summers ere the time of Christ
From out his ancient city came a Seer
Whom one that loved, and honour'd him, and yet
Was no disciple, richly garb'd, but worn
From wasteful living, follow'd – in his hand
A scroll of verse – till that old man before
A cavern whence an affluent fountain pour'd
From darkness into daylight, turn'd and spoke.

This wealth of waters might but seem to draw
From yon dark cave, but, son, the source is higher, 10
Yon summit half-a-league in air – and higher,
The cloud that hides it – higher still, the heavens
Whereby the cloud was moulded, and whereout
The cloud descended. Force is from the heights.
I am wearied of our city, son, and go
To spend my one last year among the hills.
What hast thou there? Some deathsong for the Ghouls
To make their banquet relish? let me read.

'How far thro' all the bloom and brake
That nightingale is heard! 20
What power but the bird's could make
This music in the bird?

How summer-bright are yonder skies,
And earth as fair in hue!
And yet what sign of aught that lies
Behind the green and blue?
But man to-day is fancy's fool
As man hath ever been.
The nameless Power, or Powers, that rule
30 Were never heard or seen.'

If thou would'st hear the Nameless, and wilt dive
Into the Temple-cave of thine own self,
There, brooding by the central altar, thou
May'st haply learn the Nameless hath a voice,
By which thou wilt abide, if thou be wise,
As if thou knewest, tho' thou canst not know;
For Knowledge is the swallow on the lake
That sees and stirs the surface-shadow there
But never yet hath dipt into the abysm,
40 The Abysm of all Abysms, beneath, within
The blue of sky and sea, the green of earth,
And in the million-millionth of a grain
Which cleft and cleft again for evermore,
And ever vanishing, never vanishes,
To me, my son, more mystic than myself,
Or even than the Nameless is to me.
And when thou sendest thy free soul thro' heaven,
Nor understandest bound nor boundlessness,
Thou seest the Nameless of the hundred names.
50 And if the Nameless should withdraw from all
Thy frailty counts most real, all thy world
Might vanish like thy shadow in the dark.

'And since – from when this earth began –
The Nameless never came
Among us, never spake with man,
And never named the Name' –

Thou canst not prove the Nameless, O my son,
Nor canst thou prove the world thou movest in,
Thou canst not prove that thou art body alone,
Nor canst thou prove that thou art spirit alone, 60
Nor canst thou prove that thou art both in one:
Thou canst not prove thou art immortal, no
Nor yet that thou art mortal – nay my son,
Thou canst not prove that I, who speak with thee,
Am not thyself in converse with thyself,
For nothing worthy proving can be proven,
Nor yet disproven: wherefore thou be wise,
Cleave ever to the sunnier side of doubt,
And cling to Faith beyond the forms of Faith!
She reels not in the storm of warring words, 70
She brightens at the clash of 'Yes' and 'No,'
She sees the Best that glimmers thro' the Worst,
She feels the Sun is hid but for a night,
She spies the summer thro' the winter bud,
She tastes the fruit before the blossom falls,
She hears the lark within the songless egg,
She finds the fountain where they wail'd 'Mirage'!

'What Power? aught akin to Mind,
The mind in me and you?
Or power as of the Gods gone blind 80
Who see not what they do?'

But some in yonder city hold, my son,
That none but Gods could build this house of ours,
So beautiful, vast, various, so beyond
All work of man, yet, like all work of man,
A beauty with defect – till That which knows,
And is not known, but felt thro' what we feel
Within ourselves is highest, shall descend
On this half-deed, and shape it at the last
According to the Highest in the Highest. 90

'What Power but the Years that make
And break the vase of clay,
And stir the sleeping earth, and wake
The bloom that fades away?
What rules but the Days and Hours
That cancel weal with woe,
And wind the front of youth with flowers,
And cap our age with snow?'

The days and hours are ever glancing by,
100 And seem to flicker past thro' sun and shade,
Or short, or long, as Pleasure leads, or Pain;
But with the Nameless is nor Day nor Hour;
Tho' we, thin minds, who creep from thought to thought
Break into 'Thens' and 'Whens' the Eternal Now:
This double seeming of the single world! –
My words are like the babblings in a dream
Of nightmare, when the babblings break the dream.
But thou be wise in this dream-world of ours,
Nor take thy dial for thy deity,
110 But make the passing shadow serve thy will.

'The years that made the stripling wise
Undo their work again,
And leave him, blind of heart and eyes,
The last and least of men;
Who clings to earth, and once would dare
Hell-heat or Arctic cold,
And now one breath of cooler air
Would loose him from his hold;
His winter chills him to the root,
120 He withers marrow and mind;
The kernel of the shrivell'd fruit
Is jutting thro' the rind;
The tiger spasms tear his chest,
The palsy wags his head;
The wife, the sons, who love him best
Would fain that he were dead;

The griefs by which he once was wrung
Were never worth the while' –

Who knows? or whether this earth-narrow life
Be yet but yolk, and forming in the shell? 130

'The shaft of scorn that once had stung
But wakes a dotard smile.'

The placid gleam of sunset after storm!

'The statesman's brain that sway'd the past
Is feebler than his knees;
The passive sailor wrecks at last
In ever-silent seas;
The warrior hath forgot his arms,
The Learnèd all his lore;
The changing market frets or charms 140
The merchant's hope no more;
The prophet's beacon burn'd in vain,
And now is lost in cloud;
The plowman passes, bent with pain,
To mix with what he plow'd;
The poet whom his Age would quote
As heir of endless fame –
He knows not ev'n the book he wrote,
Not even his own name.
For man has overlived his day, 150
And, darkening in the light,
Scarce feels the senses break away
To mix with ancient Night.'

The shell must break before the bird can fly.

'The years that when my Youth began
Had set the lily and rose
By all my ways where'er they ran,
Have ended mortal foes;
My rose of love for ever gone,
My lily of truth and trust – 160

They made her lily and rose in one,
And changed her into dust.
O rosetree planted in my grief,
And growing, on her tomb,
Her dust is greening in your leaf,
Her blood is in your bloom.
O slender lily waving there,
And laughing back the light,
In vain you tell me "Earth is fair"
170 When all is dark as night.'

My son, the world is dark with griefs and graves,
So dark that men cry out against the Heavens.
Who knows but that the darkness is in man?
The doors of Night may be the gates of Light;
For wert thou born or blind or deaf, and then
Suddenly heal'd, how would'st thou glory in all
The splendours and the voices of the world!
And we, the poor earth's dying race, and yet
No phantoms, watching from a phantom shore
180 Await the last and largest sense to make
The phantom walls of this illusion fade,
And show us that the world is wholly fair.

'But vain the tears for darken'd years
As laughter over wine,
And vain the laughter as the tears,
O brother, mine or thine,

For all that laugh, and all that weep,
And all that breathe are one
Slight ripple on the boundless deep
190 That moves, and all is gone.'

But that one ripple on the boundless deep
Feels that the deep is boundless, and itself
For ever changing form, but evermore
One with the boundless motion of the deep.

'Yet wine and laughter friends! and set
    The lamps alight, and call
For golden music, and forget
    The darkness of the pall.'

If utter darkness closed the day, my son—
But earth's dark forehead flings athwart the heavens 200
Her shadow crown'd with stars – and yonder – out
To northward – some that never set, but pass
From sight and night to lose themselves in day.
I hate the black negation of the bier,
And wish the dead, as happier than ourselves
And higher, having climb'd one step beyond
Our village miseries, might be borne in white
To burial or to burning, hymn'd from hence
With songs in praise of death, and crown'd with flowers!

'O worms and maggots of to-day 210
    Without their hope of wings!'

But louder than thy rhyme the silent Word
Of that world-prophet in the heart of man.

'Tho' some have gleams or so they say
    Or more than mortal things.'

To-day? but what of yesterday? for oft
On me, when boy, there came what then I call'd,
Who knew no books and no philosophies,
In my boy-phrase 'The Passion of the Past.'
The first gray streak of earliest summer-dawn, 220
The last long stripe of waning crimson gloom,
As if the late and early were but one –
A height, a broken grange, a grove, a flower
Had murmurs 'Lost and gone and lost and gone!'
A breath, a whisper – some divine farewell –
Desolate sweetness – far and far away –
What had he loved, what had he lost, the boy?
I know not and I speak of what has been.

And more, my son! for more than once when I
230 Sat all alone, revolving in myself
The word that is the symbol of myself,
The mortal limit of the Self was loosed,
And past into the Nameless, as a cloud
Melts into Heaven. I touch'd my limbs, the limbs
Were strange not mine – and yet no shade of doubt,
But utter clearness, and thro' loss of Self
The gain of such large life as match'd with ours
Were Sun to spark – unshadowable in words,
Themselves but shadows of a shadow-world.

240 'And idle gleams will come and go,
But still the clouds remain;'

The clouds themselves are children of the Sun.

'And Night and Shadow rule below
When only Day should reign.'

And Day and Night are children of the Sun,
And idle gleams to thee are light to me.
Some say, the Light was father of the Night,
And some, the Night was father of the Light.
No night no day! – I touch thy world again –
250 No ill no good! such counter-terms, my son,
Are border-races, holding, each its own
By endless war: but night enough is there
In yon dark city: get thee back: and since
The key to that weird casket, which for thee
But holds a skull, is neither thine nor mine,
But in the hand of what is more than man,
Or in man's hand when man is more than man,
Let be thy wail and help thy fellow men,
And make thy gold thy vassal not thy king,
260 And fling free alms into the beggar's bowl,
And send the day into the darken'd heart;
Nor list for guerdon in the voice of men,
A dying echo from a falling wall;

Nor care – for Hunger hath the Evil eye –
To vex the noon with fiery gems, or fold
Thy presence in the silk of sumptuous looms;
Nor roll thy viands on a luscious tongue,
Nor drown thyself with flies in honied wine;
Nor thou be rageful, like a handled bee,
And lose thy life by usage of thy sting; 270
Nor harm an adder thro' the lust for harm,
Nor make a snail's horn shrink for wantonness;
And more – think well! Do-well will follow thought,
And in the fatal sequence of this world
An evil thought may soil thy children's blood;
But curb the beast would cast thee in the mire,
And leave the hot swamp of voluptuousness
A cloud between the Nameless and thyself,
And lay thine uphill shoulder to the wheel,
And climb the Mount of Blessing, whence, if thou 280
Look higher, then – perchance – thou mayest – beyond
A hundred ever-rising mountain lines,
And past the range of Night and Shadow – see
The high-heaven dawn of more than mortal day
Strike on the Mount of Vision!
So, farewell.

Prefatory Poem to My Brother's Sonnets

MIDNIGHT, JUNE 30, 1879

I

Midnight – in no midsummer tune
The breakers lash the shores:

The cuckoo of a joyless June
Is calling out of doors:

And thou hast vanish'd from thine own
To that which looks like rest,
True brother, only to be known
By those who love thee best.

II

Midnight – and joyless June gone by,
10 And from the deluged park
The cuckoo of a worse July
Is calling thro' the dark:

But thou art silent underground,
And o'er thee streams the rain,
True poet, surely to be found
When Truth is found again.

III

And, now to these unsummer'd skies
The summer bird is still,
Far off a phantom cuckoo cries
20 From out a phantom hill;

And thro' this midnight breaks the sun
Of sixty years away,
The light of days when life begun,
The days that seem to-day,

When all my griefs were shared with thee,
As all my hopes were thine –
As all thou wert was one with me,
May all thou art be mine!

'Frater Ave atque Vale'

Row us out from Desenzano, to your Sirmione row!
So they row'd, and there we landed – 'O venusta Sirmio!'
There to me thro' all the groves of olive in the summer glow,
There beneath the Roman ruin where the purple flowers grow,
Came that 'Ave atque Vale' of the Poet's hopeless woe,
Tenderest of Roman poets nineteen-hundred years ago,
'Frater Ave atque Vale' – as we wander'd to and fro
Gazing at the Lydian laughter of the Garda Lake below
Sweet Catullus's all-but-island, olive-silvery Sirmio!

▲ ▲ ▲

From *Locksley Hall Sixty Years After* (1886)

Locksley Hall Sixty Years After

Late, my grandson! half the morning have I paced these sandy
 tracts,
Watch'd again the hollow ridges roaring into cataracts,

Wander'd back to living boyhood while I heard the curlews call,
I myself so close on death, and death itself in Locksley Hall.

So – your happy suit was blasted – she the faultless, the divine;
And you liken – boyish babble – this boy-love of yours with mine.

I myself have often babbled doubtless of a foolish past;
Babble, babble; our old England may go down in babble at last.

'Curse him!' curse your fellow-victim? call him dotard in your
 rage?
10 Eyes that lured a doting boyhood well might fool a dotard's age.

Jilted for a wealthier! wealthier? yet perhaps she was not wise;
I remember how you kiss'd the miniature with those sweet eyes.

In the hall there hangs a painting – Amy's arms about my neck –
Happy children in a sunbeam sitting on the ribs of wreck.

In my life there was a picture, she that clasp'd my neck had
 flown;
I was left within the shadow sitting on the wreck alone.

Yours has been a slighter ailment, will you sicken for her sake?
You, not you! your modern amourist is of easier, earthlier make.

Amy loved me, Amy fail'd me, Amy was a timid child;
But your Judith – but your worldling – *she* had never driven me wild. 20

She that holds the diamond necklace dearer than the golden ring,
She that finds a winter sunset fairer than a morn of Spring.

She that in her heart is brooding on his briefer lease of life,
While she vows 'till death shall part us,' she the would-be-widow wife.

She the worldling born of worldlings – father, mother – be content,
Ev'n the homely farm can teach us there is something in descent.

Yonder in that chapel, slowly sinking now into the ground,
Lies the warrior, my forefather, with his feet upon the hound.

Cross'd! for once he sail'd the sea to crush the Moslem in his pride;
Dead the warrior, dead his glory, dead the cause in which he died. 30

Yet how often I and Amy in the mouldering aisle have stood,
Gazing for one pensive moment on that founder of our blood.

There again I stood to-day, and where of old we knelt in prayer,
Close beneath the casement crimson with the shield of Locksley – there,

All in white Italian marble, looking still as if she smiled,
Lies my Amy dead in child-birth, dead the mother, dead the child.

Dead – and sixty years ago, and dead her agèd husband now –
I this old white-headed dreamer stoopt and kiss'd her marble brow.

Gone the fires of youth, the follies, furies, curses, passionate tears,
Gone like fires and floods and earthquakes of the planet's dawning years. 40

Fires that shook me once, but now to silent ashes fall'n away.
Cold upon the dead volcano sleeps the gleam of dying day.

Gone the tyrant of my youth, and mute below the chancel stones,
All his virtues – I forgive them – black in white above his bones.

Gone the comrades of my bivouac, some in fight against the foe,
Some thro' age and slow diseases, gone as all on earth will go.

Gone with whom for forty years my life in golden sequence ran,
She with all the charm of woman, she with all the breadth of man,

Strong in will and rich in wisdom, Edith, yet so lowly-sweet,
50 Woman to her inmost heart, and woman to her tender feet,

Very woman of very woman, nurse of ailing body and mind,
She that link'd again the broken chain that bound me to my kind.

Here to-day was Amy with me, while I wander'd down the coast,
Near us Edith's holy shadow, smiling at the slighter ghost.

Gone our sailor son thy father, Leonard early lost at sea;
Thou alone, my boy, of Amy's kin and mine art left to me.

Gone thy tender-natured mother, wearying to be left alone,
Pining for the stronger heart that once had beat beside her own.

Truth, for Truth is Truth, he worshipt, being true as he was
brave;
Good, for Good is Good, he follow'd, yet he look'd beyond the
60 grave,

Wiser there than you, that crowning barren Death as lord of all,
Deem this over-tragic drama's closing curtain is the pall!

Beautiful was death in him, who saw the death, but kept the deck,
Saving women and their babes, and sinking with the sinking
wreck,

Gone for ever! Ever? no – for since our dying race began,
Ever, ever, and for ever was the leading light of man.

Those that in barbarian burials kill'd the slave, and slew the wife,
Felt within themselves the sacred passion of the second life.

Indian warriors dream of ampler hunting grounds beyond the
night;
Ev'n the black Australian dying hopes he shall return, a white. 70

Truth for truth, and good for good! The Good, the True, the
Pure, the Just –
Take the charm 'For ever' from them, and they crumble into dust.

Gone the cry of 'Forward, Forward,' lost within a growing gloom;
Lost, or only heard in silence from the silence of a tomb.

Half the marvels of my morning, triumphs over time and space,
Staled by frequence, shrunk by usage into commonest
commonplace!

'Forward' rang the voices then, and of the many mine was one.
Let us hush this cry of 'Forward' till ten thousand years have
gone.

Far among the vanish'd races, old Assyrian kings would flay
Captives whom they caught in battle – iron-hearted victors they. 80

Ages after, while in Asia, he that led the wild Moguls,
Timur built his ghastly tower of eighty thousand human skulls,

Then, and here in Edward's time, an age of noblest English
names,
Christian conquerors took and flung the conquer'd Christian into
flames.

Love your enemy, bless your haters, said the Greatest of the great;
Christian love among the Churches look'd the twin of heathen
hate.

From the golden alms of Blessing man had coin'd himself a curse:
Rome of Cæsar, Rome of Peter, which was crueller? which was
worse?

France had shown a light to all men, preach'd a Gospel, all men's
good;
Celtic Demos rose a Demon, shriek'd and slaked the light with
blood. 90

Hope was ever on her mountain, watching till the day begun –
Crown'd with sunlight – over darkness – from the still unrisen sun.

Have we grown at last beyond the passions of the primal clan?
'Kill your enemy, for you hate him,' still, 'your enemy' was a man.

Have we sunk below them? peasants maim the helpless horse, and drive
Innocent cattle under thatch, and burn the kindlier brutes alive.

Brutes, the brutes are not your wrongers – burnt at midnight, found at morn,
Twisted hard in mortal agony with their offspring, born-unborn,

Clinging to the silent mother! Are we devils? are we men?
100 Sweet St Francis of Assisi, would that he were here again,

He that in his Catholic wholeness used to call the very flowers
Sisters, brothers – and the beasts – whose pains are hardly less than ours!

Chaos, Cosmos! Cosmos, Chaos! who can tell how all will end?
Read the wide world's annals, you, and take their wisdom for your friend.

Hope the best, but hold the Present fatal daughter of the Past,
Shape your heart to front the hour, but dream not that the hour will last.

Ay, if dynamite and revolver leave you courage to be wise:
When was age so cramm'd with menace? madness? written, spoken lies?

Envy wears the mask of Love, and, laughing sober fact to scorn,
110 Cries to Weakest as to Strongest, 'Ye are equals, equal-born.'

Equal-born? O yes, if yonder hill be level with the flat.
Charm us, Orator, till the Lion look no larger than the Cat,

Till the Cat thro' that mirage of overheated language loom
Larger than the Lion, – Demos end in working its own doom.

Russia bursts our Indian barrier, shall we fight her? shall we yield?
Pause! before you sound the trumpet, hear the voices from the
field.

Those three hundred millions under one Imperial sceptre now,
Shall we hold them? shall we loose them? take the suffrage of the
plow.

Nay, but these would feel and follow Truth if only you and you,
Rivals of realm-ruining party, when you speak were wholly true. 120

Plowmen, Shepherds, have I found, and more than once, and still
could find,
Sons of God, and kings of men in utter nobleness of mind,

Truthful, trustful, looking upward to the practised hustings-liar;
So the Higher wields the Lower, while the Lower is the Higher.

Here and there a cotter's babe is royal-born by right divine;
Here and there my lord is lower than his oxen or his swine.

Chaos, Cosmos! Cosmos, Chaos! once again the sickening game;
Freedom, free to slay herself, and dying while they shout her
name.

Step by step we gain'd a freedom known to Europe, known to all;
Step by step we rose to greatness, – thro' the tonguesters we may
fall. 130

You that woo the Voices – tell them 'old experience is a fool,'
Teach your flatter'd kings that only those who cannot read can
rule.

Pluck the mighty from their seat, but set no meek ones in their
place;
Pillory Wisdom in your markets, pelt your offal at her face.

Tumble Nature heel o'er head, and, yelling with the yelling street,
Set the feet above the brain and swear the brain is in the feet.

Bring the old dark ages back without the faith, without the hope,
Break the State, the Church, the Throne, and roll their ruins down the slope.

Authors – essayist, atheist, novelist, realist, rhymester, play your part,
140 Paint the mortal shame of nature with the living hues of Art.

Rip your brothers' vices open, strip your own foul passions bare;
Down with Reticence, down with Reverence – forward – naked – let them stare.

Feed the budding rose of boyhood with the drainage of your sewer;
Send the drain into the fountain, lest the stream should issue pure.

Set the maiden fancies wallowing in the troughs of Zolaism, –
Forward, forward, ay and backward, downward too into the abysm.

Do your best to charm the worst, to lower the rising race of men;
Have we risen from out the beast, then back into the beast again?

Only 'dust to dust' for me that sicken at your lawless din,
150 Dust in wholesome old-world dust before the newer world begin.

Heated am I? you – you wonder – well, it scarce becomes mine age –
Patience! let the dying actor mouth his last upon the stage.

Cries of unprogressive dotage ere the dotard fall asleep?
Noises of a current narrowing, not the music of a deep?

Ay, for doubtless I am old, and think gray thoughts, for I am gray:
After all the stormy changes shall we find a changeless May?

After madness, after massacre, Jacobinism and Jacquerie,
Some diviner force to guide us thro' the days I shall not see?

When the schemes and all the systems, Kingdoms and Republics fall,

Something kindlier, higher, holier – all for each and each for all? 160

All the full-brain, half-brain races, led by Justice, Love, and
Truth;
All the millions one at length with all the visions of my youth?

All diseases quench'd by Science, no man halt, or deaf or blind;
Stronger ever born of weaker, lustier body, larger mind?

Earth at last a warless world, a single race, a single tongue –
I have seen her far away – for is not Earth as yet so young? –

Every tiger madness muzzled, every serpent passion kill'd,
Every grim ravine a garden, every blazing desert till'd,

Robed in universal harvest up to either pole she smiles,
Universal ocean softly washing all her warless Isles. 170

Warless? when her tens are thousands, and her thousands millions,
then –
All her harvest all too narrow – who can fancy warless men?

Warless? war will die out late then. Will it ever? late or soon?
Can it, till this outworn earth be dead as yon dead world the
moon?

Dead the new astronomy calls her . . . On this day and at this
hour,
In this gap between the sandhills, whence you see the Locksley
tower,

Here we met, our latest meeting – Amy – sixty years ago –
She and I – the moon was falling greenish thro' a rosy glow,

Just above the gateway tower, and even where you see her now –
Here we stood and claspt each other, swore the seeming-deathless
vow . . . 180

Dead, but how her living glory lights the hall, the dune, the grass!
Yet the moonlight is the sunlight, and the sun himself will pass.

Venus near her! smiling downward at this earthlier earth of ours,
Closer on the Sun, perhaps a world of never fading flowers.

Hesper, whom the poet call'd the Bringer home of all good things.
All good things may move in Hesper, perfect peoples, perfect
kings.

Hesper – Venus – were we native to that splendour or in Mars,
We should see the Globe we groan in, fairest of their evening
stars.

Could we dream of wars and carnage, craft and madness, lust and
spite,
190 Roaring London, raving Paris, in that point of peaceful light?

Might we not in glancing heavenward on a star so silver-fair,
Yearn, and clasp the hands and murmur, 'Would to God that we
were there'?

Forward, backward, backward, forward, in the immeasurable sea,
Sway'd by vaster ebbs and flows than can be known to you or me.

All the suns – are these but symbols of innumerable man,
Man or Mind that sees a shadow of the planner or the plan?

Is there evil but on earth? or pain in every peopled sphere?
Well be grateful for the sounding watchword, 'Evolution' here,

Evolution ever climbing after some ideal good,
200 And Reversion ever dragging Evolution in the mud.

What are men that He should heed us? cried the king of sacred
song;
Insects of an hour, that hourly work their brother insect wrong,

While the silent Heavens roll, and Suns along their fiery way,
All their planets whirling round them, flash a million miles a day.

Many an Æon moulded earth before her highest, man, was born,
Many an Æon too may pass when earth is manless and forlorn,

Earth so huge, and yet so bounded – pools of salt, and plots of
land –
Shallow skin of green and azure – chains of mountain, grains of
sand!

Only That which made us, meant us to be mightier by and by,
Set the sphere of all the boundless Heavens within the human eye, 210

Sent the shadow of Himself, the boundless, thro' the human soul;
Boundless inward, in the atom, boundless outward, in the Whole.

*

Here is Locksley Hall, my grandson, here the lion-guarded gate.
Not to-night in Locksley Hall – to-morrow – you, you come so late.

Wreck'd – your train – or all but wreck'd? a shatter'd wheel? a
vicious boy!
Good, this forward, you that preach it, is it well to wish you joy?

Is it well that while we range with Science, glorying in the Time,
City children soak and blacken soul and sense in city slime?

There among the glooming alleys Progress halts on palsied feet,
Crime and hunger cast our maidens by the thousand on the street. 220

There the Master scrimps his haggard sempstress of her daily
bread,
There a single sordid attic holds the living and the dead.

There the smouldering fire of fever creeps across the rotted floor,
And the crowded couch of incest in the warrens of the poor.

Nay, your pardon, cry your 'forward,' yours are hope and youth,
but I –
Eighty winters leave the dog too lame to follow with the cry,

Lame and old, and past his time, and passing now into the night;
Yet I would the rising race were half as eager for the light.

Light the fading gleam of Even? light the glimmer of the dawn?
Agèd eyes may take the growing glimmer for the gleam
withdrawn. 230

Far away beyond her myriad coming changes earth will be
Something other than the wildest modern guess of you and me.

*

Earth may reach her earthly-worst, or if she gain her earthly-best,
Would she find her human offspring this ideal man at rest?

Forward then, but still remember how the course of Time will swerve,
Crook and turn upon itself in many a backward streaming curve.

Not the Hall to-night, my grandson! Death and Silence hold their own.
Leave the Master in the first dark hour of his last sleep alone.

Worthier soul was he than I am, sound and honest, rustic Squire,
240 Kindly landlord, boon companion – youthful jealousy is a liar.

Cast the poison from your bosom, oust the madness from your brain.
Let the trampled serpent show you that you have not lived in vain.

Youthful! youth and age are scholars yet but in the lower school,
Nor is he the wisest man who never proved himself a fool.

Yonder lies our young sea-village – Art and Grace are less and less:
Science grows and Beauty dwindles – roofs of slated hideousness!

There is one old Hostel left us where they swing the Locksley shield,
Till the peasant cow shall butt the 'Lion passant' from his field.

Poor old Heraldry, poor old History, poor old Poetry, passing hence,
250 In the common deluge drowning old political commonsense!

Poor old voice of eighty crying after voices that have fled!
All I loved are vanish'd voices, all my steps are on the dead.

All the world is ghost to me, and as the phantom disappears,
Forward far and far from here is all the hope of eighty years.

*

In this Hostel – I remember – I repent it o'er his grave –
Like a clown – by chance he met me – I refused the hand he
gave.

From that casement where the trailer mantles all the mouldering
bricks –
I was then in early boyhood, Edith but a child of six –

While I shelter'd in this archway from a day of driving showers –
Peept the winsome face of Edith like a flower among the flowers. 260

Here to-night! the Hall to-morrow, when they toll the Chapel bell!
Shall I hear in one dark room a wailing, 'I have loved thee well.'

Then a peal that shakes the portal – one has come to claim his
bride,
Her that shrank, and put me from her, shriek'd, and started from
my side –

Silent echoes! You, my Leonard, use and not abuse your day,
Move among your people, know them, follow him who led the way,

Strove for sixty widow'd years to help his homelier brother men,
Served the poor, and built the cottage, raised the school, and
drain'd the fen.

Hears he now the Voice that wrong'd him? who shall swear it
cannot be?
Earth would never touch her worst, were one in fifty such as he. 270

Ere she gain her Heavenly-best, a God must mingle with the
game:
Nay, there may be those about us whom we neither see nor name,

Felt within us as ourselves, the Powers of Good, the Powers of Ill,
Strowing balm, or shedding poison in the fountains of the Will.

Follow you the Star that lights a desert pathway, yours or mine.
Forward, till you see the highest Human Nature is divine.

Follow Light, and do the Right – for man can half-control his
doom –

Till you find the deathless Angel seated in the vacant tomb.

Forward, let the stormy moment fly and mingle with the Past.
I that loathed, have come to love him. Love will conquer at the
280 last.

Gone at eighty, mine own age, and I and you will bear the pall;
Then I leave thee Lord and Master, latest Lord of Locksley Hall.

From *Demeter and Other Poems* (1889)

Demeter and Persephone

(*In Enna*)

Faint as a climate-changing bird that flies
All night across the darkness, and at dawn
Falls on the threshold of her native land,
And can no more, thou camest, O my child,
Led upward by the God of ghosts and dreams,
Who laid thee at Eleusis, dazed and dumb
With passing thro' at once from state to state,
Until I brought thee hither, that the day,
When here thy hands let fall the gather'd flower,
Might break thro' clouded memories once again 10
On thy lost self. A sudden nightingale
Saw thee, and flash'd into a frolic of song
And welcome; and a gleam as of the moon,
When first she peers along the tremulous deep,
Fled wavering o'er thy face, and chased away
That shadow of a likeness to the king
Of shadows, thy dark mate. Persephone!
Queen of the dead no more – my child! Thine eyes
Again were human-godlike, and the Sun
Burst from a swimming fleece of winter gray, 20
And robed thee in his day from head to feet –
'Mother!' and I was folded in thine arms.

Child, those imperial, disimpassion'd eyes
Awed even me at first, thy mother – eyes
That oft had seen the serpent-wanded power

Draw downward into Hades with his drift
Of flickering spectres, lighted from below
By the red race of fiery Phlegethon;
But when before have Gods or men beheld
30 The Life that had descended re-arise,
And lighted from above him by the Sun?
So mighty was the mother's childless cry,
A cry that rang thro' Hades, Earth, and Heaven!

So in this pleasant vale we stand again,
The field of Enna, now once more ablaze
With flowers that brighten as thy footstep falls,
All flowers – but for one black blur of earth
Left by that closing chasm, thro' which the car
Of dark Aïdoneus rising rapt thee hence.
40 And here, my child, tho' folded in thine arms,
I feel the deathless heart of motherhood
Within me shudder, lest the naked glebe
Should yawn once more into the gulf, and thence
The shrilly whinnyings of the team of Hell,
Ascending, pierce the glad and songful air,
And all at once their arch'd necks, midnight-maned,
Jet upward thro' the mid-day blossom. No!
For, see, thy foot has touch'd it; all the space
Of blank earth-baldness clothes itself afresh,
50 And breaks into the crocus-purple hour
That saw thee vanish.

Child, when thou wert gone,
I envied human wives, and nested birds,
Yea, the cubb'd lioness; went in search of thee
Thro' many a palace, many a cot, and gave
Thy breast to ailing infants in the night,
And set the mother waking in amaze
To find her sick one whole; and forth again
Among the wail of midnight winds, and cried,
'Where is my loved one? Wherefore do ye wail?'
60 And out from all the night an answer shrill'd,

'We know not, and we know not why we wail.'
I climb'd on all the cliffs of all the seas,
And ask'd the waves that moan about the world
'Where? do ye make your moaning for my child?'
And round from all the world the voices came
'We know not, and we know not why we moan.'
'Where'? and I stared from every eagle-peak,
I thridded the black heart of all the woods,
I peer'd thro' tomb and cave, and in the storms
Of Autumn swept across the city, and heard 70
The murmur of their temples chanting me,
Me, me, the desolate Mother! 'Where'? – and turn'd,
And fled by many a waste, forlorn of man,
And grieved for man thro' all my grief for thee, –
The jungle rooted in his shatter'd hearth,
The serpent coil'd about his broken shaft,
The scorpion crawling over naked skulls; –
I saw the tiger in the ruin'd fane
Spring from his fallen God, but trace of thee
I saw not; and far on, and, following out 80
A league of labyrinthine darkness, came
On three gray heads beneath a gleaming rift.
'Where'? and I heard one voice from all the three
'We know not, for we spin the lives of men,
And not of Gods, and know not why we spin!
There is a Fate beyond us.' Nothing knew.

Last as the likeness of a dying man,
Without his knowledge, from him flits to warn
A far-off friendship that he comes no more,
So he, the God of dreams, who heard my cry, 90
Drew from thyself the likeness of thyself
Without thy knowledge, and thy shadow past
Before me, crying 'The Bright one in the highest
Is brother of the Dark one in the lowest,
And Bright and Dark have sworn that I, the child
Of thee, the great Earth-Mother, thee, the Power

That lifts her buried life from gloom to bloom,
Should be for ever and for evermore
The Bride of Darkness.'

So the Shadow wail'd.
100 Then I, Earth-Goddess, cursed the Gods of Heaven.
I would not mingle with their feasts; to me
Their nectar smack'd of hemlock on the lips,
Their rich ambrosia tasted aconite.
The man, that only lives and loves an hour,
Seem'd nobler than their hard Eternities.
My quick tears kill'd the flower, my ravings hush'd
The bird, and lost in utter grief I fail'd
To send my life thro' olive-yard and vine
And golden grain, my gift to helpless man.
110 Rain-rotten died the wheat, the barley-spears
Were hollow-husk'd, the leaf fell, and the sun,
Pale at my grief, drew down before his time
Sickening, and Aetna kept her winter snow.
Then He, the brother of this Darkness, He
Who still is highest, glancing from his height
On earth a fruitless fallow, when he miss'd
The wonted steam of sacrifice, the praise
And prayer of men, decreed that thou should'st dwell
For nine white moons of each whole year with me,
120 Three dark ones in the shadow with thy King.

Once more the reaper in the gleam of dawn
Will see me by the landmark far away,
Blessing his field, or seated in the dusk
Of even, by the lonely threshing-floor,
Rejoicing in the harvest and the grange.
Yet I, Earth-Goddess, am but ill-content
With them, who still are highest. Those gray heads,
What meant they by their 'Fate beyond the Fates'
But younger kindlier Gods to bear us down,
130 As we bore down the Gods before us? Gods,

To quench, not hurl the thunderbolt, to stay,
Not spread the plague, the famine; Gods indeed,
To send the noon into the night and break
The sunless halls of Hades into Heaven?
Till thy dark lord accept and love the Sun,
And all the Shadow die into the Light,
When thou shalt dwell the whole bright year with me,
And souls of men, who grew beyond their race,
And made themselves as Gods against the fear
Of Death and Hell; and thou that hast from men, 140
As Queen of Death, that worship which is Fear,
Henceforth, as having risen from out the dead,
Shalt ever send thy life along with mine
From buried grain thro' springing blade, and bless
Their garner'd Autumn also, reap with me,
Earth-mother, in the harvest hymns of Earth
The worship which is Love, and see no morc
The Stone, the Wheel, the dimly-glimmering lawns
Of that Elysium, all the hateful fires
Of torment, and the shadowy warrior glide 150
Along the silent field of Asphodel.

Crossing the Bar

Sunset and evening star,
And one clear call for me!
And may there be no moaning of the bar,
When I put out to sea,

But such a tide as moving seems asleep,
Too full for sound and foam,
When that which drew from out the boundless deep
Turns again home.

Twilight and evening bell,
10 And after that the dark!
And may there be no sadness of farewell,
When I embark;

For tho' from out our bourne of Time and Place
The flood may bear me far,
I hope to see my Pilot face to face
When I have crost the bar.

NOTES

ABBREVIATIONS

TENNYSON'S WORKS

1830	*Poems, Chiefly Lyrical.*
1832	*Poems.*
1842	*Poems*, 2 vols.
1847	*The Princess.*
1850	*The Princess*, third edition.
1855	*Maud, and Other Poems.*
1864	*Enoch Arden.*
1869	*The Holy Grail and Other Poems.*
1885	*Tiresias and Other Poems.*
1889	*Demeter and Other Poems.*

OTHER

AHH	*The Letters of Arthur Henry Hallam*, ed. Jack Kolb, 1981.
Buckley	Jerome Hamilton Buckley, *Tennyson: The Growth of a Poet*, 1960.
Eversley	*The Works of Tennyson*, ed. Hallam Lord Tennyson, 9 vols., 1907–8; with notes by Tennyson.
JEGP	*Journal of English and Germanic Philology.*
Killham	John Killham, ed., *Critical Essays on the Poetry of Tennyson*, 1960.
Letters	*The Letters of Alfred Lord Tennyson*, ed. Cecil Y. Lang and Edgar F. Shannon, Jr.; vol. I: 1982; vol. II: 1987; vol. III: 1990.
Lincoln	The Tennyson Research Centre, Lincoln. Holdings at the Centre include books from Tennyson's father's library to which Tennyson would have had access at Somersby; journals, notebooks, poetical manuscripts; and thousands of family letters.
Materials	Hallam Lord Tennyson, *Materials for a Life of A. T. Collected for My Children*, 4 vols., privately printed *c.* 1895.
Memoir	Hallam Lord Tennyson, *Alfred Lord Tennyson: A Memoir By His Son*, 2 vols., 1897.

PMLA — *Publications of the Modern Language Association of America.*

Rader — Ralph Wilson Rader, *Tennyson's 'Maud': The Biographical Genesis*, 1963.

Ray — Gordon N. Ray, *Tennyson Reads 'Maud'*, 1968. Includes comments on *In Memoriam* and *Maud* made by Tennyson to James Knowles in 1870–71. Some of these had originally been published by Knowles in 'Aspects of Tennyson II (a Personal Reminiscence)', *Nineteenth Century*, XXXIII, 1893, pp. 164–88.

Ricks — Christopher Ricks, ed., *The Poems of Tennyson*, 1969; second edition, 3 vols., 1987.

SB — *Studies in Bibliography.*

TRB — *Tennyson Research Bulletin.*

POEMS

Timbuctoo

Published in *Cambridge Chronicle and Journal*, 10 July 1829; then in *Prolusiones Academicae* (1829, the text adopted here). 'Timbuctoo' was announced as the subject for the Chancellor's Gold Medal in December 1828; on 6 June 1829 the announcement was made that Tennyson had won the prize. Tennyson cannibalized an earlier poem, 'Armageddon', in his writing of 'Timbuctoo'. Christopher Ricks has noted that a version of 'Armageddon' in Trinity College Notebook 18 (1828) shows that 'Broadly, the whole central vision of "Timbuctoo", from l.62 ... to l.190 ... was present ... in "Armageddon"' ('Tennyson: "Armageddon" into "Timbuctoo"', *Modern Language Review*, LXI, 1966, p.23). On the failure of confidence in high Romantic values manifest in 'Timbuctoo' see Aidan Day, 'The Spirit of Fable: Arthur Hallam and Romantic Values in Tennyson's "Timbuctoo"', *TRB*, 4, 1983, pp.59–71. The epigraph to the poem is not by *George* Chapman, presumably a Tennysonian licence. In *1829* l.196, after 'Heaven', has the note: 'Be ye perfect even as your Father in Heaven is perfect' (from Matthew 5:48).

The Idealist

Unpublished in Tennyson's lifetime; first published *Ricks*. It is dated 1829 in Trinity College Allen MS, R.7.50 (the text adopted here) and in the Fitzwilliam Museum Heath MS (compiled 1832–4).

FROM *POEMS, CHIEFLY LYRICAL* (1830)

Mariana

Published *1830*. Tennyson noted 'The *moated grange* was no particular grange, but one which rose to the music of Shakespeare's words' (*Eversley*). The epigraph is from *Measure for Measure* (III, i, 212ff): 'She should this Angelo have married: was affianced to her by oath, and the nuptial appointed ... [Angelo] Left her in her tears, and dried not one of them with his comfort ... there at the moated grange resides this dejected Mariana'. Among other influences was Goethe's *Wilhelm Meister's Apprenticeship*: 'Wilhelm's first love is an actress called Mariana ... Goethe's Mariana finds no such happy consummation [as Shakespeare's] ... she waits and watches for him in vain' (Ian Kennedy, 'Alfred Tennyson's *Bildungsgang*: Notes on

His Early Reading', *Philological Quarterly*, 57, 1978, p.93). H. M. McLuhan comments, '"Mariana" is there to prove that the most sophisticated symbolist poetry could be written fifty years before the Symbolists' ('Tennyson and Picturesque Poetry', *Essays in Criticism*, I, 1951, pp.262–82; reprinted in *Killham*, pp.67–85).

Supposed Confessions of a Second-Rate Sensitive Mind

Published *1830*, with a longer title '. . . *Mind Not In Unity With Itself*'. The uncertainties and dubieties in the poem precede the death of Arthur Hallam and look forward to 'The Two Voices' and *In Memoriam*.

Song ['*A spirit haunts the year's last hours*']

Published *1830*. Hallam Tennyson notes (*Eversley*): 'Written at Somersby'. The first stanza appears in Trinity College Notebook 18 (1828).

A Character

Published *1830*. The poem is on Thomas Sunderland (1808–67), who was at Trinity College with Tennyson. Edward FitzGerald spoke of Sunderland as 'a very plausible, parliament-like, and self-satisfied speaker at the Union Debating Society' (*Eversley*). See Peter Allen, *The Cambridge Apostles: The Early Years* (1978, chapter 3): 'Thomas Sunderland and the Cambridge Union'.

The Poet's Mind

Published *1830*. G. H. Ford, in *Keats and the Victorians: A Study of His Influence and Rise to Fame, 1821–1895* (1944, p.34) notes that the principal influence is the end of Keats's *Lamia*: 'Do not all charms fly/At the mere touch of cold philosophy?' (II.229–300). The piece is touched by the high Romantic idealism which was characteristic of Tennyson's Cambridge circle and which, in a poem such as 'Timbuctoo', Tennyson subjected to sceptical inquiry.

Nothing Will Die

Published *1830*.

All Things Will Die

Published *1830*.

The Dying Swan

Published *1830*. The tradition of the swan's death-song was discussed in William Hone's *Every-Day Book* (1825, II, pp.964–8) which Hallam Tennyson cites as a source of 'St Simeon Stylites' (*Eversley*).

The Kraken

Published *1830*. Tennyson notes (*Eversley*): 'See the account which Erik Pontoppidan, the Norwegian bishop, born 1698, gives of the fabulous sea-monster – the kraken (*Biographie Universelle*)'. Pontoppidan's description was recounted in the *English Encyclopaedia* (1802), of which there was a copy at Somersby (*Lincoln*).

FROM *POEMS* (1832)

The Lady of Shalott

Published *1832*; extensively revised *1842*. At least partly written by 5–9 October 1831 (*AHH*, p.487). Tennyson notes that it was based on 'an Italian novelette, *Donna di Scalotta*' (*Eversley*). The source is given in *Materials* (IV, p.461): 'The following is the Italian novella on which "The Lady of Shalott" was founded: Novella LXXXI . . . From the *Cento Novelle Antiche,* dated conjecturally before 1321. Text from the Milan edn, ed. G. Ferrario, 1804.' But the story is different in important respects. F. J. Furnivall cites Tennyson in January 1868: 'I met the story first in some Italian *novelle*: but the web, mirror, island, etc., were my own' (*Rossetti Papers 1862–1870*, ed. W. M. Rossetti, 1903, p.341). Tennyson also commented 'The Lady of Shalott is evidently the Elaine of the *Morte d'Arthur*, but I do not think that I had ever heard of the latter when I wrote the former' (*Eversley*). Northrop Frye, commenting on Romantic views of the imagination and on the interiority of Romantic metaphorical structures, observes: 'the attempt to turn around and see the source of one's vision may be destructive, as the Lady of Shalott found when she turned away from the mirror. Thus the world of the deep interior in Romantic poetry is morally ambivalent' ('The Drunken Boat: The Revolutionary Element in Romanticism', *Romanticism Reconsidered,* ed. Northrop Frye, 1963, p.19).

Mariana in the South

Published *1832*; considerably revised *1842*. Written 1830–1. Tennyson notes (*Eversley*): 'The idea of this came into my head between Narbonne and Perpignan', during a summer 1830 tour of the Pyrenees with Arthur Hallam. Hallam observed to W. B. Donne on 13 February 1831 (*AHH*, p.401)

It is intended . . . as a kind of pendant to his former poem of Mariana, the idea of both being the expression of desolate loneliness, but with this distinctive variety in the second that it paints the forlorn feeling as it would exist under the influence of different impressions of sense . . . the essential & distinguishing character of the conception requires in the Southern Mariana a greater lingering on the outward circumstances, and a less palpable transition of the poet into Mariana's feelings, than was the case in the former poem.

Fatima

Published *1832*, without a title but with an epigraph from Sappho's *Fragment 2*: *φαίνεταί μοι κῆνος ἴσος θέοισιν / ἔμμεν ὤνηρ*; revised for *1842*.

Oenone

Published *1832*; greatly revised for *1842*. Written 1830–2; the scenery prompted by the Pyrenees, where Tennyson noted part of it was written during the summer of 1830 (*Eversley*). The classical allusions – particularly Ovid's *Heroides* and Theocritus – have been exhaustively discussed by P. Turner ('Some Ancient Light on Tennyson's "Oenone"', *JEGP*, LXI, 1962, pp. 57–72). Oenone was the daughter of a river-god and married to the Trojan prince Paris. In this poem she is spectator of the judgement in which Paris awards the apple of discord to the goddess Aphroditè, who promises him success in love, rather than to Herè or Pallas, who promise him power and wisdom respectively. Paris deserted Oenone for Helen, whom he carried off to Troy, thus instigating the Trojan War which is anticipated at the close of this poem. A. D. Culler notes that the central judgement scene 'has echoes of the temptation scenes in *Paradise Lost* and *Paradise Regained*, and, indeed, it is less a judgement scene than a temptation. It is a temptation *to* judge, as well as to judge wrong' (*The Poetry of Tennyson*, 1977, p. 79).

The Palace of Art

Published *1832*; much revised *1842*. Completed by April 1832 (*Memoir*, I, p. 85). Possibly not begun before October 1831, the date of Arthur Hallam's *Theodicaea Novissima* (see l. 223: in *Eversley* Tennyson observes that this line parallels an expression in Hallam's *Theodicaea Novissima*: 'the power of God's election, with whom alone rest the abysmal secrets of personality'). Tennyson also notes that R. C. Trench 'said, when we were at Trinity (Cambridge) together, "Tennyson, we cannot live in Art". This poem is the embodiment of my own belief that the Godlike life is with man and for man.' There are numerous biblical and literary sources or analogues from Ecclesiastes 2: 1–17 through to Shelley's *Queen Mab* (II, ll. 56–64). A. D. Culler (*The Poetry of Tennyson*, 1977, pp. 70–72) comments on the similarity between much of the architecture of the poem and Cambridge, particularly Tennyson's Trinity College. He notes that 'the pantheon of wise men whose busts adorn the Palace of Art is virtually that of the Apostles themselves'.

The Hesperides

Published *1832*; not reprinted in Tennyson's lifetime. The epigraph is from Milton's *Comus* (ll.982–3). Tennyson later regretted withdrawing it and Hallam Tennyson reprinted it in *Memoir*, I, pp.61–5 and in the *Eversley* notes (the text here is from *1832*). The poem was recited October 1830 (H. Alford, *Life*, 1873, p.61) and appears in Trinity College Notebook 23 (1830). Together with the dragon Ladon, the daughters of Hesperus, who lived where the sun sets in the west, protected the golden apples given by Ge (Earth) to Hera at her marriage with Zeus. Hercules killed the guardian dragon and removed the apples. See G. R. Stange's suggestion that the poem is 'a symbolic statement of the situation of the artist' in 'Tennyson's Garden of Art: A Study of "The Hesperides"' (first published *PMLA*, 67, 1952, pp.732–43; reprinted in *Killham*, pp.99–112). For a differing view of the poem's treatment of Romantic ideas of creativity, see Aidan Day, 'Voices in a Dream: The Language of Skepticism in Tennyson's "The Hesperides"', *Victorian Newsletter*, 62, 1982, pp.13–21. The *Periplus* of the Carthaginian Hanno, who sailed down the west coast of Africa in the fifth century B.C., is the source of Tennyson's prologue. Douglas Bush (*Major British Writers*, 1959, II, p.382) suggests that Tennyson 'presumably used *The Voyage of Hanno*, translated T. Falconer (1797); Falconer has ... remarks on the island of the Hesperides'.

The Lotos-Eaters

Published *1832*. In *1842* the major revisions were the addition of ll.114–32 and the rewriting of ll.150–73. Composed 1830–32 (*Memoir*, I, p.86). The principal source was *Odyssey* (IX, ll.82–104), where Odysseus describes how the lotus-eaters persuaded some of his men to eat the 'honey-sweet fruit of the lotus'. These men no longer wanted to leave the land of the lotus-eaters, wishing only to feed on the lotus, 'forgetful of [their] homeward way'. Thus Odysseus brings them, weeping, back to their boat. The principal influence on style and tone was Spenser, especially the cave of Morpheus, *Faerie Queene* (I, i, st.41); the blandishments of Despair (I, ix, st.40); the 'Idle Lake' and its debilitating island (II, vi, st.10); and the mermaids and the Bower of Bliss (II, xii, st.32). The gods mentioned in ll.150–73 are derived from Lucretius's description of the Epicurean gods in *De Rerum Natura* (III, ll.18–24). Robert Langbaum (*The Poetry of Experience: The Dramatic*

Monologue in Modern Literary Tradition, 1957, p.90) argues that, considered as a dramatic monologue, the 'Choric Song' of this poem allows us little reserve of judgement, and that Tennyson the author is to be identified with the 'weariness and longing for rest' expressed by his mariners.

'Hark! the dogs howl!'

Unpublished in Tennyson's lifetime. Hallam Tennyson printed ll.7–8, 10–11, 18–21, 26 of the poem: 'On the evening of one of these sad winter days [late 1833; the news of Arthur Hallam's death was sent to Tennyson on 1 October 1833] my father had already noted down in his scrapbook some fragmentary lines, which proved to be the germ of *In Memoriam*' (*Memoir*, I, p.107). First printed in full in *Ricks*. The text here is from Harvard Notebook 16 (1833).

'This Nature full of hints and mysteries'

A fragment first published in *Ricks*. The text here is from Trinity College Notebook 20 (1833).

'Over the dark world flies the wind'

First published by Sir Charles Tennyson in *Nineteenth Century* (CIX, 1931, p.504); then in *Unpublished Early Poems by Alfred Tennyson* (ed. Charles Tennyson, 1931, p.72). Sir Charles printed it, as here, from Harvard Notebook 16, which is watermarked 1833 and includes portions of *In Memoriam*. Sir Charles noted that the poem 'is characteristic of Tennyson's nature poetry during the early *In Memoriam* period. MS evidence suggests that many sections of that poem were founded on brief mood pictures like this, written in various metres'.

'Oh! that 'twere possible'

Published, as *Stanzas*, in *The Tribute* (ed. Lord Northampton, 1837). First written, without ll.71–110 (added in 1837), in 1833–4 and apparently informed by Tennyson's feelings on the death of Arthur Hallam. It appears in two drafts in the Fitzwilliam Museum Heath MS (compiled 1832–4). The poem has many connections with *In Memoriam*: see G. O. Marshall, 'Tennyson's "Oh! that 'twere possible!": A Link between *In Memoriam* and *Maud*' (*PMLA*, LXXVIII, 1963, pp.225–9). But while the association with the death of Hallam is important, the poem also has numerous links with *The Lover's Tale*, originally composed before Hallam's death. On this see

Aidan Day, 'The Archetype that Waits: *The Lover's Tale, In Memoriam,* and *Maud*' in *Tennyson Society Lectures*, ed. Philip Collins (forthcoming). Tennyson later took 'Oh! that 'twere possible' as the germ of *Maud*, incorporating it there as II, iv, ll. 141–238.

FROM *POEMS* (1842)

The Epic [*Morte d'Arthur*]

Published *1842*. Written after 1835 (*Eversley*), possibly 1837–8, if the references to skating and geology are anything to go by (*Memoir*, I, pp. 150, 162). Edward FitzGerald notes (*Eversley*) that this frame was added to 'Morte d'Arthur' in order 'to anticipate or excuse the "faint Homeric echoes"', and 'to give a reason for telling an old-world tale'. The poem suggests Tennyson's early wish to write an epic on Arthur in twelve books, though when he later came to produce *Idylls of the King* the 'Morte' formed part of the twelfth, not the eleventh book (l. 41).

Morte d'Arthur

Published *1842*. Written 1833–4 (*Memoir*, I, pp. 129, 138) after the news of Arthur Hallam's death had reached Tennyson at the beginning of October 1833. Tennyson's first major Arthurian work, subsequently incorporated in *Idylls of the King* as ll. 170–440 of 'The Passing of Arthur'. It is based on Malory's *Morte d'Arthur*, XXI, chapters 4–5 (Tennyson owned a three-volume edition of 1816: *Lincoln*). The Homeric echoes mentioned in 'The Epic' include set lines opening and ending speeches; the expressions of one speaker being quoted by another; set epithets; and soliloquies. Tennyson noted that 'Lyonnesse' (l. 4) is 'the country of legend that lay between Cornwall and the Scilly Islands' (*Eversley*).

The Gardener's Daughter

Published *1842*. First composed 1833–4 (*Memoir*, I. p. 103, and Fitzwilliam Museum Heath MS). Arthur Hallam wrote on 31 July 1833: 'I trust you finished *The Gardener's Daughter*' (*AHH*, p. 767). Shadowing the poem is Tennyson's friendship for Hallam (the narrator's for Eustace) and Hallam's love for Tennyson's sister Emily (Eustace's for Juliet). The poem is indebted to Theocritus, particularly the seventh Idyll.

St Simeon Stylites

Published *1842*. Dated 1833 in the Fitzwilliam Museum Heath MS; written by 27 November (*Letters*, I, p. 98; *Memoir*, I, p. 130). Simeon (390–459), the first and most renowned of the Pillar-hermits, was born in Northern Syria and lived on a pillar for thirty years (Stylites, from στῦλος, Greek for pillar). The sources given by Hallam Tennyson (*Eversley*) include William Hone's *Every-Day Book* (1825, I, pp.35–9) and chapter 37 of Gibbon's *Decline and Fall of the Roman Empire*. Edward FitzGerald notes (*Eversley*): 'This is one of the Poems A.T. would read with grotesque Grimness, especially at such passages as "Coughs, Aches, Stitches, etc." [ll.13–16], laughing aloud at times'.

Ulysses

Published *1842*. Composed by 20 October 1833 (dated in Fitzwilliam Museum Heath MS). In *Eversley* Tennyson notes: 'The poem was written soon after Arthur Hallam's death, and it gives the feeling about the need of going forward and braving the struggle of life perhaps more simply than anything in *In Memoriam*.' To James Knowles, he said: 'There's more about myself in *Ulysses*, which was written under the sense of loss and that all had gone by, but that still life must be fought out to the end. It was more written with the feeling of his loss upon me than many poems in *In Memoriam*' (*Ray*, pp.37–8). The poem treats Ulysses on the threshold of his last wanderings well after the end of the *Odyssey*. In *Eversley* Tennyson identifies as sources, *Odyssey* (XI, ll.100–37) and Dante's *Inferno* (XXVI, ll.90ff.). Robert Langbaum (*The Poetry of Experience: The Dramatic Monologue in Modern Literary Tradition*, 1957, p.90) argues that it is a mistake to read 'Ulysses' as a poem of strenuousness: 'its music bears the enervated cadence of "Tithonus" and "The Lotos-Eaters"'.

Locksley Hall

Published *1842*. Written 1837–8 (*Rader*, pp.41–2). Tennyson's love affair with Rosa Baring (described in detail in *Rader*) is the principal source from Tennyson's life. The poem is influenced by Tennyson's disillusionment with Rosa and probably by talk in 1837 of her engagement and her marriage in October 1838. *Rader* emphasizes that Rosa's was an arranged marriage (ep. ll.59–62) and that the Hall may have been modelled on Harrington Hall, home of the Barings, near Somersby. Tennyson insisted that it was 'an imaginary place and imaginary hero' (*Eversley*); but his experience of 'marriage-hindering Mammon' informed, among other poems, 'Edwin Morris' and *Maud*. Hallam Tennyson suggests (*Eversley*) that 'Sir William Jones's translation of the *Moâllakát*, the seven Arabic poems . . . hanging up in the temple of Mecca, gave the idea of the poem'. The first poem – of Amriolkais – deals with a poet passing the former dwelling of his former mistress and lamenting his loss. The distinctive use of the eight-stress trochaic line may have been spurred by the fact that Jones's prose naturally fell into such a line in his rendering of the Amriolkais (see Christopher Ricks, '"Locksley Hall" and the "Moâllakát"', *Notes and Queries,* 12, 8, 1965, pp. 300–301).

The Two Voices

Published *1842* (dated '1833'). In Fitzwilliam Museum Heath MS (compiled 1832–4) and in Trinity College Notebook 15 (1833) it is titled 'Thoughts of a Suicide'. A version of the poem existed before Tennyson had been sent (1 October 1833) news of Hallam's death. J. M. Kemble wrote to W. B. Donne, in a letter postmarked 22 June 1833: 'Next Sir are some superb meditations on Self destruction called *Thoughts of a Suicide* wherein he argues the point with his soul and is thoroughly floored' (*Ricks,* I, p. 570). The poem may have been touched by Hallam's death in its post-1833 stages of composition. Edmund Lushington reports that Tennyson 'left it for some time unfinished . . . The termination . . . I first heard him read' in 1837 or 1838 (*Materials,* I, p. 246). Thomas Carlyle wrote to Tennyson on 7 December 1842: 'in the "Two Voices" . . . I think of passages in *Job*' (*Memoir,* I, p. 213).

'Move eastward, happy earth, and leave'

Published *1842*. An epithalamium, it possibly dates from the marriage of Tennyson's brother Charles in May 1836, or alternatively, from early in 1838, when Tennyson's engagement to Emily Sellwood was recognized.

'Break, break, break'

Published *1842*. Written 'in a Lincolnshire Lane' one spring (*Memoir,* I, p. 190), so apparently after September 1833, since it seems to be on the death of Arthur Hallam, and before early 1837, when the Tennysons departed from Somersby.

FROM *POEMS* (1846)

The Golden Year

Published *Poems,* fourth edition, 1846. Probably written on a visit to

Llanberis in 1839 (*Ricks*, II, p. 149). The notion of the golden year derives from the classical idea (as in Virgil, *Eclogue* IV) of the great new era.

FROM *THE PRINCESS* (1847)

Tennyson observed of the Songs (*Eversley*):

> The child is the link thro' the parts, as shown in the Songs (inserted 1850), which are the best interpreters of the poem ... Before the first edition came out, I deliberated with myself whether I should put songs between the separate divisions of the poem; again I thought that the poem would explain itself, but the public did not see the drift.

'As thro' the land at eve we went'

Written 1849 and added in *1850* to intercalate Parts I and II.

'Sweet and low, sweet and low'

Written in 1849 and added in *1850* to intercalate Parts II and III.

'The splendour falls on castle walls'

Tennyson noted: 'Written after hearing the echoes at Killarney in 1848' (*Eversley*). Added in *1850* to intercalate Parts III and IV.

'Tears, idle tears, I know not what they mean'

Published *1847*. An integral section (ll. 21–40) of Part IV. Tennyson commented: 'This song came to me on the yellowing autumn-tide at Tintern Abbey, full for me of its bygone memories. It is the sense of the abiding in the transient' (*Eversley*). See Cleanth Brooks, 'The Motivation of Tennyson's Weeper', *The Well-Wrought Urn: Studies in the Structure of Poetry*, 1947; (revised edition, 1968, pp. 136–44; reprinted in *Killham*, pp. 177–85).

'Ask me no more: the moon may draw the sea'

Written 1849 and added in *1850* to intercalate Parts VI and VII.

'Now sleeps the crimson petal, now the white'

Published *1847*. An integral section (ll. 161–74) of Part VII. Elements of form and diction are influenced by Eastern sources (see John Killham, *Tennyson and 'The Princess': Reflections of an Age*, 1958, pp. 219–20).

'Come down, O maid, from yonder mountain height'

Published *1847*. An integral section (ll. 177–207) of Part VII. Tennyson observed: '*Come down, O maid* is said to be taken from Theocritus, but there is no real likeness except perhaps in the Greek Idyllic feeling' (*Eversley*).

Lines ['*Here often, when a child, I lay reclined*']

The first stanza published *Manchester Athenaeum Album*, 1850; not reprinted in Tennyson's lifetime. Hallam Tennyson put the date of composition as 1837 when he printed this stanza, under the title 'Mablethorpe' (*Memoir*, I, p. 161). But it appears in Trinity College Notebook 17 (1833–5) along with poems of 1833 and together with the second stanza as printed here. See Sir Charles Tennyson and Christopher Ricks, 'Tennyson's "Mablethorpe"' (*TRB*, 2, 1974, pp. 121–3).

In Memoriam A. H. H. (1850)

Published, anonymously, 1850. Tennyson's close friend, Arthur Henry Hallam, died at Vienna on 15 September 1833 – 'a blood-vessel near the brain had suddenly burst' (*Memoir*, I, p. 105). Tennyson was sent the news on 1 October by Henry Elton, Hallam's uncle.

Hallam had written a favourable and acute review of Tennyson's *1830* volume of poems, 'On Some of the Characteristics of Modern Poetry and on the Lyrical Poetry of Alfred Tennyson', in the *Englishman's Magazine* for August 1831. Hallam's 1831 *Theodicaea Novissima* was, in broad terms, an influence on the religious thinking of *In Memoriam* (it was at Tennyson's request that the *Theodicaea* was included in Hallam's *Remains*, edited by his father Henry Hallam in 1834). In 1833 Hallam's engagement to Tennyson's sister Emily was recognized by his family. He was buried on 3 January 1834 at Clevedon, Somerset.

Tennyson began writing the sections of the poem in 1833 and continued right through 1848. In 1870–71 Tennyson told James Knowles that section IX was 'the first written' section (*Ray*, p. 38). It is dated 6 October 1833 in Fitzwilliam Museum Heath MS. Tennyson is reported (*Memoir*, I, pp. 304–5) as saying of *In Memoriam*:

'It must be remembered that this is a poem, *not* an actual biography. It is founded on our friendship, on the engagement of Arthur Hallam to my sister, on his sudden death at Vienna, just before the time fixed for their marriage, and on his burial at Clevedon Church. The poem concludes with the marriage of my youngest sister Cecilia. It was meant to be a kind of *Divina Commedia,* ending with happiness. The sections were written at many different places . . . I did not write them with any view of weaving them into a whole, or for publication, until I found that I had written so many. The different moods of sorrow as in a drama are dramatically given . . . "I" is not always the author speaking of himself, but the voice of the human race speaking through him. After the Death of A.H.H., the divisions of the poem are made by First Xmas (Section XXVIII), Second Xmas (Section LXXVIII), Third Xmas Eve (CIV and CV etc.).

To James Knowles Tennyson said: 'It's a very impersonal poem as well as personal . . . It's too hopeful, this Poem . . . more than I am myself . . . The general way of its being written was so queer that if there were a blank space, I would put in a poem' (*Ray,* pp. 37, 41). Knowles also records Tennyson's suggestion of nine divisions in the poem, as follows: I–VIII, IX–XX ('all connected-about the Ship'), XXI–XXVII, XXVIII–XLIX, L–LVIII, LIX–LXXI, LXXII–XCVIII, XCIX–CIII, CIV–CXXXI (*Ray,* p. 37).

Influences on the poem range from the Classics, through the Bible and Shakespeare, to Shelley. Charles Lyell's *Principles of Geology* (1830) and Robert Chambers's *Vestiges of Creation* (1844) were important for the geological and evolutionary thinking of the poem. Tennyson said of the first stanza of Section I: 'I alluded to Goethe's creed' (*Eversley*). There is an edition of *In Memoriam,* with a full collation of manuscripts, by S. Shatto and M. Shaw, 1982. On twentieth-century criticism of the poem, see J. Sendry, '*In Memoriam*: Twentieth Century Criticism', *Victorian Poetry,* XVIII, 1980, pp. 105–18. To which may be added Timothy Peltason, *Reading 'In Memoriam'*, 1985.

FROM *POEMS* (1851)

Edwin Morris

Published *Poems,* seventh edition, 1851. Written 1839 (*Memoir,* I, p. 174). The poem was inspired by Tennyson's unhappy love affair with Rosa Baring (see *Rader*) and, in this respect, is one of a group of poems including *Maud* and 'Locksley Hall'.

The Eagle

Published *Poems,* seventh edition, 1851. The date of composition is uncertain: sometime in the 1830s or 1840s, but most probably in the 1840s. C. B.

Thackeray published it from M. Brookfield's papers, with the date 2 May 1846, in the *London Mercury* (November 1925, p.620). The poem is in Tennyson's hand and is dated 30 October 1849 in a manuscript owned by the Society of Genealogists in London (*Letters*, I, p.307n).

FROM *MAUD, AND OTHER POEMS* (1855)

Maud

Published *1855*. Written 1854–5 (*Memoir*, I, pp.377, 382). The germ of *Maud* was the lyric 'Oh! that 'twere possible' (now *Maud*, II, iv, ll.141–238), first written in 1833–4 and published in an expanded form in *The Tribute* (ed. Lord Northampton) in 1837. Tennyson notes: 'Sir John Simeon years after begged me to weave a story round this poem, and so *Maud* came into being' (*Eversley*). But *Rader* argues that while Simeon may have encouraged the poet, 'Tennyson plainly intended to do something with the piece eight months before his friendship with Simeon began' (p.7), since his father-in-law, Henry Sellwood, sent by request to Emily Tennyson a copy of the poem from *The Tribute* in October 1853. The original title was *Maud or the Madness* (*Memoir*, I, p.402). '*A Monodrama*' was added to the title in 1875. Tennyson said to James Knowles in 1870–71: 'No other poem (a monotone with plenty of change and no weariness) has been made into a drama where successive phases of passion in one person take the place of successive persons. It is slightly akin to *Hamlet*' (*Ray*, p.43). There is an edition of *Maud*, with a full collation of manuscripts, by S. Shatto, 1986.

J. H. Buckley (*The Victorian Temper*, 1952, p. 63) notes that 'in form, theme and substance' *Maud* recalls the work of the 'Spasmodics' Alexander Smith and Sydney Dobell. Smith produced *A Life Drama* in 1852 and Dobell published *Balder* in 1853; Tennyson was familiar with both writers (*Memoir*, I, p.468; II, pp.73, 506). *Rader* shows how the story of a love obstructed by Mammonism is influenced by memories of the love Tennyson felt as a young man for Rosa Baring, a rich girl who lived close to Somersby (Tennyson was disillusioned by the end of 1836; Rosa Baring married in 1838). Sir Charles Tennyson suggests the influence of Charles Kingsley's *Alton Locke* (1850) and that the social criticism in *Maud* 'sprang from his long talks with Charles Kingsley and F. D. Maurice about the terrible conditions in the rapidly growing industrial cities' (*Alfred Tennyson*, revised edition, 1968, p.281).

On 6 December 1855 Tennyson wrote to Archer Gurney (*Letters*, I, pp.137–8):

I wish to say one word about *Maud* which you and others so strangely misinterpret. I have had Peace party papers sent to me claiming me as being on their side because I had put the cry for war into the mouth of a madman. Surely that is not half so wrong a criticism as some I have seen. Strictly speaking I do not see how from the poem I could be pronounced with certainty either peace man or war man. I wonder that you and others did not find out that all along the man was intended to have an hereditary vein of insanity, and that he falls foul on the swindling, on the times, because he feels that his father has been killed by the work of the lie, and that all through he fears the coming madness. How could you or anyone suppose that if I had had to speak in my own person my own opinion of this war or war generally I should have spoken with so little moderation. The whole was intended to be a new form of dramatic composition . . . I do not mean that my madman does not speak truths too . . .

Henry van Dyke records Tennyson speaking in a similar vein in 1892:

You must remember always . . . what it is meant to be – a drama in lyrics . . . The things which seem like faults belong not so much to the poem as to the character of the hero.

He is wrong, of course, in much that he says. If he had been always wise and just he would not have been himself. He begins with a false comparison – 'blood-red heath'. There is no such thing in nature; but he sees the heather tinged like blood because his mind has been disordered . . . He is wrong in thinking that war will transform the cheating tradesman into a great-souled hero, or that it will sweep away the dishonesties and lessen the miseries of humanity . . . But this very delusion is natural to him: it is in keeping with his morbid, melancholy, impulsive character to see a cure for the evils of peace in the horrors of war. [*Studies in Tennyson*, 1920, p.97.]

On *Maud* as a study in 'psychic frustration' see Roy P. Basler, 'Tennyson the Psychologist' (*South Atlantic Quarterly*, XLIII, 1944, pp.143–59).

Ode on the Death of the Duke of Wellington

Published 16 November 1852; second edition, heavily revised, published February–March 1853; then *1855*. Tennyson's first separate publication since becoming Poet Laureate, it was not, in fact, requested by the Queen and had no official publication under the terms of the laureateship. 'The doings of Wellington and Napoleon were the themes of story and verse' when Tennyson was a child at Somersby (*Memoir*, I, p. 5). On the textual history of the poem, see E. F. Shannon and Christopher Ricks, 'A Further History of Tennyson's *Ode on the Death of the Duke of Wellington*. The Manuscript at Trinity College and the Galley Proof at Lincoln' (*SB*, XXXII, 1979, pp.125–57; reprinted in Christopher Ricks, *Tennyson*, second edition, 1989). Wellington died on 14 September 1852; the funeral was on 18 November.

To the Rev. F. D. Maurice

Published *1855*, where it is dated 'January, 1854'. Hallam Tennyson observes of this poem (*Eversley*):

Mr. Maurice [1805–72] had been ejected from his professorship at King's College for non-orthodoxy. He had especially alarmed some of the 'weaker brethren' by pointing out that the word 'eternal' in 'eternal punishment' (αἰώνιος), strictly translated, referred to the quality not the duration of the punishment.

Will

Published *1855*. Two drafts of the second stanza appear in Trinity College Notebook 25 (1852) following a draft of the Wellington Ode.

The Charge of the Light Brigade

Published *The Examiner*, 9 December 1854; then *1855*. Composed 2 December 1854, 'in a few minutes, after reading . . . *The Times* in which occurred the phrase "some one had blundered", and this was the origin of the metre of his poem' (*Memoir*, I, p. 381). The *Times* editorial (13 November) had in fact spoken of 'some hideous blunder'. The Crimean charge took place on 25 October 1854. 'Not a poem on which I pique myself' observed Tennyson (*Memoir*, I, pp. 409–10). The textual development of the poem is given by E. F. Shannon and Christopher Ricks, '"The Charge of the Light Brigade". The Creation of a Poem', *SB*, XXXVIII, 1985, pp. 1–44; reprinted in Christopher Ricks, *Tennyson*, second edition, 1989.

FROM *ENOCH ARDEN* (1864)

The Grandmother

Published as 'The Grandmother's Apology' in *Once a Week*, 16 July 1859; then *1864*. Emily Tennyson's *Journal* (*Lincoln*) notes that Tennyson read it to her on 13 May 1858.

Tithonus

Published *Cornhill Magazine*, February 1860; then *1864*. A revised version of an unpublished early work 'Tithon', written 1833, the revisions were carried out in November–December 1859 after W. M. Thackeray asked Tennyson for a poem to be published in his *Cornhill Magazine*. As Tennyson notes, Tithonus was 'beloved by Aurora [goddess of the dawn], who gave him eternal life but not eternal youth. He grew old and infirm, and as he could not die, according to the legend, was turned into a grasshopper' (*Eversley*). Like its companion pieces 'Ulysses' and 'Tiresias' the poem was written soon after Tennyson had heard of Arthur Hallam's death. On Tennyson's use of language and the dramatic monologue form in this poem, see Daniel Harris, *Tennyson and Personification. The Rhetoric of 'Tithonus'*, 1986.

In the Valley of Cauteretz

Published *1864*. Written 6–8 September 1861 when Tennyson visited a 'valley in the Pyrenees, where I had been [in 1830] with Arthur Hallam' (*Eversley*).

On a Mourner

Published in *A Selection from the Works of Alfred Tennyson*, 1865. Written in October 1833 after Tennyson heard of Arthur Hallam's death, though revised towards greater impersonality in its published version.

FROM *THE HOLY GRAIL AND OTHER POEMS* (1869)

Northern Farmer, New Style

Published *1869*. On 18 February 1865 the Duke of Argyll wrote to Tennyson: 'I hear you have got something new to match the *Lincolnshire Farmer*' (*Lincoln*).

'Flower in the crannied wall'

Published *1869*. Tennyson noted that 'The flower was plucked out of a wall at "Waggoners Wells", near Haslemere' (*Eversley*).

Lucretius

Published *Macmillan's Magazine*, May 1868 and, in America, *Every Saturday*, 2 May 1868; then *1869*. Composed October 1865–January 1868 (*Memoir*, II, p.28; George Grove's *Life*, 1903, p.155). Hallam Tennyson notes that the legend of Lucretius' death in 'Jerome's addition to the Eusebian Chronicle under date B.C. 94' provides the basis of the story (this version Tennyson could have read in the *English Encyclopaedia*, 1802, which was at Somersby: *Lincoln*). The poem reworks lines from Lucretius' *De Rerum*

Natura. For an account of the textual history of the poem, see E. F. Shannon, 'The Publication of Tennyson's "Lucretius"' (*SB*, XXXIV, 1981, pp. 146–86).

FROM *TIRESIAS AND OTHER POEMS* (1885)

To E. FitzGerald

Published *1885*. Edward FitzGerald died on 14 June 1883 and Tennyson wrote to Frederick Pollock on 17 June: 'I had written a poem to him within the last week – a dedication – which he will never see' (*Letters*, III, p. 247). The poem remembers the last visit made by Tennyson and Hallam Tennyson to FitzGerald in September 1876. As originally published the poem, in its two parts (ll. 1–56 and 57–88), frames 'Tiresias'.

Tiresias

Published *1885*. Begun before Arthur Hallam's death (see D. F. Goslee, 'Three Stages of Tennyson's "Tiresias"', *JEGP*, LXXV, 1976, pp. 154–67), continued after it (Hallam Tennyson notes in *Eversley* that it was 'partly written at the same time as Ulysses', in 1833), then concluded in 1883 (H. M. Butler noted on 7 April 1883: 'He was working up an old poem written originally at the same time as *Ulysses,* and . . . was in rather anxious doubt as to the paternity of Creon!', E. Graham, *The Harrow Life of H. M. Butler,* 1920, pp. 297–8). The poem was recited on 25 August 1883 (F. T. Palgrave's *Journals,* 1899, p. 178). The most important source is Euripides, *Phoenissae*. Douglas Bush discusses the sources in *Mythology and the Romantic Tradition in English Poetry* (1937, pp. 216–19). The destruction of Thebes in Boeotia is imminent. Creon, ruler of Thebes, asks Tiresias the blind seer how the city may be saved. Eventually he gets the reply that the only way is the sacrifice of Menoeceus, Creon's son and a descendant of Cadmus who had offended the god Ares. Creon advises silence and suggests that Menoeceus flee. Menoeceus pretends to agree to do so but actually kills himself. Tennyson changes the meeting between Creon and Menoeceus to one directly between Tiresias and Menoeceus and removes Tiresias' hesitation in explaining what is required to save Thebes.

The Ancient Sage

Published *1885*. Written 1885, when the subject was suggested by Benjamin Jowett who wrote to Emily Tennyson on 6 July 1885: 'I hope *Laotsee* has prospered. I shall consider myself fortunate if I have succeeded in finding a subject for Alfred' (*Lincoln*). Tennyson noted: 'What the Ancient Sage says is not the philosophy of the Chinese philosopher Laot-ze, but it was written after reading his life and maxims' (*Eversley*).

Prefatory Poem to My Brother's Sonnets

Published 1880, with Charles Tennyson Turner's *Collected Sonnets*; then *1885*. The subtitle provides the date of composition. Charles died on 25 April 1879.

'Frater Ave atque Vale'

Published *Nineteenth Century,* March 1883; then *1885*. Written during a visit to Sirmio in June 1880 (*Memoir,* II, p.247). It refers to Tennyson's brother Charles who died in 1879. The influences are Catullus' *Poem* XXXI, joyfully celebrating the beauty of Sirmio, and his *Poem* CI, a sad elegy for his dead brother. Tennyson's work combines the two moods.

FROM *LOCKSLEY HALL SIXTY YEARS AFTER* (1886)

Locksley Hall Sixty Years After

Published *Locksley Hall Sixty Years After,* 1886. Composed 1886; recited 27 October (*Memoir,* II, pp.324, 506). *Buckley* (p.234) notes that Tennyson 'strove through heavy revision of several early drafts to control the invective'. *Rader* (p.58) suggests that Tennyson was re-estimating Rosa Baring and her husband (ll.239–40). 'Edith' is Tennyson's wife Emily ('very woman of very woman', l.51, is associated with her, *Memoir,* I, p.331). Tennyson wrote to C. Esmarch, 18 April 1888: 'I must object and strongly to the statement in your preface that *I* am the hero in either poem . . . The whole thing is a dramatic impersonation, but I find in almost all modern criticism this absurd tendency to personalities. Some of my thought *may* come out in the poem but am I therefore the hero?' (*Letters,* III, pp.366–7).

FROM *DEMETER AND OTHER POEMS* (1889)

Demeter and Persephone

Published *1889*. On 19 August 1886 the classical scholar R. C. Jebb directed Hallam Tennyson to the *Homeric Hymn to Demeter* (*Lincoln*); the poem was completed in May 1887 (*Memoir,* II, p.335). Hallam Tennyson wrote: 'The poem was written at my request . . . He said: "I will write it, but when I write an antique like this I must put it into a frame – something modern about it. It is no use giving a mere *réchauffé* of old legends". He would give as an example of the frame [ll. 126–36]' (*Eversley*). Demeter was goddess of the cornfield and mother of Persephone (Zeus was the father). While gathering flowers in the neighbourhood of the Sicilian city of Enna, Persephone was abducted by Hades and taken to the underworld. Demeter's grief was so great that she caused the earth to be afflicted with sterility until Persephone was restored to her. In the end a compromise was reached whereby Hades returned Persephone for a part of the year. It is a myth about the seasons. At the end of Tennyson's poem Demeter looks forward to the coming of Christianity and envisages a cosmic order that transcends the natural and the seasonal.

Crossing the Bar

Published *1889*. Hallam Tennyson notes: 'Made in my father's eighty-first year, in October 1889, on crossing the Solent after his serious illness in 1888–9' (*Eversley*).

INDEX OF TITLES

INDEX OF FIRST LINES

READ MORE IN PENGUIN

READ MORE IN PENGUIN

A CHOICE OF CLASSICS

Matthew Arnold	**Selected Prose**
Jane Austen	**Emma**
	Lady Susan/The Watsons/Sanditon
	Mansfield Park
	Northanger Abbey
	Persuasion
	Pride and Prejudice
	Sense and Sensibility
William Barnes	**Selected Poems**
Anne Brontë	**Agnes Grey**
	The Tenant of Wildfell Hall
Charlotte Brontë	**Jane Eyre**
	Shirley
	Villette
Emily Brontë	**Wuthering Heights**
Samuel Butler	**Erewhon**
	The Way of All Flesh
Lord Byron	**Selected Poems**
Thomas Carlyle	**Selected Writings**
Arthur Hugh Clough	**Selected Poems**
Wilkie Collins	**Armadale**
	The Moonstone
	No Name
	The Woman in White
Charles Darwin	**The Origin of Species**
	Voyage of the *Beagle*
Benjamin Disraeli	**Sybil**
George Eliot	**Adam Bede**
	Daniel Deronda
	Felix Holt
	Middlemarch
	The Mill on the Floss
	Romola
	Scenes of Clerical Life
	Silas Marner

READ MORE IN PENGUIN

A CHOICE OF CLASSICS

Charles Dickens	**American Notes for General Circulation**
	Barnaby Rudge
	Bleak House
	The Christmas Books (in two volumes)
	David Copperfield
	Dombey and Son
	Great Expectations
	Hard Times
	Little Dorrit
	Martin Chuzzlewit
	The Mystery of Edwin Drood
	Nicholas Nickleby
	The Old Curiosity Shop
	Oliver Twist
	Our Mutual Friend
	The Pickwick Papers
	Selected Short Fiction
	A Tale of Two Cities
Elizabeth Gaskell	**Cranford/Cousin Phillis**
	The Life of Charlotte Brontë
	Mary Barton
	North and South
	Ruth
	Sylvia's Lovers
	Wives and Daughters
Edward Gibbon	**The Decline and Fall of the Roman Empire** (in three volumes)
George Gissing	**New Grub Street**
	The Odd Women
William Godwin	**Caleb Williams**

READ MORE IN PENGUIN

A CHOICE OF CLASSICS

Thomas Hardy	**Desperate Remedies**
	The Distracted Preacher and Other Tales
	Far from the Madding Crowd
	Jude the Obscure
	The Hand of Ethelberta
	A Laodicean
	The Mayor of Casterbridge
	A Pair of Blue Eyes
	The Return of the Native
	Selected Poems
	Tess of the d'Urbervilles
	The Trumpet-Major
	Two on a Tower
	Under the Greenwood Tree
	The Well-Beloved
	The Woodlanders
Lord Macaulay	**The History of England**
Henry Mayhew	**London Labour and the London Poor**
John Stuart Mill	**The Autobiography**
	On Liberty
William Morris	**News from Nowhere** and **Other Writings**
John Henry Newman	**Apologia Pro Vita Sua**
Robert Owen	**A New View of Society and Other Writings**
Walter Pater	**Marius the Epicurean**
John Ruskin	**Unto This Last and Other Writings**
Walter Scott	**Ivanhoe**
	Heart of Mid-Lothian
	Old Mortality
	Rob Roy
	Waverley

READ MORE IN PENGUIN

A CHOICE OF CLASSICS

Robert Louis Stevenson	**Kidnapped**
	Dr Jekyll and Mr Hyde and Other Stories
	The Master of Ballantrae
	Weir of Hermiston
William Makepeace Thackeray	**The History of Henry Esmond**
	The History of Pendennis
	The Newcomes
	Vanity Fair
Anthony Trollope	**An Autobiography**
	Barchester Towers
	Can You Forgive Her?
	The Duke's Children
	The Eustace Diamonds
	Framley Parsonage
	He Knew He Was Right
	The Last Chronicle of Barset
	Phineas Finn
	The Prime Minister
	Rachel Ray
	The Small House at Allington
	The Warden
	The Way We Live Now
Oscar Wilde	**Complete Short Fiction**
	De Profundis and Other Writings
	The Picture of Dorian Gray
Mary Wollstonecraft	**A Vindication of the Rights of Woman**
	Mary and Maria (includes Mary Shelley's **Matilda**)
Dorothy and William Wordsworth	**Home at Grasmere**